FOLLOW

me

DOWN

FOLLOW
me
DOWN

TANYA BYRNE

headline

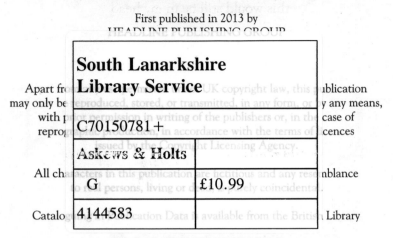

To Claire Wilson, without whom
this would still be in my head

'A ship is safe in harbor, but that's not what ships are for.'

Attributed to William G. T. Shedd

THE DAY AFTER

MAY

When I was a kid and I couldn't sleep, my father would tell me it was because someone was dreaming about me. I know now that this isn't true – it's just one of those things he used to tell me to make me feel better – but for a long time, I believed him.

I'm sure she doesn't want me dreaming about her, either, but I do – a lot – which is kind of cruel because I spend most of the day trying to avoid her, yet as soon as I close my eyes, there she is, as though my brain won't forget. I hate that, how it holds on to things and won't let go. I can't remember a thing about my fifth birthday party. I've seen photographs of it – me in that frothy pink dress, my aunts and uncles laughing so much you can see their teeth – but all I remember about that day is how my father ran over a dog that ran out in front of our car when we went to pick up the cake. Who does that? I don't know. So when I say that I dream about her, they're not always good dreams – and even the not-so-bad dreams still make me wake up gasping her name like someone running down the street shouting, 'Fire!'

I was dreaming about him last night, the two of us lying on our backs on his scratchy tartan blanket in Savernake Forest,

1

the sun weighing over us, all fat and yellow and ready to burst.
We were watching the clouds bob past, pretending each one
was a country – 'India! Let's go there . . . Australia! Let's go
there' – like we did yesterday afternoon. I saw a cloud that
looked like Africa, but when I turned to tell him, it was her
next to me. She was grinning and wearing those heart-shaped
sunglasses – the cheap red ones that she loves so much – and
for a few moments it was like it used to be, the two of us giggling
and comparing nail polish, until she asked me if I thought
death was going to be beautiful. Only she could ask a question
like that, and I told her not to be so morbid. She just laughed
and blamed Oscar Wilde, then told me to imagine it, lying in
the earth with flowers growing from my fingernails and grass
from my eyelashes. It does sound kind of beautiful, doesn't it?

I woke up with a gasp and for a moment I wasn't sure where
I was. It wasn't until the shadows began to take shape – my
closet, my desk, my noticeboard with its patchwork of photographs, the gaps where the ones of her used to be now covered
with other ones – that I remembered I was at school and my
nerves lurched back into place.

I used to enjoy it, moving around. It didn't bother me that I
might be here in Wiltshire one day then back in Lagos the
next, watching my grandmother in the kitchen in her faded
boubou, singing to herself as she chopped bitterleaf. I used to
be able to sleep anywhere, but I can't sleep here. At first it was
the strange bed, then it was the murmurs through the walls –
the girls who have to sleep with the radio on, the ones who call
their boyfriends at midnight, when they think everyone is
asleep – and now it's the dreams about her.

It's got to the point where I dread going to bed. My stomach
clenches like a fist just thinking about it because I know that

I'm going to lie there – thinking about her, about him, about what we've done – until the muffled giggles stop and the DJs shut up and all I can hear is the heavy *tick tick tick* of the grandfather clock at the bottom of the stairs.

Then I wonder who else is awake, if there's another girl in another bed in another room listening to the *tick tick tick* as well. If there's a guy on the other side of the village, or a woman fussing over a loose thread on her duvet. It's like I'm part of a club – the misfits, the liars, the lonely – who meet every night in the empty, black silence to wait for it to go grey with the promise of morning, with its cups of tea and conversations about the weather that fill the hours before we have to go to bed and do it again. And every night I tell myself the same thing, that tonight it will pass, that tonight I'll sleep – and I never do.

But I guess that's guilt, what it does to you.

245 DAYS BEFORE

SEPTEMBER

As first days of school go, today wasn't so bad. No one flushed my head down the toilet or stole my lunch money, so I shouldn't complain, but I still don't want to be here. I'm trying to be mature about it, though; it's hardly my father's fault that the Nigerian High Commissioner in London died and he was posted here, plus my mother just found out that she's going to be teaching a class at UCL, which she's thrilled about. It doesn't make being here any easier, though.

Maybe it wouldn't be so bad if I could stay in London with them, but being shipped off to boarding school feels too much like I've done something wrong. I haven't, I know. I know that they just want me to go to the best school in England – which is Crofton College – but if I had known that they were going to send me away, I would have asked to stay in New York where I had friends, a boyfriend, a favourite coffee shop, a favourite bench in Central Park. Secret places that I found, that were mine, but here I am at this dusty old school that's about ten miles south of No One Gives a Damn, where no one can pronounce my surname.

I can't tell my parents this, though, because they'd just tell me that it's only been a day and I should give it a chance, and I should, but *my God*, if New York is the city that never sleeps, then Ostley is the village that's about to nod off. I don't think I'll ever get used to it. It's almost too much – too much green, too much space, too much sky. And it's so quiet. There are no sirens, no buses panting in traffic, not the constant rumble of life you feel under your feet in New York. The rattle of the subway somewhere below the sidewalk or the far-off hum of a pneumatic drill splitting a road in two, as though the city is always shifting because there's not enough room for everyone. But in Ostley, all there is is room. The fields go on until you get bored of looking at them and you can always hear stuff – birds chattering and brooks babbling – like a cartoon.

I'd refused to look at the Crofton brochure my father tried to show me before we left New York, but it didn't matter because it's just as I imagined. It's the sort of school my father has always wanted to send me to, the sort of school he'd read about in books – that his friends from Cambridge had gone to – somewhere with hockey pitches and house badges and dining halls with long wooden tables. His eyes lit up when our car pulled onto the tree-lined drive and we got our first glimpse of it. I don't think I've ever seen him like that – wide-eyed and blinking, like a little boy – which is why I'm giving it a chance.

Crofton is stunning, I'll give it that – grand and gloriously Gothic, all spires and arches and leaded windows – but when the driver stopped to let a gaggle of girls cross the road, I realised that it has none of the glamour of my school in New York, none of the attitude. All the girls looked rather proper and seemed to be wearing their uniform with pride as though they'd chosen to wear it. No one tried to look different. There were no cute coats and matching headbands. No one had pinned a brooch to their blazer. They even seemed to be carrying the same folders. So when our car pulled up outside my boarding house and I was greeted by my housemistress, a middle-aged woman with a greying bob and sensible shoes called Mrs Delaney, I realised that I wouldn't be wearing half the stuff I'd packed.

We'd got stuck in traffic leaving London so were half an hour late. In Nigerian time – where 7 a.m. means more like 11 a.m. – half an hour isn't so bad, but in British time, it was a big deal, especially to Mrs Delaney, who made a point – three times – of telling us that she could only give us a fleeting tour before I had to get to Registration. So we left our housekeeper, Celina, in my room unpacking my luggage while Mrs Delaney showed us around.

'Burnham houses all the girls in the Lower Six,' she told us, marching back towards the stairs. 'I've been the housemistress here for six years. Your house tutor is Madame Girard, whom you will see every morning for Registration, then for your one-on-one on a Monday.'

I nodded, wondering if I should be making a note of it, not that she slowed down for me to do so. She only stopped when we got to the end of the corridor. 'I live in the cottage attached to the house and you can reach me out of hours by ringing this bell.' She gestured at the door. 'All the staff at Crofton live on campus, but we prefer if you call first, if you can.'

And that's how it went on, Mrs Delaney barking stuff – about when to get up and when to sign out and when to clear my room so that it could be cleaned – as she showed us around. My father seemed impressed, nodding at each room: the bedrooms, the Common Room, the Laundry Room, the Dining

Hall with its long tables. He didn't say a word, just followed her, hands behind his back, his long wool coat swinging as he swept in and out of each room. When we returned to my room, all he said was, 'The lock on the Common Room window needs replacing,' and it was Mrs Delaney's turn to look bewildered.

He told us that he'd wait in my room while we looked at the bathroom. Not that I was in any hurry to see it; my mother had to take me by the elbow and lead me down the corridor. I could see it at the end, steam billowing out of the door as a girl ran in with a pink towel. 'You have four minutes, Miss Avery,' Mrs Delaney barked after her and I shot a look at my mother, who smiled tightly and patted my arm.

There are fifty girls in Burnham, apparently, most of them doing A-Levels, but some are doing the Baccalaureate, like me. It felt like much more, though, and I didn't expect it to be so *chaotic*. It was the first day of term, so I don't know why I was surprised, to be honest. I thought it would be quiet – solemn – like a convent, I guess. But there were girls everywhere, darting from room to room clutching washbags and hairbrushes. I've never had to share a bathroom before and the thought of it, of having to queue to use the shower and brushing my teeth a sink away from a stranger, made my stomach knot. Where would I put my make-up on? In all the upheaval, it was such a silly thing to worry about, but it was all I could think about.

My mother must have known because when we got back to my room, she went to the window. 'What a nice view, Adamma.' She gestured at the magnolia tree. 'Isn't it lovely?'

I didn't respond, just fussed over my skirt and blazer. At least the uniform was black and white, which was more flatter-ing than the bottle-green and tartan I had worn at my school in New York, but I still sneered at my reflection in the mirror as Mrs Delaney ushered a girl in. Even though she seemed sweet, her hair wet from the shower, I still glared at her like a cornered cat.

She was struggling under the weight of a hockey bag. I waited for Mrs Delaney to tell her to put it down, but she didn't. 'This is Orla Roberts. Orla's doing A-levels – so you won't have any classes together – but she's a house monitor, so if you need anything, she's just across the hall.' She gestured at me. 'Orla, this is Adamma Okomma and her parents. They've just moved here from New York. Mr Okomma is the new Nigerian High Commissioner in London.' She turned to my parents with a smile. 'Orla is a scholarship student.'

She said it as though she was describing her eye colour. *This is Orla Roberts. She has brown eyes and poor parents.* I guess my mother noticed it too because she smiled tightly, then, with a more genuine one, turned to Orla and extended her hand. My father did too, and when it was my turn I did the same – a little sullenly, I admit, but I was too distracted as I saw Celina trying to shoehorn my clothes into the tiny closet. Mrs Delaney turned to watch her too. 'There was no need to bring everything, dear. You must learn to pack for the term.' When she laughed, I wanted to tell her *that* was my Fall wardrobe, but my father gave me a look, so I crossed my arms instead.

I guess I've seen too many movies about English boarding schools because when my parents left, I expected Orla to roll up her skirt and put on some red lipstick. Instead she told me that she'd see me later and left. As I watched her go, still struggling with her hockey bag, I won't lie, I was a little disappointed. She hadn't given me a cigarette and tried to take me under her wing, warn me who I should and shouldn't speak to, offer to show me Crofton's secret places. I suppose it served me right for being surly.

Mercifully, I didn't have to find my way to my first class because every new pupil is assigned a hen, an older girl who has to show her around and help her settle in. My hen was an Upper Sixth girl called Tara Salter. She was more what I had expected, bright eyed and shiny haired. She'd definitely drunk the Kool-Aid and she gushed and gushed about the school, introducing me to each building as if it was her friend. But, as eager as she was, she had the grace to let me go to the bathroom by myself – not before she made sure I knew where my English lit class was. I still got lost, though, and wandered up and down the long corridor several times before I had to admit defeat and get the map she had given me out of my bag.

'Going my way?' a guy asked, suddenly at my side.

He said it so smoothly – as though we were in an old black-and-white movie and he was offering me a cigarette – that I stared at him for a moment or two before I remembered that the sixth form was mixed.

Perhaps my father wasn't trying to torture me after all.

'I'm Dominic Sim.' He held out his hand. I looked at it, but that just made his smile more wicked as his hand dropped back down to his side. 'I can escort you.'

'You can? How do you know where I'm going?'

'Heaven, I assume?'

I stared at him, horrified. I thought English boys were charming. I quietly cursed my father for making me watch *Downton Abbey* and raising my expectations.

I turned to walk away, but he changed tack. 'OK. If the face isn't working,' he said, suddenly in front of me, 'I'm a billionaire.'

That didn't work, either. 'Your father's a billionaire,' I replied, looking back down at my map. 'The only thing you've earned is Air Miles.'

He laughed at that, loud and bright. 'I like you already, Miss Okomma.'

I shot a look at him again. 'How did you know my name?'

'I know things.' He gestured at the door of the classroom we were standing outside of. 'Like you're doing the Baccalaureate, right?' I arched an eyebrow at him and his smile widened. 'Me too. So this is where you want to be: English lit with Mr Lucas.' He put a hand to his chest. 'I promise never to lead you astray, Miss Okomma.'

He smiled and, as obnoxious as he was, I had to tell myself not to smile back. I kind of hate myself, but what can I say? What he lacked in humility he made up for in wit and if I have one weakness, it's funny guys.

'Come and sit next to me,' he said, turning and walking into the classroom. 'I'm new, too. We new kids need to stick together.'

'I'm OK, thanks,' I told him as I followed him in, sensing that I should probably keep as much distance between us as possible.

I headed for the empty desk in the middle of the classroom, but the girl sitting at the one behind it shook her head so emphatically that I stepped back. That left just one, in the front row, but before I could get to it, I heard Dominic say, 'Get up, then, you unchivalrous bastard. Can't you see the lady needs a desk?'

Realising what he was doing, I turned to tell him off, but was stunned to find the boy he'd barked at gathering up his books. By the time I'd recovered, he'd shuffled towards the desk in the front row, leaving just one free desk, the one next to Dominic's.

'Do people always do what you tell them?' I asked, sighing as I realised that by sitting next to him, I was answering my own question.

At least he had the decency not to comment on it; he just smiled and gave me a *whatcha gonna do?* shrug as I took my notebook out of my bag. I put it down with a petulant huff, determined not to give him any further encouragement, but after I had opened it and written the date neatly in the top right-hand corner of the first page, my gaze strayed back towards him. He was still looking at me and I looked away, my toe tapping. I glanced at the doorway as a girl with dark hair walked in. She came in with a slight swagger and for a second, I thought she was walking towards me, but she stopped at his desk.

'Dominic Sim,' she said, and I could tell that she was fighting a smile.

He did smile. 'Surprise!'

'I thought you were on a slow boat to Korea after the Eton thing?'

The Eton thing, I noted, pretending to write something in my notebook so that they wouldn't think I was eavesdropping. I was the only one who took the trouble to be subtle, though; everyone else just turned to look at them as she stood in front of his desk, hands on her hips. Not that she seemed fazed that she had an audience, she had her chin up and her shoulders back. I got the feeling that she did this a lot.

'You, more than anyone, should know not to listen to everything you hear, Scarlett,' he said, his eyes suddenly black. 'Good summer? How was rehab?'

12

'I'm off the crack, at last. Three weeks clean.' She crossed her fingers and held them up. 'How was Eton? Do you still know what a vagina looks like?'

'Feel free to remind me.'

'Like you'd know what to do with it.'

He laughed and she claimed the victory with a curtsey, then went and sat at the desk in the middle. I guess that's why that girl had shaken her head when I'd gone to sit there: it was her desk, the one in the middle where everyone could see her. Not that she needed to sit there; wherever she sat, you would see her; she seemed to reflect off the panelled walls like a new penny.

After her performance with Dominic, I wasn't surprised that she was the first to raise her hand when class started. She didn't do it with any eagerness, though – she looked rather bored, actually – but as soon as she did, four other hands shot up, and I watched Mr Lucas let go of a breath and smile, obviously grateful that his first lesson of the year wasn't dying on its ass.

'Yes, Miss Chiltern?' He pointed the copy of *Anna Karenina* he was holding at her.

He'd been clutching it a little too tightly, I'd noticed, his knuckles white. And when he asked us what our favourite opening line of a book was, he sounded out of breath. I didn't envy him. He was clearly flustered and *young* – in his early twenties, I guessed – much younger than the rest of the faculty, which must make some of the parents uncomfortable. I don't think my father would be impressed; he seemed to think that every teacher at Crofton was the best in England. I think he'd struggle to believe that a twenty-something-year-old man, with what looked like MAX BIRTHDAY scribbled on the heel of his palm in biro, was the best English lit teacher they could

13

find. His favourite line was from *Anna Karenina*. Somewhat predictable, or perhaps convenient, given that we were about to study it, so I expected her to say something similar. But she said, 'All this happened, more or less.'

'*Slaughterhouse-Five*,' he said, but there was no shake in his voice this time. If anything, he sounded pleased with himself, as though he was on a game show, announcing the million-dollar answer. 'That's a wonderful book, Miss Chiltern.'

I must have rolled my eyes, because he smiled at me. 'Not a fan, I take it?'

He looked at me, his chin raised and his lips parted, and I stared at him dumbly for a moment until I realised that he was waiting for me to tell him my name as well. I sat a little straighter. 'Adamma, Sir. Adamma Okomma.'

He nodded. 'I realise Vonnegut isn't everyone's cup of tea, so what's your favourite opening line, Miss Okomma?' He sat on the edge of his desk, arms folded.

My gaze flitted around the classroom as everyone turned to look at me and it made my cheeks burn. I took a breath. ' "It was inevitable:" ' I had to stop and take another breath as a sudden tremor in my voice made the words wobble, ' "the scent of bitter almonds always reminded him of the fate of unrequited love." '

Mr Lucas was quiet for a moment or two, then nodded. '*Love in the Time of Cholera*.' I watched his Adam's apple rise then fall. 'Excellent choice, Miss Okomma. Gabriel Garcia Marquez is—' He stopped, flustered again.

'Magnificent?' I suggested, and he blinked at me.

When I glanced at Scarlett, she wasn't smiling any more.

THE DAY AFTER

MAY

As soon as Molly knew, we all did. I'd only just caught my breath, my heart still throbbing as I remembered my dream – Scarlett in those cheap red sunglasses, the sun in her hair – when a strip of light appeared under my door. A moment later I heard it, the *slap slap slap* of Molly's bare feet on the floorboards as she ran from room to room, gleefully delivering the news as though she was announcing the birth of a baby.

Orla got to me first. I smelled her before I saw her, smelled her sugary perfume that even smells pink, somehow, and attaches itself to everything she touches. I'd never noticed it, not until I was idly trying perfumes at JFK last year. I reached for one and when I smelled it – smelled her – I smiled. I hadn't realised how much I liked her until then. I hadn't realised how much I liked Crofton, either. I guess that was the first time I missed it, when, despite its ugly uniform and my strange, hard bed, it started to feel a little like home.

Orla turned on the light. I sat up and raised a hand as it drenched me, my eyes stinging for a second or two before they came back into focus as she sat on my bed.

'What's wrong?' I asked, my voice still sticky with sleep, but then I saw the Paris guidebook on my nightstand and I was suddenly awake. I wanted to reach over and snatch it off, hide it under my duvet, but I didn't want to draw attention to it.

'Scarlett's gone,' she said, out of breath.

My heart began to beat very, very slowly. 'Gone?'

'She's run away again.'

'How do you know?'

'Molly heard it from Tara who heard it from Olivia.'

'Olivia Fisher or Scarlett's sister Olivia?'

'Her sister.'

'So it's true?' She nodded and my heart sped up again, back to normal speed then faster, faster. 'Where's she gone?'

Before she could answer, Molly was in my doorway. 'Ding dong the bitch is gone,' she sang with a nasty smile, before she skipped off again.

'She needs to pace herself.' I sighed. 'She'll be dead of glee by lunch.'

Orla frowned. 'She says you crashed Scarlett and Olivia's party on Saturday.'

'Yeah.' I tugged off my headscarf and smoothed my hair down with my hand.

'Did Scarlett go mad?'

'Not at all. She was fine. More than fine, it was the first party since –' I thought about it, then shrugged – 'I don't know when, when she didn't start anything.'

'Really? But it was her birthday.'

'I know. She was . . .'

'Nice?' Orla offered with a careful smile when I hesitated.

I raised an eyebrow. 'Not quite. But she wasn't vicious, either.'

'Is that why you went? Because things are getting better?' she asked, but it was just that – a question – there was no undertone. And that's what I love about Orla, there was no 'Why didn't you tell me?' or 'But you're my best friend' like I used to get from Scarlett.

'I don't know.' I laid my headscarf in my lap, unknotting it then folding it into a neat square. 'I thought—' Before I could finish, two girls hurried past my open door whispering. I shook my head and sighed. 'But nothing's changed, has it? She's still Scarlett.'

Orla looked confused. 'Did you think she had changed?'

I shrugged and thought of Scarlett on Saturday night. She looked so happy, dancing under the canopy of Chinese lanterns, arms in the air, the glitter from her blue eye shadow freckling across her cheeks and, for a moment, it was like old times. It wasn't perfect – it will never be perfect again – but despite the wall of people between us, it kind of felt like it was just her and me again. But then I thought about Dominic, standing too close (always too close), the smell of blackcurrant on his breath – *Do you think she'll ever forgive you?*

I didn't tell Orla that, though. I wanted to, but before I gave into the temptation, I lied and told her that I'd forgotten to file something for the school newspaper and when she left, I went to my closet, opened the doors and reached for my tuck box. The contents rattled as I took it out and put it on my bed then reached for my bag, fingers fluttering as I rooted through it for my keys. My hands were shaking so much that it took two attempts to unlock it, but when I did, I turned it upside down. Everything spilled out on to the bed: half a dozen jewellery boxes, my passport, credit cards, a memory stick, the cash my parents had given me in case of an emergency, a handful of carefully folded notes and, finally, my other cellphone. I switched it on, panic pinching at me as I paced back and forth over the rug in the middle of my room.

As soon as the menu loaded, I called him. I didn't even give him a chance to say hello before I breathed, 'Did you hear about Scarlett?'

245 DAYS BEFORE

SEPTEMBER

Crofton is confounding. I guess that's what the breast pocket of my blazer is for, a compass and a piece of Kendal Mint Cake, because I will *never* find my way around here. Everything looks the same. Even the oil paintings are beginning to look the same; I'm sure they're all of the same white guy in different positions.

I'm not being melodramatic, but I will die here. They are going to find my desiccating body at the end of one the corridors, gnarled fingers still curled around my map. It's my own fault; Tara was getting on my nerves, so I told her I'd be fine and, in an effort to avoid any further advances from Dominic, I'd refused his offer to show me around. I shouldn't have because I'm hopeless with maps so I got lost *three times* on the way to lunch. I don't even know how that's possible (that has to be some sort of record, right?) but when I finally saw the doors to the courtyard, I had to stop myself running out into the midday sun and throwing my arms out like Andy Dufresne in *The Shawshank Redemption*.

I'd only taken a few steps before someone marched over to me and snatched the map out of my hands. I looked up to see

19

Scarlett and stepped back, as I remembered the time Darcy Young put a cigarette out on a girl's Chanel purse for laughing at her when she said the wrong answer in Calculus. I hoped my disdain of Vonnegut wouldn't provoke a similar reaction from Scarlett.

'Where are you going?' She sounded irritated, as though I had interrupted her.

'I . . .' I stopped as I watched her scrunch up the map and hand it back to me. I looked at it with a frown. 'I was going back to my boarding house for lunch.'

'No one eats lunch in the dining hall.' She sighed heavily. 'Come.'

'Don't I need to sign in?'

She ignored me and continued walking across the courtyard. I watched her go, hips swaying, and when she realised that I hadn't followed, she turned to smile at me over her shoulder. 'Come on, Alice. Don't you want to follow the white rabbit?'

I trotted after her and when I caught up, I introduced myself.

'I know,' she said, without looking at me. 'I'm Scarlett Chiltern.'

'I know.'

She turned to look at me, and when I held her gaze, she smiled. 'I like your shoes.'

I don't know whether it was her red lipstick or the fact that she still hadn't taken it off even though Madame Girard had scolded her for it during French, but I immediately felt drawn to her. She reminded me of the girls I went to school with in New York and the way she walked through the busy courtyard without hesitating – just kept going like a bowling ball, the crowd parting so that she could pass – reminded me of my best friend Jumoke. I was trying so hard to be OK with all this – with moving to the UK, starting at Crofton with its LEGO green lawns and stupid house badges – but I missed Jumoke so much then. We've been best friends for nine years and it was strange not having her there to complain with me in pidgin about having Latin at 8.30 a.m. on a Saturday morning or to question when the sheets were last washed.

I think that's why I followed Scarlett, because there was something so familiar – almost *comforting* – about her swagger, about the way she lifted her chin and pushed her shoulders back, like Jumoke always does. Jumoke would hate her, though, she would say she was stuck up, which is kind of funny, because that's what everyone says about Jumoke. Mind you, people say the same thing about me. 'You're so aloof, Adamma,' they say with a smile as though they're telling me something I'd want to know about myself. If not hugging girls I don't know outside of class and telling them that I love them makes me aloof then, yeah, I guess I am.

I hesitated when we reached the Green. During my tour with Tara this morning we'd walked on the path. 'Are we allowed to walk on the grass?'

'Only sixth formers can.'

When Scarlett stepped on to it, I followed, walking with her as she headed towards the wall of oak trees at the end of the Green. As we passed through them, I realised that we were near the car park and wondered if she was going to drive me somewhere, but she led me to the left, towards another lawn, then turned to look at me with a smirk.

'If you're going to survive at Crofton, you need to know where to hide, Adamma.'

I started to smile back, but then felt each of my nerves tighten as it occurred to me that it might be a boarding school initiation, that she was taking me somewhere she knew I'd never find my way back from. I looked around, hoping to recognise something from my tour. As we got closer, I realised with some relief that she was leading me to the hockey pitch. I'd gone a different way with Tara, but it was on my map, so I could find my way back.

Then I began to wonder if it was another sort of initiation and slowed, half expecting to find a gang of girls waiting to steal my uniform or shave my head. But the pitch was empty except for a sprinkler sputtering water across it. We walked along the edge and headed up another small grass-covered hill towards a crooked tree. When we reached the top we stopped under it and I realised that we were by the canal. Tara and I had passed it that morning, but, as there are no buildings near it, she'd only waved her hand at it, and we hadn't got close enough to see it. From there, we were only a few feet away and suddenly, everything slowed.

It wasn't like the canal I'd walked along when I was in London last summer, the one in Camden with the brick bridges bruised with graffiti. Like the rest of Crofton, it was edged with green. The other side was as well, but it was more overgrown, and, as I listened to the whisper of the willow trees, their branches leaning over the edge as though they were trying to drink the water, I realised that it was the first moment of quiet I'd had since I'd left New York. Even the light was different here, green and white all at once, like a peeled pear.

'It's so pretty,' I said, a little breathless.

'It leads to my house.' She nodded up the canal. 'When my sisters and I were little, we'd joke about swimming to school.'

22

'You don't board?'

She shook her head then shrugged off her blazer, laying it on the grass and sitting cross-legged on it. 'We don't have to; we only live a few minutes away, in the house on the hill.' She said it like I should know which one. 'Your first time?'

'How did you guess?' I said with a small sigh, copying her and taking off my blazer. I laid it on the grass in front of her. 'I thought my last school was strict.'

She watched me sit down, then smiled. 'You'll get used to it.' I gave her a look that told her I didn't believe her and she laughed. 'It's not that bad.'

'Didn't you just get told off for wearing lipstick?'

'*Red* lipstick.'

'Still.'

'I'm sure your school in New York was much cooler,' she conceded with a shrug and I don't know how she knew that I went to school in New York, but then how did Dominic know my name? So I let her go on. 'But we know how to have fun.'

'Oh yeah? Watch all the *Harry Potter* films at Saturday Film Club kind of fun?'

'Hey.' She pointed at me. 'Don't hate on Harry.'

I held my hands up. 'I would never.'

'Yes. Well, as fun as that is,' she went on with sly smile, 'a school like Crofton is nothing without its rules, but rules are meant to be broken, right?'

I perked up at that. 'So they say.'

She glanced over her shoulder, then leaned in. She was loving it, I could tell – the drama of it, teasing me a little – and her eyes were bright. 'The first Alphabet Party is on Saturday.'

'What's that?'

'It's a stupid name, but they've been having them here since the forties. Not everyone is invited,' she told me, and I could tell she loved that, too, 'but the first Saturday of the year, Abbott hosts a party in Savernake Forest, then the month after that Bedwyn does it, then Burnham and every house takes it in turns until the end of the year.'

'Yeah, but next Saturday isn't an exeat weekend.'

'That doesn't matter.'

'Yeah, because you don't board. I'm not allowed out.'

'What was it I said about rules?' She heaved her bag into her lap with a smug smile. She rooted through it for a moment or two, then took out a key and held it out to me.

I stared at it, my lips parted. 'What's that?'

'It's a master key. It will open pretty much any door in Crofton.'

'How did you get it?'

'Don't worry about that.' She rolled her eyes, then handed it to me. 'There's a window in the broom cupboard on the first floor of Burnham that opens on to a flat roof. If you walk across it then climb down the trellis, you can get out without anyone seeing you.' I must have looked horrified, because she shrugged. 'It sounds so Katniss Everdeen, I know, but if you don't want to spend your Saturday nights watching *Clueless* and going to bed early, Adamma, you'd better learn to climb down trellis with your shoes in your hands.'

I tried to picture it and couldn't. Jumoke won't even use the Subway because there are too many stairs. She'll choke with laughter when I tell her.

'Thanks.'

I guess I didn't look grateful enough, because she tilted her head and looked at me. 'Do you know how much that key is worth, Adamma? Molly Avery could pay her fees with the amount she charges girls for master keys.'

'Thank you, Scarlett,' I breathed, closing my fist around it.

'You're welcome,' she said, taking off her jumper. I heard a crackle of static as she pulled it over her head, her dark hair rising then spilling over her shoulders and down her back. I could see her red bra beneath her cotton shirt and when I looked away, I wondered if that was something she did on purpose, if she always wore something red.

'You don't sound African,' she said and I looked at her again.

'What do Africans sound like?'

'You sound American.'

'Do I?' I'd never thought about it.

'I'm so jealous that you got to live in New York!' She swooned. 'I love New York. I go there all the time. I always stay at the Bowery Hotel,' she said, hands everywhere. 'I'm obsessed with the theatre. I was there last month; I went to see John Malkovich in *Waiting for Godot*. Were you born there?' she asked before I had a chance to tell her that I'd seen it as well.

I shook my head. 'No, Nigeria. My father's a diplomat. We lived in Lagos until I was five, then he was posted to Madrid, then to New York when I was seven.'

'You speak Spanish?' She didn't wait for me to answer. 'I love Barcelona.'

'Me too. I much prefer it to Paris.'

'I know, but I have such a soft spot for Paris. That's where my parents met. My older sister Edith was born there. I'm thinking of going to uni there.'

'Is that why you're doing the Baccalaureate not A-levels?'

'That and I'm applying to a few American universities. It makes life easier.'

25

She opened her bag and took out a series of Tupperware tubs, piling them on to the grass between us. She peeled off each lid, revealing bright green salads and shiny cherry tomatoes. When she pulled out a roll and split it in half with her fingers, I watched the flour puff up in the air like dust and thought of the girls at my school in New York who were absurdly proud of the fact that they hadn't eaten bread since they were twelve.

'So which American colleges are you applying to?'

'Juilliard, Duke, Carnegie Mellon, DePaul and Yale.'

'Ah. An actor.'

Her eyes lit up. 'Wannabe Judi Dench.'

I didn't expect that. Most girls our age would have said Angelina Jolie.

'The funny thing is,' she said, unwrapping a slab of cheese, 'my parents aren't like the other parents here. They're total hippies so they just want me to be happy. They aren't putting pressure on me to even *go* to university if I don't want to. I'm too scared to tell them that I want to go to Yale. They'll be so disappointed.'

I giggled, then pretended to nod solemnly. 'My father just wants me to be happy, too. Happy at Cambridge.'

'Is that where he went?'

I nodded.

She rolled her eyes and handed me a piece of cheese, then opened a jar. 'Butternut squash chutney.' She dipped her cheese into it and held the jar out to me. When I copied her, she asked what I thought. 'Dad's trying a new recipe,' she explained and I finally made the connection: Scarlett Chiltern of Chiltern Organics.

'So good,' I told her, holding up the piece of cheese. 'My mother would love it. She's obsessed with your Scarlett Tomato

Chutney. She has a nervous breakdown if she goes to the Fairway Market and they don't have it.'

'Scarlett Tomato!' She pointed at herself. 'That's my recipe! I invented that. I say *invented*, I accidentally put apple in the wrong saucepan, but still. It would never have happened if it wasn't for me.' She giggled and handed me a celery stick. 'It's so funny that you can buy it in New York. I remember the first batch Dad made. He did it in this massive saucepan. I was so little I had to stand on a chair to stir it.'

I smiled. My father can't even make coffee. Neither can my mother; she writes the most beautiful poetry which makes you feel like you can touch the sky, but is confounded by the microwave. But imagining Scarlett on that chair, adding chopped apples to the wrong pan, made me think of our house in Lagos and our cook, Comfort. When I was little, I loved watching her in the kitchen as she hummed to herself while she plucked the bones from stockfish or pounded cocoyams in the mortar. It was so hot in there, though – there was always a huddle of pots boiling gleefully on the stove, steam puffing out of them like smoke – that I couldn't stand to be in there for more than a few minutes.

'Now I'm jealous,' I admitted, biting into the celery and thinking about the dining hall. I was yet to eat there, but didn't have high expectations. I doubt I'd be having moi moi any time soon. 'Do you just get to eat delicious things all day?'

'Pretty much. Dad's trying potato and rosemary bread today. I'll tell him to make extra so we can have it for lunch tomorrow.'

I smiled. 'The French make the best bread.'

She frowned. 'The French?'

'You said your parents met in Paris.'

'Oh, yeah. No. They met in Paris, but they're both English. My mother's a Lister.'

As with her house, she assumed that I knew that too, but I had no idea who the Listers were. Very important, I guessed, so I just smiled sweetly as she told me about her mother who was an only child and, like most of the girls at Crofton, was raised by a nanny. I had a similar upbringing. That surprises some people, they seem to think all Africans are desperately poor. Someone at my last school once asked me if I lived in a house in Nigeria. I guess she thought I lived in a mud hut. I don't. I live in a house. A very nice house, in fact.

I felt a sudden ache as I thought about home, about my big white house and the garden, with its hot, bright flowers and the curved palm leaves that cast shadows on the lawn like black eyelashes in the afternoon sun. I could never run away like Scarlett's mother did; I'd miss my parents too much. Miss how my mother still likes to plait my hair before I go to bed and how my father eats breakfast in a suit while frowning at his copy of *The Vanguard*. But I suppose I can understand why her mother did it, why she felt like she had to run away. I'm an only child, too. I understand the burden of knowing that my family's name ends with me. But that's a good thing, too, I think. When I marry, I can shuffle it off. Make a new name for myself. I guess that's what her mother was trying to do.

The story is hopelessly romantic, and, to be frank, a little cliché, but it is what it is: her mother packed a bag, left a note for her parents, and fled in the middle of the night to Paris. Scarlett spoke of it with such joy: of how her parents met in a café and fell in love; of the top-floor apartment they shared in the twentieth arrondissement and their second-hand brass bed that they dragged into the living room so that they could

28

wake to a view of the rooftops and the Eiffel Tower in the distance. And it was a charming story, one Scarlett was clearly proud of, even though I'm not sure that what her mother did was remarkable enough to warrant being spoken of with such reverence. When I thought about it, it was actually pretty selfish; she was in Paris for a year before she told her family where she was. But I couldn't say that, could I? So I nodded and smiled in all the right places and waited for her to finish.

'So what are your co-curriculars?' she asked without stopping for breath.

'Running, tennis and lacrosse. And I'm thinking, maybe, swimming as well.'

'Oh God, I couldn't.' Her eyes widened as she reached for a grape. 'I hate swimming pools. I can't go near them. My sister, Olivia, swims, though.'

'Does she go to Crofton?'

'Yeah.'

'What year is she in?'

'Ours,' she said with a shrug, offering me the last cherry tomato, then putting the lid back on the Tupperware tub. 'We're twins. She's doing A-levels, though.'

I grinned. 'You're a twin? I've never met a twin before.'

'I was born first,' she said with a grand wave of her hand that told me she was done talking about it, then pulled a magazine out of her bag and started flicking through it. 'So what other co-curriculars are you interested in?'

'I want to go for the *Disraeli*. I used to write for my school newspaper in New York, but I hear it's super hard to get on to.'

'I know the editor, Hannah. I'll introduce you.'

'Really?'

'Of course,' she said, ripping a page out of the magazine, then pulling a pen out of her bag and scribbling something on it.

I didn't know what to say so I just smiled clumsily and said, 'Thank you.'

'Plus Mr Lucas is going to be overseeing it this year and he's a family friend.'

'Really?'

'Yeah. My parents rent out rooms in our house to artists, and—' She stopped folding the page and looked up. 'I almost told you his name then!' she said with a smile, savouring the secret as though it was a truffle. '*Mr Lucas* is a poet. He stayed with us a couple of years ago, after he graduated from Oxford and again when he got the job at Crofton, while his cottage was being decorated. I've never had so many girls drop by unannounced to see how I was.'

She winked then held up her hand, a folded paper boat cupped in her palm.

'That's so cute!'

'It's a ship. I used to make them with my dad when I was little. His were much better, though. He'd find a toothpick and stick a sail on it with my name on. The *HMS Scarlett*.' She smiled to herself and touched the top of it with her finger.

'Why ships?'

She shrugged. 'No idea, but it was our game. We have a globe in our nursery and he'd tell me to find a country. I'd look for somewhere really random like Kazakhstan and we'd go down to the library and find out as much as we could about it, then we'd make a paper ship, walk down the garden to the bridge over the canal and set sail to it.'

'That's lovely.'

30

'Now I write secrets on them, send them off to Kazakhstan.' She smiled at me, then handed me the paper ship. 'So that's your thing, huh?' she asked when I took it, then started gathering the empty Tupperware tubs. 'You want to be a journalist?'

I nodded, putting the paper ship in the pocket of my blazer. 'Wannabe Gwen Ifill.'

'I have no idea who that is,' she admitted with a chuckle. 'But I can tell you who'll also be going for the *Disraeli* – ' She paused for effect – 'Dominic Sim.'

'Let him.'

'Oh really?' she said, shoving the last Tupperware tub into her bag.

'What do you mean?' I asked, watching as she stood up and shook the grass off her blazer. 'He just helped me find Mr Lucas's classroom this morning.'

'Dominic Sim doesn't *just do* anything.'

'You think he likes me?' I stood up and shook my blazer too.

'Just hold on to your knickers around him, Adamma, that's all I'm saying.'

I laughed. 'Thanks for the tip, but he isn't my type.'

'Dominic's *everyone's* type. Didn't you hear why he got kicked out of Eton?'

When I shook my head, she smirked. 'He got a teacher pregnant.'

THE DAY AFTER

MAY

The first time she ran away she was six. She announced it over breakfast, apparently, and I can just see her, a spoon in her hand, little chin raised, telling her parents that she was going to live in Darkest Peru. She even packed a suitcase, a tiny brown leather thing that belonged to the Paddington Bear that stood next to the bookcase in her nursery. She packed the essentials – her toothbrush, her bridesmaid's dress and her grandmother's pearls – then added the round of marmalade sandwiches her father had made her and put on her coat.

Her parents were amused by the whole thing, she says, and even took a photograph (I've seen it, Scarlett in her yellow wellington boots, pouting and clutching the tiny suitcase, the lace from her bridesmaid's dress trapped in the clasp) as they stood by the back door waving her off. Edith and Olivia did too, but as she walked down the stone steps towards the lawn, Olivia began to cry. Her father told her that Scarlett would get scared and turn back, but she didn't, she just stomped and stomped, and when she'd almost reached the end of the lawn (quite a feat for a six year old given it was almost half a mile long), her father ran after her. He grabbed her just as she reached the bridge that arced over the canal and she wriggled in his arms all the way back to the house.

It's in her DNA, apparently, that restlessness, that need to run. She inherited it from her mother, she says. That's why no one was surprised when we found out that she'd run away this morning; she bounces off every wall she touches, like a butterfly trying to find an open window. She's done it so many times – when she went to Glastonbury with Dominic the summer before we met, last October when she went to New York to audition for *Hamlet* and didn't tell anyone because she didn't want to jinx it – that it's just become her 'thing'. Some people play the ukulele, some collect stamps, Scarlett Chiltern runs away. So before Ballard had even finished telling us in assembly, Sam had started a book on when she'd be back. Most people went for twenty-four hours, Molly put £50 on thirty-six because she was sure she was in New York again. When Dominic found out, he told Sam to stop being a dick.

It didn't take long before the theories began to circulate. I was only in the dining hall a few minutes before I heard three: she was in Vegas with a guy she'd met on the Internet, she was doing a campaign with Stella McCartney and she'd got a part in a film with James McAvoy. It's a shame she missed it, she would have loved it.

When I spoke to him earlier, he told me to sign in for lunch then meet him in the prop room. We haven't done that in months, not since we first got together and the thought of waiting until 3 o'clock was unbearable. It feels like it's always me calling – breathless and a little desperate – asking to see him, so I was so excited that I didn't even bother to pretend to queue in the dining hall. I just signed in, then slipped out again. But of all the people to catch me, of course it was Molly.

'Off to meet Dominic?' she said with a satisfied smile.

'Jesus. Will you let it go? I'm not seeing Dominic,' I said over my shoulder, turned and ran towards the theatre, my bag knocking against my hip.

By the time I got to it, my heart was pounding. My fingers trembled as I reached for the handle on the door. It's been five months but I feel that every time and I love it, love how every bit of me shudders at the thought of seeing him again. I held my breath as I ran through the warren of corridors behind the stage, past the dressing rooms and abandoned ladders, checking over my shoulder every other step until I got to the prop room. I sucked in a breath and blew it out again, hoping it would satisfy my throbbing lungs as I stepped into the dim light. But as I walked past the metal shelves of wine bottles and candlesticks, and the rails and rails of costumes, to the back – where the painted wooden cut-outs of ships and cars stood propped against the wall – I couldn't catch my breath.

I went to the corner, to the red-velvet couch we'd claimed as our own, to find it cloaked in a paint-splattered dust cloth. I was tugging it off when he jumped out from behind a painted crocodile, clearly thrilled as I screamed. I slapped his arm, but he was unrepentant, grabbing my waist and pulling me to him.

'I've missed you, Miss Okomma.' He breathed, nose in my hair, mouth on the shell of my ear and, I don't know how, but I knew he was smiling.

'I haven't missed you,' I lied, slapping him again.

He laughed and I could feel his whole body humming as he pulled me closer and it was like when we first got together and he couldn't stop smiling, couldn't stop looking at me, touching me, his finger turning in my hair then tracing the curve of my bottom lip then playing with a loose button on my blazer.

'Are you OK?' I breathed.

He looked at me, then pressed a kiss to my mouth. 'I am now.'

When he held me again, I felt him shaking. He was nervous, I realised – jittery – like when I'm swimming a medley relay and I'm on the starting blocks waiting my turn. I stood back, sweeping his dark hair out of his eyes with my hand.

'Hey, you.'

'Hey.' He smiled, but he wasn't looking at me. His finger and thumb pinched my chin as though he was trying to memorise the shape of my mouth.

'Look at me.' When he did, I tilted my head. 'Are you OK?'

'I just needed to see you.'

'I saw you yesterday.'

He pinched my chin. 'You know I love you, right?'

'Of course.' I moved my hand and let his hair fall back over his eyes.

'Don't say of course.' He frowned and took my face in his hands, the pads of his fingers pressing into my cheeks. 'Say you know, Adamma, because I wouldn't be doing all of this, all of this sneaking around and lying, if I wasn't in love with you.'

'I know.'

He kissed me again, then pressed his cheek to mine. When I'd caught my breath, I put my hand in his hair again and started playing with it.

'This Scarlett thing hasn't got you spooked, has it?'

'Of course not. I just hate this.' He took a step back and looked at me. 'I saw you with Molly. I hate that I can't *just be*

36

with you, that you can't even sneak out of the dining hall without someone seeing you.'

'I know.' I closed the gap between us, pressing my palms to his chest. 'But it's May, this year is almost over and then we have one more before we can move to Cambridge and be together.' He shook his head, but I reached for his lapels and tugged. 'My parents will be pissed as hell, but I'll be eighteen.'

'A year.'

'I know.' Panic plucked at me as he took another step back and rubbed his forehead with his hand. 'But it'll fly by. The last five months have felt like nothing.'

He reached for me again, one hand on my cheek. 'Not nothing.'

I immediately felt better, pressing my cheek into the curve of his palm with a smile. 'So stop fretting.' But when he didn't smile back, I knew it was more than that and I tugged on his lapel again. 'What? Talk to me.'

He sighed and stepped back. 'Why did you go to her party?'

'I told you—'

'You pissed her off,' he interrupted, hands on his hips.

'How do you know?'

Before he could tell me, my cellphone rang. I took it out of the pocket of my blazer to reject the call, but when I saw that it was Mrs Delaney, I muttered, 'Damn.'

'Hello, Mrs Delaney.'

He sighed and shook his head again and when he walked over to the painted crocodile he'd just jumped out from behind, I knew what he was thinking, that there was always an interruption, always *something*.

'Where are you, Miss Okomma?'

37

If it was anyone else, I would have lied and said I was in the dining hall, but it was Mrs Delaney. 'By the canal. I wasn't feeling well so I thought I'd get some fresh air.'

'Well, that's hardly surprising. It is Tex Mex Day in the dining hall,' she said with the sort of contempt usually reserved for paedophiles. 'But you must remember to sign out, Miss Okomma.'

'Sorry, Mrs Delaney.'

'I need you to go to the car park,' she said, pausing to tell someone to do up his tie. 'It seems that someone tried to break into your car last night.'

'My car? Are you sure?'

'Quite sure, Miss Okomma. Security have arranged for it to be towed—'

'Towed?' I interrupted with a gasp.

'I don't know the extent, but there seems to be some damage. Security need you to sign the relevant paperwork.'

'Yes, Mrs Delaney,' I muttered with a sullen sigh.

When I ended the call, he asked me what was wrong and, even though he was sympathetic enough, I knew he was still pissed about Scarlett's party.

'I'm sorry. I'll call you later,' I promised, pressing a quick kiss to his mouth, before hurrying out of the prop room.

I was about to cross the Green when Olivia started walking towards me and my heart sank. I haven't spoken to her since, I don't remember the last time I spoke to her, but it was probably about Scarlett so I knew she didn't want to chat about the weather.

'I can't stop.' I put my head down. 'Someone tried to break into my car last night and the Mercedes garage are coming to tow it.' She followed and the shock of it almost made me break into a trot. 'I have to go, Olivia. If I don't give them the keys now I'll be late for my one-to-one with Madame Girard.'

She's as stubborn as her sister and caught up with me. 'Didn't you write a piece for the *Disraeli* about how Crofton is the safest boarding school in England?'

She wasn't giving me a reason to slow down, but she kept pace as I crossed the Green and I realised that she wasn't going to leave me alone so I slowed down. 'Irony wins again,' I muttered, reaching into my bag and pulling out my sunglasses.

Given all the drama, the weather should have been grim, but today was perfect, the sky clear and the sun gilding all of Crofton's edges. I hadn't expected it to be so warm; last week everyone was wearing scarves and gloves. But that's England; one day I'm wearing a sweater, the next I'm in sandals.

I think that's what I love most about the English: as soon as there's a hint of sun, everyone goes outside. The Green was cluttered with girls sitting on their blazers watching the boys play an impromptu game of rugby. As Olivia and I walked past, heads popped up from each huddle, eyes wide, like meerkats, and I knew what they were thinking: Why was I talking to Olivia Chiltern? I'd wondered the same thing as I weaved between the clumps of girls, stepping over piles of bags and discarded sweaters. I heard a roar and turned to look as a boy skidded across the grass, hugging the ball.

'What are you working on now?' Olivia asked, as we took the short cut to the car park through the trees.

I was startled by her attempt at polite conversation and answered robotically. 'A profile on Mr Lucas,' I told her, ducking under a particularly low branch.

'A profile on a teacher? Wow.' She shook her head and whistled. 'That's front page news, Adamma. That'll get you that Pulitzer.'

I shot a look at her, but when I saw her red eyes and unwashed hair, I softened. I wanted to ask if she was OK, but she wouldn't look at me. Her gaze was on the rows of cars below us at the bottom of the hill, their roofs glistening in the sun, and it was kind of beautiful; if you squinted hard enough it looked like the ocean.

'It's the *Disraeli*, Liv,' I said, then caught myself; Liv sounded too much like we were friends. 'It's for the parents and governors. They only care about exam results and if we beat Cheltenham in the hockey.'

'And teachers.'

'He sold a collection of poems to Faber,' I told her with a sigh. She knew that – everyone did, it was announced in the *Disraeli* last month – so I don't know why she was giving me a hard time. 'Ballard's asked him to revive the *Crofton Review*.'

'Because a lit mag is so much more important than my missing sister.'

So that's why she was so upset.

'Of course it isn't, but parents don't want to read about pupils running away.'

'Scarlett didn't run away.'

I was about to walk down the hill towards the car park when I realised that she'd stopped and walked back over to her. When she crossed her arms and glared at me, I had to resist the urge to roll my eyes because I didn't know what to say. I didn't want to lie and say I was sorry, that I was worried too, and it was suddenly so quiet that I could hear the trees trembling in the wind.

The sun was so bright, even though I had sunglasses on, that I had to shield my eyes with my hand to see her. I'm rarely warm enough to sweat in England – usually I'm the one in a coat while everyone else is in shorts – but my shirt was sticking to my back under my cardigan. I wondered if she'd noticed, if she'd seen the skin around my hairline glisten and asked herself if I was nervous, if I knew something that I wasn't telling her. After all, I'd noticed how pale she looked, how she was holding on to the strap of her satchel with both hands.

Olivia has never been more than Scarlett's sister to me, but I suddenly felt protective of her. She isn't like her sisters. She isn't as restless, as reckless. She doesn't have Scarlett's swagger or their older sister Edith's charm. She's named after her grandmother – a formidable woman who, when introduced to Winston Churchill at the age of seven, told him that she didn't like him much – which isn't as cool as Edith who's named after Edith Piaf or Scarlett who's named after *that* Scarlett and is just as stubborn as Miss O'Hara. So Olivia always describes herself as the boring one, even though she isn't. She may be quieter than her sisters, more careful, but she's the bravest one. She must be to come to me asking for help. Not that I was in any mood to give it to her.

'She's fine,' I told her with a sour sigh. 'It's Scarlett. She'll be back in a couple of days with another tattoo and an epic story about how she got it.'

'She didn't run away, Adamma.'

I shook my head as I remembered last October, the rolling boil of panic from the moment Olivia called to ask if I'd seen Scarlett until I tracked her down to the Bowrey Hotel and she answered with a bored *Hello?*

She'd laughed when she had realised it was me.

Even Dominic was out of his mind with worry and got into a fight with Sam on the Green when Sam said that she'd run off with another guy. It's kind of funny because I know what everyone thinks – that she and I fell out because of Dominic – but all we ever talked about was Scarlett, so if she hadn't run away that day, I would never have gone to him for help and we might never have become friends.

'I know what you're thinking,' Olivia said, and when I saw the tears in her eyes, I had to look away. 'But something's happened to her. I know it has.'

I crossed my arms and made myself look at her. 'Why?'

'She didn't take her passport this time.'

'So?' I shrugged. 'That just means she didn't leave the country.'

'She didn't take anything, her bag – ' she counted off each thing on her fingers – 'her purse, her keys, her mobile. She just left, Adamma.'

That made me hesitate, but I tried not to show any concern. 'Was she upset?'

'She seemed fine. She just said that she'd be back for supper.'

'Did she say where she was going?'

'To see a friend.'

'Who?'

'She didn't say.'

'Did she walk?'

When Olivia crossed her arms and looked away, I realised that Scarlett had taken their Land Rover – a muddied, broken-down thing affectionately known in Ostley as The Old Dear because you heard it wheezing towards you ten minutes before you saw it – and I sighed. She always took The Old Dear, even though she knew her parents needed it for the farm.

The brat.

'See? She's fine, Olivia.'

'But she didn't take any clothes.'

'Like you'd know if she took anything,' I said with a bitter laugh. 'Her room is a disaster. You need a shovel to find the bed.'

'I just know, OK!' She threw her hands up, her cheeks suddenly flushed. 'She's my twin sister and I know that something's happened to her, Adamma!'

'What do you want from me, Olivia?' I said, trying not to lose my temper too.

'I want you to believe me, Adamma.'

'I don't.' I shook my head. 'I'm sorry. I did this the last time, remember? I cried my heart out, sure that she was dead in a ditch, and she was in New York.'

She wouldn't listen. 'Why did she book theatre tickets then?'

A tear rolled down her cheek and she wiped it away with her sleeve before she opened her satchel and pulled out a piece of paper. She handed it to me and I realised it was a ticket confirmation from the Theatre Royal in Bath.

'How the hell did you get into her email?'

'It wasn't hard.' She shrugged. 'Scarlett is impossible with passwords so she has the same one for everything: *password*. But don't worry about that.' She pointed at the confirmation. 'The play was last night. Why hasn't she come back?'

But I wasn't looking at that, I was looking at how many tickets she'd bought – two – and I felt something in me finally snap. 'Because she – ' I shook the confirmation at her – 'and whoever this second ticket was for, probably stayed in a hotel last night,' I said, trying to hide my disdain and failing.

'She wouldn't miss school.'

I tipped my head back and laughed.

'She wouldn't,' she insisted a little sheepishly. 'OK, she did when she went to New York, but that was the beginning of the year. Her first rehearsal for *Pygmalion* is this afternoon.' She must have sensed that I wasn't convinced, because her voice got higher. 'Plus, she got a written warning the last time. Headmaster Ballard told her that if she did it again, she'd be suspended. Even Scarlett wouldn't be so stupid.'

I didn't know that. 'Well, she's an idiot. She'll never get into Yale now.'

'Adamma—'

'Olivia, *enough*.' I held a hand up. 'I don't care. I've left Planet Scarlett and I'm not going back. I don't care where she is.'

She looked horrified. 'You don't mean that, Adamma.'

'I do,' I said, turning and continuing on down the hill to the car park.

'No, you don't,' she called after me. 'You wouldn't have come to our birthday party on Saturday if you didn't still care.'

'I don't,' I said over my shoulder, but *Goddamn Scarlett*, because as soon as I was out of sight, I looked at the confirmation email again.

I was so angry that the words blurred together for a moment, but when they came back into focus, I saw that she had opted to collect the tickets from the box office. Every cell in my body screamed at me not to, not to let her suck me back into her drama, but I took my phone out of my pocket and called the theatre.

'You're the second person to call about these tickets today,' the guy said when I got through to the box office. 'Are you from Wiltshire Police as well?'

My heart stopped then started again, twice as fast. 'Yes. Yes,' I breathed, the lie rolling – too quick, too easy – off my tongue. 'Did she collect the tickets?'

I hadn't realised until that moment that Olivia was right – I did still care – not until I caught myself holding my breath as I heard a voice in my head saying, *Please say yes. Please say yes. Please say yes.*

'No, she didn't.'

224 DAYS BEFORE

SEPTEMBER

In Nigeria we have a saying: hold a true friend with both hands. Scarlett does this too, it seems, because it's been three weeks since I started at Crofton and we've been inseparable. We have lunch by the canal every day and I spend almost every afternoon at her house, in that precious hour between classes finishing and co-curriculars starting, swapping clothes and eating whatever her father has made that day.

It's nice, kind of like it used to be with Jumoke. Even her great, cake-coloured house is beginning to feel like home, despite me being completely overwhelmed by it the first time I went there. It's not that I'm not used to houses like that; my parents are friends with families like the Chilterns, so I've been to parties on the Upper East Side and spent weekends in the Hamptons in vast white houses with porches dusty with sand. I mean, if I could pad around Jumoke's East 82nd Street condo in sweats and that had been featured in *House and Garden*, I didn't expect to be intimidated by Scarlett's house.

But for all of New York's glamour, for all its marble and black lacquer and fringe, I'd never seen a house like Scarlett's. If Jumoke's condo had commanded an entire floor, then

Scarlett's house was the size of a city block. It looked like something from a BBC period drama – big and square with three rows of white-framed windows – and even though I'd heard so much about it (it's talked about at Crofton almost as much as she is) I couldn't help but be a little in awe the first time she led me around it; from the hall into the big yellow music room with its glossy piano and wireless, to the library with the buttery leather armchairs that remember the shape of you until you sit on them again.

She announced each room with no fanfare, as though it was normal, as though every girl lived in a house with a name and a chandelier in every room, but when we got to the drawing room, she smiled. Everything in it looked so stiff, from the huge carved fireplace to the heavy silk drapes, that I couldn't imagine relaxing in a room like that, but I do. We lie in there all the time – her lying on one couch, me on the other – eating fistfuls of popcorn and talking about where we want to go to university, where we want to live, what we want to see. Or, when the sun is out, we open the French windows and sit on the uneven mossy steps that lead to the lawn, the grass rolling out in front of us down, down to the canal with its rickety wooden bridge, and it feels like we have the world at our feet.

That's the thing with her house, it's grand, but they really *live* in it. They don't have a housekeeper (I didn't know this until I noticed the dust on the piano and the white wax weeping from the candelabras in the dining room), which makes sense – her mother didn't want her daughters to have the upbringing she had – but my father would have been appalled. An old house like that needs care, he'd say. He wouldn't approve of the unpolished floors and rumpled rugs. He'd say it was neglect-ful. But Scarlett's house is like a vintage bag; it has so many scuffs because it's used. *Loved*. It's not like Jumoke's magazine-perfect apartment with its white sofas and bowl of green apples in the kitchen that no one is allowed to eat.

The Chilterns live in every corner of their house. It has a smell, a nice smell: old, but kind of comforting, like a spent match or a second-hand book. There are photos of the girls on every wall. The one of six-year-old Scarlett in her yellow wellington boots, pouting and clutching her leather suitcase, is by the door in the mud room, presumably where it was taken before they waved her off. And there's one of the girls in the drawing room, the three of them huddled together and giggling. It's impossible to tell them apart, their faces and white cotton dresses covered in red, pink and blue powder. I guess they were in India for Holi and whenever I look at it, I can almost hear them screaming and chasing one another.

That's what I love about her house: it's a home. There are tulips from their farm in every room and a bowl of browning bananas in the kitchen. Normal things. In the summer, I'm sure she sunbathes on the lawn in her heart-shaped sunglasses – Olivia next to her, reading a book – and slams doors when she doesn't get her way. Every scratch tells a story, every dent, every repaired vase. Even the paintings say something, because that's another thing her mother does that infuriates her grand-mother: she rents rooms to writers and artists – like Mr Lucas – most of whom pay their way with poems or paintings. I've seen the paintings dotted around the house, wild splashes of colour between the dour portraits of the house's previous residents.

Every time I go to her house, I think of my house in Lagos, of its high gates and marble floors, and wonder what it was like to grow up in a house like that. I've never really felt the loss of being an only child, until I imagine the girls skidding in their socks along the floorboards outside their bedrooms and trying to pick out the animals from the dusty tapestry in the dining room while they eat dinner. And I imagined Olivia sitting on her pink meringue of a bed while Scarlett stomped around hers, refusing to tidy it or tugging on the tattered bell pull demanding juice and ginger cake, and I wished I'd known her then, that we'd discovered her hiding places together and counted the steps from the house to the canal.

Everyone at Crofton asks me about it, about what shampoo she uses and what book she's reading and they want to know what her room looks like. I just smile and shrug, but if they thought about it, they'd know that her room is like her – a mess. After all, she can never find anything in her locker and is always hastily putting chewing gum into a folded-up receipt before class, then tossing it in her bag, only to find the gum stuck to a notebook two days later. Her room is much the same; she never makes her bed and clothes hang from everything they can hang from: door handles, chairs, open closet doors. There's stuff all over the place – folded paper ships dotted everywhere, magazines on the floor, a pile of orange peel on her nightstand. It sounds disgusting, but it's so gloriously *Scarlett* with its Mucha posters and aura of Chanel that it's impossible to turn your nose up at it.

It's kind of strange how well I know her house already. Nice strange. I know that the cutlery drawer in the kitchen sticks and that they keep a spare key under the mat outside the back door. I know to avoid the creaky floorboard under the rug in her bedroom in the same way I knew to avoid the creaky step on the staircase at my old house in New York that tried to betray me every time I snuck in when I'd missed my curfew.

50

I know her house better than my new one in London, which I'm yet to sleep in. I saw photos of it before we left New York, so I know that it has square windows like Scarlett's house and a black front door flanked by bay trees and that my room has a tiny fireplace and a view of the garden, but that's it. It's a house in a photograph, not my home. I'd never tell my parents that, though, because it would upset them and I know that sending me away to school hasn't been easy for them, either. Which is why they're so relieved that I've made a friend, particularly my mother who teases me mercilessly whenever I mention her. 'Scarlett, Scarlett, Scarlett. Did you do anything else today, Adamma? Perhaps go to a lesson?'

Jumoke isn't as amused, though. 'Replaced me already, have you?' she said the last time we spoke, making no effort to disguise her contempt. I don't blame her; I was just as petulant when she told me that she was going to Sabrina Earl's seventeenth birthday party. We used to hate Sabrina Earl. How can so much have changed in three weeks?

If Jumoke met Scarlett, she'd understand. She kind of dazzles you. I'm trying to persuade her to fly to London on Friday for my first exeat weekend so that she can meet her. I think they'd love each other and even if they didn't, a weekend with them still had to be better than the horror of last night – my first Crofton social. Scarlett had warned me about them, but I didn't think it would be that bad. After all, it was just a dinner in honour of the *Disraeli* and the sixth formers who want to join the staff, but, as we gathered in the teacher's dining room in Sadon Hall, I counted twenty-two of us. Twenty-two. One girl I spoke to had a short story published in *Granta* last month and another just won Young Photographer of the Year, so what I thought would be a nice, quiet dinner turned out to be more like a job interview with twenty-two other people while trying not to spill soup down my dress.

That's Crofton, it seems. I thought my last school was competitive, but Crofton is in a different class. I used to feel so grown up when Jumoke and I went to bars, sipped cocktails and talked about sex, but I felt like such a kid at the social last night compared to everyone else. There was no trace of awkwardness; they were all so charming and funny and told the sort of anecdotes I'm used to hearing at my parents' dinners at the embassy.

It was kind of weird, though, because while they're all so polite – so proper, like Stepford kids – if you say the word 'penis' to some girls, they immediately revert to being thirteen and collapse into helpless giggles. I think that's why I like Scarlett so much. There's something so hopelessly human about her. She isn't putting on an act; she bites her nails and doodles in class and sulks when she doesn't get her own way, like every other teenager. She's normal, I guess, and at a school where everyone says the right thing and wears the right thing and laughs at the right jokes, she's a splash of graffiti on the wood-panelled walls.

Last night everyone was dressed the same. Even me. I was told it would be informal, but I know that schools like Crofton don't really do 'informal', so I didn't take it literally and rock up in jeans and sneakers. I also resisted the urge to wear one of the bright, patterned dresses I would have worn to an event at my old school. I opted for a simple black one instead and as I stood among the boys in their tweed blazers and the girls in their pretty tea dresses, I was glad I did. But then she swept into the dining room in a floor-length red gown that was enough to make my philosophy teacher, Mr Crane, spill wine down his shirt and I was besotted.

Only Scarlett.

As she drifted around the room, I looked down at my black dress and wished that I'd been brave enough to wear what I wanted. Headmaster Ballard wasn't as impressed, though, and handed Mr Crane a napkin and told us all to sit down.

I was so surprised that it didn't occur to me to question why she was there. It wasn't until I saw her stop to kiss Hannah on both cheeks that I realised why.

'I didn't know you were trying out for the *Disraeli*,' I said, stepping into her path as she made her way to the table.

She stopped and blinked at me – as though she'd never seen me before – then beamed and kissed me on both cheeks, too. 'I'm not trying out,' she said, and there was a slight edge of, *Silly Adamma*. 'Hannah's asked me to do the theatre reviews.'

'Oh. OK,' I started to say, but she just continued on to the table.

I'm not sure how, but I lucked out and the seating plan sat me between Mr Lucas and Hannah. I wondered if it was Scarlett's doing, her way of introducing me to Hannah, as she'd promised to, but when she just waved across the table at her, I realised that she wasn't going to. She had probably forgotten, so I did it myself. I introduced myself to the boy sitting opposite, as well, a guy called Sam Wolfe who held my hand for a moment too long and, when he repeated my name, managed to make it sound dirty, which I didn't think was possible.

British boys continue to disappoint me.

There was an empty chair opposite Hannah and I was wondering who would be foolish enough to be late for an event like this when Dominic strode in in a black suit, which he wore so well it made Hannah blush a little when he introduced himself with a smile. He then turned to me, his smile a little wider, and told me I looked divine. My reaction wasn't as obvious so I hope he didn't see my fingers flutter as I tugged my pashmina onto my shoulders. I hope Mr Lucas didn't notice, either. If he's going to be overseeing the *Disraeli* this year, I don't want him to think I'm a silly schoolgirl easily distracted by compliments.

'I hope my cousin isn't being too lecherous,' Dominic said, then winked at Sam. 'Hands on the table where we can see them, Samuel.'

I was a little startled; they couldn't have looked more different. Dominic's surname was Sim, so I guessed they were related on Dominic's mother's side because they were almost direct opposites of one another; where Dominic has dark hair and eyes, Sam has a tangle of white-blond hair and eyes so blue that they were almost unreal. Disney-prince blue. When Dominic saw me looking between them, he winked and I turned away, determined not to let him distract me as I continued my conversation about Wole Soyinka with Mr Lucas.

As I had suspected, the informal dinner was rather formal. It wasn't unlike the ones at the embassy, but much more English, with white table linen and white plates and perfect medallions of pink lamb, that made me miss my parents' rowdy parties with the decanters of palm wine and bright centre-pieces of lilies and amaryllis.

The conversation was as sober as the food, mostly about school and the upcoming year. Unfortunately, despite chatting animatedly for ten minutes about Wole Soyinka, Mr Lucas wouldn't look at me after resting his knee against mine under the table while we were being served our soup. I was startled, but when I moved and he flushed, apologising clumsily, I realised that he'd thought my knee was a chair leg and had to swallow a laugh.

He didn't look at me again, didn't utter another word, in fact, until the cheese course, when he said how excited he was to be assisting Crofton's Drama department, which has an excellent reputation. It was clearly for the benefit of Headmaster Ballard, who noted the compliment with a nod, but when he went on to say that he would be directing the production of *Hamlet*, Scarlett's eyes lit up. She spent the rest of the evening batting her eyelashes at him until she heard Dominic and Sam trying – and failing – to woo me in French, and couldn't resist joining in.

Where my French was competent, if a little awkward, she chatted breezily, bantering with Dominic and Sam, who were also fluent. Within a few moments, everyone at the table was rapt and when she had their attention, she explained why she spoke French so well. She told them the story of her mother running away to Paris, about her parents' apartment with its second-hand brass bed and how her sister Edith was named after Edith Piaf, who was born under the lamp post across the street. When she was done, you could have heard a pin drop.

It's impossible to describe Scarlett to anyone who hasn't met her, which is why I'm so desperate for Jumoke to meet her. I'm in awe of her, I know, and it's silly – like I have a hopeless crush – but at a school like Crofton, she is nothing but light and colour. I don't know if I would have survived the last three weeks without her. After dinner last night, when everyone was on the lawn outside the teacher's dining room trying to impress Hannah with better – brighter, funnier – stories, Scarlett stopped me as I was about to join in and pulled me into the shadows around the side of Sadon Hall. When we were far enough away, she grinned, the light from the dining-room window hitting her cheek, making her blue eyes look like they were made of glass.

'This is so boring, Adamma. I want to dance.'

'I covet that dress,' I told her as she raised one arm and twirled.

She perked up at that. 'Olivia's going to kill me dead. I bought it with her credit card.' She threw her head back and laughed, clearly unrepentant.

I sniggered, too. 'What about your card?'

'Daddy cut it up after the *Waiting for Godot* incident.'

'Ladies,' Sam said, appearing from nowhere.

Scarlett put her hand on her hip with a playful smile. 'Got a fag?'

He pulled a pack of cigarettes out of the pocket of his jacket and opened it. Scarlett took one, put it between her red, red lips and waited for him to light it. When he did, he held the pack out to me, too, but I refused, stunned as I watched Scarlett inhale then blow the smoke towards the sky. I had no idea she smoked.

'I have some of this, if you prefer,' he said, taking a silver hip flask out of his other pocket and holding it up to me with a proud smile.

'What is it?'

Scarlett didn't wait for him to answer, just thrust her glass at him. I had a moment's hesitation as I watched him pour some of whatever it was into her glass, thinking of who was gathered a few feet away. When she saw me watching, she smiled and I knew what she was thinking, so I held my glass out too and she cheered. She thinks I'm so prim; *You're such a princess*, she tells me whenever she watches me pour a can of soda into a glass or

56

catches me checking my make-up between classes. Maybe I am. I've never drunk from a hip flask before.

I hadn't even taken a sip before Dominic came around the corner, his eyebrow arching when he saw us huddled in the shadows.

'And then there were four,' Scarlett said with another grin.

He looked at her and nodded towards the party. 'Hannah's looking for you.'

'Shit,' she muttered, flicking her cigarette into the bushes.

I watched as she downed her drink then walked around the corner towards the light of the lawn. When we lost sight of her, Dominic turned to Sam, who took the hint and followed her back to the party. When we were alone, I tensed, waiting for Dominic to smile and say something charming, but he frowned.

'What are you doing?' He took the glass and sniffed it, then tossed the contents into the bushes. 'Is that how you're going to impress Hannah? With the smell of Jack Daniel's on your breath?'

'Give me a break. It wasn't even a shot,' I snapped. Of all the people I expected to get a lecture on drinking from, I didn't think it would be Dominic Sim. He sounded like my father. 'Scarlett just downed a whole glass. Go tell her off!'

He shook his head, then turned back towards the party. 'Keep doing what Scarlett does, Adamma,' he said over his shoulder. 'See how far you get.'

I was furious, but I've been thinking about it all day. He's right, I know. Scarlett has her spot on the *Disraeli*, she doesn't need to try out like I do, so drinking wasn't my brightest moment. I'm not usually so easily swayed, but there's something about Scarlett. She reminds me so much of Jumoke – she's wicked and funny and has an answer for everything. I love our lunches by the canal, waving at the brightly painted barges as they go past and, when it's too cold to sit outside, giggling on the top row of the bleachers, the pool below us, big and bright and blue. She makes me do things I would never usually do, like sneak out of Burnham on a Sunday afternoon and drive around Ostley in The Old Dear with the windows down and the sun on our cheeks.

She shouldn't be driving, because she's only sixteen and doesn't have a licence yet, but her parents don't seem to mind as long as she stays in the village. They don't seem to mind about a lot of things, actually. They're so cool, much cooler than my parents. I mean, I know my parents could be way worse, but they're not as liberal as they think they are; they think I'm too young to be in a serious relationship (another reason they were so keen to move to the UK, because it would put some distance between me and my boyfriend, Nathan, who my father thought I was seeing far too much of) and they never let me drink apart from a glass of champagne on special occasions. But Scarlett's parents aren't like that *at all*. Last Sunday, her mother didn't say anything when we took a bottle of red wine from the kitchen and drunk it in the big yellow music room. She just grabbed a glass and came in and danced to Fela with us.

I guess that's why Scarlett is the way she is – so brave, so restless – because her parents let her do whatever she wants. She always knows a window at school that's been left open or a door that's unlocked, and if it isn't, we have the master key. Today we got into the new observatory, which still smelt of paint, the chairs covered in canvas drop cloths and the new telescope wrapped in plastic ahead of the unveiling on Saturday.

'Be sure to thank Dominic for this the next time you see him,' she'd told me, giving the telescope a playful pat. 'His family donated it.'

'Wow.' I raised an eyebrow. 'That's quite a donation.'

'Almost every boarding school in England has one. Or a new library. Dominic would never go to school otherwise; in the last year he's been kicked out of Harrow and Eton. It's a good thing his family have more money than God.'

'What do they do?'

'I don't know, but they're obscenely wealthy. His father invented the Internet, or something,' she said with a regal shrug. 'His parents spend most of their time travelling between Seoul, California and here, so Dominic never sees them, which is why he's so horribly misunderstood.'

'Have you known him long?' I asked, stepping over a paint tray and roller and walking over to where she was standing.

'As long as I can remember,' she said, tipping her head back to look up at the domed roof. 'He's the boy next door.'

'Really?'

'Sort of. Technically he lives in Burbage. His house is on the other side of the canal, directly opposite mine. When we were little, we used to meet on the bridge, make paper ships and race them.' She turned to look at me. 'I always made mine out of a different coloured paper because he cheated.'

'I didn't realise you were so close.'

'He was my first –' she shrugged – '*everything*.'

I looked away, suddenly out of breath. 'I had no idea.'

I was about to ask her if she loved him, but she'd already moved on, her eyes bright and a brush in her hand as she dared me to paint something rude on the wall.

I've never met anyone like Scarlett. Dominic has flirted relentlessly with her since I started at Crofton, but Scarlett hasn't said a word. Yet she wants to know everything about me, about every boy I've kissed, every girl I've thought of kissing, about every crack in my heart. It's as if my life is a cake she wants to gorge on while she doesn't tell me a thing. Just the same old stories about her mother and Paris and the second-hand brass bed.

If I told Jumoke, she'd say that she had something to hide.

THE DAY AFTER

MAY

Signing the paperwork to get my car towed took forever, so I was late for my meeting with Madame Girard and had to run back to Burnham. I was in such a rush that I didn't see Orla waiting for me until she grabbed my sleeve and led me around the side.

'Orla, wait,' I gasped, almost tripping on a tree root that had punctured through the grass. 'I can't. Not now, I'm late.'

She ignored me, finally stopping outside the door to the laundry room. 'I saw him,' she said, eyes wet, her fingers still curled in the sleeve of my cardigan.

'Who?'

'That policeman, DS Bone. The one you wanted me to speak to after –' she stopped to suck in a sob – 'after –' she tried again, but couldn't say it. 'You know?'

I knew.

'Bones was here?'

'I saw him coming out of Headmaster Ballard's study.'

'Did he see you?'

She shook her head. 'I hid behind a tree.' She laughed and sucked in another breath. 'How pathetic is that?'

61

'It's not pathetic, Orla.' I frowned. 'It's not pathetic at all.'

'Is that why he's here?' she asked, her eyelashes sticky with mascara.

'He can't be. That was *months* ago.'

'But what if he is? What if he tells everyone?'

'He won't.' I reached over and wiped a tear away with the pad of my thumb.

'How do you know?'

'Because he *can't* tell anyone. He doesn't even know your name.'

'So why is he here, Adamma? What if everyone knows?' Her gaze flicked to the path and I turned to see Molly walking out of Burnham, the sun on her hair making it look even blonder. Orla lowered her voice. 'What if it's around school already?'

'If it was, one of us would have heard.'

She nodded, but when I took a step back, she asked me where I was going. I told her that I was going to speak to him and I heard her release a breath.

'You are?'

'Don't worry.' I squeezed her arm. 'I'll find out, OK?'

'Thank you.' She pulled me into a hug. I could feel her trembling and when I smelled her sweet, pink perfume, I hugged her tighter. When she let go, she wiped her cheeks with the heels of her palms. 'You won't tell him my name, will you? I don't want my father to find out. He'll blame himself. He saves me from everything.'

'Of course I won't. Now go inside. I'll text you when I've spoken to him.'

'Thank you, Adamma.'

'I have my one-to-one with Madame Girard, so I need you

to cover for me, OK?' She nodded. 'Tell her that I can't make it because someone tried to break into my car last night and I'm in the car park getting it towed.'

She nodded, but she looked so scared that I hugged her again.

I waited for DS Bone on the hood of his car, a battered green thing I'd nicknamed Kermit. I'd almost finished reading my newspaper when finally I saw him walking through the car park, his white shirt too bright in the sunlight, like something from a commercial for laundry detergent. I haven't seen him since February, but he looked the same, tall and lean, though his cake-batter-coloured hair was shorter and noticeably lighter than the moustache/beard combo he was experimenting with, no doubt in an attempt to look older. It wasn't working. But at least he hadn't surrendered to the cheap suits police detectives seem to insist on wearing and was in jeans and a pair of aviator sunglasses that were too nice to be chasing criminals in.

He didn't see me, he was too distracted as he undid the top button on his shirt and loosened his tie, so when I jumped down from the hood of his car, he stepped back.

'Hey, Bones,' I said with a grin.

'Adamma,' he said, hands on his hips, the corners of his mouth twitching.

'How's it going?'

'Good,' he said warily. 'You?'

'I'm good. How funny! Bumping into you here.'

'I know, *how funny*, bumping into me, here, by my car.' I saw the top of his eyebrow spring up over his sunglasses. 'What do you want, Adamma?'

63

'Why so suspicious, Bones? I'm just saying hello.'

'OK. Hello, Adamma,' he said, reaching into the pocket of his jeans and pulling out his keys. He opened the car door, then said, 'Goodbye, Adamma.'

'So why are you here?'

He stopped, fingers curled over the top of the open car door. 'There it is.'

'Come on, Bones.' I winked theatrically at him. 'You can tell me.'

The corners of his mouth twitched again. 'You know I can't.'

'Please, Bones,' I said as he started to get into the car. 'My friend, the one I told you about, is worried sick. She thinks you're here to talk to her.'

He stopped, then turned to face me again. 'Tell her not to worry.'

'So you're not here about that?'

My heart thumped suddenly, but I tried to ignore it.

'No.'

'You're here about Scarlett, aren't you?' I blurted out when he turned back to his car.

'The case has been passed on to me, yes.' I wanted him to take his sunglasses off, even though I didn't know what would be more unnerving: being able to see his eyes or not.

'I thought you were CID?' I said, trying not to give into the panic punching at me. 'Why has the case been passed on to you? Why? She ran away.'

'Look, don't panic, OK—' he started to say, but I didn't let him finish.

'What's this got to do with CID? She hasn't even been gone a day.'

'Actually, she has; she left this time yesterday."

'Yeah. But . . .' I breathed, but he interrupted me this time.

'CID being called in doesn't mean anything, OK?' He held up a hand. 'We're just being careful. If her family didn't own half of Ostley, no one would give a shit.'

'You weren't called in last time.'

'I have to get back to Swindon and I'm sure you have a lesson to go to.' He nodded towards the main hall. 'If you have any questions, speak to your housemistress.'

'My *housemistress*? What the hell? Don't give me that, Bones.' My hand curled around the strap of my bag. 'What's going on? Her sister's going out of her mind.'

'It's fine. I just spoke to her.'

'Fine?'

'Yes. *Fine*.'

'So Scarlett's OK? You know where she is?'

He sighed heavily and I thought he was going to fob me off again, but he took his sunglasses off, rubbed the bridge of his nose, then put them back on. 'If she isn't back by tomorrow morning, which she will be, then we'll issue an appeal.'

'An appeal?' I repeated, but the word didn't feel real – *appeal* – like a sweet that fizzes on your tongue then disappears. 'So she hasn't run away?'

'That's all I can say right now, Adamma.'

He turned and climbed into his car, but before he closed the door, I grabbed it with my hand. 'It was you. You called the theatre about the tickets.'

'I have to go,' he said without looking at me.

I let him close the door, and watched as he drove out of the car park. As soon as he turned out of Crofton, I ran back to my room and got my other cellphone out of my tuck box. It took an eternity for the menu to load, but as soon as it did, I called him. It went straight to voicemail and something in me wilted. I wanted to hang up, but I made myself wait for the beep, then breathed, 'It's me. We need to talk about Scarlett.'

212 DAYS BEFORE

OCTOBER

Today I got my first assignment for the *Disraeli*. It wasn't much, I was just asked to cover the Crofton/Cheltenham hockey match, but it was something. The trouble was, Dominic was the photographer assigned to work with me and that was never going to end well, was it? It didn't help that I was still prickly after what he had said at the social last week, and when he showed up an hour late – sauntering with no trace of urgency towards the door to the girls' changing rooms where I'd been waiting for him – I had to fight the urge to club him with a hockey stick.

'I've already done the interview with Chloe,' I told him, arms crossed.

'Fine,' he grinned, holding up his camera, 'I'll just take some shots.'

I grabbed him by the sleeve of his coat and tugged him back. 'Like hell you're taking photos in the girls' changing rooms. This article is for the *Disraeli*, not *FHM*.'

'I love cross Adamma. She's my favourite.' The skin around his mouth creased as his smile widened, but I ignored him.

'Let's just head over to the pitch, the match is about to start.'

'Is that what you're wearing?' He frowned and I had to take a deep breath; I hate it when guys think they can comment on what I'm wearing. He must have known I was pissed, because he held his hand up. 'Not that you don't look ravishing, as always, but you do know that it's October and this match is outside, right?' He pointed up at the ominous black clouds.

'This is waterproof.' I ran my hands down my Burberry trench coat. My Lois Lane trench coat purchased especially for my *Disraeli* assignments.

He didn't look convinced. 'If you say so, Miss Okomma.'

He stopped to talk to so many people on the way to the pitch – mostly girls whose hands lingered on his shoulders when he leaned down to kiss them on both cheeks – that I went on without him. I was nearing the pitch when I felt the first drop of rain, as it hit the top of my ear with a cold splash that made my shoulders jump up. I shivered and turned the collar of my coat up, wondering if there was enough time to head back to Burnham for an umbrella, but when I looked back at the changing rooms to see the players jogging out, I settled for a spot on the edge of the pitch next to a kind man with a big umbrella.

By the time the match started with a roar, the rain was biblical. To make matters worse, there was no sign of Dominic, so when Crofton scored early, I was livid and took some photos on my phone so I had *something* to include with my story.

Luckily, the shower was fierce but quick and after about fifteen minutes, it stopped. People began to close their umbrellas and that's when I saw Dominic, the hood of his Crofton sweatshirt up as he weaved through the crowd, taking photos of the game and the mothers pacing the sidelines in their Hunter wellies, their hands balled into fists.

When he worked his way around to me, he grinned and said, 'Let's go.'

'Dominic!' I stopped to grab his coat as he turned to walk away. My fingers were so cold I thought they were going to snap. 'The match has just started.'

'Don't worry.' He held up his camera. 'I have everything and you know what you're going to write, right? Chloe Poole, scholarship girl done good. What more do you need?'

'The score might be useful.'

'Someone will tell you that!' he shouted as the crowd cheered.

I looked at the pitch to see who'd scored and when I turned back to him, he was walking away. I went after him and snatched the camera out of his hands.

'You've been taking photos for all of fifteen minutes, Dominic,' I hissed, wiping the raindrops from the screen with the pad of my thumb. 'You can't have enough.'

As I scrolled through them, I was surprised to find that he did. There were dozens of the players, some great ones of Chloe and one of a little girl in a Cheltenham sweatshirt looking forlorn as the girl in the Crofton scarf next to her cheered. I probably should have stopped there, but when I saw the other ones he'd taken, I kept going. I expected to find a series of pictures of him and Sam with a parade of pink-lipped girls holding champagne glasses, but there was one of a farmer stopping outside a newsagent to frown at a poster in the window advertising pints of milk for 40p and another of a Google logo stuck to the door of a boarded-up library, and I was impressed. Then I got to one of Scarlett and stopped. She had her eyes closed and one hand covering her face as she laughed, but I knew it was her. When I realised that her shoulders were bare and saw her dark hair spilling across the pillow under her head, I almost dropped the camera.

The photograph was taken in the last week because Scarlett had bangs in it, but I had no idea when. She hadn't mentioned it, yet there she was, in bed, laughing, and I felt like an idiot, not just because I didn't know, but because she didn't tell me. Did she think that I was going to judge her?

Would I judge her?

'OK. You have enough.' I handed him back the camera.

'This way,' he called out to me when I started to head towards Burnham.

'What way?'

'I have to show you something.' He nodded towards the car park.

'I can't just leave, Dominic. I need to go back to Burnham and get a pass—'

'We'll go through the car park,' he interrupted. 'No one will see.'

'Forget it, Dominic. I'm cold and wet and I just want to go back to my room,' I muttered. The rain may have stopped, but I was still shaking, my breath puffing out in front of me as I crossed my arms and told him that I'd see him on Monday.

But before I turned away again he said, 'Fine. But you were at that dinner last week, Adamma. Do you think this –' he nodded at the hockey players charging across the pitch – 'is going to be enough to get Hannah and Mr Lucas's attention?'

'What can we do, Dominic? This is what we were assigned,'

I told him with a defeated shrug. But I can't lie, I'd wondered the same thing.

'Did you know that there are only two spots on the *Disraeli* for sixth formers?' I didn't. 'One Senior Features Writer and one Senior Photographer. I'm up against someone who won Young Photographer of the Year. This face can get me pretty much anything I want –' he sighed theatrically – 'but I don't think it can compete with *actual talent*.'

I sighed too and glanced at the pitch. Earlier, when I'd been looking for him in the crowd, I'd recognised some of the faces, but was too pissed at him to think much more about it. I still didn't know everyone's names, so I'd assumed I knew them from class or had seen them around school. But then I saw her, the girl whose short story was published in *Granta*, holding out a Dictaphone to Orla Roberts, who didn't play today because she'd sprained her knee, and realised what Hannah had done: she'd assigned us all the same story.

I turned back to Dominic with another sigh. 'Fine. What've you got?'

He licked his lips, then grinned. 'Fuck this shitty hockey game. I have a story.'

It had stopped raining, but I still wanted to cry. I wanted to be in Lagos. I find myself missing home at the strangest times – not just when I'm frowning at a plate of shepherd's pie in the dining hall or laughing at my grandmother on Skype because she won't talk to me until she's changed out of her old boubou – but on days like today, after the rain, when my limbs suddenly felt heavier as I followed Dominic away from the hockey pitch. It was probably because my hair was wet and I could smell my mango shampoo and it made me think of Comfort's mango cake, of sneaking slices of it with my father when she'd gone to bed. I even began to miss New York. At least there autumn is lazy and golden. As my shoes squelched in the muddy grass, I thought of the colours changing in Central Park – green to red to gold – and wondered if Ostley would be as beautiful, if the leaves would fall from the trees like brown paper butterflies.

'I love this weather,' Dominic told me as we took the short cut to the car park.

When we approached the top of the hill, he held out his hand and I refused, until the sole of my shoe skidded in the mud, and I took it. At least he wasn't offering to carry me.

'You love rain?' I muttered, horrified.

'When it's fierce like that.' When we got to the bottom of the hill, he started unbuttoning his coat, then he shrugged it off. 'It feels like the world is about to end.'

I looked up at the grey sky as we walked through the car park. 'I think it might be.'

His eyes lit up. 'We should probably do it in case it is.' I sighed wearily, but when he tugged off his sweatshirt, the black T-shirt underneath riding up to expose a strip of skin and the waistband of his underwear, I tensed, sure that he meant it. But then he handed me the sweatshirt. 'Put this on, Miss Okomma. Your magical waterproof trench coat has failed you and I don't want you to catch pneumonia.'

I stuck my nose up at it. 'I'll be fine.'

'Stop being a princess.'

'I'm not. I just don't get why I can't go back to Burnham and change.'

'Because it might be raining again in ten minutes. We won't be able to see anything if it's raining.'

'See what?'

'Patience, little one. Now take it. Quick, before the heavens open again.'

I glanced at the grey sweatshirt. It looked so tempting – all soft and warm and fluffy – that my disdain dissolved. 'Fine,' I muttered, peeling off my trench coat.

'You should probably take that off too.' He nodded at my sweater. 'It looks soaked.' It was, but I had no intention of removing any more clothing in front of him. 'Fine. I won't look,' he said, turning his back and putting his coat over his head. I considered leaving him like that, but instead ducked behind the Range Rover we were standing beside and tore off my sweater, then tugged on his sweatshirt so quickly that I banged my elbow against the window.

'That sounded like it hurt,' he said from under his coat.

'Let's get this over with,' I said, emerging from behind the Range Rover.

He pulled his coat away and grinned. 'That's the spirit!'

'This had better be worth it.'

He put his coat back on with a laugh and I thought it was at me, until he told me that he'd never seen me like that before.

'Like what?'

'I dunno. Like *you*, I suppose. You're so quiet when you're with Scarlett.'

'Am I?'

'Yeah. You never say anything. *This*', he pointed at me, 'is the Adamma I met outside English lit last month. I've missed her.' He turned to me with a loose smile. 'I know Scarlett's a human tornado, but you shouldn't let her overpower you.'

I didn't realise I did.

'I'm about to say a whole lot more if you don't tell me where we're going,' I warned, as I stopped to check my make-up in the wing mirror of a car, licking my thumb and wiping away the black smudges of mascara from under my eyes before we carried on.

'You'll see.'

When we passed his car, I frowned. 'Aren't we driving?'

'Don't worry, it's only a few minutes' walk.'

I knew where we were going then. 'So what's in Savernake Forest?'

He shot me a look, gaze narrowing as I smiled smugly. 'How did you know?'

'You don't walk anywhere, Dominic, so we have to be going to Savernake Forest because you don't want to damage your precious car.'

'That,' he thumbed over his shoulder, 'is a 1964 Aston Martin DB5 and the road through Savernake Forest is barely a road. It's some gravel held together with tree sap and the tears of drunk Crofton girls.'

I knew what he meant, it was fine to run on, but if I had a car, I'd think twice about driving on it, too. That didn't mean I couldn't tease him about it, though.

'It's just a car.'

'Sssh!' he said theatrically, waving his hands about. 'She'll hear you.'

'How come you even have a car? Don't you have to be seventeen to drive here?'

'I'm driving it illegally.'

'No you're not.'

'Scarlett drives The Old Dear all the time.'

'Not *all the time* and definitely not to school. You love that car, if you were driving it illegally, you wouldn't risk parking it at Crofton. Security would notice.'

74

'OK, Nancy Drew.' He shrugged. 'Maybe I'm a bit older than you think I am.'

'How much older?'

'Forty-two. That's my car. My wife drives the Volvo.' I raised an eyebrow at him and he sighed dramatically. 'Fine. I'm already seventeen.'

'How come?'

'I lost a year.'

'How do you lose a year, Dominic?'

'I'm quite the scatterbrain, Miss Okomma.' He smiled, but when I didn't smile back, he turned away and shook his head. 'It's a long story.'

'Give me the CliffsNotes, then.'

'Harrow. The Headmaster's daughter.'

I sighed and shook my head. 'Jesus, Dominic.'

'What?' He feigned innocence. 'I loved her.'

'Of course you did.'

'I love them all,' he said with an unrepentant smile, then kicked at a particularly large piece of gravel. 'I was blacklisted after that. If Scarlett and her parents hadn't sweet-talked Mr Lucas into giving me a reference to Eton I would have ended up at school in Alaska. They still made me retake the year, though.'

'I had no idea.'

'There are lots of things you don't know about me, Miss Okomma,' he said with a lascivious wink and I realised that he still hadn't answered my question.

'So what's in Savernake Forest?'

'You'll see.'

'I'm guessing a hot shower is out of the question?' I asked with a shiver.

'It can be arranged.' He waggled his eyebrows.

'Hands up who's not going to get punched in the face in a minute.' I put my hand up and looked around at the neat rows of cars still dripping with rain.

He laughed, nudging me with his hip.

'Face. Punched,' I reminded him with a scowl.

He went quiet and I wondered if he thought I was being serious. But then he said, 'You've seen the photo, then.'

'Which photo?'

'You know which photo.'

I feigned nonchalance, waving a hand at him. 'I don't care.'

'Clearly. You've only threatened to punch me twice in the last five minutes.'

'Like I'm the first person to do that.'

'OK, Miss Okomma,' he said with a slow smile.

We walked the rest of the way in silence and when we turned left out of Crofton towards the forest I relaxed. I'm very fond of Savernake Forest; I go running in it every morning. It's been a relief to have somewhere to run where I know I'm not being watched, where I can just run and run without worrying about the sweat patches on my T-shirt and my messy hair; where I don't have to think about Crofton's sharp spires and green, green lawns and homework and what universities I'm applying to next year and why Jumoke hasn't replied to my last two emails. I guess it's kind of funny, how it takes running until my lungs feel like they're going to burst until I can take a breath.

As we approached the stone pillars that mark the entrance, the light began to change. It went from grey to gold as we passed under the canopy of trees towards the road that runs through the middle of the forest, cutting through the beech

76

trees, neat as the parting my mother used to comb into my hair when I was a kid. The four-mile-long road leads from the entrance to a pair of iron gates that are just known at Crofton as 'the gates', which is as far as Mrs Delaney permits me to run. I don't know what's behind them, they probably belong to one of the private houses, but there are several stories at Crofton: an old insane asylum, a mansion where the lady of the house was murdered and now haunts the forest in a white dress, and my personal favourite, an abandoned coaching house where the girls from Crofton used to go with bottles of gin and knitting needles if they found themselves 'in trouble'.

The gates are usually locked, but someone at Crofton has a key, so that's where the parties are usually held. Every Halloween, Scarlett says, the Upper Sixth host one there that's invitation only. It's a huge deal, apparently, especially as you only know if you're invited on Halloween morning, when the chosen ones wake up to a white postcard with a black cat on it. Scarlett already knows what she's going to wear. She showed me the dress with great glee the last time I was at her house and when she did, I thought of the one I'd bought in London our first exeat weekend, the black one with the lace that kind of looks like cobwebs. It wasn't an accident that I'd picked it out, not after she'd said, 'You're new, so you shouldn't be invited, but I go every year, so you'll probably get a postcard.' I was too distracted by the thought, so didn't notice when Dominic started to veer off the road towards the trees.

'Where are we going?' I asked when I caught up.

'It isn't far.' He looked down at my muddied ballet pumps. 'Are you gonna be OK?'

'I'll be fine.'

'If you say so, Miss Okomma,' he said with a shrug, taking my trench coat and sweater from me and throwing them over his shoulder. 'This way.'

He began walking through a break in the trees, towards a path. It wasn't a proper path, it had just been worn into the ground by years of people walking over it, so it was narrow and uneven, and my shoes slipped on the wet leaves as I followed him. The trees were still heavy with water and dripped on us as we passed under them. The smell made me think of something I read in an article once about the smell of rain. Apparently, rain doesn't smell of anything, it's the moisture in the air that heightens the smell of everything around you so you smell what you couldn't before. This afternoon, the forest smelt earthy, of wet soil and mushrooms and piles of raked-up leaves and it was a smell I knew, that I found comforting, even though I usually only smell it in those scented candles you buy in gift shops.

After a few minutes, the sunlight began to push through the trees, sieving through the browning leaves into white threads that illuminated the forest floor and the spider webs shivering in the breeze. He kept turning back to check I was OK as we stepped over the stray tree roots, twigs snapping, loud and sharp as bones beneath our feet. I could hear the birds too, chattering in the trees above us and making the leaves rustle as they darted from branch to branch. As we passed under one tree, we startled them because they flew away in such a rush that it showered us with leaves that fell around us like brown confetti.

Eventually he reached an oak tree that must have fallen over in the last storm and lay on its side, its pale, torn belly exposed. He slapped it with his hand as he went past, turning left and heading into a thicker, darker part of the forest. He turned back to make sure that I was following him, his forehead creased and his arm outstretched as it got darker. I didn't want to take his hand, but common sense prevailed and I reached for it; his palm warm against mine as he led me towards a clearing. When we got to it, he let go, as the trees parted to expose the open, blue-grey sky above our heads, flooding everything beneath them with light.

'This is it,' he said, out of breath.

'What is?'

'A couple of kids from Crofton were running through here last night.'

'Running through *here?*' I interrupted, looking back the way we came. 'Why didn't they stick to the road? You can't run through here, it's too uneven.'

'OK, they were looking for somewhere to shag.' He rolled his eyes. 'Stop being so judgmental, Adamma.'

'I'm not being judgmental.'

'Yes you are. You have Adamma face.'

He didn't give me time to retaliate, he just ran ahead, and by the time I got to him, he was standing in the middle of the clearing, his lips parted.

'Look, Adamma,' he gasped, eyes big and black.

I looked around at the scene and it made my heart beat too fast. Stick figures hung from the trees, the twigs tied together with string so that they looked like people, and on the forest floor, there were piles of rocks. Each pile was spaced out across the clearing and as I watched him run between them, taking photos, I realised what was going on and let go of a breath.

'Um, Dominic,' I said, unsure whether to tell him, because he was so excited.

79

He wasn't listening, he was taking photos of a pile of twigs that were tied together with a strip of plaid material. 'Hannah will lose her shit when she sees this.'

'Dominic,' I said again, trying not to giggle. 'I think you've been had.'

'Had? What?' he asked between snaps as I walked towards him.

'I think this is a joke.'

He looked up at me, bewildered. 'A joke?'

'Yeah.' I gestured at the pile of twigs at our feet. 'The Blair Witch.'

'What?'

'The movie, *The Blair Witch Project*. Haven't you seen it?' He shook his head. 'This is pretty much it. Someone's obviously playing a prank. It's Halloween this weekend, maybe they're trying to scare some of the kids at Crofton.'

He looked around at the scene, eyes wide, then muttered, 'Fucking Sam.'

'This is actually pretty clever, for him,' I conceded, but Dominic was livid and stomped around, kicking at the piles of rocks as I tried not to laugh. 'What did you think this was? Some sort of pagan sacrifice?'

'Fucking Sam,' he hissed again, then marched back to where I was standing. As he did, my coat and sweater slipped off his shoulder and he tugged them back on with an angry huff. 'I'm gonna kill him.'

'OK.' I crossed my arms. 'But can we go now? I'm freezing.'

He looked a little despondent as we turned to walk back the way we had come, this time side by side. 'Are you pissed that I made you come here for nothing?'

I wasn't, actually. 'You didn't make me do anything. I was

curious,' I said as I watched him put the lens back on his camera. 'Plus I got to see a different side of you.'

He looked up with a big smile. 'A more doable side?'

'A more annoying side.' I retracted with a sneer.

'Are you pissed about Scarlett?'

I stiffened. 'I told you: I don't care.'

'I'd be pissed-off if my best friend was keeping stuff from me, but you should get used to that.'

'So it seems.' I looked down at my shoes. They were ruined.

'Welcome to Planet Scarlett. Population: everyone,' he chuckled, then licked his lips. 'She's always been a brat, you know. When we were kids, we used to meet on the bridge over the canal between our houses, make paper ships and race them.' He raised an eyebrow. 'I always made mine out of newspaper because she cheated.'

I thought of her again, in the observatory, looking up at the domed ceiling – *He was my first everything* – and felt the itch of something.

'Is that why you're doing this?' I asked.

'Doing what?'

'Flirting with me. To make her jealous?'

'No.' He looked horrified. 'Of course not.'

'So what's going on here, then?'

'I don't know.' He shook his head and looked down at his camera again. 'I don't know.'

'Are you two together?'

'She doesn't want to be in a relationship.'

It wasn't a no.

'But you do?'

'It doesn't matter what I want.'

'Of course it does, Dominic.'

'Not with Scarlett. You'll see,' he said with a bitter laugh, then thought better of it, his face softening. 'But don't be pissed at her, Adamma. It's not her fault, it's us.' He sighed. 'We're a fucking train wreck. Don't try and get in the middle of it.'

'Why are you trying to put me in the middle of it, then?'

He *oofed* and missed a step as though I'd punched him in the chest. 'You're right. I am. Sorry.' He shook his head then glanced sideways at me, his cheeks suddenly pink. 'I used to think she was the one, you know?'

I nodded, but I didn't. I thought of my ex-boyfriend Nathan with a sting of shame. As nice as he was – as *perfect* – he was hardly the love of my life, even if I had thought he was a month ago. I used to get so mad when my mother referred to it as 'puppy love', but she was right. I didn't realise until then how little I'd thought about him since I had got to Crofton. I'd missed brunch at Sarabeth's more than him.

'What about you?' he asked, reading my mind.

'Me?' I stalled, walking around a cluster of toadstools.

'Yeah. Who's your Scarlett?'

I shrugged. 'I had a boyfriend in New York, but we weren't a train wreck.'

'Had?' he asked with a cheeky grin.

'Yeah, we broke up before I moved here.'

'What was his name?'

'Nathan.'

'*Nathan*,' he said, as if he was tasting it. 'How long were you together?'

'Not long. A few months.'

'So you're single, then?' nudged me with his hip. 'Duly noted.'

'I thought you weren't going to put me in the middle, Dominic?'

'I know.' He smiled slowly. 'But you're already there.'

We walked the rest of the way in silence and when we got back to the road, he apologised again. I thought he meant for flirting with me, but when he looked back the way we had come, I realised that he meant for dragging me out there.

'It's cool,' I said, with a shrug. 'I'm sure Sam will have fun with that at the Halloween party this weekend.'

'It's been called off.'

'What? Why?'

'After what happened at the Alphabet Party last weekend.'

'I thought that was called off when the housemaster at Abbott found out?'

'Who told you that?'

'Scarlett.'

He chuckled, the skin around his eyes creasing. 'She was there, Adamma.'

'She can't have been. We went to the theatre that night.'

'She came late, about midnight, I think. But she was definitely there.'

He wouldn't look at me and I realised that was when the photo on his camera had been taken.

'You mean to tell me,' I stopped and pointed at him, 'that I ripped my leather jacket climbing out of a goddamn window so that I could go to Bath with Scarlett to see a stupid play, then she drops me back at Crofton and goes to a party without me?'

He shrugged and I might be mad, but I'm sure there was a hint of, *Of course.*

'Why would she do that, Dominic?'

'I don't know what to tell you. Scarlett has two modes: lying and asleep.'

'I don't understand. Did she want to go without me?'

'When I asked after you, she said that *you* didn't want to come.'

'It was the first Crofton party of the year, why wouldn't I want to go?'

'She said it wasn't your thing. *As if Princess Adamma would come to a party in a forest*,' he said, mimicking Scarlett perfectly. '*She might get her shoes dirty.*'

He laughed and when I didn't, just crossed my arms and tried not to look down at my ruined pumps, the corners of his mouth fell.

'Look,' he said with a sigh, and I hoped he couldn't see the tears in my eyes. I tried to blink them away, but that seemed to make them worse. 'I'm sorry, Adamma. I'm not trying to upset you, but if you and Scarlett are going to be, like, totes BFFs, you need to get used to this.'

'To what?'

'To her secrets. I've known her for ever and I still have no idea why she does the things she does. It's part of her charm, I guess.'

That didn't make me feel better, but I didn't want to talk about it any more because I could feel my throat getting tighter and tighter.

'So what did I miss?' I turned and carried on walking up the road towards the stone pillars. When he followed, he looked confused, so I added, 'At the party?'

'Oh. Nothing. Much drunkenness.'

'So why has the Halloween party this weekend been called off, then?'

He went quiet, the skin between his eyebrows pinched as he looked down at the road, kicking at the tear in the tarmac before he walked over it. When he started fiddling with his camera, idly flicking through the shots he'd taken, I felt something in me tense.

'Are you OK, Dominic?'

He nodded, but didn't look at me.

'You don't seem OK. You haven't said anything that's made me want to punch you in at least ten minutes. Do you need medical attention?'

He didn't laugh, but he did smile. 'It's nothing. It's stupid.'

'Probably, but tell me anyway.'

He didn't and when he started fiddling with his camera again it was suddenly so quiet that I could hear the *bat bat bat* of the birds in the trees, fluttering from branch to branch. I tried to look at him, but when he avoided my gaze, playing with the strap on his camera and wrapping it around his wrist, my nerves began to twitch.

'Dominic?'

He shrugged. 'It's probably just a rumour.'

My heart clenched. 'Tell me.'

'It's probably bullshit.'

'But?'

He lifted his eyelashes to look at me. 'If I tell you, you can't repeat it, because that's how these things start and I don't know anything for sure.'

'I promise.'

'And you have to promise that you won't put it in your story for the *Disraeli*.'

'Why the hell would I do that?'

He looked me in the eye then. 'Because it's about Chloe Poole.'

'*Chloe Poole* . . . Chloe Poole? The hockey player I just interviewed?'

He nodded.

'What about her?'

He looked away again and when he started chewing on the inside of his cheek, I thought he wasn't going to tell me, but then he said, 'I think she was raped.'

I stopped and stared at him. 'Raped?'

'Yeah.' He stopped as well. 'Here.'

'*Here?*' I pointed to the road. 'In Savernake Forest?'

He nodded.

'What?' My stomach turned inside out so suddenly that I almost reached for his arm to steady myself. 'When?'

'At the Abbott party last weekend.'

I shook my head. 'No.'

'Some asshole pulled her into his car when she was walking back to Crofton and now everyone is too scared to come back, which is why the Halloween party's been called off.'

'A man in a car?' I couldn't catch my breath.

'That's what I heard.'

'What sort of car?'

'I have no idea.'

'Do you think he was following her?'

'I don't know.' He shook his head. 'But you know what this place is like. Girls walk back to Crofton by themselves all the time. He would have had his pick.'

I felt another fierce wave of nausea at the thought. 'Poor Chloe.'

'Are you OK?'

'I had no idea.' I sucked in a breath, but then I thought of something and shot a look at him. 'Does Scarlett know?'

'Everyone does.' I must have looked horrified, because he added, 'She probably didn't tell you because she didn't want to worry you.'

'I run in this forest every morning.'

'It's probably bullshit.' He frowned. 'Chloe didn't report it to the police.'

'That doesn't mean it didn't happen, though. She's probably too scared to tell them.' I stopped to take another breath. 'And you're sure it was Chloe Poole?'

'I heard it was a hockey player. But it has to be Chloe. There's only one hockey player anyone talks about at Crofton. Chloe plays for the England Under Eighteens.'

I pressed my hands to my face. My cheeks were hot. 'Poor Chloe.'

I heard something then, and it took me a moment too long to realise that it was The Old Dear, so it pulled up next to us before I could step away from Dominic.

With some effort, Scarlett wound down the window and looked at us. 'Well, well,' she said with a *Mona Lisa* smile that didn't tell me whether she was pleased to see us or not. 'Need a lift or am I disturbing something?'

'Of course not,' I snapped, still flustered from the Chloe thing, although, with hindsight, she probably took it as an admission of guilt.

Dominic and I exchanged a glance, then went to climb into the back seat.

'I'm not a chauffeur,' she said tightly, but her smile was still perfect. 'Unless you'd both rather be in the back seat, of course.'

I stumbled in my haste to get into the front seat, banging my shin as I climbed in next to her. It hurt so much that it brought tears to my eyes, but I still smiled as I sat next to her, thanking her for the ride as I tugged on my seat belt.

The road through Savernake Forest is pretty narrow, too narrow to turn around on, especially in a Land Rover, so we had to drive for a bit before she could use one of the lay-bys. I say a bit, but it felt like for ever. Mercifully, the growl of the engine and the rattle of our bones as the car dipped in and out of the potholes filled the awkward silence. Scarlett seemed to be enjoying it, though, humming to herself, then making a show of fighting with the steering wheel, huffing and puffing as she heaved the car around. When we were finally heading out of the forest, she lifted her chin to look at Dominic in the rear-view mirror.

'Red's your colour, Mr Sim,' she said, with her *Mona Lisa* smile.

He looked bewildered, then realised that she meant my sweater, which was still slung over his shoulder. He handed it, and my trench coat, back to me while Scarlett watched us, eyeing my Crofton sweatshirt. She'd obviously made the connection that it was Dominic's and was waiting for an explanation and I would have given her one, except that I thought of the photo on his camera and realised that she hadn't given me one, so I said nothing. It was petty, I know, but there was a thrill to it. I'd tell her eventually, but until I did, it made me feel better to know that she'd know how I felt when I saw that photo, even if it was only for a few hours.

If she knew that I was mad at her, she didn't show it, she just smiled as The Old Dear wheezed up the road. I wanted to ask her about it, ask her why she had lied about the party, but it wasn't the time, not with Dominic in the backseat, so in the few minutes it took to drive out of the forest, the silence became increasingly awkward until I almost opened the door and jumped out to avoid it. When she finally turned out of the forest and the mouth of the car park came into view, I was faint with relief and told her that if I wanted to sneak back into

Crofton I should probably walk from there. After all, The Old Dear was hardly stealth.

Scarlett agreed and pulled over. We hugged, as we always did, albeit not as tightly, and I was careful to just wave at Dominic before I climbed out. I didn't look back as I heard The Old Dear chug off, just dipped my head and ran through the car park towards the hill as it started to rain again.

When I got back to Burnham, I took advantage of having the bathroom to myself, for once, and stood under the water until the pads of my fingers were as rough as almond skin. But when I reached for my towel and stepped out, Molly was waiting for me.

'What were you and Dominic Sim doing in Savernake Forest?' she asked and the shock of it made me gasp and reach for the shower curtain.

'Jesus,' I said when I'd recovered, readjusting my towel.

'I knew you'd give in,' she said smugly, her hips swinging as she followed me over to the row of sinks. 'Everyone does.'

'Isn't there a Year Eight girl you should be bullying into bulimia, Molly?' I asked, the mirror squeaking as I rubbed the steam away with the palm of my hand. But I was impressed, I admit. I'd only been back at Burnham for half an hour. That must be a record.

She laughed, too loud, too bright, like cheap canned laughter on a sitcom. 'I know you and Scarlett are best friends, but sharing boys, too? Really, Adamma.'

Am I the only one who doesn't know they are together? I wondered, trying not to huff as I inspected my reflection in the mirror. Best friends, my ass.

When I didn't acknowledge her, I expected her to poke me some more. Instead, she looked over her shoulder at the bathroom door, then stood next to me at the sink and lowered her voice. 'Just be careful, OK? Scarlett doesn't like to share.'

I turned to look at her, expecting to find her staring at me with a vile smile, but she was gone. The shock of the cold air from the corridor when the bathroom door opened, then closed again, made me shiver.

I told myself that she was being melodramatic, yet when I got back to my room, I called Scarlett, explaining about Dominic and the hockey match and Sam's prank. I can't be sure, but I'm fairly certain from the sounds I heard on the other end of the phone that she stopped listening about halfway through, which wasn't like her. I'm not saying that she hangs on every word I say, but I know she listens. She even asks me to repeat myself sometimes – 'What bar? The one off Old Street?' she'll ask, as though she's taking notes in class. But this afternoon she just hmm-ed and yeah-ed then told me she had to go.

I felt sick when I hung up. I hate it when people are pissed at me, but it didn't occur to me that I should have been pissed with her as well. After all, she'd been keeping things from me, too. I think that's why I started to think about Chloe again, because I was trying not to think about Scarlett. So I threw myself into my story for the Disraeli and spent the rest of the afternoon trying to make it sound vaguely exciting. I didn't succeed. Not that there was anything wrong with it, it was fine, it just didn't sound like me. I could imagine it sitting neatly beneath a glossy photograph of Crofton Scholarship Student Chloe Poole in the brochure, her hockey stick aloft, and almost printed it out, just so I could rip it up again.

It was dark by the time I gave up and went to stand by the window. When I looked towards Savernake Forest, I felt the prickle of something and closed it. I've never felt that here – fear, I guess. I've always thought of Ostley as perfect with its green hills and Blyton-bright afternoons. Jumoke said it wasn't – that it couldn't be – and it's not that I didn't believe her, but I expected Ostley's deviancy to stray as far as wife-swapping parties or cheating at the church Christmas cake bake-off, I didn't expect *this*. This was the sort of thing that would make me think twice the next time I snuck out of Burnham. The sort of thing that made me close my window. And it's kind of funny, that I felt that here. Not in Lagos, or New York – sitting in an empty carriage on the 6 Train at one in the morning – but in a tiny village in Wiltshire. A village where Scarlett and I ordered red wine at the pub one Sunday afternoon and Mrs Delaney knew about it by the time I got back to Burnham.

I glanced at my copy of *The Times* on the desk next to my laptop and wondered if Chloe would ever be brave enough to report what had happended. I wished she would because, until she did, he was out there. That's why I find newspapers so comforting, I think. Comforting is the wrong word to use when reading stories about murderers and paedophiles, but I guess I like my monsters where I can see them, held to paper, with ink, in Times New Roman.

So I went back to my laptop and typed up what I knew. It wasn't much, but dealing with the facts made it easier. It didn't make me feel better, but the words on my screen didn't seem as black, either. Then I called Chloe. When she answered, she sounded as though she was at Balogun Market and for the second time that day, I missed home.

'Hey, Adamma! How's it going?' she shouted over the din.

'Celebrating your win?'

There was a sudden roar through the phone and I jumped.

'Sorry,' Chloe howled. 'Lauren just walked into a tree!'

'Where are you?'

'Savernake Forest.'

My nerves twitched. 'You're in Savernake Forest?'

'Yeah? Why?'

'I . . . I just—'

'Oh God,' she interrupted with a groan. 'Is this about that rumour?'

My heart started to beat too hard. 'Rumour?'

'Please tell me that's not why you called, Adamma?'

'No. I guess. It's just that I heard—'

She wouldn't let me finish. 'Who told you? Molly Avery?'

'Of course not. Molly's too busy trying to find out if I'm shagging Dominic Sim.'

I heard a rustle and when the sound of the music began to fade, I realised that she was walking away from the party. 'Who told you, then? Was it Scarlett?'

'Does it matter, Chloe?'

'So everyone's talking about it?' When I didn't respond, she let out a long sigh. 'I'm going to start wearing a I WASN'T RAPED T-SHIRT.'

'You weren't?'

'No,' she said so sharply that it made my cheeks burn. I hope she didn't think I sounded disappointed. 'Nothing happened. I was walking out of Savernake Forest after the party when some pervert stopped and tried to get me into his car. I told him to get stuffed and that was it.'

'That was it?'

'Yes! I don't know how that turned into me being raped.'

'Did you see what the guy looked like?'

92

'No. When he pulled up next to me, I didn't look, I just ran.'

'I probably would have, too,' I admitted, stopping to chew on the lid of my pen. 'Did you see his licence plate?' She scoffed. 'Not even part of it? A letter? A number?'

'You know what the forest is like, it was so dark. I couldn't see a thing.'

'Did you see what his car looked like?'

'Adamma,' she sighed, clearly weary of the interrogation. 'I didn't see a thing. It was dark and I was *shitfaced*. Just before he stopped, I was sick in a bush.'

'I'm sorry,' I said, covering my eyes with the back of my hand. 'I shouldn't be grilling you. I just hate the thought of this guy driving around, looking for girls.'

'You're not going to put it in the *Disraeli*, are you?'

I was mortified. 'Of course I won't.'

The line was quiet for a moment or two, and I could hear the party in the distance. I almost recognised the song that was playing and strained to make out the words, like at night when I can't sleep and I try to guess what song is playing on Orla's radio.

'I'm sorry,' she said with a long sigh. 'It's just that I told one person and look what happened? I guess that explains why Sam Wolfe just commented on my short skirt. I thought he was taking the piss because it was from Primark,' she said with a huff. 'Oh well. Looks like I've been upgraded from the Girl With the Cheap Clothes to the Girl Who Was Raped.'

She made an excuse then and hung up. When she did, my mouth was so dry, I downed the glass of water on my desk in a few gulps. I was still struggling to catch my breath when I heard a knock on my door and had to wait a second before I could say, 'Come in.'

Orla edged in, her face flushed, and when she closed the door behind her, I stood up, a little startled. She hadn't been in my room since the day I started at Crofton.

'Are you OK, Orla?'

She clearly wasn't, her hands were shaking as she tucked her blond hair behind her ears. 'Were you just talking to Chloe Poole?'

'How did you know that?' I asked and her cheeks went from pink to red.

'I was just walking past and—'

'Were you listening?' I stepped forward. This place is like a damn goldfish bowl. 'That was a private conversation, Orla. How dare you? What did you hear?'

'Nothing,' she said, shoulders shuddering, then she dissolved into tears. I felt awful for snapping at her, but when I went to reach for her hand, she wouldn't let me touch her. 'You know, don't you? Everyone knows!'

'Know what?' I asked, but when she lifted her sticky eyelashes to look at me I knew.

I knew before she said it.

'That I was raped.'

2 DAYS AFTER

MAY

Scarlett isn't back.

I don't know how Molly knew that Scarlett's parents were doing an appeal on BBC *Breakfast* this morning but, just before it started at 6 a.m., I could hear her opening doors and waking everyone up. I didn't want to watch it in the Common Room with everyone, but Orla made me, saying it would look bad if I didn't. So I checked my other cellphone again and when I discovered that he still hadn't called me back, I reluctantly joined the sleepy shuffle down the stairs into the Common Room.

It filled up quickly, girls chomping on slices of toast and passing around mugs of tea as though we were waiting for Saturday Film Club to start, not waiting to hear what had happened to one of our school friends. I sat huddled next to Orla on the couch, cupping a mug of tea in my hands while Molly sat cross-legged in her pyjamas on the coffee table.

'This is it,' she said with the air of a girl about to be made queen, 'we knew it was going to happen.' She looked around to check that everyone was listening and when she got to me, her gaze narrowed. Perhaps I didn't look as awed as the other girls, or maybe she was concerned that with Scarlett gone, I was going to make a grab for the throne as well.

I glared at her until she turned back to the television. 'You can't keep running away like that. Something was bound to happen.' She flicked her hair. 'Daddy says the police are putting MISSING posters up in Marlborough this morning. He just saw someone walking around with a pile of them. They've used last year's class photo.'

My stomach clenched so suddenly I thought I was going to be sick. 'Posters?' I sat forward, tea spilling over my knuckles, but I didn't feel it as I asked myself why I didn't talk to Olivia yesterday.

I should have talked to Olivia yesterday.

Molly didn't acknowledge me. 'They've never put up posters before, have they?' she went on, and the urge to reach over and push her off the coffee table was unbearable. 'She's usually back before they've finished printing them.'

A girl began crying and I felt another long roll of nausea. Molly was enjoying it too much, her shoulders back, as though we were gathered around a campfire and she was telling us scary stories. I couldn't take it, but as I was about to leave, Mrs Delaney came in. She was fully dressed, her hair immaculate as she sat on the arm of one of the couches.

'I don't want you to worry, girls. Scarlett will be fine,' she said, her voice steady, but I saw her playing with her wedding ring. 'She'll be fine. Just fine.'

Three fines.

'Oh my God. This is it. This is it. Turn it up!' Molly said, hands everywhere, as though the radio was playing her favourite song.

I looked up as the photograph of Scarlett came on screen. She was in her Crofton uniform, her hair down and falling over her shoulders in dark waves. As soon as I saw it, I looked down at the drying tea stain on the rug and I didn't lift my head for the rest of the segment. But I heard it all: how Scarlett had left home to meet a friend on Sunday afternoon and hadn't come back. It was strange hearing her reduced to a few facts – age, height, hair colour – the presenter describing her in a dull, flat voice that made her sound so ordinary. Then, when he described The Old Dear, referring to it as a 'green Land Rover' – not the car she charged around in, singing to herself because it didn't have a stereo, or the car her father drove me back to Crofton in when I went to her house for dinner, gushing about a recipe he'd found for yam porridge – I started playing with my necklace to distract myself from crying.

I didn't realise until that moment how much I missed her, how much I used to like her, so when Orla reached for my hand, I was grateful, especially when I heard Scarlett's mother's voice, small and broken, begging for information. If Orla hadn't been there, I might have given in to the urge to run out of the room.

As soon as the segment finished there was a moment of silence then Molly turned to Mrs Delaney. 'Oh my God. Do they think Scarlett's dead, Miss?'

I jumped up. 'Shut up, Molly!' I hissed, tea splashing over the rim of my mug and soaking through my socks. 'You don't know what you're talking about!'

She leapt off the coffee table to stand opposite me. 'Like you care, Adamma.'

'We may not be friends any more, Molly, but I'm still a decent human being. Olivia must be worried sick,' I reminded her, guilt

97

biting at me again. 'She shouldn't have to come to school today to hear everyone talking about how her sister is dead.'

'Decent human being?' Molly cocked an eyebrow up at me. I knew what she was going to say and I wanted to cover her mouth with my hand. 'You were her best friend and you threw her away for Dominic. So get off your high horse, Adamma.'

'I don't know how many more times I can say this, but I'm not with him!'

Molly rolled her eyes. 'Yeah. Yeah.'

'That's enough, girls,' Mrs Delaney said, suddenly between us.

She ushered Molly towards the kitchen and Molly stomped off to be comforted by a group of girls, not before she had called me a *two-faced bitch*, which earned her a swift telling off from Mrs Delaney. Ordinarily, I would have stuck around to enjoy it, but I was so desperate to see if he'd called back that I rushed to my room.

I pulled the pillow and blanket off the shelf in the closet in my impatience to get to my tuck box, almost tripping over them as I walked to my bed. As soon as I opened it, I snatched my phone. It was on top and I had left it switched on after checking it at 3 a.m., then again before I went to the Common Room, so I didn't have to wait long to find out that he hadn't called. My heart sank. I thought he might have seen *BBC Breakfast*, too. So I texted him – *Call me. Please.* – and managed to put the phone back into the tuck box a second before Orla came in.

'Are you OK, Adamma?' she asked, running over to me and pulling me into a hug. 'I just told Molly off. I don't know why she said that. Everyone knows that isn't true. You didn't steal Dominic from Scarlett. She didn't even want him.'

98

I contemplated defending myself again but sighed and shook my head instead.

'I don't know what's got into her,' Orla went on. 'She's behaving like—' She stopped, her cheeks suddenly pink. Yesterday she would have said Scarlett.

What a difference a day makes.

'I don't care any more,' I muttered, stuffing everything back in my closet and closing the doors. Luckily, Orla was too distracted to notice that I had my tuck box out, and if she did, she didn't think it was worth asking why.

I was pulling my towel off the radiator when Mrs Delaney came in and told Orla to give us a moment. I thought she was going to tell me off for what had happened with Molly, but when Orla left, she closed the door and told me to get dressed.

'Of course, Mrs Delaney,' I said, reaching for my washbag and checking that my wide-toothed comb was in it. 'I'm just getting in the shower.'

'Be as quick as you can please, Miss Okomma.'

I looked up with a frown. 'Why, Miss?'

'We need to get to the police station.'

211 DAYS BEFORE

OCTOBER

I don't know what to do. I begged Orla to tell the police, I even offered to go with her, but she won't. She says that she doesn't want her father to know and I get that. I could probably deal with being the Girl Who Was Raped at Crofton, I might even be able to stomach the questions about what I was wearing and how much I'd had to drink and why I'd walked home by myself, but I couldn't tell my father. Not because he'd be ashamed, but because he'd never forgive himself for not being there and I don't want him to stop thinking that he can protect me from everything. The day he realises he can't is the day I stop being his little girl and then what will I be? That's all I've ever been. I don't know if I can be anyone else.

So I promised Orla I wouldn't tell a soul, but I don't know if I can keep my promise. I lay awake all night with it scratching at my insides and now I need to get it out. I've just written it all down, because I had to do something. She says that she doesn't remember anything, but she told me enough to make me sure that the guy in the car at Savernake Forest is more than just another Crofton rumour. Now that I know that, now that it's all typed up and I have half a page of words and a stack of printouts about how to report it, and details about a rape sanctuary in Swindon that can help if she decides not to, I want to do something even more. I suppose that's why I ended up lingering outside the newsroom when classes were over this afternoon.

I guess Mr Lucas saw me pacing in the corridor through the glass panel in the door, because he opened it and asked if I was OK. He wasn't wearing his glasses so he looked strange – young – and he'd taken his jacket off to reveal a navy pinstripe waistcoat that I hadn't noticed him wearing when I'd seen him earlier in class.

It was odd to see him in something so fitted. I could see the shape of his arms beneath his shirt, the curve of his shoulders. Most of the girls in my year are besotted with him. I don't know why, he isn't my type at all; tall and thin as a toothpick with a mop of brown hair which he is incapable of willing into sub-mission, no matter how many times he runs his hand through it. But it made sense, I suppose; compared to the grumpy, grey-ing faculty at Crofton, he's Adonis. Put a dozen teenage girls in a classroom with a twenty-three-year-old teacher who wears waistcoats and quotes Bob Dylan and they're bound to find him attractive.

I wonder sometimes what the other teachers think of him; he's at least twenty years younger than most of them. They must walk past his classroom and see him charging around, hands everywhere, or hear him from their classrooms, quoting Shakespeare until he's out of breath, and think he's mad. Last month, when we were studying *Richard III*, he made us all stand on our chairs and we could only sit down when we had answered a question correctly. He'd only managed to ask three before the assistant headmaster swept in and told us all to sit down, reminding Mr Lucas that it was a Health and Safety violation. As soon as he left, Mr Lucas rolled his eyes and told us to stand on our chairs again, *but more quietly this time.*

'Miss Okomma?' he prompted with a frown.

'I'm fine, Sir,' I said, breathless from pacing.

'You don't seem fine. Is something bothering you?'

'No, Sir.'

'Are you here to file something?' He nodded at the folder I was hugging.

'I did this morning, Sir. But I need to speak to Hannah. Is she here?'

'She's with Headmaster Ballard getting his message for the first issue.' He stepped back and gestured at me to come in. 'But you can speak to me.'

'It's OK, Sir. I don't want to bother you.'

'No bother, Miss Okomma. Come in.'

Before I could object, he turned and walked back into the newsroom.

The newsroom sounds so fancy. I'm sure most people would be underwhelmed by it. It's just a classroom with a long desk in the middle and computers around the edges, but I love it. It's the only place I've ever felt a buzz at Crofton. It's loud and untidy, the bins spilling over with balled-up pieces of paper and the walls covered in huge, messy noticeboards of printed-out photos and newspaper clippings, their corners curling. Mr Lucas swept past one on his way to the desk at the far end, the strips of paper fluttering as he did.

I followed him in gingerly, as though everyone in the room was asleep and I didn't want to disturb them. I wouldn't have, of course. It must have been 3.15 p.m. by then, so the room was cluttered with pupils trying to get their pieces in by the 4 p.m. deadline. It was hardly *The New York Times*, but the chaos (chaos for Crofton, anyway), still made my heart stutter. Cellphones rang and keyboards rattled while, in the corner, two girls stood in front of a computer screen, bickering over two photos that looked identical to me.

'How do you spell vociferous?' a guy called out as I walked over to Mr Lucas.

But before I could tell him, Mr Lucas said, 'Try to keep it simple, Lambert. You're writing about a hockey match.'

When I got to his desk, Mr Lucas was putting his glasses on. He reached for a piece of paper, the skin between his eyebrows pinching as he read it.

'Ah. Yes!' he said, looking up and waving it at me with a smile. 'I have read your story, Miss Okomma. It's good. I could almost hear the sticks clashing.'

I don't know what was worse, the *good* or the fact that he'd forgotten he'd read it. Either way, I knew, I hadn't got in. I felt my ego wrinkle as I imagined *Granta* Girl's piece making him weep, and I held the folder a little tighter to my chest.

'But that's not what you need to speak to me about, is it?' he said, before my brain could engage with my feet and tell them to start walking.

I went rigid. 'Sir?'

'You're clearly anxious about something. You were distracted in class today and please don't take this the wrong way, but it looks like you haven't slept. A perfectly pleasant piece about a hockey match doesn't usually incite such anxiety.'

He smiled, but when I didn't respond – just stared at him – he nodded at the folder. 'I'm guessing whatever you're concerned about is in that folder.'

'I. Um –' I went to take a step back, but stopped myself. I had to do something. 'Is there somewhere we can speak privately, Sir?'

He gave me a look that pleaded with me not to tell him I was pregnant and, for a second, I wondered if he could deal with what I was about to tell him. But then he caught himself and gestured towards the door at the back of the newsroom.

It led to what would have been the darkroom. I guess it hasn't been used much since everyone started using digital cameras, but it still smelt strongly of chemicals. I don't know if it was that or the panic suddenly pulsing through me, but I felt very dizzy.

'Are you OK, Miss Okomma?' he asked, catching me by the elbow as my eyes swam out of focus, then steering me towards a stool.

When I'd caught my breath, I climbed onto it and watched as he dragged another one across the small darkroom and sat opposite me.

'What's wrong, Adamma?' he asked with a frown. He'd never called me by my first name before and I don't know why, but it made me feel better.

So I took a deep breath and made myself say it, 'Sir, has anyone ever told you a secret that you think is too big to keep?'

He considered this for a moment, then leaned a little closer and looked at me from under his eyelashes. 'Is there something that you'd like to tell me, Adamma?'

I nodded and when I did, my chin trembled.

He must have seen it, because he said, 'Do you need a moment?'

I nodded again and took another deep breath, but I still couldn't do it. I kept thinking of Orla and the promise I'd made. I've never broken a promise before.

He waited for me to say something, but when I didn't he folded his arms and said, 'I can't say that I know you as well as your classmates do, Adamma, or even Mrs Delaney, but I do know that you're very bright.' He stopped to sweep his hair back with his hand. 'So if there's something you want to tell me, then I'm assuming it's because you haven't been able to resolve it by yourself.'

I nodded.

'And you think maybe I can help.'

I nodded again.

'So please let me.'

I must have looked like I was about to erupt into tears, because he tugged a handkerchief out of the pocket of his pants and handed it to me. I took it and balled my fist around it, grateful that I didn't need to use it. Given how much of a klutz he is in class sometimes, tripping over his words – and his laces – I don't imagine he'd know what to do with a sobbing teenage girl.

'I've never betrayed a friend before,' I said at last.

'Unfortunately, you have to sometimes, Adamma.'

He was right. And it's funny, not funny *ha ha*, more funny fucked-up, how twenty-four hours ago, I wouldn't have given Orla Roberts a second thought, let alone referred to her as a friend. What a horrible thing to be united over.

I looked at my hands. 'My friend was raped,' I said, finally, and the room suddenly felt smaller. I felt the nearness of the walls, the ceiling.

He went very quiet and I couldn't look at him, so I started fiddling with the edges of the handkerchief while I waited for him to respond.

After a minute or so, he said, 'When did this happen, Miss Okomma?'

106

'This weekend in Savernake Forest.'

'Does your friend know who did it?'

I shook my head. 'Some guy in a car.'

'A car?'

I nodded. 'There were two girls, actually,' I told him, rolling one of the edges of the handkerchief between my forefinger and thumb.

'Two?' he asked, his voice a little higher.

'He stopped one girl when she was walking back here and tried to get her into his car, but she ran away. My friend wasn't as lucky.'

He didn't say anything for a long time and I could hear the murmur of the newsroom – a cellphone ringing, followed by a long laugh. But then I heard him take a breath and panic pinched at me. He was going to ask for names and I couldn't.

I couldn't.

But he said, 'You spoke to both of these girls, Miss Okomma?'

I nodded.

'And you're sure they're telling the truth?'

'Of course.' I looked up to find him frowning at me. 'Do you think I should tell the police, Sir?'

He thought about it for a moment longer than I expected him to. 'I don't know,' he said, and the shock of it nearly knocked me off my stool. But then he caught himself, 'I mean, *of course* you should tell them, Miss Okomma,' he said, flustered. 'But they won't be able to do much if these girls won't speak to them.'

He was right, and I felt the injustice of it pinching at my insides. It was so unfair. This guy – this asshole – did this awful, disgusting thing. Why should he get away with it because Orla was embarrassed? It wasn't fair.

It wasn't fair.

'So I should get my friend to report it?'

'Why won't she?'

'She was drunk. She thinks it was her fault.'

He took off his glasses and rubbed the red mark on the bridge of his nose, then sighed heavily. 'That's what most girls think, sadly.'

'But I have to do something, Sir.'

'I get that.' He was quiet while he cleaned his glasses with the end of his tie, then he sighed, and when he put them back on again, he said, 'When I was your age, something similar happened to someone I knew.'

I lifted my eyelashes to look at him. 'That's horrible, Sir.'

He nodded. 'Her name was Charlotte and the same thing happened: she was walking home alone after a party and someone offered to give her a lift.' He stopped and I didn't want him to, I wanted him to tell me what had happened, that she was OK, but I wonder now if he had to stop. 'If you want my advice, and I think you do, then the best thing you can do right now is get your friend to speak to someone.'

'But what if she won't go to the police?'

'There are other people she can speak to. The school has a counsellor. I'm sure we can arrange for them to meet.'

That was a good idea. 'Thanks, Sir. But what about the police?' He hesitated again, and when he did, I stuttered out, 'Even if she won't report it, I should warn them, right? What if this guy does it again? What if he's done it before?'

He waited for my breathing to settle, then he nodded. 'So wise so young.'

I tried to smile, but when I thought of us in class, standing on our chairs as we answered his questions about *Richard III*,

Scarlett with her arms out saying, *So wise so young, they say, do never live long*, my heart started to throb.

Throb and throb.

I knew I was doing the right thing, but a voice in my head still told me to leave it as I walked out of the newsroom. *Leave it. Leave it. Leave it.* But I didn't listen, didn't think, I didn't even miss a step, as though I was out for a run and I had to keep my heart rate up. I had to keep going before I thought about it too much, like Orla with her list of reasons why no one would believe her. I believed her and someone would believe me, too. But as soon as I walked out into the courtyard, someone stepped into my path, and I screeched to a cartoon halt.

It took me a moment to recover, but when I did, and I realised it was Scarlett and Olivia, I was relieved.

'Olivia, thank God,' I gasped, reaching for her arm.

'Oh good. You're late, too. *Someone*', she turned to glare at Scarlett, 'made me late running lines with her. Frailty, thy name is sister.'

I know they're twins, but they look like day and night – Olivia with her paper-straight blond hair and Scarlett with her mess of dark waves – but when Scarlett glared back, as distracted as I was, I still noted that they'd never looked so alike.

'Actually—' Scarlett started to say, but I interrupted.

'I can't make Debating Society today. Can you cover for me, Liv?'

Usually, Scarlett would have been livid at being talked over, but her eyes lit up. 'What's this? Princess Adamma bunking off? I am shocked. *Shocked*.'

Olivia didn't look impressed. 'You've been spending too much time with her.'

When she thumbed at Scarlett, I shook my head. 'You know I wouldn't. I mean, I've never.' I stopped to suck in a breath. 'It's important.'

'Of course O will cover for you,' Scarlett said. Olivia raised an eyebrow, but Scarlett ignored her. I barely had time to thank her before Scarlett took me by the elbow and tugged me away. 'What's going on at the *Disraeli*? Did you get in?'

'I don't think so,' I said, and it should have stung, but with everything going on with Orla, it suddenly didn't seem as important.

Scarlett tutted. '*Granta* Girl?'

'Probably.'

'Bitch,' she hissed, hooking her arm through mine. 'Forget the *Disraeli*. Who needs it? Print media is dead. Come home with me. Dad's making risotto.'

Easy for you to say, I almost said, *you're already in*, but I shook my head. 'I can't. I'm on a mission,' I said as we rounded the fountain and headed for the Green.

'Intriguing,' she cooed. 'What's going on? Tell me everything.'

She was so eager, her blue eyes bright, that I hesitated. This wasn't another juicy piece of gossip about a girl buying a pregnancy test from the chemist in the village or a couple being caught doing it in the A/V Equipment Room. It was serious. *Horrible*. But it was Scarlett, I could trust her and, I reasoned, she might know something.

'OK. But you must promise not to tell anyone.'

'Cross my heart.'

When we stepped onto the Green, I steered her away from the group of girls walking towards us onto an empty stretch of grass, then lowered my voice. 'I think there's something going on in Savernake Forest.'

'There's always something going on in Savernake Forest.' She waggled her eyebrows.

'Not that. Things happening to girls.'

The corners of her mouth fell. 'What sort of things?'

'I'm not pissed at you, OK –' I waited for a guy hugging a rugby ball to pass us – 'but Dominic told me you were at the Abbott party.'

She didn't deny it, just shrugged. 'It was a spur-of-the-moment thing. I was driving back from Crofton and Sam flagged me down. I was there for, like, a minute.'

I knew she was lying and almost told her that I knew about the photograph Dominic had taken, too, but stopped myself. It wasn't the time.

'So you heard what happened to Chloe Poole?'

She didn't say that she had, but when she looked away, she didn't have to. I don't know why I was so surprised. I guess I was more surprised that she didn't tell me and it hurt. She knows I run in Savernake Forest every morning. I tried not to think about it as we passed through the wall of oak trees, telling myself that she mustn't be worried. Scarlett may have her secrets, but there's no way she'd keep something like that from me if she thought I was in any danger. No way.

'Apart from Chloe, I haven't heard a thing.' She shook her head, then stopped. 'Hang on,' she said, looking at her feet as we began to walk down the hill to the car park, 'do you know Rachel Flock?' I shook my head. She thought about it for a moment more, then frowned. 'I overheard her saying that the last time she was there it felt like she was being watched.'

'Watched?'

'That's what she said, she said she was with some guy and it felt like someone was there, but then she thought she was being paranoid because she'd had too much to drink.'

'When did you hear this?'

'On Monday, in the girls' toilets.'

My stomach tensed. 'Do you think she was talking about the Abbott party?'

'She must have been.'

'Did she say anything else?'

'Nope. That was it,' Scarlett said with a shrug when we got to the bottom of the hill. 'I was in one of the stalls and by the time I came out, she was gone.'

'Rachel Flock, right?'

'Sure you don't need to write it down, Lois Lane?' She winked as she took out her make-up bag and put on her red lipstick.

'I'm like Rain Man when it comes to names. I never forget them.'

'So what do you think is going on?' she asked, rubbing her lips together.

'I don't know.' I realised I was biting mine, and stopped. 'Something.'

'Like a peeping Tom?'

My eyes darted across the car park, then I took a step closer. 'OK. This is the bit you can't tell anyone, Scarlett, not even Olivia.'

'I never tell Olivia anything, anyway.'

That was true.

'Someone was raped,' I said it so quietly, I wasn't sure she heard me over the crunch of gravel beneath our feet, but then she rolled her eyes.

'Chloe wasn't raped. Some perv just tried to get her in his car.'

'No. Someone else. On the same night.'

She turned to me and gasped, her cheeks suddenly pink. 'Who?'

'I can't say.'

She stopped and grabbed the sleeve of my blazer. 'Adamma, it's me.'

I stopped too. 'I can't, Scarlett.' I shook my head. 'I promised.'

'But I'm your best friend, Adamma. You know I won't tell anyone.'

'I know, but I *swore*.'

'Fine.' She tossed her make-up bag back into her bag and I thought she was going to give me the silent treatment, but as we were about to walk out of the car park, she crossed her arms. 'So you think there's a rapist in the forest?'

'I don't know. Maybe.'

'Where are you going now?' she asked as we turned left out of Crofton.

'I spoke to Mr Lucas about it and I'm going to tell the police.'

'When did you speak to Mr Lucas?'

'Just now.'

'What did he say?'

'Nothing. Just that.'

'I'm surprised he's encouraging you to speak to the police. Ballard will go batshit when he finds out. Every parent will pull their daughter out of school.'

'I know. But I think I should warn them. What if it happens again?'

She went quiet as we walked under the shadow of the forest. I could see that she was chewing on the inside of her cheek and

113

I wondered if she was worried, if she knew something she wasn't telling me. But as we stepped into the daylight, she resumed her usual swagger.

'You could just *call* the police, you know?' she said, flicking her hair.

She was right, I didn't have to go to the police station, I could just call. There was still time. I could run back to Crofton and endure a telling-off from Mr Crane for being late for Debating Society, but there was something about Scarlett's attitude, about the way she flicked her hair, that made me more determined. Then she said it: 'The police won't do anything, you know.'

My heart clenched like a fist and I had to take a breath before I could speak. 'So I should just do nothing? I should let him get away with it?'

'Look.' She stopped when we got to the police station and turned to face me. 'Adamma, you are so sweet and kind and I know that you're just trying to do the right thing, but you can't fix this. I know you want to, but you can't.'

I felt something in me hold on, *dig in*. 'Why not?'

'I don't know the details, but if this girl – whoever she is – won't report it, then it's probably because she knows there's no evidence.'

'Or because she thinks no one cares.'

Scarlett frowned at that. 'Is that what she told you?'

'She thinks it's her fault for drinking too much.'

Scarlett started chewing on the inside of her cheek again, then, after a second or two, she sighed. 'Go.' She nodded at the police station. 'Do what you can.'

'That's all I can do, right?'

'Do you want me to come in with you?'

I told her I'd be OK and we hugged – for a moment longer

114

than we normally do – then she was gone. I watched as she made her way across the village green towards the hill that led up to her house, her ponytail swinging, then I turned to look at the police station. I pressed my palm to the door and was startled when it didn't move. I tried again and, when it still didn't move, I reached for the brass handle and pulled, but the door didn't budge, just rattled loudly in its frame.

It was closed.

I took a step back and stared at it, then reached into the pocket of my blazer for my cellphone. I checked online and cursed myself: it had just closed. It's Ostley, of course it closes early. I should have looked it up before I stormed down here.

Deflated, I decided to head back, but as I was putting my cellphone back in my pocket, it rang. I don't know how he knew – how he *always* knows – but it was my father.

'*Kedu*, Ada, when is your next exeat weekend?' he asked when I answered. I could hear him flicking pages back and forth in his diary and imagined him in his office, glasses perched on the end of his nose as he tried to decipher his handwriting.

'October the twenty-fifth, Papa.'

'Excellent.' I heard the scratch of his fountain pen as he wrote it down. 'I'll be in Lagos that weekend if you'd like to come with me.'

'OK.'

He was quiet for a moment and I thought he was going to ask about another date, but he said, 'What's wrong, Ada?'

I went rigid, my heart beating desperately as I grasped for something to tell him – I wasn't feeling well, I'd had an argument with Scarlett, school was kicking my ass, *anything* – but I'm a terrible liar, which is his fault, ironically. It was also his fault that I was standing outside Ostley police station when no one – not Mr Lucas or Scarlett, even Orla – thought I should be there. That's why I answered my phone, isn't it? Because I knew what he'd say.

So I closed my eyes and took a breath. 'Papa, something happened to my friend and she won't tell the police and I don't know what to do,' I said, all at once, and I felt five years old again, tearing home to tell him that someone had stole Mbeke's bicycle, back when my first instinct was to tell my father when something went wrong.

I think it still is.

'Where are you now, Adamma?'

'Outside Ostley police station.'

'Then you know exactly what to do.' I heard his chair creak and imagined him sitting back, his forehead creased. 'I know I'm always pleading with you to think before you do things, Adamma, but, in this instance, you don't need to.'

I let go of a breath and, when I opened my eyes again, I saw a man walking towards the tiny three-bay car park in front of the station, to the only car parked in it, a battered green thing that should probably be put out of its misery.

I thanked my father, then told him I'd call him back and took a step forward.

'Excuse me, Sir?'

I don't think he heard me, because he just opened the car door, reached across to grab a cellphone from the passenger seat, then closed it again and started walking back the way he had come. The voice in my head told me to *Leave it* again as I watched him go, but it felt too much like giving up on Orla, so I went after him.

'Excuse me, Sir?' I said again when I'd caught up with him.

He eyed me warily. 'Why are you following me?'

116

I hesitated. What if he wasn't a police officer? Maybe he'd just parked his car outside the station and there I was, chasing him down the street. As I watched him tuck his cellphone into the back pocket of his jeans, I realised that he didn't look like a police officer. But what do police officers look like? Do they wear fitted black T-shirts and jeans? I guess they do.

I slowed to a stop, letting him go. 'Sorry, Sir.'

'Stop calling me Sir,' he snapped, turning to face me. The sun must have been in his eyes, because he squinted at me, his blond eyelashes suddenly invisible. 'It's DS Bone.'

'DS? That's Detective Sergeant, right?'

He didn't say anything and I don't know if he was impressed, but I earned an arched eyebrow. 'I'm CID,' he said, finally, putting his hands on his hips.

'Ostley has a CID branch?'

He turned away from me with a chuckle. 'Of course not,' he said, continuing up the road. 'I'm meeting a friend for a drink and I left my phone in my car. You can't be too careful around here,' he said when I'd caught up with him again, 'what with all the Crofton kids hanging around, hopped up on Earl Grey.'

I stared at him. I think he was trying to be funny. I didn't laugh.

'Would you be able to help me, DS Bone? My name is Adamma Okomma and I need to speak to someone, but the police station is closed.'

'Dial nine nine nine.'

I thought he was joking, but when we got to the pub, he didn't stop, he just strolled into the beer garden and around the picnic tables towards the door. There was a sudden spill of voices as he opened it and when it snapped shut behind him, I stood there, staring at it. It was like walking into a lamp post. I stepped back, picturing cartoon bluebirds chirping and circling my head. I should have taken the hint, but I'm not very good with no, so, before I could stop myself, I was pin-balling off the picnic tables and charging through the door.

The Crown is the sort of pub that when you walk in – especially in a Crofton uniform – everyone looks up so it was one of the most stupid things I've ever done. If someone had reported me, I would have had a letter sent home to my parents for sure. But I didn't think, I just looked for him among the people sitting at the small, dark wood tables. The pub is so tiny that I thought I'd see him straight away, but I had to hunt for him. Eventually I found him in the nook between the fruit machines, sitting at a table with a group of men in rugby shirts. He didn't seem surprised as I approached them, my hands balled into fists at my sides.

'I don't like being wrong,' I told him, ignoring his friends as they looked up from their pints. 'In fact, I think this might be the first time it's happened. But my friend was raped and she won't report it because she thinks the police won't listen.' I had to stop and suck in a breath. 'Of all the things to be wrong about, I wish it wasn't this. Enjoy your drink, DS Bone.'

The fruit machines chirped – as if in applause – as I stormed back out of the pub, my legs weaker as I wondered what my parents would think of me shouting at a police officer. They'd be mortified.

I was about to turn and run back to Crofton when I heard someone say, 'Hey, Buffy the Conversation Slayer.'

'This isn't funny,' I hissed, turning to face DS Bone as he ambled towards me.

'Come on. Talk to me.'

He nodded at one of the picnic tables, but I didn't move.

'There's no point.' I crossed my arms and I suddenly felt flat, like the sail of a boat, sagging on a calm day.

'Humour me.'

I shook my head. 'I shouldn't have come.'

I didn't realise I was crying until I saw him put his hand into the pocket of his jeans. He pulled out a Greggs napkin and held it out to me, but I couldn't look at him as I took it, mortified that he was seeing me like this. I didn't even cry at my grand-father's funeral. Not in front of anyone, anyway.

'I'm tired,' I explained, turning away to wipe under my eyes.

He nodded at the picnic table again and I sat down this time.

'I didn't sleep much last night,' I said, with another heave and a sob as I dabbed at my eyes again. But when he didn't say anything, I felt the need to fill the silence. 'I don't know what I'm doing, I just know I need to do something.'

He sat next to me, his legs spread. 'Do you want to tell me what happened?' He clasped his hands together and leaned forward to rest his forearms on his knees.

'I don't know much.'

'It doesn't matter.'

I told him everything I knew between sobs. He listened and when I was done, he took a deep breath and looked up at the sky. The sun was setting – it must have been about 4.30 p.m. – and I felt a prickle of panic. I hoped Olivia had covered for me, otherwise Mrs Delaney would be ready to release the hounds.

'So this happened to your *friend*?' he said, finally.

I nodded, circling one of the knots in the wood of the picnic table with my finger, then realised what he was asking. 'No. This is about my friend. Really.'

And it was, but as I sat there, under the marmalade-coloured sky, I thought that maybe it was about me, too. Me and my body and how I'm responsible for it now, not my parents. I can drink and smoke and cut my hair and get a tattoo and when I have sex, it should be because I want to, not because I'm wearing a short skirt or I've had one too many cocktails and some asshole thinks he can make that decision for me. I guess that's why I was so upset – so involved – because if what happened to Orla happened to me, I'd want someone to give half a shit.

'And this happened last Saturday?'

I nodded.

'Did you get a description of the car?'

'No – ' I had to stop myself before I said Chloe's name – '*my friend* doesn't remember anything about it. She said it was too dark.'

'Did your other friend see it?'

'No, she doesn't remember anything, just going to the party then waking up in her room. But it has to be the same guy, right? It's too much of a coincidence.'

He looked at his hands. 'And she's sure she was raped?'

'She said that when she woke up, she wasn't wearing underwear anymore.'

'That doesn't mean she was raped.'

'And *that*,' I pointed at him, 'is why she won't tell the police.'

He looked at his feet, then rubbed his face with his hands. He was quiet for a second or two, then he stood up and I thought he was going to go back into the pub, but he reached into the back pocket of his jeans and pulled out his wallet. When he sat back down again, he opened it and handed me two business cards.

'The top one is for my wife, Lisa. She works for the New Swindon Sanctuary.' I knew it from my research last night. 'Your friend needs to go for an exam, if she hasn't already. And she needs to speak to someone. If she won't speak to the counsellor at Crofton, Lisa can help. The Sanctuary is nothing to do with the police so tell your friend not to worry.'

I nodded. 'Thank you.' I stopped myself adding *Sir*.

'The second card is mine, for when she's ready to talk. She doesn't have to speak to me, she should probably talk to a SOLO—'

'What's a SOLO?' I interrupted.

'A Sexual Offences Liaison Officer. I can arrange for her to meet one, or she can talk to me, if she prefers. I don't care as long as she talks to someone and I hope she does.' His gaze narrowed in mock disdain. 'I haven't known you long, Adamma, but if anyone can persuade her, I think you can.'

I felt a tickle of hope at that. 'So you don't think it's too late?'

'At the risk of sounding like a poster: it's never too late.'

'Even though she can't remember anything?'

He shrugged. 'She might.'

'Not if she was drugged. I looked it up.'

'She might not have been. It's strange that she doesn't remember anything. Most people usually remember stuff up until they were drugged.'

'So you think she has short-term memory loss?' I'd read something about that last night, too. 'That fits, I suppose. It can be triggered by stress.'

He nodded, but I could tell that he wasn't convinced.

'What?'

He scratched the corner of his mouth, then let out a long sigh. 'Sometimes it's triggered because the victim doesn't want to remember.'

I frowned. 'Why wouldn't she want to remember?'

'Because she knows who did it.'

TWO DAYS AFTER

MAY

Ostley Police Station wasn't what I expected. I think I've watched too many cop shows, because I thought it would be chaotic. I thought the phones would be ringing off the hook and there would be police officers pacing up and down, knocking back cups of coffee. I don't know why, it's hardly Scotland Yard. I must have passed it a dozen times before I knew what it was. After Scarlett's house, it's the second largest building in the village, which isn't saying much. It's only fractionally bigger than the pub so, with its pitched roof and leaded windows, it looks like the other houses around it. If it wasn't for the blue-glass POLICE lantern over the door, I might never have noticed it.

With a population of just under a thousand, Ostley shouldn't have a police station. Like the Post Office, its days are numbered, and every now and then there's a polite protest outside. I've seen the pictures in the local newspaper; lots of men and women in wellies waving grammatically correct signs. DOWN WITH THIS SORT OF THING.

I could see why they wanted to keep it; it was kind of lovely, with its tub of pansies and the posters about missing bicycles and bake sales pinned to the noticeboard by the door, but when

I walked into it today, I held my breath. I can't say that I'd thought too much about what it looked like inside, but I was surprised to find that the reception was white-walled and tidy, like a dentist's waiting room, just without the dog-eared magazines. There were no surly prostitutes smacking gum, like on television, no crying mothers with crying babies on their hips, no drunk men singing 'Danny Boy', just a few plastic chairs and a yucca plant in the corner.

I don't know how long we had to wait, but it felt too long, long enough to make me fidget. Mrs Delaney did too, she fussed over her hair and crossed and uncrossed her legs several times before she eventually stood up and wandered around the tiny waiting room. She peered through the window, then took a tissue out of her purse and wiped the dust from the leaves of the yucca plant.

It made me fidget more. 'Are you sure it's nothing serious?' I asked for the fourteenth time when she sat down again. 'Did they say what it was about?'

'Don't worry, dear.' She patted my knee. 'You're not in any trouble. The police just want to ask you some questions about Scarlett.'

'What sort of questions?'

'I don't know, dear.'

She didn't look at me and I felt a shudder of dread. It wasn't the first time the police had wanted to speak to me about Scarlett running away, but they always spoke to me at Crofton. They'd never asked me to go to the station.

'Don't we have to tell the Foreign Office?' I asked when I noticed her fiddling with her wedding ring. I wished she'd let me bring my cellphone. I wanted to call my father, hear him tell me that it was going to be OK.

'I've left a message for your father.' She patted my knee again.

'When?'

'When DS Hanlon called asking you to come in. About an hour ago.' She checked her watch and arched an eyebrow. 'Actually, more like two hours ago now.'

'Did you speak to anyone at the embassy?'

'To someone called Chinwe. She told me that it was fine for you to speak to the police as long as you're not under caution.'

I knew Chinwe, so that made me feel better, but I still had to close my eyes and take a deep breath as I felt the muscles in my legs begin to twitch. *Run*, a voice in my head said as I looked across at the door. *Run*.

Mrs Delaney sighed and checked her watch again. 'They're making us wait an inordinate amount of time given that this is urgent,' she said, raising her voice for the benefit of the police officer at the reception desk who wasn't paying attention. She sighed again. 'We've been waiting over half an hour.'

Finally, the door next to the reception desk swung open and PC Hill looked across the waiting room at me. 'Adamma Okomma?' he said, as if we'd never met, as if he wasn't the person who I spoke to every time Scarlett did this.

'Hello again, PC Hill,' I said with a pointed smile, standing up. But he didn't flinch, just gestured at me to follow him.

Mrs Delaney and I followed him through the door and up a flight of stairs to the first floor. When he led us through a set of double doors into the main office, I was startled. It was more what I had expected – busy. Noisy, even. I don't know what it looked like before, but it was clear that the room, which wasn't much bigger than one of the classrooms at Crofton, with two smaller offices on either side, had never seen such

125

chaos. There was a bank of untidy desks in the middle – two worn ones and three newer beech ones – suit jackets hanging on the back of each of the swivel chairs next to them. The phone was ringing and a woman in a creased white shirt, who was standing in the middle of the office, talking into a cellphone, interrupted her conversation to lean down and answer it, 'CID?'

I missed a step, then missed another as we passed a white-board with green writing all over it. Scarlett's name was in capital letters at the top and I turned away, stepping on Mrs Delaney's toe as I did. I apologised and when I stopped to catch my breath, I glanced through the open door to one of the offices and saw Dominic in his Crofton uniform sitting slumped at the desk next to a man in a suit.

'Dominic,' I gasped.

He blinked at me a few times, as though I'd just woken him up. 'Adamma.'

'What are you doing here?'

Before he could respond, I heard someone bark, 'Keep them apart,' and looked up as Bones marched across the office towards us.

'Bones.' My heart stopped. 'I thought you were based in Swindon?'

'What are you doing here?' he asked and when his jaw clenched, I wished that I could take it back. I shouldn't have called him Bones there.

'I called her in,' the women in the creased white shirt said from across the office as she hung up the phone.

That seemed to irritate him more. 'Take them into room two,' he said, pointing the manila file in his hand at PC Hill, before marching over to the woman.

I heard them whispering furiously while PC Hill led Mrs Delaney and me to the office on the other side, and, as we sat in the grey plastic chairs he gestured at, I heard her hiss, 'I got it, Mike,' a moment before she appeared in the doorway.

'Sorry to keep you waiting,' she said with a quick smile, nodding at PC Hill as he left, then closing the door and sitting on the other side of the desk. 'Thanks for coming in to have a chat with me, Adamma. My name is DS Hanlon and I'm one of the officers investigating Scarlett Chiltern's disappearance.'

'What's wrong?' I breathed, my hands balling into fists in my lap. 'Is Scarlett OK? Did something happen?'

'No.' DS Hanlon put the manila folder and legal pad she was holding down on the desk in front of her. 'I just want to ask you a few questions about Scarlett.' She looked at me, her green eyes suddenly brighter. 'Is that OK?'

I nodded, waiting for my heart to settle. It didn't.

'I've asked your housemistress to join us because you're seventeen.' She glanced down and opened the folder. 'Just.' She smiled at me. 'By a month.'

When she reached into the pocket of her jacket and pulled out a Dictaphone, I felt Mrs Delaney tense. 'That's rather formal for a *chat*, isn't it, DS Hanlon?'

'I'm sure Adamma understands. You have one of these for when you do interviews for the school newspaper, right?' She held it up and when I nodded, she smiled again, but it didn't quite reach her eyes. If she was trying to put me at ease, it wasn't working. 'I don't know shorthand so I have to record everything.'

I watched Mrs Delaney sit back in her chair, her hands folded neatly in her lap, then turned to look at DS Hanlon again. 'How can I help?'

She asked me to confirm a few details – my full name, date of birth, address – and when I did, she asked me when I had met Scarlett. 'Last September,' I told her, trying to control the tremor in my voice, 'on my first day at Crofton.'

She wrote that down. 'Were you close?'

'We were.'

'When was the last time you saw Scarlett?'

'On Saturday night.'

'Where did you see her?'

'At her seventeenth birthday party.'

'Where was that?'

The tops of my ears burned as I remembered that Mrs Delaney was next to me. I don't know what was worse, being questioned by a police officer or knowing that I'd just admitted to sneaking out in front of Mrs Delaney. But I couldn't lie.

'In Savernake Forest.'

'Did you speak to her?'

I started fiddling with my necklace and told myself to stop. 'No.'

'Why not?'

'We haven't spoken in a while.'

'You fell out?'

I nodded, looking down at the scuffed desk.

'Why?'

'We grew apart,' I lied, and even though I knew the words – I'd said them so many times – they still felt strange, like a pair of jeans that were suddenly too short.

'Grew apart?'

I nodded.

'When was the last time you spoke properly?'

'Not for a while.'

She looked up from the notepad. 'A while?'

'Not since last year, I guess.'

'Since her sister Edith's wedding?'

I had to take a breath before I said it and I hoped she didn't notice. 'Yes.'

'I hear you argued.'

I nodded again.

'About Dominic Sim?'

I felt it like a punch in the jaw and was too stunned to speak for a moment. I blinked at her and when she held my gaze as if to say, *Go on*, I looked at Mrs Delaney. She was so used to Scarlett and our drama that I thought she would give me a withering look, but she reached under the table and squeezed my hand.

When DS Hanlon realised that she wasn't getting a response, she opened the manila folder and took out a photo, sliding it across the table at me. 'We found this in Scarlett's bedroom.' I lifted my eyelashes to look at the photo, then looked away again, as my heart began to thump and thump. 'Do you know what it is, Adamma?'

'It looks like a credit card,' I lied.

'Really, Adamma? Why don't you look at it again?'

I didn't have to. I knew what it was. I knew the colour, the shape, recognised the grey line scratched back to reveal the number, but I made myself look at it as I wondered when the trash in my room was last emptied. 'It looks like a top-up card.'

'A top-up card?'

'For a disposable phone.'

'Why would Scarlett Chiltern have a disposable phone, Adamma?'

'How would I know?' I didn't mean to sound so surly, but when I heard myself, I looked at the door. *Run*, the muscles in my legs twitched again. *Run*.

'You've never seen her with one, Adamma?'

'No.' That wasn't a lie, at least.

'What phone have you seen her with, Adamma?'

'An iPhone with a red case.' I stopped for breath. 'The screen was cracked.'

She nodded. 'Why would Scarlett have two phones?'

My heart was beating so hard she must have heard it. 'I don't know.'

'Was she seeing someone?'

'I'm the last person she'd tell.'

'That doesn't mean you don't know.' She sat back and looked at me. 'You're a very bright girl, Adamma. You write for the school newspaper, don't you?' She waited for me to nod. I didn't – couldn't. I was too scared that, if I moved a muscle, she'd know I was lying. 'You know that Scarlett bought two theatre tickets for a play on Sunday night. I know you called the theatre to check that she'd picked them up. That was very clever.' She paused again and I don't know whether she was waiting for me to thank her for the compliment, but I didn't. 'Who was she seeing, Adamma?'

'I don't know.' And I don't.

I don't.

'Don't worry,' she said, sitting forward with another faint smile. 'You won't be getting her into any trouble. Her family just needs to know that she's OK.'

I felt dizzy and made myself take a breath. 'I don't know.'

She licked her lips and sat back. 'Could she be seeing Dominic Sim?'

I thought of Dominic sitting slumped in the other office and panic started kicking at me. 'Scarlett is capable of anything.'

'Yes. But what is Dominic Sim capable of?'

Mrs Delaney raised a hand. 'I think that's enough.'

But before DS Hanlon could object, I heard my father and my heart leapt. 'Where is my daughter?' I heard him say and we looked up in unison at the door.

My father isn't a big man, even if that's what my grandmother likes to call him. 'My son the Big Man,' she tells him whenever we visit, fingers lingering on the collar of his pinstripe suit as she hugs him. But he isn't big. Sure, he isn't as fine as my uncle Som, who, as my mother always says, has to run around the shower to get wet. But then he isn't as big as my uncle Oluchi, either. He doesn't have uncle Oluchi's big hands and great big laugh. My father is average, I suppose. Neither fat nor thin, tall nor short. Yet there is something solid about him, something immovable. He doesn't raise his voice and throw his hands about when he loses his temper, like my uncle Oluchi. He doesn't lose his temper at all, in fact. I've never heard him raise his voice, never even heard him curse. But I've seen him silence a room with a look and make men twice his size step back.

It's a look that would derail a freight train, but it's never been directed at me. He always has time for me, even when I call and interrupt a meeting or linger in his study, complaining about school or another hopeless crush. He never tells me that I'm disturbing him, just listens and nods in all the right places until my breathing isn't as furious, then tells me to go to bed. And I miss that. I can't talk to him about those things any more. The exams are harder and there's more at stake – university, a future, freedom – and the crushes aren't so hopeless.

131

I'm seventeen. This isn't puppy love any more. The boys are nearly men, when they bite they leave scars.

I suddenly wished that I was four years old again, back when my heart still felt new and my father would make me think that I could do anything. He'd stand in the doorway of my room while my mother plaited my hair before bed, and when she'd kissed me goodnight, he'd come in and tell me a story. There was one about a drummer boy and one about a leopard who gets his claws, but my favourite was the one about the little boy who had to cross the Niger River. Every time he finished it, I would tell him that even though I was a girl, I was that brave. 'Of course you are, Adamma,' he'd say, tucking me in so tightly that I couldn't move and when I'd stopped giggling, he'd kiss me on the forehead and say, 'You have a light.'

It would make me feel the surge of something in my chest and I wouldn't be able to sleep. My legs would shiver under the sheets until I had to kick them away. Then I'd creep down to his study and stand in the doorway in my pink nightgown, watching him at his desk, the nib of his fountain pen whispering words and words and words into the quiet room. I would look through the window at the trees in the garden while I waited for him to notice me – the breadfruit tree, the palms with their sharp green leaves, the cashew tree, red fruit hanging like Christmas-tree ornaments – and when he finally looked up, he'd smile and gesture at me to come to him.

I was lucky to see him like that, I know, without his armour, in just a shirt, his jacket and tie discarded on the leather chair by the door and his top button undone to reveal an inverted triangle of perfect skin. I'd press my cheek to his chest and wait until I could hear the steady beat of his heart, then I'd ask him

132

where my light was because I couldn't see it. 'Here,' he'd say, tickling my chest until I'd nearly choke giggling.

I don't know when I forgot that. It's still there, I think – I hope – the light. I can feel it sometimes, at night, when I can't sleep and I try to remember what it was like to be the girl who thought she could do anything. But then the morning comes and I tell a lie, then another and another. One more and I'll never feel that light again.

One more.

When I think of the nights that I fell asleep in my father's lap, lulled to sleep by the steady scratch of his fountain pen, the cotton of his shirt cool against my cheek, I wonder how I can lie to him. But you'll never know what you're capable of until someone takes your heart in their hand and shows it to you. That's another thing I never thought I'd do: love another man as much as I love my father. But I do and oh it's scary. I love him more than the doubt that nudged at me as I thought about where Scarlett could be and why she had a disposable cellphone like mine, but I knew she couldn't be with him, so I wasn't going to say a word.

'Adamma,' my father said, suddenly sweeping into the room.

I couldn't look at him and I realised then, as he stood over me, why I've been sneaking around – lying – why I haven't told him about any of this. I thought it was because he wouldn't understand, but it's because I don't want him to know who I am now. I want him to see me as that four year old forever, asleep in his lap, hand fisted in his shirt, not the seventeen year old who is lying to protect her boyfriend.

'Mr Okomma,' DS Hanlon gulped, the legs of her chair scraping on the lino as she jumped to her feet. 'Who let you up here?'

'I did,' Bones said, appearing in the doorway.

'Mike,' she hissed, her cheeks red, which seemed to piss my father off more.

'He was right to,' he said, tightly. 'What on earth is going on here?'

'I'm ever so sorry, Mr Okomma,' Mrs Delaney interjected. I'd never seen her so flustered. 'You were on a conference call with Australia—'

'That's fine, Mrs Delaney,' he interrupted, lifting a hand. But he wasn't looking at Mrs Delaney. 'I was led to believe that this was an informal chat at Crofton, not at the police station, DS Hanlon, but that doesn't seem to be the case.'

'She isn't under caution, Mr Okomma,' DS Hanlon said, hands on her hips.

'I should hope not. Adamma is under eighteen, so my diplomatic immunity extends to her and you can't interview her without permission from the Nigerian Embassy, as you well know.'

'I do, Mr Okomma. I was just asking Adamma some questions about Scarlett Chiltern. She's been missing for thirty-six hours and we're anxious to find her.'

'Of course. But why are you talking to her here and not at Crofton?'

'Because it's easier.'

'Easier? I assume that's why you're recording this, because it's *easier*.' He arched an eyebrow and held out his hand. 'Give me the tape.'

She shot Bones a look, who sighed. 'Just do it, Marie. You can't use it.'

'It's digital.'

My father nodded. 'Delete it, then.'

She snatched the dictaphone from the desk and pressed a button. 'Done.'

'Thank you, DS Hanlon,' he said, with a polite nod. 'Come along, Adamma.'

Bones and I exchanged a look as I shuffled after my father across the office to the double doors. 'Adamma,' he barked, holding them open as I stopped to look over to the office where I'd seen Dominic waiting. I jumped and followed him down the stairs and out of the station.

When I got outside, my mother was pacing back and forth on the pavement, muttering something in Igbo into her phone. When she saw us walking towards her, she ended the call with a swift, *Kaomesia*, then raised an eyebrow at me. I knew that she was livid, but I still felt the same surge of joy I feel every time I see her. My mother is magnificent. That's the only word big enough to describe her. There we were – my father and Mrs Delaney in their dull, dark suits, me in my black and white Crofton uniform – and there was my mother, in an ankle-length, strapless dress with a lime-green and purple print, her hair down, dark, tight curls frothing in all directions. Next to us, she looked like a piece of turquoise in a box of buttons.

Mrs Delaney stared at her, as she always does, as everyone does. Whenever she comes to Crofton, people stop and gape. 'You'd think they'd never seen a black person,' Scarlett says whenever they do, but it's nothing to do with her being black; people stare in Nigeria, too. Men rush to open doors while women mutter under their breath that she should relax her hair. Not that she notices; she's usually too busy asking me about school or trying to persuade my father to try a restaurant. Today she didn't notice the man staring at her as he walked his dog past the police station, she just nodded at me to get in the car. I didn't wait for her to tell me twice, and as I was climbing in, I heard my father offering to give Mrs Delaney a ride back to Crofton.

'It's fine, Mr Okomma. Thank you. It isn't far to walk at all.'

'Are you sure?' he offered, if a little half-heartedly.

When she refused again, he waited for my mother to get into the car next to me, then slid in himself. He didn't look at me as he did, just unbuttoned his suit jacket and asked the driver to take us to Crofton.

I waited for them to tell me off, but my mother just asked, 'Is there anything you need to tell us, Adamma?'

I closed my eyes as everything inside me fizzed up – the guilt, the confusion – like bubbles in a champagne glass, as I wondered what had happened to Scarlett. And it was right there – *I'm so scared, Mama* – right there on the tip of my tongue, but I just shook my head. 'No, Mama.'

190 DAYS BEFORE

NOVEMBER

The last few weeks have been strangely quiet. Half-term helped, but still, no one has got together or fallen out or been caught in the A/V Equipment Room.

Even Scarlett's been behaving herself, probably because she got the part of Ophelia in Crofton's production of *Hamlet*, so with her rehearsals, and my desperation to make up for not making it onto the staff of the *Disraeli* by taking any assignment Hannah is willing to offer, we've hardly seen each other. It's my fault too, because I've kind of been avoiding her. We haven't had an argument or anything, but things have been weird between us since she ran away to New York last month. I've calmed down and I even get that she didn't want to jinx it, having to come back to school and tell everyone that she didn't get the part would have been excruciating, but she could have told me. I was worried out of my mind.

I miss her, of course. I miss going to her house for tea in that hour before I have to get to swimming practice or Debating Society or Spanish Club or the hundred and one other things I have to do now. I can't remember the last time I had a conversation with my parents that lasted more than ten minutes.

It feels like all I say to them now is, *I'll call you back*. Jumoke thinks it's amusing, though. 'I'll give your regards to Bendels,' she told me yesterday me when I said I'd call her back because I needed to take a shower after Cross Country and it made my heart ache a little.

But being apart from Scarlett has been kind of nice, too. I do my own thing now. I have a routine (frantic as it is). I've learned everyone's names and can find my philosophy classroom without leaving a trail of breadcrumbs. Crofton is starting to feel like my school, too. And I'm not the only one who's busy; everyone else has been settling into the slog of sixth-form life, too, which is probably why it's been so quiet. They've even stopped whispering about Chloe Poole, so Orla has been venturing out of her room more. We have dinner together now and, as we share a weakness for bad horror movies, we sit in bed on Sunday nights, watching them on my laptop and scaring ourselves silly. Mrs Delaney has threatened a *Saw* intervention.

But all of this good behaviour also means that everyone is bored out of their minds, so I wasn't surprised when word went out this morning that the Alphabet parties are back on. Thanks to the promise of drama, everyone seems to have forgotten why the last one was called off. I suppose it helps that Sam Wolfe 'accidentally' sent everyone a video of Rachel Flock going down on him yesterday so everyone's too busy discussing that to worry about what happened to Chloe Poole the last time there was a party in the forest. Besides, this school would be nothing without its traditions and the Alphabet parties have been happening here since the forties. They're as much part of Crofton as tartan skirts and tantrums.

Speaking of tantrums, today was the first time Scarlett has shown any regret for running away to New York. Of course she isn't sorry for worrying us all sick, rather, she is sorry for herself because she's grounded and can't go to the party. A few weeks ago, I would have raged with her, but I stopped listening halfway through her rant as I wondered if I had my Kate Spade dress with me or if I'd left it in London.

I must admit, it was kind of satisfying to see her sulking. That's mean, I know, but I keep hoping that absence will make the heart grow fonder and we can go back to how things were before, before I knew that she'd lied to me about Dominic, before she ran away and went to parties without me. Back when she was my bright, fearless friend who made me feel like I could do anything. So I figured another weekend apart would do us good, but who was the first person I saw when I got to Savernake Forest tonight?

She was dancing with Dominic, her back to him and her arms up as he held on to her hips with his hands. She saw me, I know she did, I saw the red curl of her mouth as she flicked her hair back and forth. If I hadn't walked there with Molly, who was standing next to me, all but panting as she waited for a reaction, I might have turned around and gone back to Burnham. Sam came over, his hand lingering on my waist as he kissed me on both cheeks. He kept it there as he leaned over to kiss Molly, and I pulled away as it began to edge over my hip to my ass.

'Got any ice?' I asked, holding up the bottle of vodka in my hand. I'd bought it for the first Alphabet party with my fake ID the last time I was in London. It had been hiding at the back of my closet since then in case Mrs Delaney found it.

He reared back, registering the threat, then grinned. 'On the table.'

It was my first forest party and I was impressed; the Bedwyn boys had done a good job. I mean, Martha Stewart wouldn't be calling them any time soon, but they'd strung some lights between the trees, which swayed lazily over our heads, and there was a DJ, a fire pit (which I'm pretty sure they weren't supposed to dig, but I was too grateful for the heat to care) and a table with an impressive array of bottles given most of us are under eighteen. But then you never truly understand the resourcefulness of teenagers until it comes to acquiring alcohol; I'm sure there are drinks cabinets and wine cellars all over Wiltshire that are a bottle or two lighter this morning.

Molly was immediately distracted by a couple who were kissing against a tree and went off to investigate, cellphone in hand, which left me rooting around on the table for a clean plastic cup. I was scooping one into a bag of ice when Scarlett bounded over, squealing as though she hadn't seen me for three weeks, not three hours. She gathered me up into a huge hug, smelling of cider and Chanel, and when I didn't give her the satisfaction of asking what she was doing there, she told me anyway, regaling me with her epic tale of how she snuck out of the house, which probably involved elves and trolls and dragons, but I wasn't listening.

'Yum!' She thrust her cup at me as I poured myself some vodka. She watched me fill her cup, then arched an eyebrow at me. 'So. Why are you so late?'

'Am I?'

'I've been here ages.'

'I would have been here earlier, but I was trying to persuade Orla to come.'

Scarlett laughed, but when I didn't, she stared at me. 'You're joking.'

'No. Why?'

'Orla? *Orla Roberts?*'

'Yes, Orla Roberts. What's the big deal?'

'She would never come to this party!'

'Why not?'

'Not after Sam dumped her.'

I blinked at her. 'She went out with Sam?'

I tried not to look horrified, but I must have failed, because her eyes lit up. 'Yeah. For *ages*. He dumped her after the last Alphabet party.'

'Orla dumped him,' I muttered, turning to check if there was any cranberry juice. When I couldn't find any, I settled for Coke, my hands shaking as I picked up the bottle.

'You didn't even know they were going out,' she told me when I turned back to her. She tried to hide her smile behind her cup as she took a swig from it, but I saw and I made myself take a breath in case I bit back and gave her what she wanted.

'I knew she was seeing someone.' I did. Orla had told me that she'd broken up with her boyfriend after what happened because she couldn't bear him touching her, but she didn't say that it was Sam. It made sense when I thought about it; he didn't seem the type to be sensitive about something like that. 'But I'm not surprised she left out the fact that it was Sam,' I added with a sweet smile.

I knew that she wasn't going to agree with me, but I was still surprised when she feigned confusion and asked, 'Really? Why's that?'

I humoured her. 'Because he's vile.'

'And Orla isn't?'

I thought she was joking, so I laughed.

She didn't.

'You weren't at the Abbott party, Adamma. You should have seen her—'

141

'Oh yeah,' I interrupted, and I don't know whether I lost my temper or the music got louder, but I raised my voice. 'And why wasn't I there, Scarlett?'

She knew what I was getting at, but waved her hand at me and carried on, raising her voice as well. 'Orla was a *mess* that night. She was absolutely wasted, falling all over the place in a dress that she really shouldn't have been falling all over the place in,' she said and I was astonished. I would never describe Scarlett Chiltern – Scarlett Chiltern with her unbrushed hair and red lipstick and bread-making father – as sanctimonious, but *my God*.

I stared at her. 'And you didn't think to check that she was OK?'

'Why would I?' She looked equally bewildered, then she gasped, her blue eyes wide. 'Holy shit! Is Orla the girl you think was raped at that party?'

I looked around, my cheeks burning as I wondered if anyone had heard. The only people close enough to hear were two girls, who were standing behind Scarlett, but they didn't seem to be listening as they bickered over the last bottle of gin.

When I didn't deny it, Scarlett laughed, long and hard. 'Oh, Adamma.'

All of my muscles clenched at once. 'What?'

'Silly, Adamma,' she sang, tilting her head at me with a nasty smile that I wanted to slap right off her face. 'Orla wasn't raped.'

I was so angry, I couldn't breathe, my heart thumping. 'Says who?'

'Says me.'

'And how would you know, Scarlett?'

'I know.'

'Why? Were you there?'

'I didn't need to be. Everyone thinks it's bullshit. Even Dominic.'

My heart reared up like a startled horse mid-gallop. 'Dominic knows?'

'He told you, Adamma.'

'He told me about Chloe Poole, not Orla.'

'Same thing.' She flicked her hair and looked at me like I was mad. 'He told you about the pervert in the car, didn't he?'

'So?'

'So, Orla heard about that and is using it as an excuse.'

It was my turn to stare at her like she was mad. 'An excuse for what?'

'For shagging a random.'

I took a step back and stared at her. 'What the hell, Scarlett?'

'I'm just saying, Adamma —' she snapped, so loudly that the girls behind her stopped wrestling with the gin bottle and looked at us — 'she can't go around behaving like that, drinking herself silly and fawning all over boys, then cry rape.'

I wanted to tell her to lower her voice, but I knew that would make her worse, so I took her by the arm and tugged her towards the other end of the table.

'You're disgusting,' I hissed when we were far enough away from the girls with the gin.

'Why? It's true, Adamma. You didn't see the state of her.'

I couldn't look at her. My hands were shaking so much that I put my cup down on the table, terrified that I was going to drop it. I would never give her the satisfaction. 'God forbid something like that ever happens to you, Scarlett.'

I don't know whether what I said registered or she was horrified at being compared to a drunken slut like Orla, but she was suddenly furious and pointed at me. 'And you're gullible, Adamma. She's just saying this for attention.'

'Why in God's name would she say something like that for attention?'

'You'd be surprised the lengths some girls will go to, to be noticed.'

I arched an eyebrow at her. 'Ain't that the truth.'

I didn't mean it to sound as nasty as it did, but as soon as I said it, her eyes went black and I couldn't hear a thing over the sound of my heart in my ears. I thought she was going to slap me, but then Molly was between us, gushing about catching two Year 10 girls kissing. When we didn't react, she frowned.

'What are you two talking about?'

I gave Scarlett a look that pleaded with her not to say anything and when she smiled, I thought that was it, that was her retaliation for what I'd said, but instead she sighed. 'We're just talking about what a drama whore Orla Roberts is.'

She said it with such relish, the word rolling long and loud from her tongue – *whore* – but I was so relieved that I reached for my cup and drained it in two gulps. However, I shouldn't have been relieved, because when I looked at Scarlett, she was still smiling and I knew that it wouldn't be the end of it.

She'd call the favour in soon.

Molly laughed. 'Oh God. Remember last year? With Mr Lucas?'

They both laughed and it made my nerves rattle. 'What about Mr Lucas?'

Molly turned to face me, standing next to Scarlett. 'She had this ridiculous crush on him. She wrote him poetry and everything.' She and Scarlett exchanged a glance then giggled again. 'It was pathetic. She let me read it.'

'She probably let you read it because she thought you were friends.'

'Oh well,' Molly said with a smirk as she reached for a bottle and refilled her cup. 'I was only friends with her for the key to the broom cupboard.'

She and Scarlett laughed again and it made me shudder.

'Didn't she say they did it?' Scarlett laughed, her nose wrinkled.

'They kissed.' Molly rolled her eyes. 'And then she gave him a hand job.'

'As if!' Scarlett squealed.

At least Scarlett and I agreed on that.

'Come on, Molly.' I crossed my arms. 'Orla's gone from having a ridiculous crush on him to giving him a hand job? Which is it? Either it happened or it didn't.'

'That's my point,' she said slowly, the way the kids at my last school did when I started, as though they didn't expect me to speak English. 'She's a fantasist.'

'Pot, kettle, black, Molly.'

She and Scarlett exchanged another glance, then Molly turned back to me, her gaze narrowed. 'She is. She makes stuff like this up all the time for attention.'

Scarlett looked at me as if to say, *Told you so.*

I could feel myself losing my temper and I couldn't, not in front of Molly, of all people. So I took a deep breath. 'I'm not saying that she didn't have a crush on him,' I said, carefully. 'I'm just questioning the bit where it was reciprocated.'

'Exactly! My family has known him for years and he *never* would,' Scarlett said, completely missing that it wasn't Orla I was doubting, rather Molly's version of events. I almost corrected her, but it would have been futile; Scarlett was on a roll. 'Besides, *Daniel* is gorgeous,' she added, saying his name grandly, as though it was something we were lucky to know. 'He'd never go for someone like Orla Roberts.'

I wanted to scream, but bit down on my lip. The pair of them were either too drunk – or stubborn – to respond to logic. I have no idea what Orla did to piss them off, but she'd been shunned like the Amish girl who'd been caught with the flat irons.

'*Now* he is.' Molly shook her head. 'But Dominic Sim says that there are photos of him up at Eton and he was *really* ugly when he was our age.'

'No way!' Scarlett looked appalled.

'Yeah. He was lanky and his nose was too big for his face. He's definitely grown into his looks.' Molly nodded when we stared at her. 'He must be *loving* the attention he's getting now. He could have any girl at Crofton he wanted. Abbey Ascot found out his mobile number and has been texting him pictures of her breasts.'

'Yes. Well,' Scarlett said with a shake of her head before she finished her drink. 'He's gorgeous *now* and there's no way he'd risk losing his job here for someone like Orla Roberts.'

I shouldn't have, but I couldn't help it. 'What's that supposed to mean?'

'I'm just saying, Adamma,' Scarlett said, sighing and waving her empty cup. 'Orla was fifteen last year. Even if he could prove consent, it's still Statutory Rape. He'd never work again. There's no way he'd risk it. His family isn't like ours. His father's a mechanic, or something. He went to Eton on a scholarship. If he lost this job, he'd be back to living with his parents on a council estate in Sheffield.'

'A council estate?' Molly asked and when Scarlett nodded, she said, 'Ew.'

'He wouldn't risk that for someone like Orla Roberts.'

I held my hands up and stepped back. 'I have to go.'

I'd heard enough. Scarlett had said nothing to convince me that Orla was lying, but had said more than enough to convince me that she wasn't who I'd thought she was. I tried not to look at her, but I couldn't help it, I was so disappointed.

I guess she knew that, because she stared at me, her cheeks flushed. 'What? We're not saying anything that isn't true, Adamma.'

'Exactly,' Molly added. 'Everyone knows that Orla's a lying bitch, Adamma.'

I shot a look at her. 'Don't call her that.'

Molly stared at me, her lips parted, and I could hear my heart in my ears again as Scarlett took a step towards me. But I wasn't scared this time, I was livid. 'Sorry, Adamma. Did we say something about your new best friend?'

It was so juvenile, I almost laughed. But I didn't want to dignify it with a response, so I just shook my head as Sam swaggered over.

'Everything OK, ladies?' he asked with a smile so smug that, if he was a cat, he would have had feathers poking out of the corners of his mouth.

'Fine,' we said in unison.

He chuckled, then reached between us for a bottle of beer, but before he swaggered away again, he reached for Scarlett's hand and squeezed it. I don't think they knew I saw, but I did, and I would have dismissed it because it was Sam, but he squeezed her hand, not her hip or her ass, but her *hand* and finally – *finally* – I put two and two together and got, OH GOD. I'M GOING TO BE SICK.

Scarlett was seeing Sam.

That explained why she said all of that about Orla. But that made it worse, somehow. If she'd said it because she actually *believed* it, I'd understand, but the fact that she'd said it out of jealousy made it more despicable, especially as, if the photo I'd seen on Dominic's camera was anything to go by, she'd been seeing him, as well.

I couldn't look at her, scared that I would say something I couldn't take back, so I turned and walked away, my heels sinking into the damp forest floor as I wove between the trees towards the road. After a few minutes, the sound of the music began to fade and I stopped to suck in a long breath that seemed to make each of my bones rattle. I sighed it back out again and in the moment of quiet that followed, I heard it, a twig snapping – then another and another and another – and suddenly my breathing was hysterical again as I looked around frantically.

I'd held my breath during the walk to Savernake Forest with Molly, my heart jumping up in my chest like a startled cat each time I heard something or saw a shadow between the trees. I guess I was so angry when I stormed away from Scarlett and Molly that I'd forgotten about the threat, about what had happened to Orla, but I was suddenly achingly aware of it: a voice in my head roaring at me to run. But before I could tug my heel out of the earth, someone emerged from between the trees and I put a hand to my chest.

'Jesus, Dominic,' I gasped, my heart still thundering.

'Where are you going?'

'I'm getting the hell out of Dodge,' I told him, turning and continuing to walk towards the road. It hadn't felt this far when I'd come with Molly earlier.

'What was that about?' he asked, walking alongside me.

I eyed him carefully. 'What do you think you're doing?'

'You're shit out of luck if you think I'm letting you walk back to Burnham by yourself.'

'I'll be fine.'

'Really?' He nodded in the opposite direction. 'The road's that way.'

'I knew that,' I told him with a scowl and began stomping the other way.

'OK, Miss Okomma.'

We walked in silence, him watching and offering his hand every now and then as I navigated over the cluttered forest floor in my heels. I refused it each time, so was grateful when the trees parted and the road finally came into sight. It wasn't lit, but the break in the foliage let the moonlight in so I could see the long line of the tarmac and the chewed-stone pillars further up. He turned to hold out his hand as he stepped onto it, but I didn't take it, too concerned for my heels as I heaved my feet out of the mud. You'd think I'd have learned my lesson after the day of the hockey match.

'So what's up with you and Scarlett?' he asked when I joined him on the road, but I ignored him and he chuckled. 'I told you so.'

I crossed my arms. 'Told me what?'

'That if you want to be friends with Scarlett you'd better get used to that.' He nodded back down the road towards the party.

'That *what*?'

'Whatever you were arguing about. Sam, I assume.'

I thought of Sam, reaching for Scarlett's hand, and almost missed a step.

'You know?'

He wouldn't look at me. 'I don't know anything,' he said, pausing to chew on the corner of his mouth. 'Sam says nothing's going on, so I guess nothing's going on.'

'Do you believe him?'

'He's my cousin.'

'That isn't a yes, by the way.'

I turned my cheek towards him, but when he wouldn't look at me, his forehead creased as he stared at the stone pillars at the top of the road. I suddenly felt so sorry for him. It must be awful to be in love with someone like Scarlett, to hope that she takes you with her the next time she runs. To hope you'll love her more than the next guy promises to. And the next guy. And the next guy. And the next guy.

'We weren't arguing about—' I started to say, then jumped, my hand flying to my chest as I heard a twig snap somewhere between the trees next to me. But before I could look to see what it was, Dominic took me by the arm and tugged me back so that I was behind him.

'I thought the Chloe Poole thing was bullshit?' I breathed, and I had to suck in a breath before I did, my heart hammering as he peered at the black tangle of trees.

'It's nothing. Just a bird,' he muttered, letting go of my arm, but he sounded almost robotic, like an automated message. *Press 0 to connect to the Operator.*

When my breathing had settled and we began walking in step again, I turned to look at him. 'I spoke to her, by the way.'

'To who?' he asked, glancing at the trees again.

'Chloe Poole.'

He looked at me then and the skin between his eyebrows creased. 'When?'

'The day you told me.'

'What did she say?'

'It's a long story, but let's just say you got the wrong hockey player.'

It was suddenly so quiet, I could hear him breathing and it made me uneasy. Perhaps he was processing it, but there was something about his gait, about the way his chin was up and his hands were in his pockets, that seemed a little too relaxed.

'You don't seem surprised, Dominic.'

'Nothing at this school surprises me any more,' he said, but I knew.

'Scarlett told you.'

He sighed and shook his head. 'Don't be mad at her.'

'I'm already mad at her.'

'She was worried.'

I almost choked on a laugh, too angry to respond as I crossed my arms and recalled what she'd just said about Orla.

'What did the police say?'

She'd told him that, too? So much for crossing her heart.

'They can't do anything unless she reports it.'

He stopped. I did, too, and when I eventually lifted my chin to look up at him, I was so surprised to find him looking sad, that my arms dropped to my sides.

'I hope she's OK,' he said, softly. 'Do you think she'll be OK?'

'She will be.'

He nodded, looking at me from under his dark eyelashes, and I don't know if I reached for his hand or if he reached for mine, I just remember thinking that I had to do something a second before I felt his fingers between mine. But before our palms touched, I heard someone say, 'Well, this is becoming quite a habit, isn't it?' and we sprang apart to find Scarlett watching us.

When I caught my breath, I held my hands up. 'Scarlett, *please*. I'm cold and tired and my feet hurt. I can't argue with you any more tonight.'

'I came to apologise, actually,' she said, her arms crossed, and I know it was an effort for her to say something like that. I guess Dominic did, too, because he told me that he'd wait for me by the pillars and started walking up the road.

When he was far enough away, she took a step towards me, her arms still crossed. 'You drive me nuts, Adamma, you know that, right?'

I stared at her. I know it was as close as Scarlett Chiltern got to an apology, but I still wasn't going to let her get away with it.

'I know you've never done this before, Scarlett, but you should know: telling someone you're trying to apologise to that they drive you nuts? Not an apology.'

'You're going to make me say it, aren't you?' Her gaze narrowed and when I returned the favour, she threw her arms out. 'Fine. *I'm sorry.*'

I continued staring at her for a moment or two, then gave in with a huff.

'See?' I arched an eyebrow at her. 'That wasn't so bad, was it?'

'It actually physically hurt, Adamma,' she said with a theatrical sigh.

When she pouted, I had to fight a smile, and I kind of hate that, how the line between wanting to slap her and hug her is usually only a sentence. But she knows that, too, I think. She knows that line better than I do, it's her catwalk.

'But don't you feel better?'

'No. I still don't like Orla.'

I could feel myself losing my temper again. 'All of this for a boy? You said all of those nasty things about Orla because of a boy? Really, Scarlett,' I snapped, and I didn't realise that I was looking over her shoulder at Dominic until I told myself to stop.

'A boy?' She blinked at me, then threw her head back and laughed.

I didn't know what was so funny until she nudged me with her hip and *God help me*, I want to kill her sometimes, but then she does something like that.

'I've missed you too,' I told her, nudging her back and she grinned.

We hugged wildly, giggling and grinning like a couple reunited after the war, and when we turned to walk back up the road towards Dominic, she said, 'You have to do me a favour, though, Adamma, you have to stop being so bloody perfect all the time. I can't decide if I love or hate that about you. You make me feel like shit.'

I elbowed her in the side. 'I'm not trying to.'

'Well, stop.' She elbowed me back. 'You're making me look bad.'

'Sorry.'

'I have a reputation to maintain, Adamma –' she paused to flick her hair – 'and here I am, apologising and trying to be a better person. Olivia will be thrilled.'

'I won't tell her, I promise.'

'Don't tell her what I said about Orla, either. She'll beat me to death with Mum's copy of *The Female Eunuch*.'

We walked the rest of the way, chuckling, but just before we got to the stone pillars where Dominic was waiting, she looked at me. 'I don't mean everything I say, you know,' she said with a shrug, and I almost laughed.

That's the trouble.

2 DAYS AFTER

MAY

I've never lied to my parents before. I mean, I have, of course. I've told white lies, *I got it half off* lies and *I promise there won't be any boys there, Papa* lies, but I've never lied like that. I've never been unable to look them in the eye when I told them.

Mercifully, my father was too pissed at DS Hanlon to notice and after giving me another thorough telling-off about talking to the police without telling him, he and my mother told me that they didn't want me to miss any more classes and headed back to London. As soon as they did, I got my other cellphone out of my tuck box and called him. It went straight to voicemail, which it always does now, so I left a message telling him to meet me in the prop room at the end of the day. I went back to my room to check my phone at lunch, but when he hadn't replied, I felt a slow curl of dread and instead of heading to the prop room at 3 o'clock, I went to the car park and, sure enough, I saw him getting into his car.

I had to run, otherwise I would have missed him. He must have heard me, feet splashing in the gravel, because he looked up. When he saw that it was me, his face hardened and there was a moment – I saw it, I'm sure – when his gaze flicked to the door of his car as he wondered if he could get in before I got to him.

'Adamma,' he hissed, one hand still on the car door. 'What are you doing?'

'I've been calling and calling,' I said, breathless.

'I left our phone at home.'

'You never leave it at home.'

'I know,' he said lowering his voice as his gaze darted around the car park. 'But everyone's been on high alert since the appeal this morning; I was worried someone would see it.'

That made sense, but it still didn't make me feel better.

'But aren't you going out of your mind? Don't you want to know what happened at the police station earlier?'

'Of course, but not here. *Please*.'

As if on cue, a car rolled past and I humoured him, taking a book out of my bag and handing it to him.

'Let's go somewhere,' I pleaded when he took it, nodding at his car.

'Now? School's kicking out and you want to go somewhere *now*?'

'Please. I need to speak to you.'

I was so dizzy with panic I could barely get the words out and I think he was too, because when he opened the book and pretended to leaf through it, his hands were shaking. 'Not here,' he said, so quietly I almost didn't hear him. 'We need to be careful.'

'But what about Paris this weekend? We're still going, right?'

He looked up from the book. 'What? *Now*? We can't. Are you mad?'

'But—' I started to say, taking a step towards him, but before I could finish, I heard someone say his name. He looked over, giving them a nod and a smile, then muttered something about Thomas Hardy at me before giving the book back.

'I'll call you,' he said through his teeth, turning to get in his car.

I panicked, my heart racing as I reached for the door with my hand before he could get in and close it. 'Why does Scarlett have a disposable cellphone?'

He looked at my hand, then at me. 'What?'

'Why does Scarlett have a disposable phone?'

'How should I know?'

I stared at him as I waited for my heart to settle, but it wouldn't. And I love him – I *love him* – so I should have left it, but I couldn't.

I couldn't.

'It's a bit of a coincidence, don't you think? That we have the same phone.'

He straightened and turned to face me, the car door between us.

'Come on, Adamma, this isn't like you. Just say it.'

'Fine.' I lifted my chin and took a breath. 'Are you seeing her as well?'

He didn't flinch. 'We have a history, you know we do, but no, I'm not.'

I waited for my heart to settle, for it to make me feel better. It didn't.

I think he knew that, because he frowned. 'Do you believe me?'

I hesitated as I looked over his shoulder to see a guy walk past carrying a cricket bag. I waited until he was out of sight, then let go of a breath.

157

'Hey.' He reached around the car door to squeeze my hand and it was nothing – not the hug I needed, the kiss – but it was enough to bring me back. I looked at him, my heart rattling for a different reason as he smiled. 'Do you trust me?'

I arched an eyebrow. 'I don't trust her,' I told him and he smiled.

I forgot that it was Tuesday and swimming practice started early, so I was late and I had to do forty lengths, which was a relief; I needed the distraction, especially when I realised that Olivia wasn't there, her red and white spotty towel not on the hooks with the others in the changing room. But even after a two-hour practice, my brain was still jumping in all directions, like a bird flying from rooftop to rooftop, so before dinner, I asked Mrs Delaney if I could go for a run. I was already in my running gear, which, with hindsight, was a little presumptuous, but she seemed more anxious than put out. I thought she was still recovering from what had happened at the police station this morning, but when I told her that I was going to Savernake Forest and she started playing with her wedding ring, I realised that she was nervous.

'Just to the gates and back, Miss Okomma,' she said, zipping up my vest and giving me a look that made something in my chest feel too tight.

I don't think I've ever seen Mrs Delaney scared.

As I was jogging down the path towards the Green, I met a group of Lower College girls shuffling down it towards the library. I stepped out of their way and onto the Green and when they watched me do it, bumping into one another as they did, I felt my whole body tense as I realised that it was more than the usual awe of watching an Upper College girl who is allowed to walk on the grass. They were *staring*.

I pretended not to notice, but I felt a sudden weakness in my legs as I continued across the Green. I'd hoped it would pass, but it's been happening all day – the whispers, the stares – ever since I got back from the police station, and while being talked about at Crofton is something I've come to accept since I fell out with Scarlett, I don't think it's something I'll ever be used to. So I ran and ran, all the way to Savernake Forest. My legs were shaking by the time I got there and I was tempted to stop when I got to the mossy stone pillars at the entrance, but I kept going.

Every morning, the forest gets greener, the skeletons of the trees filling out with new leaves so bright, they look freshly painted. Today it smelt fresher too. I know green doesn't have a smell, but if it did, it would smell like Savernake Forest in May – sharp and crisp and new, like green apple peelings.

Last week, the ground beneath the trees erupted with thousands of bluebells until the forest floor was Monet-painting purple, just like he said it would be. They were so beautiful that I swooned the first time I saw them, their bell-shaped petals, heavy with dew. But this afternoon I didn't look at them, I just ran and ran, up the uneven road towards the gates. *Keep going*, I told myself when finally I saw the shape of them in the distance. I don't know why I turned my head, how I saw the flash of green between the pencil-thin trunks of the beech trees, but I did and I stopped.

I knew, before I approached it, before I saw the thick back bumper and the muddied tail light. But I had to stare at it for a few moments before it registered.

The Old Dear.

I stumbled towards it, approaching it with my hands up as though it was a rabid dog that might go for me. I hesitated before I looked inside and it took a few attempts before I was brave enough to peer through the dirty window. It was empty except for a half-empty bottle of water and an A *to* Z on the passenger seat and I let go of a breath. I don't know what I had expected, whether I thought she'd be in there, but I could feel my heart throbbing as I took a step back and reached into my pocket for my cell.

'Buffy,' Bones sighed, answering on the second ring. 'I'm sorry about this morning. Hanlon has a thing about Crofton kids,' he babbled on while I tried to catch my breath. 'She's worked on too many cases that have fallen apart because *Daddy's a QC* that I guess she just assumes the worst and—'

'Bones!' I didn't mean to shout, but I had to make him stop.

'What? What's wrong?'

'I've found her car.'

189 DAYS BEFORE

NOVEMBER

Ever since Orla told me what happened to her, it feels like I've been holding my breath. I hold my breath if I hear someone crying in the shower or if I pass a huddle of girls in the dining hall, heads stooped and whispering furiously, and I do it every time I reach for my phone to check the news. I hold my breath and think, *This is it*. He's done it again.

It's become a habit, I guess. I don't even notice I'm doing it any more. This morning, I caught myself doing it again, before I even got out of bed, my lips pressed together as I waited, hoping not to hear doors opening and the excited *slap slap slap* of Molly's bare feet on the floorboards as she darts from room to room, delivering the news. *He's back. He's back.* I held my breath and waited, but there was nothing, just the cranky creak of the radiators and the far off howl of a magpie.

One for sorrow.

I still held on to the breath, though, and didn't relax until Orla and I were walking to chapel and I half-heard my name. Normally, I would have turned around to see who had said it, maybe even blushed, but when I heard Scarlett's name a second later, I let go of the breath because it meant that nothing happened last night; the biggest news from the Alphabet party was my argument with Scarlett.

I wouldn't usually be so cool about it; I'm not like Scarlett, hearing my name in the corridor doesn't make me lift my chin and smile, but I could live with it if it meant that the creep who was driving around Savernake Forest hadn't come back. Besides, the whispering waned briefly when Scarlett and I saw one another going into chapel and hugged fiercely, then started again a few minutes later when Dominic saw me and winked.

It continued right through brunch and it must have been bad because Orla noticed and asked if I was OK. I was – *really* – I just wanted to go to the library and finish the piece I had to file for the *Disraeli* about Mr Crane retiring, but when Orla offered to go for a walk, I was so surprised that I almost erupted into tears. She's been reluctant to leave her room, let alone school grounds since the last Alphabet party, so I didn't hesitate, the relief making my hand shake a little as we signed out of Burnham then walked together into Ostley.

Today was one of those perfect November days; tensely cold but bright, the browning leaves making everything slightly yellow, like an old photograph. Orla laughed at me as I tugged on a pair of leather gloves, her cheeks pink as she told me that it wasn't that cold. I ignored her, huffing and making a show of fussing over my scarf before woefully reminding her that it was 31 degrees in Lagos. She conceded with a giggle, kicking at the leaves under our feet. I did it too, and I can't remember the last time I did something so silly, the last time I kicked at a pile of leaves without worrying about what might be underneath or if I'd scuff my shoes, and it felt kind of nice. More than nice; I was happy, I realised, and so was Orla, if just for that second, before we passed under the shadow of Savernake Forest and she went rigid.

My instinct was to reach for her arm and ask if she was OK, but she wasn't like Scarlett. We didn't hug or play with each other's hair or elbow one another. It always felt like there was something between us, a fence she'd let me get close enough to peer over, no more than that. So we walked in silence and when we passed the forest and stepped into the midday sunshine, I started babbling about the hockey social and asked her what she was going to wear, but she wasn't listening.

'You and Scarlett weren't arguing about Dominic last night at the party, were you?' She didn't look at me. 'You were arguing about me, weren't you?'

I stared at her, hoping that she was guessing and hadn't heard, because that was another thing I could live with: everyone thinking Scarlett and I were bickering over Dominic if it meant that Orla didn't find out what Scarlett had really said.

'I – we –' I fumbled, the words fighting with one another on their way out.

She sighed and shook her head. 'She told you about Sam, didn't she?'

'She—'

'I know what you're thinking.' She interrupted with a frown, crossing her arms. 'But whatever she told you, don't believe her. He's completely different when it's just us.' She shrugged, her voice a little higher. 'He's sweet. He doesn't talk to me like he talks to everyone else. Even his smile is different. She doesn't know him like I know him.'

I thought of Sam squeezing Scarlett's hand at the party and it turned my stomach inside out. I didn't know what to say so I looked away, the spent leaves under our feet suddenly louder as we continued on towards the village.

She tried to fill the silence. 'I know he's a bit of a bastard,' I stopped myself from raising an eyebrow at *bit*, 'but he isn't like that with me.'

There was another moment of silence and I don't know whether she was waiting for me to refute that, but when I didn't say anything, she shrugged. 'He's no Nathan, he's not perfect. He's never given me flowers or a Chanel bag,' she said bitterly, kicking at another clump of leaves. 'I don't expect you to understand.'

I'd heard that before, of course, heard friends question whether their bad boy boyfriends were really *that bad* while I smiled and nodded and resisted the urge to roll my eyes. So it's not that I was surprised (even if I doubted if Sam Wolfe was capable of such depths of emotion), it was that I found myself nodding.

'Perfect is overrated,' I told her, but I wasn't thinking about Nathan, I was thinking about him and I found myself doing exactly what she was doing: wondering if he was different with me, if his smile was different, if he spoke more quietly to me, more softly. And it's ridiculous – *insane* – he and I. The moment I let myself consider it, the same thoughts darted through my head – it will never work, my parents will never approve, he'll never be the boyfriend I need him to be – but they suddenly weren't as loud, as *certain*, as I thought about all the times I've caught him looking at me and asked myself if it was in my head.

I think Orla knew that, because she smiled for the first time in weeks. 'I guess I'm not the only one with a weakness for bad boys.'

If she'd done that yesterday, I would have denied it, but something told me to keep quiet as I thought about the dream I'd had about him, my hand in his hair, trying to see his eyes, as he turned his face away.

So I changed the subject back to the hockey social and what she was going to wear. That was it for the rest of the afternoon, as we tested the lipsticks on the rickety plastic stand in the chemist (it's hardly Space NK, but needs must); then we went to the newsagent and stocked up on magazines that I'd never have time to read and candy bars I really shouldn't eat, while she asked me more about the party.

I was approaching the counter when I was aware of someone next to me.

'Hey, Buffy.'

'DS Bone,' I gasped, falling against it and almost decapitating the tiny woman behind it as a copy of *Marie Claire* flew from my grasp.

'I didn't come in here for cigarettes,' he said, putting his hands on his hips and raising an eyebrow at me. 'Because smoking's bad, OK?'

'OK.' I pretended not to notice as the woman behind the counter put a box of Marlboro Lights back on the shelf. 'But I can still binge drink, right?'

'Not until you're eighteen.'

Orla approached with an armful of magazines of her own and I hoped she would be too distracted by the candy bar she was devouring to notice him, but he turned to her, his gaze narrowing. 'Have you paid for that Dairy Milk, young lady?'

She stared at him, startled, then at me as my brain clumsily grabbed at an excuse to get her out of the store, but before I could find one, she made the connection. I thought she was going to choke, but then she yanked the chocolate bar out of her mouth and pointed at him. 'He's that policeman you were telling me about! Is this a set-up? Did you tell him that we'd be here?'

'Of course not, Orla.' I was mortified, but she wouldn't listen.

'Was the I *didn't come in here for cigarettes* thing code?'

'This isn't a le Carré novel, darling,' he laughed, and I turned to glare at him, but when I turned back to Orla, she'd abandoned the magazines on the counter and was running between the narrow aisles towards the door.

I barked an apology at DS Bone, then ran after her. We were halfway to Crofton before I got close enough to reach for her sleeve. 'Orla, please.'

She pulled away, furious, but it was enough to make her stop. 'I can't believe you did that, Adamma,' she said with a sob. 'I can't believe you did that.'

'I didn't do anything.'

'I can't believe you did that,' she said again and she was *shaking*. When I saw a tear roll down her cheek, I wanted to cry too, cry and tell her that I would never do that to her, that we'd been having such a lovely day and I was *so* proud of her. I'd never ruin it by confronting her with a police officer.

'It was just a coincidence, Orla, I swear.'

'Oh yeah,' she put her hands on her hips, '*big coincidence*. You've been telling me for weeks to speak to the police and guess what? The police officer you were speaking to just *happens* to be in the newsagent while we're in the newsagent.'

'You think I'd do something like that? You think I'd ambush you like that?'

I stared at her and she stared back and for a moment I

thought she was going to shout at me again, but she seemed to calm down. 'So why was he there?'

'I don't know.' I put my hands up. 'I swear.'

The skin between her eyebrows smoothed. 'So it's just a coincidence?'

'They happen sometimes.'

'You didn't tell him to come and speak to me?'

'No. I said I'd leave you alone and I meant it.'

'OK.' She took a breath, then puffed it out again. 'OK.'

I watched her pace on the spot for a minute or so and, when her breathing had settled and she turned to look at me again, I frowned at her. 'Are we good?'

She nodded. When she'd caught her breath and her shoulders fell, I thought that would be it, but then she said, 'So what did you tell him?'

'About what?'

She gave me a, *You know what I'm talking about, Adamma* look. 'About me.'

'Just what happened.'

'Did you tell him my name?'

'Of course not. You told me not to.'

'Did you tell him that I don't remember anything?'

I nodded.

'And what did he say?'

I shivered as I recalled what he'd said and hoped she didn't notice. 'Nothing.'

'Nothing?'

I nodded.

'So he thinks I was roofied?'

'I guess,' I muttered and immediately regretted it.

She jumped on it. 'You *guess*?'

167

My heart started pounding with panic, so I made myself take a breath and chose my words more carefully. 'He thinks you might have short-term memory loss.'

'You said the same thing. You said it might be triggered by stress.'

I nodded.

'So what aren't you telling me?'

'Nothing.'

'You're such a bad liar.' She crossed her arms and tilted her head at me.

'Forget it, Orla.' I sighed and crossed my arms as well.

'Absolutely not.'

'Please, Orla. You're upset enough as it is. I think we should just leave it.'

'No. I want to know. I want to know what he's been saying about me.'

'He hasn't been saying anything.'

'Well, he said something that you won't tell me.'

'It's not that I won't tell you, it's just that I don't think this is the right time.'

'When is it going to be the right time? Tomorrow after registration? Or how about before my hockey match on Saturday, in front of my parents?' She laughed, then smiled sourly. 'It's never the right time, Adamma.'

I shook my head, but she was right. 'Fine,' I said with a defeated shrug. 'He said that you might not remember because you don't want to remember.'

She frowned. 'So? What's so bad about that? That makes sense.'

I should have stopped there – I *wanted* to stop there – but I could feel something digdigdigging at me and I wanted to know. I had to know.

168

I had to know.

I licked my lips, then lifted my chin to look at her. 'He said that you might not want to remember because you know who did it.'

She went from hot-cheeked to deathly pale in a second and I took a step forward, sure that she was going to faint. She took a step back. 'What?' She didn't wait for me to respond. 'So he thinks I know who did it, I'm just not telling anyone?'

'No.' I shook my head. 'No. I think he means *subconsciously.* I looked it up,' I said and I wished we were at Burnham where I had my laptop and printouts. Things I could show her. 'Sometimes, when something really bad happens, you forget the details. It's like your brain's way of protecting you. It's called dissociative amnesia.'

She considered this for a long moment, then sucked in a breath and said, 'Do you think that's what happened to me?'

'I have no idea. I wish I did, but I don't.'

She started pacing again and I watched her, watched the skin between her eyebrows crease as she bit her lip. 'If it is memory loss, how do I get it back?'

'You need a trigger.'

'Like what?'

'I don't know.' I shrugged. 'Like a smell or a song.'

She stopped pacing and looked at me. 'What if I never remember?'

'That's why you should talk to someone.' I said it carefully, as though it was a magic trick that wouldn't work if I didn't say it properly, but it didn't work.

She still looked livid.

'It always comes back to this, Adamma!' I could feel myself losing my temper so I looked down and kicked at a chestnut, its

169

spiky green shell split to expose its mahogany heart. When I didn't respond, Orla took a step towards me. 'Why do you keep telling me to talk to someone?'

I tried not to let her provoke me. 'Because that's the only thing you can do.'

'No. I can move on.'

I shouldn't have, but I lost it then. 'And how are you going to do that? This isn't the flu, Orla,' I snapped. 'You aren't just going to get over it. You were raped. You can't keep pretending it never happened. OK, you don't want to tell the police, I get that, but you're not sleeping or eating. You need to see a doctor. What if you're pregnant or he gave you an STD? I'm guessing he didn't use a condom.'

She staggered back as though I'd slapped her. 'Jesus, Adamma.'

'I'm sorry.' I couldn't look at her; tears stung the corners of my eyes and my hand shook as I pressed it to my mouth.

'I wish I'd never told you.'

'Don't say that.' I shook my head. 'Please.'

'I do.'

'I'm sorry. I shouldn't have said that, but I'm just trying to help.'

'Why don't you get it, Adamma?' she hissed, hands balled into fists at her sides. 'Not everyone is like you. I'm not as brave as you.'

'You're so much braver than you think you are, Orla.' I wanted to reach for her hand. I wished she'd let me reach for her hand, but she wouldn't look at me. 'You are. I wouldn't even be able to get out of bed if that happened to me.' She turned her cheek towards me again. 'I know it's hard, but I'm here, and DS Bone and I told you that his wife, Lisa, works for that rape sanctuary in Swindon.'

170

'Stop it!' she spat. 'Stop saying that word!'

'Orla –'

'No. You don't get it, do you? I'm at Crofton on a scholarship. What do you think Ballard's going to do if I tell the police what happened at a Crofton party he didn't know anything about? The parents will freak and start pulling their daughters out of school! A school like Crofton is only as good as it's reputation and there's no way Ballard is going to let me call that into question.'

'But what if he does it again, Orla?'

'That's not fair!' she roared, fresh tears suddenly rushing down her cheeks. I shouldn't have, but I didn't think and reached for her hand and it seemed to make her worse. 'That's on him, not me!' she roared again, pulling away. 'Don't put that on me! I have enough to live with! You don't know what I have to live with!'

'I'm sorry, Orla. I'm sorry.'

'Why are you doing this to me?' she sobbed and my heart split open.

'Sorry, I just want to help. *Please*. Just tell me what to do.'

'Just leave it. I want to forget it ever happened.'

'OK.'

'Just help me do that, OK?'

'OK.'

We stood facing one another for a minute or two, our arms crossed as we tried to catch our breath. When she had, she sighed. 'Sorry,' she muttered, wiping her cheeks with her fingers. 'I didn't mean to shout at you. I know you're just trying to help and I appreciate it.' She shook her head and looked at her feet. 'I just can't.'

'I know.' I nodded. 'I'll stop pushing, I promise.'

'Thank you,' she said with a dull smile, but when I took a step back, she looked panicked again. 'What are you doing? Where are you going?'

'I have to go back to the newsagent.' I thumbed over my shoulder, trying to lighten the mood. 'You totally shoplifted a Dairy Milk in front of a policeman.'

'Is he going to arrest me?'

'Of course not! But I should pay for it, and *Maire Claire*. I want that free nail varnish.'

I smiled, but she looked terrified. 'I'm not going back there.'

'I know.' I nodded. 'It's up to you. Do you want to wait for me here or would you rather walk back to Crofton?'

I knew what she was going to say before she took a step back. 'I'll see you back at Burnham,' she said, looking down the road towards the newsagent as though it were on fire, then turning and all but sprinting back to Crofton.

When I got to the newsagent, DS Bone was sitting on the hood of his car, waiting for me. As I approached he raised an eyebrow and handed me a blue-and-white striped plastic bag. 'Twenty quid on magazines. How the other half live.'

I went to take my wallet out of my purse, but he shook his head and motioned at me to sit next to him on the car. I've never sat on the hood of a car before and had a sudden flash of Dominic's Aston Martin. He'd have an embolism.

'So women are running from me now?' he said with a theatrical sigh when I sat next to him. 'Good to know.'

I wanted to laugh, but couldn't. When I didn't respond, he rubbed his mouth with his fingers, then sighed again. 'So that's your friend?'

'That's my friend.'

'How's she doing?'

I didn't know what to say, so I just shrugged.

He nodded. 'All you can do is be there for her, Adamma.'

'It's not enough.' I shook my head and looked at the plastic bag, sure that I was going to cry in front of him again and I didn't want to. 'It's not enough.'

I jumped down from the car before he could tell me that it was, because I couldn't bear it. I didn't want him to give me a speech about how Orla just needs time and I'm doing the right thing, the one that he's probably given dozens of times to dozens of silly girls like me, who still believe in things like justice and redemption and a world where the good guys win and the bad guys go to prison.

'Thank you for the magazines,' I managed to say before I gave in to the tears.

I ran so fast that by the time I got back to Burnham, I had to stop to let my eyes come back into focus before I ran up the stairs. I knocked at Orla's door, but she didn't answer, she didn't come out of her room for the rest of the day, in fact, not until I knocked at her door again before lights out. I didn't think she was going to answer, but when she did, she did what she always does and answered with a too-big smile, as though nothing had happened. She babbled on for a while, complaining about how hard her Latin homework was and how quickly the weekend had passed and I humoured her, not because I particularly wanted to talk about either of those things, but because I was just happy she was talking, even if it was about nothing. So I nodded and agreed and when she turned on her radio, I took the hint and said goodnight.

'She's nice,' she said, as I was about to close the door. 'Lisa, his wife,' she explained when I frowned at her, her voice a little smaller. 'She's nice.'

I froze, my hand still on the door handle. It was like being approached by a nervous cat, I didn't want to make any sudden movements, I just wanted her to come to me, so I nodded, but inside, my heart was beating so fast I felt dizzy.

She started running a brush through her hair and I thought that was it, but then she turned her cheek towards me. 'Will you go with me to see her tomorrow?'

I couldn't speak, I just nodded, and when I went back to my room, I cried.

Cried and cried.

3 DAYS AFTER

MAY

Headmaster Ballard called an assembly during breakfast this morning to tell us that the police would be searching Savernake Forest. There must have been almost sixty of us huddled in the dining hall – everyone in Burnham and what looked like most of the staff, from Mrs Delaney to the people who worked in the kitchen and laundry room – but I've never heard a silence sound so loud. It seemed to scream out as we all looked at one another. I thought the windows were going to break.

I didn't see Bones until Ballard introduced him and the man standing next to him as Chief Inspector Tom Bracken, who was exactly what I pictured a Chief Inspector to look like: greying and a little overweight. The sort of man who has a favourite mug and walks the dog every day and carves the chicken on a Sunday. He told us that he was co-ordinating the search with Bones who, despite being in a clean shirt and a tie, still looked in need of a hot meal and a good night's sleep.

He handed back to Headmaster Ballard who suddenly looked very solemn. 'I know that some of you helped Scarlett's parents search Savernake Forest after the Chilterns' Land Rover was discovered yesterday –' he didn't, but it felt like he looked right at me – 'but the police have taken over and have been conducting a search of the area since dawn. I know how keen you all are to help, so I said we'd assist.'

He turned to look back at Chief Inspector Bracken, who added, 'We know that Scarlett took the Land Rover with her when she left, so we can only assume she was in Savernake Forest at some point. We think that she might have met someone there before she went on somewhere else, so at this stage we're just looking for clues as to where that might be.'

Everyone looked at each other and Ballard held up his hands. 'Don't be afraid, girls. As Chief Inspector Bracken says, we're just looking for *clues*,' he said and it wasn't until he did that it occurred to me we might find something more sinister. I felt a shiver of dread at the thought, as though there was a spider under my shirt, scuttling across my back, but waited for the feeling to pass as I told myself that she was in New York again.

She was in New York.

No one said a word when Ballard told us to return to our rooms and change into mufti, not even Molly, who glanced at Orla and me as we were leaving the dining hall; her eyes wet. As we headed towards the stairs, Mrs Delaney pulled Orla to one side and asked her to stand with a small group of worried-looking girls. None of them seemed to know why they were there, but as I went up to my room, I could hear Orla crying and saying that she wanted to help. I guess Mrs Delaney couldn't reach her parents to get permission.

A moment later, I heard my cellphone ringing in my room and thought it might be him so I ran to it, grabbing it and answering it with a breathless, 'Hello?'

'Adamma! *Kedu ka i mere?*' my mother gasped, breaking into Igbo.

176

I told her I was fine and she was quiet for a second or two before I heard her say, 'Thank God,' her breathing settling as I pictured her in my parents' big white bedroom, pacing back and forth. 'What's going on, Ada?'

'Nothing, Mama,' I told her, trying to sound nonchalant as I rested my phone between my shoulder and ear and unbuttoned my blazer. I didn't want her to worry, especially after what had happened at the police station. 'They think Scarlett ran off with some guy. You know what she's like. She'll be OK. She always is.'

'Are you sure?'

My stomach quivered, but I ignored it. 'Yes, Mama.'

'That child.' She tutted. 'Why are the police searching the forest?' I told her about The Old Dear and she sucked in a breath. 'Be careful, Ada.'

'I will. I promise.'

I heard Orla in the corridor then, crying – 'I'm going anyway, Miss. I'll sneak out while you're gone. You can't stop me' – then slamming her door.

'I can and I will,' Mrs Delaney called after her. 'One missing girl is enough.'

'I'd better go. I'll call you later. *Ahuru m gi n'anya, nne.*'

She managed to tell me that she loved me too a second before Orla flew into my room, hair everywhere, and I hung up.

'Can you believe this?'

'It's bullshit,' I told her as I unzipped my skirt. 'But what can Crofton do? They're not allowed to take you out of school without permission.'

'This isn't a school trip, Adamma!'

'I know. But don't give Mrs Delaney a hard time; she's just doing her job,' I said with a shrug, hanging my skirt back in

177

the closet. 'Parents are being super over-protective since Scarlett ran away. I just overheard Ella Sanderson saying that her parents are threatening to pull her out and send her to Cheltenham.'

She softened a little at that and sat on my bed with a pout as I tugged on a pair of jeans. 'But I want to help.'

'Keep trying to call your parents.'

'Dad's on a bloody submarine and Mum's on a flight to Nice.'

'OK,' I said, walking over to my chest of drawers and taking out a fleece.

She saw me contemplating it and said, 'It's too warm for that.'

'Yeah, but it's me.'

'Put it on.'

I did. 'So. OK. France is what, a two-hour flight? Call your mother when she lands and get permission. You can do it later. We'll probably still be there.'

'I suppose,' she muttered, arms crossed.

Talking to her had settled my nerves, but I still struggled to lace my walking boots. I guess she noticed, because she asked me if I was OK as I struggled with the zip on my Gore-tex jacket as well. 'I'd better go,' I told her, running over to kiss her on the cheek, before dashing out the door and down the stairs.

Mrs Delaney must have known that with everything that was said over breakfast, none us had eaten, so she handed a breakfast bar and a banana to each of us as we left Burnham, telling us that there would be more food there, but that if we felt faint, to let her know immediately. I wasn't hungry, but forced mine down because she kept barking, 'Eat, girls! Eat!' as we walked over to the main hall, holding out her hand for our breakfast-bar wrappers and banana skins as proof that we had. Then, when we'd gathered outside the main hall, she separated us into five groups of ten by surname. I was in the third group with Madame Girard who frantically counted us four times before we'd even left Crofton.

It had rained heavily overnight, but you'd never know it, the sun was cartoon-yellow and the sky was clear. It wasn't hot – not what I regard hot – but it was warm enough to make some girls shrug off their jackets during the walk. Even I was comfortable.

It was strange seeing Savernake Forest so busy. When I run through it in the morning I rarely see anyone. Maybe someone walking their dog, but usually it's just me. But this morning there must have been at least a hundred people gathered on Postern Hill. Mrs Delaney kept telling us to keep together as we navigated our way through them and gathered to one side where we wouldn't be in anyone's way. The police were in uniform, so the rest must have been volunteers, most dressed as we were, in walking boots and waterproofs.

A small group of people had already started setting up folding tables. There was a tea urn on one, with a woman behind it, peeling the plastic from a stack of polystyrene cups. It's such a silly thing to think, but my first thought was that Scarlett's parents are so environmentally conscious that they would never use polystyrene cups, but then I realised it was Edith and panic licked at my palms. I wandered over to her before I could tell myself that it was a bad idea. I hadn't seen her since her wedding so I didn't know how she was going to react. She was thinner than the last time I saw her, but not as pale, her cheeks freckled from the sun and her dark hair threaded with gold. But that brightness had gone, her eyes dull from lack of sleep. 'Adamma,' she said when she saw me, running around the table to give me a hug. 'What happened?' she said into my hair. 'What happened?'

Before I could answer, Mrs Delaney was next to me. 'Miss Okomma,' she said, so loudly that everyone around us turned around. 'What part of *stay with your group* do you not understand?' She took me by the sleeve and dragged me away so brusquely that I could only manage to mouth *I'm sorry* at Edith over my shoulder.

She had a long stick, I don't know from where, and marked a cross in the mud by my feet. 'Stand on this, Miss Okomma.' I did with a sigh. 'Now don't move.'

I heard Bones before I saw him. 'If you could gather around, please,' he called out, holding a hand up. 'OK,' he said, when everyone had gathered in a clump in front of him. 'My name is Detective Sergeant Michael Bone from Wiltshire Police. I'd like to thank you for assisting us with this search. We've been searching since dawn, but we still have a lot of ground to cover, so we really appreciate your help. I know it's a Wednesday and some of you have taken time off from work and school to be here, so Scarlett's family has asked me to extend their gratitude. They will be providing refreshments, so once everything is set up, please help yourselves and dispose of any rubbish in the bins provided.

'A couple of basics before we start. Savernake Forest is about four thousand five hundred acres. It's very easy to get lost so I need you to pay attention. OK?' He waited for us to nod. 'OK. First, there are some maps being passed around, please take one. If there aren't enough, let me know. If you haven't already done so, please sign in.' He pointed towards a woman in a red waterproof coat standing behind one of the folding tables. 'It's kind of rough around here and muddy from the rain last night so if you don't feel up to it, I understand. But if you are feeling up to it, thank you. If you haven't brought any water with you,' he pointed at Edith, who was still fussing over the cups, 'please grab a bottle on your way out. Does everyone have a mobile?' We all mumbled *yes* and he nodded. 'Good, but I still don't want you to go off on your own. If you are on your own, let me know and I'll pair you up with someone.

'OK. This is the important bit.' He held up a hand. 'Only search where we tell you to search. If you think you see something outside the area you have been asked to search, please tell a police officer. And while we're telling police officers stuff, if you find anything, don't touch it. Just report it to a police officer immediately.' He turned to the table behind him and held up a box. 'There are gloves for people who want them and please, *please* don't forget to sign out with a police officer when you leave.

'Any questions?' He waited a moment, but when no one said anything, he nodded. 'Good. We're going to be working in a straight line from here through the forest, focusing on the undergrowth. We're looking for any clue as to where Scarlett might have gone, even knowing what way she left the forest will help, so nothing is too small. A receipt. An earring. *Anything.* And remember: take your time. This isn't a race. We have plenty of volunteers. OK?' He clapped his hands. 'Thanks, everyone. Good luck.'

Our group of ten girls had two teachers – Madame Girard and Mrs Delaney, who hadn't left my side – and a uniformed police officer. We worked slowly, flattening the carpet of bluebells under our feet as we kicked and poked through them, looking for something, *anything*. With each step, I held my breath, then let it out when I kicked a tuft of bluebells to find nothing beneath it but a leaf or a twig. Then I saw something white and my heart tumbled against my ribs as though it had fallen down a flight of stairs. Mrs Delaney must have seen me stop, because she peered down, poking at the bluebells with her stick to find a white feather and my legs went weak with relief.

'Thank God,' I muttered and she told me it was OK, rubbing my back with her hand. 'I hope I don't find anything,' I confided in a whisper and she nodded.

We were almost finished with our first small section of the forest when the police officer with us stopped to mutter something into his radio. It had been wittering away, like a television left on in another room, and I'd been trying to listen but could only make out the odd muffled word. I stopped to listen, but was distracted by someone's cellphone ringing. It was Mrs Delaney's and she answered with a gruff, 'Hello?' then immediately softened, saying, 'Yes. Right now? Of course. Yes.' She took a breath, then turned to us with a smile. 'That's it, girls. Let's begin making our way back.'

'Back?' we muttered, all at once.

'To school,' Mrs Delaney said breezily, trying to usher us towards the road.

I wasn't convinced. 'But we've been searching for, like, twenty minutes.'

'Come along, Miss Okomma,' she said, hand on the small of my back.

It took a moment for me to realise what she was saying. It was like a coin rolling into a jukebox. Rollrollroll SPLASH. Then I was running, crushing the bluebells under my boots. I didn't even know where I was going, but when I got onto the road and saw a group of policemen at the end of it, blue and white police tape fluttering in the wind like bunting, I ran faster, faster, towards the gates, until I saw that they were open. Then Dominic was there, in front of me, arms around my waist. The force of it knocked the air right out of me and my feet left the ground, so I don't know how he didn't fall over, but he was solid, this wall between me and the gates.

'Is it her?' I gasped, trying to get past him. But he wouldn't let me, telling me not to, to go back, but I couldn't. I couldn't. 'Scarlett!' I screamed and the force of it sent a flock of birds fleeing from the trees.

I managed to wriggle away and ran to the end of the road, under the blue and white tape and through the gates. I ran and ran, over the bluebells, frantically weaving between the trees until I saw another huddle of police officers. As I approached them, I saw something on the forest floor, something my heart recognised before I did, because it felt like it had broken into a gallop. I stopped, just as Bones broke away from the huddle. He said something, but I didn't hear. 'Is it her?' I gasped, but he reached for my arm and led me away, back the way I'd just run, back between the trees, over the bluebells, lifting up the police tape with his free hand as we approached it. 'Is it her?' I asked again when he tugged me under it.

My head was spinning and spinning, then suddenly it stopped and my eyes lost focus as I realised what I'd seen – Scarlett's hair spread out on the forest floor.

'It's her,' I breathed, and it came back to me all at once: Scarlett by the canal, in her heart-shaped sunglasses, face tilted towards the sun. Scarlett in that red dress. Scarlett dancing with me to Fela in her big, yellow music room. Scarlett on my first day at Crofton. *Come on, Alice. Don't you want to follow the white rabbit?*

Scarlett.

Scarlett.

Scarlett.

'Take her,' Bones said, handing me to someone as everything in me – my heart, my lungs, my bones – flew apart, hung there for a moment, then crashed into each other again with such force that I doubled over.

When I'd caught my breath, I lifted my head again to find it was Dominic. He was shaking and holding on to me tight enough to leave bruises. Or maybe, I was holding on to him tight enough to leave bruises, I don't know. I just know that I could hear myself breathing *It's her* as I lifted my eyelashes to look at him. Then I heard a scream and I don't know how, but I knew it was her mother, and when she screamed, 'Scarlett!' loud and desperate, everything went black.

167 DAYS BEFORE

DECEMBER

When Hannah called this afternoon to say that Scarlett had blown out on a play she was supposed to review, I was thrilled. I mean, I'd rather it wasn't something Scarlett couldn't be bothered to do, but I'm not a staffer on the *Disraeli* so I have to take my bylines where I can get them, right? Plus, I like going into Bath, with its glossy bars and restaurants; it's practically Manhattan compared to Ostley and it was a way out of Crofton on a Saturday night that didn't involve having to climb down some trellis, which was no bad thing. But when Hannah told me that I had to go to the theatre by myself, my enthusiasm waned.

I guess Scarlett didn't mind if she only requested one ticket, but I've never done anything like that by myself. I travel alone all the time, but there's a thrill to that, to being fussed over by the cabin crew while I read *Ovations* magazine, but I've never done anything sociable on my own. I might have a coffee by myself, but I've never eaten alone and I'd rather miss a movie than see it by myself. I had hoped my parents would say no when Hannah asked for their permission, but the one time I would have welcomed them being overprotective, of course they weren't. My disappointment must have been obvious because Hannah told me not to be silly, that even if I went with someone, we wouldn't be able to talk during the play. She was right, but I still felt a pinch of embarrassment as I walked into the theatre alone.

I was in such a rush to get to my seat that I wouldn't have seen him if he hadn't said my name. I almost didn't stop, sure that I'd imagined it because I'd been thinking about him, so when I heard him say my name and turned to find him next to me in the cluttered foyer, I still thought I was imagining it, kind of like when you stare at your phone, then it rings.

'Miss Okomma. What a lovely surprise,' he said with a smile that made me need to catch my breath before I could say hello back.

He'd never smiled at me like that, like he really meant it, a big, helpless smile he had no control of, the way I used to smile in school photographs before I cared that my parents were going to frame it and put it on the mantelpiece. There was an honesty to it that made me feel a bit silly, and I found myself fussing over my pashmina as I watched him tuck his hands into the pockets of his jeans.

I'd never seen him like that, either, so relaxed. We were away from Crofton so I guess he didn't need to try as hard, he didn't need to tuck in his shirt or say something to make everyone in class laugh. He could just be himself. He hadn't shaved and he was wearing a scuffed pair of Converse and it's such a silly thing to note – a pair of sneakers – but they were so *normal*. It's not that I don't change into my own clothes as soon as I can, but he hadn't just worn them at Crofton to walk to the library or the dining hall, he'd worn them *out*, the laces grey and the canvas coming away from the soles in places. He'd been to places in them – the gas station, the supermarket, the dry cleaner's. Normal places that I used to go to, to do normal things. It's easy to forget that outside of Crofton – with its tartan skirts and tuck boxes and Saturday Night Film Club – people still do that sort of stuff.

'Are you here for the *Disraeli*, too?' I asked, hoping I sounded nonchalant.

'No. My cousin Toby is playing Dorian.'

'I had no idea,' I said, smiling clumsily.

'I mentioned it to Scarlett. She said she'd come. Have you seen her?'

When he looked around for her, my shoulders fell. *That's why she only wanted one ticket, because she was meeting him.* I didn't realise I liked him so much until I had to fight the urge to run back out of the theatre.

'I'd better get to my seat,' I said, my gaze falling away from his as I fussed over my pashmina again. 'The play's about to begin.'

He started to say something, but I didn't wait to hear it, just turned and let myself become lost in the push of people making their way to the stalls.

With hindsight, I don't know why I was so surprised. I don't know how I hadn't noticed that her smiles had been more mischievous since she got back from New York, her comebacks more wicked. I thought it was just Scarlett being Scarlett, but maybe that's when it started. Did he realise how much he cared for her when she ran away?

I felt my heart in my throat as I thought about them plotting to meet at the theatre. I don't know why she didn't go, I just knew that there I was, in the middle again. I stared at my ticket, unable to read the seat number as tears stung my eyes. The usher came to my aid, gesturing towards the middle of a row a few back from the stage and I sat down, my hands fisted in my pashmina as I wrapped it around me.

The middle-aged woman in the seat next to mine – who reminded me a little of Mrs Delaney – must have known I was upset, because she offered to let me read her programme and gave me a wine gum. Reading the programme helped, plus focusing on it meant that I wasn't looking for him, so wouldn't know where he was sitting and spend the first act glancing at him in the dark. I still thought of him, though, when I read about his cousin having been in several television shows and movies. He was also rumoured to be the next Doctor Who, which explained why the theatre was so busy. For one bitter moment, I wondered if that's why she wanted to come, not because she liked him, but because she wanted to meet his cousin, and I felt awful. But that's what she's done, she makes me question everything I know about her.

The play was a pleasant surprise – sharp and funny enough to stop me thinking about him. Until, that is, I found him waiting at the end of my row when the curtain fell for the interval and my legs almost gave way. He suggested I join him and his friends for a drink and it made my heart beat so hard, he must have heard it.

We went to the bar and he introduced me to his friends simply as Adamma. He didn't mention Crofton, we didn't even talk about it, and it was strange, not talking about school or what universities I was applying to next year. Good strange. We talked about things, *real* things. Compared the countries we'd been to, bickered about films we hated. One of his friends had even read one of my mother's poems in the *New Yorker* and recited a line of it to me and it made me feel so grown up.

Really grown up – not just playing at being grown up like I did with Scarlett and Jumoke – and I was overwhelmed, not just at how different he was – how sweet, how cool, how laid back – but how nice his friends were. It was odd to think that he had friends outside of school. He knew a world beyond Crofton's neat lawns and spires and I realised that he'd had a life before he met me and I was suddenly murderously jealous of it, as though it were a tactile ex-girlfriend we'd bumped into in the street. Then one of his friends asked me if my name meant anything.

'It means beautiful in Igbo,' he said, before I could.

He'd looked it up, I realised, and when the bell rang to signal the end of the interval and I had to return to my seat, I was giddy at the thought of him at his computer, dark hair in his eyes, Googling my name.

The play ended with a standing ovation. Even I was on my feet. I couldn't stop smiling and when I found him waiting for me at the end of my row, I felt giddy again, especially when, in the shuffle through the doors into the foyer, someone pushed past me and I fell into him. He caught me, his hand cupping my elbow, and it was nothing, just a moment, the tiniest touch, but you know how they say that you fall for someone? My heart fell then. Fell and fell.

In the commotion, my pashmina slipped off and he leaned down to pick it up. When he hung it back on my shoulders, the tips of his fingers grazed my skin and every hair on my body bristled. It wasn't the first time I was aware of someone else's body, of their hands, their mouth, but it was the first time I was aware of my own body. I could feel my heart, my lungs, each of my long, tight nerves. I felt my pores open, my blood fizz, my cells spark then spin like pinwheels. I'd say it was like feeling alive, but it wasn't, it was the opposite. It felt like I was going to die if he didn't touch me again.

'Sorry,' he gasped, as someone knocked into him and he stepped on my toe. 'This is a nightmare.' With a hand still on my elbow, he led me out of the foyer and onto the pavement. As soon as we were outside, he let go. 'Is someone coming to pick you up?'

'Mrs Delaney.'

He looked concerned, his eyes darting around at the people spilling out of the theatre. I told myself that he was looking for his friends, but it felt like something more than that. 'I'll wait with you.'

'No. It's fine,' I told him, my cheeks stinging as I wondered if he didn't want to be seen with me. But he didn't move, just slid his hands into the pockets of his jeans and lifted his chin to look at me.

'How's your friend?' he asked with a frown.

'Better,' I said, startled. I expected him to ask about the play, perhaps make polite conversation about the weather, but of all the things he wanted to talk about, he wanted to talk about that.

His frown deepened. 'I've been thinking about her a lot,' he said, reading my mind and the muscles in my shoulders relaxed.

'I got her to speak to someone.'

'She reported it to the police?'

'No.' I shook my head and sighed. 'But I got her to speak to someone at a rape sanctuary last weekend. I went with her on Monday for a medical exam.'

'Is she OK?'

'Yes, she's fine. Physically, at least.'

'That's something.'

'She won't report it, though. She's terrified of being kicked out of school.'

'What?' He looked stunned. 'Why on earth would she be kicked out?'

'She's a scholarship student. She's worried that if she says something, Crofton will want to distance itself from her.'

I shouldn't have said that, because I know he was going through a list of names in his head. There are only two scholarship students who play for the hockey team in my year.

If he did realize it, he had the grace not to push it. 'That's terrible.'

'I know.'

A red car pulled up outside the theatre and for a moment, I thought it was Mrs Delaney, but when a woman began leading a man with a walking stick toward it, I relaxed. He must have thought the same thing because he seemed agitated again – his gaze darting in all directions – and it was making me nervous, too, so I started to babble about the play and how good it was. He started to babble back and, as predicted, mentioned the weather (an infuriatingly English thing to do, Africans don't discuss the weather. Spoiler alert: it's hot) and I don't know what happened, but suddenly everything was awkward and formal and when he said that Scarlett would be devastated that she had missed the play, my cheeks stung at the mention of her name.

I crossed a line then, I know, when I changed the subject. I've never done anything like that before, never gone after someone I shouldn't have, someone I knew my friend was seeing. But there was a thrill to it, not in trying to hurt her, but in admitting that I liked him, that he might like me, too, in putting myself first, for once. She would have done the same. And with that, I felt something shift between us. I found myself edging towards him, then backing away again, unsure what an appropriate distance was between us any more. I didn't know what to do with my hands, my fingers curling around my clutch in case I touched his arm or reached out to tuck the label back into his sweater.

It was so strange, so *awkward*, but it was a nice awkward, a nervous awkward, like on the limo ride to a dance when you can't wait for everyone to see you in your dress. When I finally saw Mrs Delaney's car pass and stop next to the bus stop at the top of the road where we'd arranged to meet, I knew that she'd be worried that I wasn't there waiting for her, but I still fussed over my dress so I could have a few more moments with him. He leaned in and I found myself holding my breath, wondering if he was going to kiss me, but he tugged my pashmina back over my shoulders and it was nothing – his fingers didn't even graze my skin – but when he lifted his eyelashes to look at me, I knew that I wasn't mad, that whatever I was feeling was reciprocated because he needed to touch me too, even if it was just the wool of my pashmina. And all I could think was: *Do it again.*

4 DAYS AFTER

MAY

They say that denial is the first stage of grief. If denial is not being able to move then, yes, I was in denial. I don't know when Mrs Delaney put me to bed, but I couldn't sleep. I just lay there until it was dark, wanting to cry, but it didn't feel like enough. I would have screamed if I thought someone would scream back, but there's nothing up there, I know that now, just the stars, like eyes, watching. Watching.

I don't think I've ever heard Burnham so quiet. As I lay in bed, I couldn't hear a thing, not Orla's radio, not the murmur of the television in the common room that had been on the BBC News channel since they'd reported that the police had found The Old Dear yesterday. I couldn't even hear my parents on the other side of my door any more. I guess they thought I was sleeping. *Leave her to rest*, Mrs Delaney has been telling them since they got here, as though that's all I needed – sleep and the mug of sugary tea going cold on my nightstand – and everything will be OK. Not that my mother listened; she kept coming into my room to stroke my hair, but I couldn't feel it. I wouldn't let myself because to feel anything other than the roaring white noise of pain in my chest would be a betrayal.

It's no less than I deserve.

But I guess I did sleep, because eventually it was light and I peeled my eyes open to find my father, immaculate as always in a dark grey suit, sitting on a chair by my bed, wire-rimmed glasses perched on the end of his nose as he frowned at the front page of *The Times*. I shivered like a cat and when someone pressed a kiss to my temple, I realised that my mother was next to me, all soft and warm and smelling of the shea butter she uses on her hair, and I cried then, cried like a little girl, because I don't think I've ever needed them so much, and there they were.

'Ada,' my father breathed, putting the paper on my bed and wiping my cheeks with his long fingers. 'Pack a bag. We're going on home.'

I nodded, kicking off the duvet with stiff legs, then padded over to my chest of drawers as my mother opened the closet. I don't know what I was doing, just grabbing handfuls of clothes so I had something to do, I think, but when I'd almost emptied the top drawer, I saw the box and knew why I'd gone to that one. It was nothing, a black and white box I was given last Christmas that used to have a gift set in it – perfume and hand lotion, I think – but now held the remains of my friendship with Scarlett. My hands shook as I took the lid off to find a stack of photos and notes and, on top, the paper ship she'd given me when we had lunch by the canal on my first day at Crofton, all of it smelling faintly of Chanel.

I reached for the paper ship, fingers fluttering as I unfolded it. And I don't know why – I'd never felt the urge to before – but I kept thinking about that day, how she'd told me that she sends her secrets to Kazakhstan, and opened it, making sure to note each fold so that I could put it back together again. As I opened each flap, I saw the curl of a word then another and another, until the ship was undone and there it was – her secret – scribbled across an ad for waterproof mascara:

I'm so bad at this friend thing, Adamma, but I'll try.

It fell from my hand, fluttering quietly to my feet, then I was running, out of my room, down the stairs and out out out of Burnham. I could hear someone calling after me – Orla, I think – then footsteps on the path, but even in socks, I knew that she couldn't outrun me and I just ran and ran until I was across the Green and fighting through the wall of oak trees. I couldn't even feel the gravel of the car park, or the pavement when I got out of Crofton and ran towards the village. And I should have stopped – I should have stopped – but I couldn't, not until I got to the police station.

There was one advantage to being dragged into Ostley police station the other day: I knew the layout. So I pushed through the door and ignored the officer behind the desk as I ran through the neat, white reception and pushed through the double doors. When I ran up the stairs and into the office, DS Hanlon was the first person I saw. She gave me a filthy look and I countered it with a filthier one as I charged over to Bones who was standing with his back to me, staring at a whiteboard. I reared back when I saw it, my heart catching in my throat as I saw the photographs of Scarlett with her red, red lips, lying pale but perfect on the forest floor, like Ophelia, a crown of green leaves in her hair.

I must have gasped, because Bones spun around to face me. The skin between his eyebrows creased as he took me by the arm and pulled me into the nearest office.

'What are you doing here, Adamma?' he hissed, shutting the door.

I flew at him, shoving him with both hands. 'I can't believe you did that!' I roared, shoving him again when he stumbled back. 'How could you, Bones?' I shoved him again, tears burning down my cheeks. 'How could you let us search the forest?'

'Adamma, listen to me.' He grabbed my wrists and waited for me to look at him. 'I didn't know.'

'You must have! You must have suspected something!'

'I didn't. We thought Scarlett met someone there and went somewhere else.'

'Stop treating me like a kid, Bones,' I said. I pulled away and stared at him. 'You don't do searches like that unless you're looking for a body.'

'Unless she's a Crofton kid and her family owns half of Ostley,' he snapped, his face red. 'We thought she was in fucking New York again!'

I turned away from him, wiping my cheeks with the cuff of my sweater.

'You seriously think that we would send a load of school kids into a forest to look for the dead body of their classmate? This is a PR *disaster*, Adamma. Ballard wants my bollocks. Parents have been calling all night, threatening to sue.'

I shook my head. 'You should never have let us go there.'

'I know,' he sighed and when I turned to look at him again, he was rubbing his face with his hands. 'I know. This is a fucking mess.'

My heart thumped and thumped as I waited for him to look at me, and when he did, I had to get it out, I had to get out the words that had been stuck in my throat since I'd found the paper ship. 'Was she raped?'

He shook his head. 'You know I can't tell you that.'

'I told you!' I roared, burning with a fresh wave of anger. 'Everyone thought I was mad, but I told you! I told you about that man in Savernake Forest.'

'I didn't say that she was raped, Adamma.' He reached for my arm again, but I wriggled away, running to the door and out of the police station, back to Crofton.

My lungs were ready to explode by the time I got there, my eyes stinging with tears, but I didn't stop and charged into Orla's room without knocking.

'It was him!' I ran towards her and she jumped back, her eyes wide as she reached for the edge of her desk. 'He murdered Scarlett! You have to remember!'

I went to take another step towards her, but felt an arm around my waist, tugging me back. It was my father, I realised, and he told me to calm down and led me across the hall, back to my room. I tried to pull away, but he wouldn't let me and I managed to shout, 'You have to remember!' once more before he closed my door.

Despite my father's threats to throw me over his shoulder and carry me out, I refused to leave Crofton. I couldn't. I couldn't leave her. I had to know what had happened to her. My parents eventually gave up just before midnight and, content that I was asleep and that Mrs Delaney would look after me, reluctantly checked into a hotel in Marlborough. A few minutes after they left, I heard my door open and a pair of socked feet on the floorboards followed by a whoosh of cold air as my duvet lifted.

'I'm trying,' Orla whispered, wriggling behind me, her head on my pillow.

197

'I know. I'm sorry,' I said, reaching for her hand. 'I'm sorry.'

I guess I fell asleep, because I woke with a start. I turned on my lamp to find Orla gone, no doubt ushered back to her room by Mrs Delaney, and when I looked across the room at the paper ship, now folded and sitting on the top of my chest of drawers, I reached over to my nightstand and snatched my phone.

Bones answered on the third ring.

'Red lipstick,' I gasped into the phone.

'What?' he muttered. I don't know if I woke him, but I don't think I did; he sounded very much awake. I was so tired that it took a second to place, but I heard it then, the squeak of a marker on a whiteboard.

'Red lipstick.'

'You're worrying me now, Adamma.'

'No. Listen, Bones.' I made myself take a breath – then another and another – as I tried to untangle my thoughts. It was like trying to sort laundry. 'Listen. I keep thinking about that photo of Scarlett.'

'Which photo?'

I had to take another breath. 'The photo I saw earlier, at the station.'

'You shouldn't have seen that—'

'Did you move her or is that how she was found?' I interrupted.

'Adamma—'

'Because if that's how you found her, then she had her arms crossed, right?' I didn't wait for him to respond, because I knew he wouldn't. 'That shows remorse.'

'Stop watching *Criminal Minds*.'

I ignored him. 'So the guy in the car must have known her, right?'

He was quiet for a moment too long and I thought he was going to say that he couldn't tell me, and tell me to go back to bed, but he sighed grumpily. 'Not necessarily.'

'Yeah, but she was wearing red lipstick.'

'She always does. In almost every photo I have she's wearing red lipstick.'

'Exactly! Everyone who knows Scarlett *knows* that she only wears red lipstick. It's her thing. It's the first thing she does when she finishes school.'

It was such a petty rebellion, but we all did it. Some girls smoked, some changed into mufti as soon as they could. Scarlett put on her lipstick.

'Yeah so?'

'So I know I only saw that photo for a second, but her lips were bright red. It looked like she'd just put lipstick on.' He didn't say anything and I took that as my cue to go on. 'So let's say that –' I had to stop and take another deep breath as my stomach turned at the thought – 'that she's been there since Sunday, wouldn't it have faded? And didn't it rain Tuesday night? Don't you remember how muddy it was when we were doing the search? How does her lipstick look so fresh, Bones?'

He said it before I could. 'Because he went back and put it on her.'

'Why would he do that, Bones?'

'Because he knows she'd want to be wearing it.'

'So Scarlett knew him?'

'I have to go,' he said, then hung up before I could ask if that meant Orla did, too.

166 DAYS BEFORE

DECEMBER

I don't think I've ever been so excited for a Monday. I was up before Mrs Delaney came to wake me and once I'd perfected my eyeliner, I all but ran to breakfast.

I couldn't get my food down quick enough, knocking over a mug of coffee and getting oatmeal on my skirt in my haste to get to class, but when I glanced through the window on my way out of the dining hall to see Scarlett swaggering across the Green, the reality of it set in and I realised that it wouldn't be as I had imagined. He wouldn't ask about my weekend with a secret smile, he'd do what he always does and sweep into class with a smile for me and one for her and that would be it. It would be as though nothing had happened at the theatre, as though I'd imagined the tips of his fingers lingering on my shoulders and the sudden stutter of his eyelashes, and I would be left wondering if it was in my head again, like a passing fever that was making me see things that weren't there.

But when I got through registration, then history, then finally – finally – I knew I'd see him in my second class, he was already there and the shock of it made my heart leap into my throat. I was supposed to get there first and be doodling nonchalantly when he arrived so he'd have to say something to me first. But there he was, his head stooped and a hand in his hair to keep it back as he leafed through a book and I didn't know what to do. So I stared at him and when finally he looked up to find me lingering in the doorway, he smiled, the skin around his mouth creasing and I wanted to touch each line with my finger. But before I could reciprocate, I heard my name and turned to find Mrs Delaney standing behind me.

'Come with me, Miss Okomma,' she said, holding out her hand.

'Is something wrong?' I asked with a frown, but she didn't respond, just put her hand on the small of my back and led me out of the classroom.

I asked her again as we walked towards the foyer, but she told me to 'Come along' as the doors around us closed, one by one, and classes began. Then it was just us, the corridor stretching out in front of us, long and empty and suddenly endless as I wondered what was wrong, where she was taking me.

I could feel the cold from the courtyard as soon as we stepped into the foyer and as we approached the open doors, a rush of wind made the ivy clinging to the frame flutter wildly. It made me shiver and I thought of last night and how I had woken up convinced that I'd left the window open. When I got up to check, the corners of the leaded window were clouded over, the point of each diamond tipped with frost and I remembered thinking, *This is it*. And it is; it's almost December and for the first time this morning, I felt the wet promise of winter in the air. Most of the trees are bare now, exposing views of Crofton I've never seen before: the red clay roofs of the science block, the glint of the canal, the hills that seem to roll on and on.

I'm not the only one to notice; I heard everyone grumbling

about it in the shower this morning. 'It's bloody miserable,' Molly said, hopping around in the stall next to mine, which elicited a chorus of mumbled *yeahs* from the other girls. I was too excited about seeing him to care, but I felt it then, walking through the courtyard with Mrs Delaney, the breeze scratching at my cheeks as we walked past the groundsman who was pushing an empty wheelbarrow across the Green.

The sky was the colour of salt and when I looked up at it, I felt a flutter of panic. It was a turnout day. Had Mrs Delaney found something in my room? She couldn't have; apart from the bottle of Patron hidden in one of my boots, there was nothing to find. Even so, a bottle of tequila wasn't enough to pull me out of class for. But when we got to Burnham and she led me to her office, the flutter of panic became a rattle that made each of my bones shudder.

She made tea and when she sat next to me on the couch and reached for my hand, every part of me started shaking, all at once. She didn't say anything for a very long time and I willed her to, because that's what scared me most, the silence, the fact that she couldn't say what she had to say. That it was too hard, too awful.

Finally, she squeezed my hand. 'I have some news, Adamma.'

I felt my heart in my throat then, thumpthumpthumping as I waited for her to look at me again. But she didn't, so I stared at her eyelids, at the pale blue eyeshadow caught between the creases of her skin, like veins in marble.

Say it, a voice in my head murmured as I squeezed her hand. *Say it.* She squeezed my hand back, a little too tightly, her wedding ring digging into my knuckle, and that was the last thing I felt before she said, 'Your father's been shot.'

The world stopped; I felt this sudden shudder, then nothing.

I glanced out of the window and up at the sky, sure that I would find the birds stuck, mid-glide. I imagined cars on the freeway, suddenly still, trains stuttering to a halt. And my heart was suddenly quiet, like a clock stopping mid-tick. I felt nothing as my gaze darted around her office, landing on the framed photograph of the blond boy on her desk and the mugs of tea she'd made that were going cold. I felt no shiver of panic, no pinch of fear, and I don't know how long I was quiet, but it was long enough to make her ask if I was OK. When I turned to look at her again, I wondered how many times she'd done this. How many girls she'd sat in this room and said, 'I have some news.'

What a thing to be practised in.

'Adamma.' She squeezed my hand again and suddenly I felt everything, my heart, the panic, the fear, her wedding ring digging into my knuckle.

The words were in my mouth – *Is he dead?* – but they didn't feel like my own, as though I was in a classroom running lines with Scarlett, me the Hamlet to her Ophelia.

But break, my heart, for I must hold my tongue.

'Adamma,' she said again and I made myself look at her. 'Your father has been shot, do you understand?' I nodded. 'I don't know the details, but I know that he's been taken to hospital and we need to get you to Lagos as soon as possible.' I nodded again. 'The Nigerian Embassy has booked your flight so let's go to your room and I'll help you pack a bag.'

She went to get up, but I wouldn't let go of her hand. 'My mother,' I breathed. 'She's giving a lecture at Brown today. She flew to New York last night.'

She squeezed my hand again. 'The Nigerian Embassy is trying to reach her.'

'Ear plugs,' I remembered, pointing to my ear with my free

204

hand. 'She can't sleep without them. She probably can't hear her phone.'

Mrs Delaney nodded. 'Come on. Let's get your bag ready.'

'I don't know where my passport is,' I muttered as she helped me to my feet, still holding my hand. I felt like a sleepy toddler being taken to bed.

'It's probably in your tuck box.' She patted my hand. 'If not, we'll find it.'

She led me down the corridor and into my room. With everyone in class, Burnham was strangely quiet. I didn't hear anyone giggling in their room or blow-drying their hair, didn't hear the murmur of the television as we passed the lounge.

My room was as I left it: strange, bare, the surfaces clear – the desk, the nightstand, the shelves – everything piled on the bed so that they could be cleaned. The smudge of purple on the carpet under the mirror where I'd dropped an eyeshadow was gone, as was the smell, the strange but comforting smell of my perfume mixed with a hint of chlorine from my damp bathing suit and the towels that always fester in my hamper until I take them to the laundry room. This morning my room smelled of lemon. Not real lemon, synthetic lemon. Cartoon lemon, my mother calls it. I usually like that smell, it reminds me of home, of Comfort in her neat white apron shooing me out of the kitchen while she cleans the floor, but today it smelt different. Stronger. All I could smell was lemon, no perfume, no chlorine. My room didn't smell like my own and it made me feel even more disoriented.

Mrs Delaney took my holdall out of the closet, put it on the desk and unzipped it. 'Come, Miss Okomma,' she said, walking over to the chest of drawers.

I didn't move. 'Is there enough time to get to the airport?'

'Of course. The embassy has arranged for a car to collect you at six o'clock.'

'Six o'clock?'

'Yes. You're booked onto the twenty-two twenty from London Heathrow.'

'What?' I felt a punch of panic. 'There must be a flight before then.'

She shook her head. 'Unfortunately not. That's the first available one.'

'That can't be true! There are dozens of flights from London to Lagos.'

'Not direct ones. Not at this short notice.' She didn't look at me, just opened my washbag and inspected the contents, before putting it in the holdall.

'I'll get an indirect one then. Emirates fly to Lagos. What about KLM?'

'The embassy doesn't want you to change. They'd rather you got a direct flight. Besides, an indirect flight won't get you there any faster, especially if there's a delay and you miss your connection. It's all much of a muchness.'

It was like running up a flight of stairs, trying to breathe became harder and harder. 'But I can't wait until six o'clock. What am I supposed to do? Sit here?'

She didn't acknowledge me, just walked back to my chest of drawers, opened one and pulled out a cardigan. 'I've only packed you one jumper, but I don't think that will be enough. Hospitals can get very cold.'

'Mrs Delaney—'

A girl appeared in the doorway. 'The administration office sent me to fetch you, Mrs Delaney. They've been trying to put a telephone call through to you.'

'Tell them to take a message,' she said, tucking the cardigan into my holdall.

'It's the Nigerian Embassy. They say it's urgent.'

She nodded. 'I'll be right back.' She stopped in the doorway and smiled at the girl. 'Please stay with Miss Okomma until I return. She's had quite a shock.'

The girl stepped into the room. She said something – asked me if I was OK, I think – but I wasn't listening as I took my cellphone out of the pocket of my blazer and checked the time. 10.43 a.m. English lit was about to finish. That gave me seven hours and seventeen minutes. It was too long. I thought of my father, alone in the hospital, bleeding into the white sheet beneath him and the panic overwhelmed me and I ran to my closet.

'Are you OK, Adamma?' the girl said again, but I didn't look up.

My hands were shaking so much, I couldn't find my keys in my purse, and when I did, I dropped them before I opened my tuck box. When I did, I looked under the jewellery boxes and photos and when I saw the green cover of my passport, I pulled it out.

'Can I get you anything, Adamma? Would you like a cup of tea?' I heard the girl ask as I zipped up my holdall and darted past her towards the door. When I didn't answer, she asked me where I was going, but I didn't stop, just ran and kept running until I was at the front door, then through it. I don't think I stopped for breath until I was halfway across the Green. The groundsman shouted something, but my heart was beating so hard in my ears that I couldn't hear what he said as I ran for the road.

I glanced over as everyone wandered out of the main hall into the cold, breath puffing from their mouths in clouds as they exchanged gossip on their way to their next lesson. Someone called my name, but I didn't stop, I just kept running, the thought of my father, broken and alone, making me desperate to close the distance between us. It was miles – miles and miles – 4,484 miles, five countries and two deep blue seas, and it felt impassable, but with each step I was closer, closer. Then I was across the Green and approaching the road.

I looked at the horizon of tarmac beyond the trees and ran faster. Then it was in front of me and it was like running towards the sea. I heard the car before I saw it, heard a howl of brakes and leapt back, just as the car skidded in front of me, braking so hard I don't know how it didn't run over my toes. The tyres scarred the road. I stared at them, at the two black lines on the frosted tarmac, my heart trying to fight its way out of my ribcage, and when the car door flew open, I took another step back.

'Adamma! What on earth?' Mr Lucas said with a gasp, leaping out.

I gasped too, my eyes losing focus for a moment. I shouldn't have stopped, it was like I'd been swimming and someone had pulled me out of the water by my hair. I couldn't see. I couldn't breathe, the cold air as heavy as damp towels on my lungs. I wanted to reach for his arm to steady myself, but I told myself not to touch him.

'My father's been shot.'

He stared at me as I panted. 'What?'

'He's been shot!' I could hear myself saying it, but it didn't sound like my voice. I was going to wake up in a moment, I was sure, wake up in my room at Burnham, in my narrow single bed, frost clinging to the corners of my window.

He reached for my arm as my legs were about to give away. 'Oh goodness, Adamma. Where? In London? Is he OK?'

'I have to go,' I breathed, but I couldn't move. I could feel myself leaning into him and tried to pull away, but the more I tried, the more I leaned into him. It was as though everything had turned around and up was down and left was right.

'I'll take you back to Mrs Delaney.'

'No. I have to go.'

I dropped my holdall as I tried to pull away, but he wouldn't let me, putting an arm around my shoulders and picking up the holdall. 'Go where, Adamma?'

'To the airport.'

'Come on,' he said, opening the car door.

When he steered me towards his car, I remember thinking how pretty it looked, the dark blue roof frosted over so it looked sugared. The tan leather was cold, and it groaned as I took my holdall from him and sat in the passenger seat. He was listening to Radio 4, to *Book of the Week*, and as I listened to the voice describing a snowy scene in Alaska, I suddenly felt awful that he'd missed it because of me.

He waited for me to put on my seat belt, then closed the door. I watched him walk around the front of the car, frowning and smoothing down his tie as he did, and when he climbed into the car next to me, I thanked him again. But he didn't say anything, and when he started the engine and began reversing, I realised what he was doing and threw my hands out, grabbing the dashboard. 'No!'

He didn't stop, the vein in his neck throbbing as he looked over his shoulder, reversing his car back up the narrow road towards Crofton. In a fit of panic, I opened the door. It flew open and he slammed on the brakes so hard, I jerked forward, and reached for the dashboard again, the holdall tumbling off my lap onto my feet.

209

'What are you doing?' He leaned across me and pulled the door shut.

'Let me out!'

He stared at me. 'Adamma.'

I stared back. 'I thought you were taking me to the airport?'

'That wouldn't be appropriate.'

'Why?'

He put his hands back on the wheel. 'I'm taking you back to Burnham.'

'I have to go to the airport! I have to see my father!'

'I'm sure Mrs Delaney has made the proper arrangements.'

'You don't understand.' I shook my head. 'I have to go now.'

He closed his eyes and sighed. 'I know you've had a horrible shock, Adamma, but you can't run off to the airport by yourself. How are you going to get there?' He waved a hand at the windscreen. 'Are you going to run all the way there?'

'If I have to. I can't sit around Burnham all day waiting for the car.'

'What time is it coming?'

'Six o'clock.'

'Six o'clock?' He wavered then. 'Why on earth is it coming so late?'

'My flight isn't until ten o'clock tonight.'

'Ten o'clock? Goodness.' He took his glasses off and wiped them with the end of his tie. 'That is an unbearable amount of time to wait.'

'I know.' I stopped to take a breath. 'I just want to be at the airport. At least if I'm there, I'll feel like I'm doing something, like I'm closer.'

He thought about that while he put his glasses back on, then said, 'Of course. That makes perfect sense. I'm sure Mrs

Delaney will think so too.' He put his hands back on the wheel. 'Let's go back to Burnham and explain that to her.'

I wasn't listening. 'What's that?' I pointed at the windscreen.

He stopped and leaned forward, peering at the sky. He wrinkled his nose. 'Oh,' he said, sitting back again, looking a little bewildered. 'It's snow.'

'Snow?' Panic rushed through me again. 'We have to go to the airport now.'

'Yes, but—'

I interrupted, my voice suddenly too loud, too hard. 'What if it gets worse?'

'It's just a few flakes.'

'Now it is. What if we're snowed in by six o'clock?'

He started to protest again, but my cellphone was ringing. 'It's my mother,' I gasped before I'd even pulled it out of the pocket of my blazer. I swallowed a sob and answered it. '*Nne m, keekwanu?*' I said in a rush, breaking into Igbo.

She was in a cab to JFK airport and as hysterical as I was. I didn't recognise her voice, it was too high, too quick. She kept breaking into English to bark at the cab driver, telling him to go faster, to take Second Avenue, there would be less traffic. She sounded so far away and I thought of the three of us – me, my father and her – scattered across the globe, trying to get back to one another.

I'd never thought about it before, about how much time we spend apart. Even when we go on vacation, one of has to leave early – there's an emergency at the embassy or I have to get back to school or my mother has to teach a class – so I'm used to travelling on my own. I enjoy it. I catch up on the television shows I've missed and when I have to stay in a hotel by myself, I order room service and eat it in bed, which I'm never allowed to do at home. It had never felt like a hardship until then, on the phone to my mother, the two of us separated by miles of wire. But when she asked me how I was, I lied and told her I was fine. '*Adi m mma.*'

I held my breath as she told me what she knew, that someone had tried to carjack my father at a gas station and when my father refused to hand over the keys, the man shot him. Other than that, all she knew was that he was in surgery.

'Poor Papa,' I breathed.

'He shouldn't be on his own,' she murmured and I don't know if she meant to say it out loud, but I felt it like a needle in my heart. My chin trembled and I pressed my lips together. I didn't want her to have to hear me cry.

When she got to JFK, I heard the cab driver muttering the fare. She told me she'd call me back and I had to swallow another sob before I told her that I loved her. '*Ahuru m gi n'anya, nne,*' I blurted out before she hung up.

It was a moment or two before the dizziness passed and I could lift my head, and when I did, Mr Lucas was driving down the narrow road. When he got to the bottom and turned left out of Crofton, I managed a small smile. 'Thank you.'

He didn't look at me, just nodded. 'You'd better call Mrs Delaney.'

'OK.'

My phone buzzed then, then again and again as the news about my father spread and everyone got in touch to check I was OK. I read each text message before I called Mrs Delaney – in case any of them were from my relatives in Nigeria – but it wasn't until Mr Lucas drove past Scarlett's huge cake-coloured house that I realised that none of them were from her. I got one from Olivia, sending her love and asking if there was anything she could do, but that was it and I shouldn't have been so surprised; I knew what Scarlett was like, but that didn't make it right and for the first time in a long time, I didn't make an excuse for her.

Mrs Delaney was relieved to hear from me, but was far from amused. When I told Mr Lucas that she wanted to speak to him, he seemed reluctant to take the phone and when he did and his cheeks went from pink to red, I realised that she was telling him off. I felt awful, it wasn't his fault, and when I offered to take the phone to tell her so, he mouthed, 'It's OK.'

Eventually, she let him respond and they began discussing the logistics of getting me to the airport. I could only hear his half of the conversation, but it sounded unnecessarily complicated. He had to give her his full name, his registration number, the make, model and colour of his car, then tell her what time he thought we were going to arrive at the airport. When he ended the call and handed me back the phone, he looked exhausted and I apologised.

'I'm so sorry, Sir. The embassy are mad strict about security.'

'It's not just them. Virgin Atlantic are just as strict. I had no idea travelling first class was so difficult,' he said with a smile that drooped when he saw that the snow was getting heavier. He turned on the windscreen wipers and when they began sweeping back and forth, he caught himself, turning to me with a brighter smile. 'Mrs Delaney is going to call back shortly with directions and a code. It seems Virgin's First Class lounge is contained in an underground bunker somewhere at Heathrow!'

I bit my lip, turning to look out the window at the snow settling in clumps on the hedges that lined the narrow road.

When my gaze flicked to the rear-view mirror, I looked at the road rolling away from us, the tarmac dusted with snow and the tyres of his car leaving two black lines, like the ones they'd left at Crofton.

He began apologising, fiddling with the various knobs on the console until the fan on the dashboard in front of me blasted heat, hot and fast, like a hairdryer. 'Sorry. As much as I love this old thing, Triumph were yet to discover heated seats when it was made in the seventies, but we should be there in an hour or so,' he said over the scrape of the wiper blades. 'I hope they don't frown at my car when I drop you off.'

'It's fine. Just drop me outside Departures.'

He chuckled. 'Are you ashamed of my car, too?'

I didn't laugh. It was such a British thing to do. If he could, he'd be making tea, no doubt, and, while I appreciated the effort to distract me from the searing pain I felt each time I thought about my father, it was taking every crumb of energy I had not to collapse into a sobbing heap so I just wanted to focus on not doing that.

So I looked out at the road, at everything going from green to white. When we moved onto the freeway, relief gave way to dread as the snow got heavier, sticking to the cars rolling past us. After a few minutes, they began to slow until all I could see was a string of brake lights ahead of us and I felt panic fizz up in me again.

We weren't going to make it.

Mr Lucas must have known what I was thinking, because he patted the dashboard and said, 'Don't worry, Adamma, she'll get us there.' I couldn't look at him, a hand on my stomach as it knotted at the thought of my flight being delayed, or worse, cancelled. He must have known I was thinking that too, because he persisted, 'A concierge from the airline is going to meet us and escort you to the lounge. You can wait there until your flight leaves. At least you'll be comfortable. They have a masseuse, apparently.'

I turned to glare at him. 'Can I have a facial, too? Maybe I can get my hair done. Look nice and pretty for my dying father.'

He stared at me for a moment, the corners of his mouth falling into a straight line. When he turned to look back out at the road, I felt awful. 'I'm sorry.'

'It's OK,' he said, his tone suddenly sharper. 'I know you're upset.'

But it wasn't OK and, with that, I felt a curtain drop between us.

By the time we got to the airport, it was snowing heavily. The concierge had to dash from the door to the car, his head dipped, fat flakes settling on the shoulders of his black suit. Mr Lucas kept the engine running. It made me feel wretched, but it was probably for the best; he hadn't said a word except to enquire after my father when my mother called again, so if he'd gotten out of the car with me, I might have tried to hug him in a clumsy effort to apologise and make things more awkward.

'Have a safe flight, Miss Okomma,' he said with a tight smile. 'I hope your father is out of surgery soon and makes a speedy recovery.'

I started to apologise, the words tumbling over themselves as I tried to force them out, but before I could open my mouth, the concierge opened the car door and let in a gust of cold air. 'Good afternoon, Miss Okomma,' he said with a smooth smile.

My heart sank. I glanced at Mr Lucas, my jaw juddering with panic, but before I could speak, before I could tell him how sorry I was for being so rude when he'd been trying to help, the concierge reached down for the holdall by my feet. I watched him and when he stood up again, standing to attention with his hand on the top of the open car door, waiting for me to get out, I began to shake and turned to look at Mr Lucas again. He wasn't looking at me, his hands wringing the steering wheel, obviously waiting for me to get out.

'I'm so sorry,' I said in a breathless rush, and immediately dissolved into tears. I didn't mean to, it seemed to just *spill* out of me.

My outburst must have surprised him too, because he let go of the wheel for the first time since he'd clambered in next to me back at Crofton. As he turned to me, he clearly didn't know what to do with his hands and I tensed, sure that he was going to touch me, but instead, he asked the concierge, 'Can we have a moment, please?'

I heard the concierge close the door and as soon as he did, Mr Lucas leaned towards me and said all the right things. He told me that it would be OK, that my father would be fine, that he was in the best hands. He reminded me that I used to live in New York, that planes take off in worse snow, that my aunt would be at the hospital soon so my father wouldn't be alone. He smoothed each of my nerves as I sobbed and sobbed and as soon as I'd caught my breath, I thanked him.

'Will you be OK, Adamma?'

I wiped under my eyes with my fingers. 'I kind of have to be.'

I probably should have lied, flashed him a brave smile and told him I'd be fine, but I didn't have the energy. It was all I could do to keep breathing. He thought about what I'd said, his eyebrows knotted, then sighed. 'Here,' he said, reaching across me and opening the glove compartment. He rooted through it for a second or two, before pulling out a red biro and a receipt. He scribbled something down and stared at it, his lips pressed together, then handed it to me. 'This is my mobile number.' He waited until I looked at him, then leaned a little closer. 'If you need anything, call me, and I'll come straight back, OK?'

I nodded. 'Thank you,' I said softly, and he smiled at me.

He got out with me, walking around the front of the car to greet the concierge who darted back through the snow towards us. He put his hand on his shoulder and lowered his voice as we walked towards the glass doors, but I still heard him, 'I don't know if the airline has explained the situation, but Miss Okomma has had an awful shock. I hate the thought of leaving her to wait alone for her flight, but I can't wait with her unless I'm flying, too, so I need you to keep a close eye on her.'

'Of course, Sir.' The concierge nodded.

He turned to me and took off his glasses, the snow catching in his eyelashes. 'You're going to be OK, Miss Okomma. And if your father is half as stubborn as you are, then he will be too.' He smiled and I couldn't help but smile back.

'Thank you, Sir.' It was almost impossible to say it around the lump in my throat, but I think he heard me. 'I'll text you when I land.'

He nodded. 'And I'll let Mrs Delaney know.'

When the concierge opened the glass door for me, he smiled and asked if there was anything he could do. I turned to watch Mr Lucas's car roll out of view, then sighed. 'I just want to go home.'

* * *

217

The First Class lounge was busier than I had expected. It wasn't full, but there was a buzz; half of the tables were taken and there was a string people sitting at the bar. Some sat sipping coffee, flicking aimlessly through magazines, while others muttered into their cellphones, asking their assistants to look into alternative arrangements if their flights were delayed. A group of women sat around one of the tables, laughing and clapping, clearly drunk on champagne, and it should all have been comforting – the noise, the heat and bustle of other people – but I still felt alone, the hours before my flight departed suddenly stretching out in front of me like an endless black road.

The staff were more than attentive, a stream of glossy men and women in neat red uniforms stopping to ask if I needed anything when I retreated to the Viewing Deck to watch the snow fall onto the runway. I appreciated the kind smiles and the urges to eat something, but after half an hour, it began to wear thin, so I asked for a glass of Diet Coke and some potato chips just so that they'd leave me alone.

I only got a few minutes' peace before someone else approached. I almost barked at them, but managed to stop myself when I looked up to find Dominic standing over me with a brown leather holdall in his hand.

'Dominic.' I looked around, half expecting a security guard to come charging after him, shouting at him to get out.

He smiled smoothly. 'Fancy meeting you here, Miss Okomma.'

I watched as he dropped the holdall onto the floor by my feet and sank into the leather chair opposite mine. 'What are you doing here, Dominic?'

'Just off to see a friend in Dubai.'

'Dubai?'

'Yeah, for the night.'

'The night?'

'Stop repeating everything I say, Miss Okomma,' he said, tugging off his black leather gloves. 'It's very annoying.'

'What are you doing?' I sat forward, suddenly livid that he was doing something so foolish, every emotion I was feeling piling on top of one another, all at once until I was breathless. 'You can't just go to Dubai for the night! What about school? You'll be kicked out!' I hissed but then he tilted his head and smiled and with that, I realised. Fresh tears pooled in my eyes and his face went out of focus. I had to take a breath before I could speak again. 'You're here to be with me.'

My chin trembled and his face softened when it did. Usually, I would have been furious that he'd seen that moment of vulnerability, but I didn't care and found myself resisting the urge to climb over the table between us and hug him.

'You gonna eat those?'

'They'll make you fly to Dubai, you know.'

'Good,' he said, stopping to reach for a chip. 'I haven't done anything to piss my father off this week. At least I'll get a holiday out of it.'

I tried not to laugh, because it wasn't funny. 'Ballard will kill you.'

He didn't seem bothered and gestured at a woman in a red suit, who came over with a bright smile. 'Two Diet Cokes, please.' He held up two fingers. 'And a menu. Miss Okomma needs to eat something more substantial than a bowl of crisps.'

'Of course, Mr Sim.'

He watched her walk away and when he turned to look at me again, I arched an eyebrow at him. 'How does she know your name?'

219

He licked his lips and sat back with a slow smile. 'They all know my name.'

I rolled my eyes and sat back too. 'How did you know I was here?'

'Mrs Delaney.'

I was impressed. 'I thought she was beyond being charmed.'

'It seems the lady is for turning.'

I bit down on my lip to stop myself smiling. 'I'm surprised she told you. I didn't think they gave out that sort of information. I thought it was private.'

'It is.' He stopped to lick the salt from his fingers, then reached for another chip. 'But she's worried about you. She doesn't want you to be here on your own.'

'*She's* worried?'

His gaze dipped to the bowl of chips. 'Are you OK?'

'Changing the subject. Duly noted, Mr Sim.'

He didn't let me get away with it, either. 'You've been crying.'

He looked up at me again and it was my turn to stare at the bowl of chips. Luckily, I was saved by the waitress who brought our drinks and menus. I opened mine, avoiding his gaze. 'I'm tired.'

'So how's your dad? Any news?'

Before I could respond, my cellphone rang. It was my mother and then my heart was beating too hard for another reason. '*Nne m, keekwanu?*'

She was about to board her flight to Lagos and sounded much calmer. She must have been, because she responded in English. She usually only broke into Igbo in public when she was saying something she didn't want anyone to hear. 'I have no news. Papa is still in surgery. I just wanted to call to let you know that I'm boarding. Are you at Heathrow yet?'

'Yes, I'm in the Virgin lounge now.'

'Are you on your own?'

I considered responding in Igbo so Dominic wouldn't understand, but knew it would make her suspicious. 'No,' I said, looking at my nails. I'd forgotten to take off my blue nail polish and had already been told off about it in History, and I knew that my father would tease me mercilessly. *Kedu, sisi?* he'd say when he saw it. Then I realised that he might not be able to and felt a fresh wave of tears.

I waited until I'd caught my breath and said, 'I'm with Scarlett.'

I knew Dominic was looking at me, but I just stared at my nails as I heard my mother's breathing relax. I could have said I was alone, I suppose, but the lie was for her, not me. I didn't want her thinking I was stuck in an airport by myself. And she liked Scarlett, I mean, she wasn't as fond of her after the New York thing, but she still liked her.

For a horrible moment, I thought she was going to ask to speak to her, but then I heard them calling her flight. 'I'll call you as soon as I land. *Ahuru m gi n'anya.*'

I told her that I loved her too and blew some kisses down the phone. When I hung up, I looked up to find Dominic smiling at me. 'How's your dad?'

I put my cellphone down on the table between us. 'Still in surgery.'

There was a moment of silence as I waited for him to say something, but when he didn't, I sighed with defeat. 'Go on. Say it.'

His licked his lips, then crossed his legs, sitting back in his chair with a smug smile. 'Lying to your mother about me already. This bodes well.'

I rolled my eyes. 'I love my mother. She thinks she's super liberal, but if she heard I was alone at an airport with a boy, she'd flip out.'

I opened my menu again so I wouldn't have to look at him, neglecting to mention that his reputation – the fight he had with Sam the day Scarlett ran off to New York, the rumours about why he got kicked out of Eton – had reached her and she'd be furious if she knew I'd even *spoken* to him. Lord knows what she'd do if she knew he was at the airport with me. I couldn't tell her. She was stressed enough about my father, she didn't need to spend the flight to Lagos worrying that Dominic was getting me knocked up, too.

'Have you heard from her, by the way?' I tried to sound nonchalant.

He knew exactly who I was talking about, but still said, 'Who?'

'Scarlett.'

I heard him sigh. 'She's done another runner.'

'What?' I snapped the menu shut. 'When?'

'This morning. She's fine, she just texted Olivia to tell her she's in London auditioning for a summer school at RADA, or something. She'll be back tonight.'

'Why didn't she tell anyone?'

'She didn't want to jinx it.'

I put the menu on the table between us, no longer hungry. 'Unbelievable.'

'I don't want to talk about her.' He leaned forward to pick up his glass and took a long sip, then licked his lips and sat back again. 'Tell me about your dad.'

I felt a sudden stab in my stomach. 'Why?' I asked, fidgeting a little.

'It's called a conversation, Adamma.'

It felt more like he was trying to find a raw nerve. Mercifully, my phone buzzed and I reached for it, frowning at the screen so I wouldn't have to look at him. It was a text message and I was sure it would be from Scarlett, but it was from Tara Salter. I realised then that Scarlett might not know about my father if she was in London and, as annoyed as I was with her for running off again, I felt myself soften. She would get in touch if she knew. Even Scarlett wasn't that self-absorbed.

'Shall I tell you about mine, then?' he said when he realised that I was replying to the text and he wasn't going to get a response from me about my father.

I didn't look up from my screen. 'If you want.'

'I love him, but I wish he was a normal Asian dad sometimes. Dominic!' he said, screwing up his face and talking like an old Korean man. 'You so ungrateful. I come to this country with £1. Why you not a doctor?' I pressed my lips together so I wouldn't laugh. 'At least then I'd have something to rebel against, but *no*.' He shook his head. 'He's all, like, "I just want you to be happy, son." What good is that?'

I put my phone on the table and reached for my glass. 'It can't be that bad.'

'He invented a piece of code in his bedroom when he was fourteen. I don't know what it does, but the Internet would burst into flames without it, apparently. By the time he was my age, he was a billionaire.' He sat forward. 'He didn't go to college. He had a kid with a white girl, whom he wasn't even married to, and is now married to someone who used to be in a band called The Weeping Vaginas. He's given my grandfather two heart attacks. How am I supposed to compete with that?'

I couldn't hold it in, and laughed. 'Dominic!'

'The only way I can rebel now is by becoming a doctor, but I can't because I'm shit at maths.'

'He sounds pretty awesome.'

'I guess.' He smiled loosely. 'When I was at Eton, I got shitfaced one night, took all my clothes off and climbed onto the roof saying I wanted to make love not war. I got expelled and Dad wrote to them, threatening to sue them for obstructing my right to peaceful protest and they had to readmit me.'

I covered my mouth with my hand as I almost choked on my Diet Coke. He watched me with a smile. 'So, yeah. He just wants me to be happy, but I don't even know what I want.' His gaze dipped away from mine, the corners of his mouth falling. 'I just know it isn't this.' I sat forward, but before I could say anything, he caught himself, and sat back, opening his menu with a brighter smile. 'So are we going to order something? I'm bloody starving.'

I humoured him, and reached for mine. 'So what's your mum like?'

'Dead.'

I almost dropped my menu. 'What?'

'She died in childbirth with me.'

'Dominic,' I breathed. 'I had no idea.'

He peered at me over his menu. 'She didn't tell you that, did she?' I shook my head. 'Bet she told you all about her parents' apartment in Paris, though. All about their second-hand brass bed and her dad's pots of basil on the balcony?' I didn't know what to say and just looked at him. He sighed and shook his head. 'Of course. Why would she mention my dead mother? Such a minor detail.'

I felt an itch to defend her, tell him that perhaps she didn't feel right telling me. After all, it wasn't common knowledge at

Crofton. But as he began flicking through the menu, I realised that he didn't want to talk about it any more.

'My father is very different,' I said.

He closed his menu and looked at me again. 'What's he like?'

'Tall,' I said, closing my menu as well. 'Solid, like a tree. He never changes. He always wears either a black or a grey suit, always has oatmeal with brown sugar for breakfast, which he has at the dining table while he's reading the paper. If he's in the country, he always comes home for dinner. Always. He's just *there*, you know? He's always there.' When I looked at him, he was nodding. 'I've never needed him and he's not been there.' My chin trembled again and I looked down.

'Are you a daddy's girl?'

'Absolutely,' I said with a small chuckle. 'My mother says that when I was a baby, he carried me everywhere, couldn't put me down. As soon as I could sit up, he would put me in a high chair next to him at the dining table and every morning we'd have oatmeal together and he'd read to me from the paper.'

'Is that why you want to be a journalist?'

I nodded. 'He says I notice everything. Even when I was little, I would walk into a room and know if the housekeeper had moved something or if my mother had bought a new cushion. He says that everything was a story. A car would drive past us too quickly and I'd say the driver was being chased, or if one of my friends didn't come to school one day, I'd come up with an elaborate reason why.'

'Does he want you to be a journalist?'

I tilted my head at him and smiled. 'He just wants me to be happy.' He rolled his eyes. 'He says that's all he wants. So much so that he can never give me bad news, he always makes my mother do it. He even made her tell me about Santa.'

Dominic raised an eyebrow. 'And you didn't take advantage of that at all.'

I giggled, covering my face with the menu for a second. When I looked at him again, his eyebrow was still arched. 'When I was younger,' I admitted, putting the menu back on the table, 'and I didn't want to go to school, I went to him before my mother, because he'd always let me have the day off. It used to drive my mother crazy. But by the time I was thirteen, he cottoned on and whenever I went to him, looking pathetic, he would pretend to be hysterical and holler at the housekeeper to call the dibia.'

'The dibia?'

'Like a medicine man.' He nodded. 'He'd call for Celine roaring, "Fetch the dibia for my only child!"' I said, mimicking my father's warm voice. 'Then he'd shake me and tell the evil spirits to leave me alone. "Tell them it is not yet your time, Adamma!" he'd say. "*Gwa ha, kitaa!*" and I'd laugh so much, I couldn't pretend to be sick.'

I chuckled again, but when I thought of my father in hospital, strung up to all of those monitors, like a marionette, something in me finally buckled and tears suddenly spilled out of me. 'It's not yet his time.'

I covered my face with my hands. A moment later, I was aware of Dominic next to me, rubbing my back with his hand. When I calmed down, I turned to look at him kneeling next to me, but when he started to say something, I shook my head.

'Don't, Dominic. I can't bear it.'

He frowned. 'Don't what?'

'Don't say that you know it'll be OK.'

He tucked my hair behind my ears and when he took my face in his hands and wiped the tears from under my eyes with the pads of his thumbs, I curled my fingers around his wrists. I could feel his pulse against my fingers, as quick as mine.

'Promise me, Dominic.'

He looked at me, then smiled. 'What the hell do I know?'

10 DAYS AFTER

MAY

I've only been to two funerals, my grandfather's and my friend Mariya's. My grandfather's was more a celebration, because that's how it is in Nigeria when people have lived long, happy lives – we honour that. Funerals are big. *Rowdy*. There are drums and trumpets. We sing, dance, eat. But Mariya was thirteen when she died of leukaemia, so her funeral was a suitably dour affair, all black suits and handkerchiefs. I just remember everyone in our class sitting in stunned silence in the church trying not to look at her coffin as the realisation crept over us that death wasn't necessarily something that would happen when we were old. It could happen any time: when we were asleep, when we were crossing the street. It might already be there – like with Mariya – in our blood, our bones.

It's not like I ever thought I'd live forever – or wanted to – but it had never occurred to me that I might die before I'd lived. Before I'd driven a car and drank red wine and worn a ball gown and had an argument in the street. Before I had loved and been loved back. Before I'd even had my braces taken off. And that scared me more than anything, more than the tears and the lilies and the coffin. I just wanted enough time to live.

That's all I could think about this morning, before Scarlett's funeral; how much she'd lived. Every moment was hers, she didn't waste it on anyone else or anything she didn't want to do. I only know a bit of what she did, and while it will never be enough – she should have gone to Yale, she should have had an apartment in Paris with a second-hand brass bed – she had loved, and when I looked around at everyone huddled outside Burnham as we waited for Mrs Delaney to lead us to the church, I knew that, as infuriating and distracting and selfish as she was sometimes, she was loved.

Mrs Delaney told us to wear our Crofton uniform, which was good because I had hardly slept so I was too tired to contemplate what to wear. I did sleep for long enough to have another dream about her, though. It was more of a memory of the last time we hugged, on the dance floor at Edith's wedding. She was drunk on champagne and we were watching Edith and her husband dancing – so she was probably a little drunk on the promise of being loved like that one day, too – when she pulled me into a hug. Even in the dream her skin was sticky, her cheekbone digging into mine, and it was like we'd just met, when it was just her and me against the world. Before she ran away to New York, before my father was shot. Before. She even smelt like she did that night, of that perfume she bought at Selfridges during our last exeat weekend in London. Light. Sweet. Like she might float away if I didn't hold on tight enough.

I woke with a gasp. It was 5 a.m. and my instinct was to go for a run. I kicked the duvet away and just for that tiny second, I forgot. But by the time my feet touched the floor, it came charging back at me – the smell of trampled bluebells, the blue and white police tape fluttering like bunting – and I had to lie down again.

A moment later, I heard my door open and lifted my duvet so that Orla could slide under it. I must have fallen asleep again because Mrs Delaney found us like that a couple of hours later. She said that we could have another ten minutes, but it wasn't enough; it still took several attempts to button my shirt and tie back my hair. I lagged behind on the walk into Ostley, my limbs stiff as I tried to keep up. Orla looped her arm through mine when we passed the road to Savernake Forest. 'Keep going,' she whispered. 'Keep going.'

When we approached the village, I shivered. It was too quiet. It was almost 11 a.m., the stores should have been open – the smell of bread wafting from the bakery – but they were closed. There were no baskets of vegetables outside the grocer, no newspapers in the rack outside the newsagent.

When we passed the telephone box, there was a MISSING poster still taped to it and Mrs Delaney marched over to it. 'The cars will go past here,' she muttered, ripping it off. 'Her family shouldn't have to see this.'

Until then, she'd been so composed, as though we were on a school trip. But then everyone was. There was no weeping, no wailing, as we walked through the village. I'd heard girls crying in their rooms this morning and seen them stopping in the corridor to hug before they went to bed last night, but that was it. I wanted to scream. Cry. Break something. In Nigeria, death isn't something we speak of in hushed voices. We don't cry behind closed doors. But in England, grief is wrapped up. Locked away. The only display of emotion Mrs Delaney allowed herself this morning was a huff as she ripped another MISSING poster off a lamp post.

As soon as she did, I heard a camera click and my heart stopped, sure that it was Dominic, but it was a man in a black

T-shirt and jeans. 'Go away!' Mrs Delaney shooed at him with the posters in her hand, but he ignored her and continued taking photos of her.

When he turned the camera at us, Headmaster Ballard marched over to him. 'Please stop.' He held up his hand. 'This is beyond inappropriate.'

The man shrugged. 'I'm just taking photos. There's no law against it.'

'Well, I'm *asking* you to stop.'

'Fine.' He sniffed. 'I got what I need.'

Headmaster Ballard walked back to us mumbling, 'As if today isn't difficult enough,' then continued ushering us towards the church.

St Matthew's is an old stone church that sits on the far side of Ostley in the middle of a graveyard. As we approached it, I could see that there was already a mess of people dressed in black outside. They looked like beetles, squirming in the sun, but as we got closer, I realised that they were hurrying up the path and into the church to avoid the pack of photographers squatting on the other side of the road. I saw them then, the news trucks parked further up, by the village green, and the men and women in tidy suits clutching microphones, and panic kicked at me.

'Stay together, girls,' Mrs Delaney said, corralling us past the photographers as quickly as she could and up the gravel path towards the church doors.

Cameras clickclickclicked as we passed and when I glanced at Molly, who was at the front near Headmaster Ballard, I saw that her head was up. But as soon as we got inside, she feigned nonchalance. 'Why do they care?' she asked, loud enough for me to hear at the back. I guess Mrs Delaney heard too, because she took her by the sleeve of her blazer and dragged her over to the candles, telling her to light one. I didn't hear what she said to her after that, but when they came back to us, Molly was crying so much she was hiccupping.

The church was too small to hold everyone at Crofton plus everyone in the village so only the Lower Sixth went to the funeral. Headmaster Ballard told us to leave the pews for the other mourners and made us stand at the back. We were separated on either side of the church, so as not to get in anyone's way. I looked for my parents in the crowd and found them quickly, sitting in the middle of one of the pews, looking around for me as well. My mother saw me first, and even in black she shone, her glossy curls the colour of paw paw seeds under the church lights, her familiar smile making my twitching nerves suddenly settle.

There's a chapel at Crofton, so I haven't been to St Matthew's since Edith's wedding. Today, it was just as packed and the faces were the same, but it was so quiet. There was no fidgeting on the crammed pews, no chatter like when we had waited to hear the Bridal March. One woman even tiptoed down the aisle when her heels starting clacking, as though we were in a library. But like Edith's wedding, it was very elegant. There were candles everywhere and all the flowers were white. For one awful moment last night, I thought the flowers might be red, that someone would tell the florist it was her favourite colour and I'd walk in to find arrangements spilling over with blood-coloured roses. She would have hated that ('So predictable,' she would have said, rolling her eyes), but then she would have hated the white flowers, too.

We talked about her funeral once, when she asked me what they were like in Nigeria. When I told her, she said that that

233

was what she wanted her funeral to be like: colour and sound and food. For everyone to get drunk afterwards and dance like no one was watching. But what she got was a church full of white flowers and people slumped in black suits reading a pink programme with her photo on it. As I saw her grandmother striding up and down the aisle, directing the ushers and fussing over the flowers, I realised that funerals aren't always for the ones who are being buried.

I looked at the arrangement nearest me and when I noticed the white tulips poking out from between the roses and hydrangea heads, I wondered if they were from the farm. I pictured the gardeners cutting them, hands shaking as they remembered Scarlett in her yellow wellington boots, chasing Olivia down the neat rows of lettuces with a snail in her hand. Then I pictured her mother going from room to room in the house, her thin gold bangles clanging as she snatched the vases of tulips from each table and windowsill, leaving behind circles in the dust, and it made my heart ache.

Just as I leaned back against the door – the faint breeze a relief as I asked myself if my legs would survive the service – Mrs Delaney found me. 'Follow me, Miss Okomma,' she said, taking me by the hand and leading me through the knot of girls to the top of the aisle. I was sure my legs were going to betray me as we walked towards the altar and when we stopped by the first pew and I saw her family assembled in a row, each of them pale and creased with grief, I was glad Mrs Delaney was still holding my hand.

'Adamma,' Scarlett's mother said, struggling to her feet then hugging me tightly. The last time I saw her, she didn't see me. It was a couple of months ago and she was crossing the court-yard at school. Her dark hair was down and she was wearing a blue and white-striped Breton shirt and ballet pumps, her jeans rolled up to expose her ankles. If I'd just glanced at her, I might have assumed she was another pupil, but today she looked old – *exhausted* – in a dull black suit that she'd probably never wear again.

Her father hugged me, too, as did Edith, who thanked me for coming. But Olivia didn't stand up and I wasn't surprised – she hadn't replied to any of my messages and wouldn't let me near her when I helped her parents search Savernake Forest the afternoon I found The Old Dear – but it still stung when I sat next to her and she turned her face away.

'I'm sorry,' I breathed, but she didn't flinch. It made the guilt dig in a little deeper, but before I could say anything else, the organ started, grim and throbbing, and everyone shuffled to their feet. I knew it was the coffin and I couldn't look at it, so I squeezed my eyes shut, although that just seemed to amplify everything – the smell of the flowers, the soft scuff of the pallbearers' shoes as the coffin approached – so I forced myself to open them again as the priest, a tall man with hair as dark as shoe polish, asked everyone to be seated.

'"I am the resurrection and the life,' saith the Lord",' he began, pausing to smooth down his robes with his hands, before raising them again, '"he that believeth in me, though he were dead, yet shall he live, and whosoever liveth and believeth in me shall never die.'"'

When he began reading 'The Lord is my Shepherd', I looked at Olivia again, the pink programme fluttering in her hands as she stared at it. I waited for her to look up at me, but when she didn't, I looked over my shoulder at the congregation instead, hoping to see him. Not that I could see much in the full church. He didn't come with us, perhaps he was standing behind one of the pillars or standing at the back. Maybe he hadn't come at all.

The thought jabbed at my ribs as I made myself look at the coffin, at the perfect wreath of white roses on top of it, studded with one red one, and my stomach turned. It turned again when the priest invited me up to the podium. There was a flurry of whispers and it knocked the bravado right out of me. I could feel the collar of my shirt sticking to my neck so I hooked a finger in it and tugged, then took a deep breath as I put the piece of paper I was holding on the podium and flattened it with my hand.

I took another deep breath and when I forced myself to look out over the miserable faces, I felt a flower of pain in my chest that seemed to *pop* open when I saw Olivia. I could see her face then, the skin around her eyes red raw from crying, as though someone had taken a brillo pad to it. I had to look away and it made me feel wretched because people must have been doing that all morning and it wasn't fair; we got to look away while she had to live with it.

I had no intention of saying anything, not because I was scared of being crucified by Molly and everyone at Crofton for being a hypocrite, but because I didn't want to upset her family. But then her father called last night and pleaded with me to say something. 'You have to put it behind you, Adamma. You have to,' he said and the way he said it made me think of the last time I saw him, the afternoon of Scarlett's party, when he told me to come – *Buy her a present and she'll forgive you anything!* – and I had to move my cellphone away so that he didn't hear me heave and sob before I told him that I would.

I hope he wasn't disappointed, but I read the lyrics to Leonard Cohen's 'Anthem'. I shouldn't imagine it meant much to her family other than that it was pretty. They probably thought, after everything that had happened, that I was too embarrassed to say anything more personal. They probably thought I didn't even know her any more, but I did. And that broke my heart all over again, because of all the people I wanted to be there to hear it, it was Scarlett. She would have loved it, loved that I was talking about her tattoo, the one no one knows about, the one on the patch of skin 'where my heart should be' she'd told me with a grin when she'd first showed it to me, her finger stroking the words. And just for that moment it felt like I was the only person in the world who knew her.

When I finished my reading, I couldn't go back to my seat – to that pew – so I walked down the aisle and out of the church into the brilliant sun. I intended to keep going – back through the village, past the closed shops and the MISSING posters, past Savernake Forest, with the gas station carnations tied to its locked gates, back to Crofton – but as soon as I stepped outside, I heard cameras clicking and panicked, heading around the side of the church instead.

They didn't follow, but I kept going, into the shade of the graveyard and I didn't stop until I had to, until I had to reach for one of the old, leaning headstones to steady myself a moment before my legs gave way. I'd barely caught my breath before I heard someone say, 'Thanks for that,' and turned to find Dominic watching me.

I wanted to run at him, grab him and shake him, ask why he hadn't called me back, ask him what the hell was going on, but as soon as I saw him, it was all forgotten. I've never seen him like that, as though a light had gone out somewhere. It was like returning home after a vacation to find everything closed.

Locked. I just wanted to hug him, but he was wearing that black suit, the one he wore to my first social at Crofton, and I almost smiled at the memory, Scarlett twirling in that red dress, her arm in the air. But I turned away from him again.

'Thank you for reading that, for saying something real. She'd hate this.' I turned to face him, but when I saw his wet eyelashes, I couldn't look at him, and I looked at the back of the church as they began singing 'Amazing Grace'. 'The poem, the organ, "The Lord is my Shepherd". All of it. It's not her.' When I didn't agree, he pushed on. 'And what's with the white flowers? Scarlett's not white, she's yellow.'

'Highlighter yellow.' I lifted my chin to look at him then.

'And flamingo pink,' he said with a faint smile.

'And Saint Patrick's Day green.'

'And red. Scarlett red.'

'But not white,' I said, crossing my arms, and he nodded back.

'I couldn't stay in there. They're all crying, girls she's never spoken to. They don't even know her.' He turned to the church again, suddenly livid. 'You don't even know her!' he roared, hands balled into fists.

I was stunned. I'd never seen him like that and it scared me, seeing the rawness of his grief, like red paint splashed over the church walls. When my heart began thrumming, I felt it again – doubt – creeping back into my bones and suddenly I heard DS Hanlon's voice. *What is Dominic Sim capable of?* Not that, I told myself, like I tell myself every time the words drift into my head now. Not that. But looking at him then, his cheeks flushed and his jaw hard, I didn't know what he was capable of.

When I took a step back, he looked mortified. 'I'm sorry, Adamma,' he said, his hands on his hips as he took a deep breath. 'It's just that, before the service started, I heard her grandmother telling someone that the programme is pink because it's her favourite colour and –' He stopped with a frown. 'I'm not going mad. It isn't pink, is it?'

I shook my head. 'Pink is Olivia's favourite colour. Hers is red.'

'Actually,' he said with a bitter chuckle, 'she's too fickle to have a favourite colour. It changes every week.'

I nodded, the corners of my mouth lifting for just a second, and when he saw, he smiled, his eyes even heavier. 'Sometimes I think we're the only ones who really know her.'

My cellphone rang then and it made me jump. My hands shook a little as I took it out of the pocket of my blazer and rejected the call.

'Don't you want to get that?'

'It's the Mercedes garage about bringing my car back. I'll call them later.'

He nodded then looked at his feet. 'I'm sorry I haven't called you back.'

'I've been going out of my mind, Dominic,' I breathed, slipping my cellphone back into my pocket. 'I've been calling and calling.'

'I know.' He rubbed his face with his hands. 'I know.'

'Why haven't you called me back?'

'I tried to, about four times, but I didn't know what to say.'

There was a moment of silence as my thoughts flew around my head again, knocking together but not sticking. I was so mad, but then I wasn't because there he was in his black suit, looking at me with those sad, sad eyes and when I heard 'Abide With Me' coming from the church, something in me began to crumble. I could feel it falling away, slowly, then quicker,

239

quicker, like an avalanche and I understood it then, why the girls at Crofton keep things behind closed doors.

I closed my eyes, but a moment later, I was aware of him in front of me, the muscles in my shoulders clenching like fists when I felt his knuckles brush against my wet cheeks, but when I opened my eyes to look at him, I saw someone standing behind him, watching us, and my heart stopped.

I shook my head and stepped away from him. 'Olivia, this isn't—'

He spun around to face her and she lurched forward so suddenly, I thought she might punch him.

'You can't stay away from each other, can you?' She looked between us, hands balled into fists at her sides as a tear rolled quickly down her cheek.

'Olivia –' he tried, but she ignored him, looking back at the church, then at us.

'I couldn't take it, I had to get out of there. I came outside for some air and I see you and I think, *That looks like Adamma and Dominic*.' She blinked, sending a fresh tumble of tears down her cheeks. 'But then I think, *They wouldn't. Not at her funeral*.'

'Olivia, please,' I tried again.

'We haven't even buried her yet!' she roared, and the look on her face.

I wanted to be sick.

'We were just talking, 'Liv,' he said, and he sounded tiny. Like a little boy.

I made myself look at her. 'Olivia, I'm so sorry.'

She didn't listen and walked away, but when I tried to go after her, she stopped and raised an unsteady finger at me. 'You picked the wrong one!' she said, and her voice had changed. It was harder, there was a little spite in it, a little Scarlett.

'What do you mean?'

'Ask him!' She pointed at Dominic. 'Ask him! Ask him who was the last person she spoke to before she left the house on Sunday.'

My heart stopped. 'No.'

He stepped between us then. 'Olivia, stop it.'

'Stop what, Dom?' She licked her lips and smiled and there was a little Scarlett in that, too. 'Stop telling the truth? Tell her where your Aston Martin is.'

'No.' I shook my head at her, then I turned to shake my head at him too. 'No, Dominic. It was that guy. The guy in Savernake Forest. The one in the car.'

'Tell her, Dom.' She crossed her arms, suddenly calm as I watched his cheeks get redder and redder. 'Tell her how someone saw you driving through the forest on Sunday.'

'It wasn't me,' he said through his teeth. 'I was with Sam.'

'It wouldn't be the first time Sam covered for you, Dom.'

He ignored her and turned to look at me. 'Adamma, it's me. It's *me*,' he said – whispered – and reached for my hand, but I pulled away.

'No.'

'I was the last person she *called*.'

I shook my head. 'What's the difference?'

'I rejected the call.'

'Why?'

'I was with Sam. He was skateboarding and he called to tell me that he tried to grind down a hand rail, or something, and landed funny. He hurt his wrist and couldn't drive so he asked me to take him to the hospital.'

I shook my head again, but I felt a quick quiver of dread as it came back to me: Sam on the morning Scarlett ran away,

241

asking how much I wanted to put on when she was coming back while I ignored him and asked him why his arm was in a sling. 'Sprained my wrist thinking of you, baby,' he'd said with a filthy smirk, pretending to jerk off with his other hand, which earned him a shove from Dominic.

'I was in the hospital when she called,' he went on, his voice low. *Familiar*. 'The nurse told me off for having my phone on so I rejected it. Call Great Western if you don't believe me. The police did. That's why they haven't arrested me.'

Olivia scoffed and he shot a look at her. 'It's true.' He looked at me again and when I stepped back, his face folded. 'It's true.'

But it was too late, it was there – the doubt – needling its way in. Then I was walking away, away from him, from Olivia, towards the sound of 'Amazing Grace'.

I slipped back into the church as quietly as I could, covering my mouth with my hand as I tried to catch my breath so that no one would hear me panting. But Mrs Delaney saw me, of course, and smiled, a gentle, *It'll be OK* smile that should have made me feel better, but then everyone turned and began to file out of the church and my heart started banging again.

It wasn't the time, but I had to find Chloe – I had to – and when I did, I reached for the sleeve of her blazer and tugged her into the corner, next to a statue of Mary, her palms outstretched. The urge to grab the lapels of her blazer and shake her was almost impossible to fight. I guess that was obvious because she frowned at me.

'What's wrong, Adamma?'

'You know that guy?'

'What guy?'

'The one from Savernake Forest.'

She closed her eyes and sighed. 'Not this again, Adamma. I told you—'

'I know. I know. But are you sure you don't remember anything about him?'

'I was shitfaced,' she hissed, then blushed and turned to check over her shoulder at everyone shuffling down the aisle towards the doors, before turning back to me and lowering her voice. 'I don't even remember what I was wearing.'

'What about the car?'

'I barely saw it. It was too dark.'

'Chloe, please.' I swiped a tear from my cheek with my fingers. 'Was it Old? New?'

'Adamma—'

'Please, Chloe,' I interrupted, then made myself take a breath and lowered my voice as I remembered that we were surrounded by her family. 'I think he murdered Scarlett.'

'What?' she gasped. 'No.'

I nodded and she was quiet for a moment, her lips parted.

'So if you can remember anything, Chloe.'

'OK.' She tucked her hair behind her ears. 'OK. Let me think.'

'Close your eyes,' I suggested. She did. 'What can you see?'

She frowned. 'Nothing. I just saw his car for a second.'

'Was it new?'

'No, but it was nice.'

'Nice?'

'I don't know.' She opened her eyes again. 'It was shiny. Taken care of.'

'Did you see a badge?'

'I only saw the side of it.'

'That's something.' I jumped on it. 'Do you remember the shape of it?'

'I don't know anything about cars, Adamma.'

'It doesn't matter.' I pushed, breathless with panic as I willed her to say something to eliminate Dominic's Aston Martin. 'Come on, Chloe. You must be able to remember what type of car it was. Was it a four by four like The Old Dear?'

She thought about it for a moment. 'No. It was small.'

'Small? Small like a sports car or small like a Mini?'

'Small like a sports car, but that's all I remember, I swear. I saw the car stop and when I heard him ask if I wanted a lift, I ran. I didn't even look at him.'

'OK,' I said, forcing myself to let go of the breath I was holding on to.

But then she said, 'He had to wind down the window,' and I went rigid.

'What?'

'When he asked me if I wanted a lift,' she said, almost to herself, 'he had to wind down the window and I remember thinking a car that cool should have electric windows.'

'Cool? You didn't say it was cool.'

'*I* don't think it's cool.' She shook her head, like I was mad. 'It wasn't a Range Rover or anything, but my dad would have loved it.'

'Why?'

'It was like something James Bond would drive.'

146 DAYS BEFORE

DECEMBER

When I was four, I helped our gardener, Jide, plant a hibiscus in our garden. It's one of my earliest memories, crouched down next to it, my tiny hands clumsily patting at the soil. My mother bought me a yellow plastic watering can and I watered it every day, anxiously poking at the cloud of leaves for some sign of life, and when it finally bloomed – the delicate heart-coloured flowers erupting overnight – I don't think I'd ever been so excited. I would sit at my bedroom window for hours staring at it and thinking, *That was me. I did that.* But when we moved to New York, the hibiscus died. 'A *na-amacha*. Sometimes these things happen,' Jide told me with an elegant shrug when I asked him what we'd done wrong.

I know now that he was right – it probably wasn't getting enough sunlight or maybe it got tip-borer (yes, I looked it up) – but I was sure that it was my fault, that I'd stopped paying attention to it so it died. I think that's what happened with Scarlett. Apart from a couple of texts, I haven't heard from her, not since I've been at home with my father. I don't know if she's just being Scarlett or if I've done something, but something's changed between us. If you hold a true friend with both hands, then when I got her sister Edith's wedding invitation, I realised that we weren't even in the same room any more.

It had been two weeks since my father had been shot and everyone who was going to send a card already had, so when I grabbed the pile of mail from the kitchen counter before I left for the hospital, I expected to find bills and junk, but there it was, a heavy cream envelope with her scruffy handwriting scratched across it.

My first thought was that it was a card, a letter even, something to let me know that she was thinking of me, and my heart relaxed, but before I could open it, my father took off his glasses and shook his newspaper at me.

'Have you read this nonsense, Ada?'

'Calm down, Papa,' I told him, patting his arm.

That made me feel better as well, him sitting up in bed, about to rant, because that meant he was better, and after sitting through two surgeries and seeing more of his blood than I ever wanted to see, I needed him to be better. But before he could launch into whatever had pissed him off, I opened the envelope to find a wedding invitation and my heart tensed again.

'What is this, Adamma?' he asked, peering over the top of his newspaper as a shower of pink rose petals fluttered onto his bed.

'Scarlett's sister's getting married,' I said with some relief before the lump in my throat formed as I realised there was no note, no *I hope your dad's better* or *I miss you*. The only thing she'd written was my address on the front of the envelope.

'The big one, I hope.'

'Yes.'

'How old is she?'

'Eighteen.'

He went back to his newspaper with a humph. 'Listen to this, Ezi,' he muttered when my mother came in with a vase of flowers.

'Pretty!' she said, nodding at the rose petals.

'Wedding invitation,' I muttered, trying to stuff them back into the envelope.

'Who's getting married, Ada?'

'Scarlett's sister, Edith.'

I saw her eyebrow quirk up in the reflection of the window as she put the vase on the windowsill. 'How old is she?'

'Eighteen.'

'What's his name?'

'Nishad.'

I knew that Edith was in love, much to her grandmother's horror. She had been for months and I think Scarlett was a little put out; she was the one who was supposed to fall in love with a guy her grandmother hated.

'Have they been together long?' my mother asked, her voice a little higher.

I considered lying but went with, 'He's a doctor,' instead.

'A doctor! How did they meet?'

'They're volunteering together in India.'

I saw her eyebrow quirk up again. 'Didn't she just go to India?'

'In August.'

She exchanged a glance with my father, muttered something I couldn't make out in Igbo, then went back to the flowers, taking one of the orange lilies and putting it in a glass of water

247

next to my father's bed. 'Don't tell Papa any more, Ada.' She kissed him on the forehead. 'We don't want him to have a heart attack, too.'

He chuckled from behind his newspaper. 'I'm in the right place.'

'Uche!' She frowned. '*I choro ihe a?*'

'No, I don't want that, Ezi. I'm just saying.'

It's the only time my mother treats me like a child, when she argues with my father. She insists on arguing in Igbo, as though I won't understand what she's saying, but my father never humours her, which infuriates her more.

She put her hands on her hips. '*Amuna m amu.*'

'I'm not laughing at you, my love. Merely noting the convenience of it.'

She turned to me with a huff. 'When is this wedding?'

I checked the invitation. 'December the twenty-second.'

She blinked at me. 'This year?'

I nodded.

'But that's next Saturday, Ada.'

'They're not getting any younger, Ezi,' my father said from behind his paper.

'Well.' She clapped. 'We must book you a flight. Get you a dress.'

'I'm not going.' I looked at her like she was mad and she returned the favour.

'Why not?'

'I can't leave, Papa.'

She huffed. 'You see, Uche.' She tugged at the sleeve of his pyjamas. 'All this talk of heart attacks and now the child is too scared to leave your side.'

'Adamma,' he said, moving his hand and letting the corner

of his newspaper droop down so he could look at me. 'You have to go. You've been invited. It would be rude not to. Besides, it's been two weeks. You must miss your friends.'

As if on cue, my cellphone buzzed.

Did you get the invite to the Wedding of the Year? – D x

'Ada,' my mother snapped.

'Sorry, Mama.' I pressed my lips together so she wouldn't see me smile.

He'd been in touch constantly since we parted at the airport. It began with a text to let him know I'd landed safely, then he texted back to check on my father, then on me, then, within a day or so, we were texting each other every few minutes. It was driving my mother nuts; she told me off every time I got a message. I'd even turned my phone on silent, but she still heard it when it vibrated.

'Fine. I'll go,' I said with a sigh, picking up the rest of the petals and putting them in the envelope. But my heart fluttered at the thought of seeing him again.

Fluttered and fluttered.

As soon as I RSVP'd, Scarlett didn't leave me alone. She still didn't call, but I gathered from the string of emails she sent that the wedding was going to be a bit like a Nigerian one in that everyone in the village was involved. The butcher provided the meat, the florist the flowers and the poor old lady in the bakery was going blind piping a lace design onto the cake to match Edith's dress. It was like a Royal wedding, Scarlett insisted, everyone was talking about it.

She loved it, of course, loved emailing me every day before I left Lagos with photos of the bunting hanging in the village and her bridesmaid's dress and the flowers she'd be carrying. Anyone would think she was the one getting married. And while she finally said all the right things – *Have a safe flight . . . Can't wait to see you . . . I'll make sure your dad gets the biggest piece of wedding cake!* – it was always an afterthought at the end of her message.

She invited me to the rehearsal dinner the night before the wedding. I wasn't in the wedding party so I have no idea why they wanted me there, but as soon as her father opened the door to me and gathered me into a hug, I realised why.

'Adamma, darling,' her mother gasped when she saw me walk in, pulling me into a hug, then feeding me a quail egg hors d'oeuvres while telling me that I must be famished after my flight.

Hearing the commotion, Olivia wandered out of the dining room, then flew at me, hugging me as well – even though she never had before – asking how my father was. That's when I saw her, coming down the staircase in a Merlot-coloured gown that Edith must have been grateful she was wearing the evening before her wedding. She didn't flinch when she saw me, just smiled that *Mona Lisa* smile, and when she got to me, she put her hands on my shoulders and kissed me on both cheeks. 'How lovely to see you, Adamma. Thank you for coming,' she said, as though I was a distant cousin she only saw at weddings, then she gestured at one of the staff lingering in the hall with a tray of hors d'oeuvres to take my coat.

When he had, I noticed her smile tighten as she turned to her parents and Olivia, who were still next to me, waiting for me to finish telling them about my father. It took them a moment, but they took the hint and dispersed in different directions as she led me towards the dining room.

'That's a lovely dress,' she said with a slight swing of the hips as we rounded the table in the middle of the hall, the vase of paper white roses on it almost yellow under the light of the chandelier. 'I wish I had the courage to wear orange.'

I registered the jab with a wounded frown, but she didn't look at me, just carried on towards the voices and the ring of crystal spilling out of the dining room. But as we approached the doorway, she stopped and pushed her shoulders back.

'I'm glad your father's better,' she said with a warmer smile, and it was her way of apologising for the swipe about my dress, I know, but it didn't feel like enough.

'Why haven't you been in touch, Scarlett?'

She seemed startled by that and blinked at me a few times, before catching herself and waving her hand. 'I didn't want to bother you,' she said with a long sigh that told me to stop making a fuss. 'Not when you were with your family.'

A couple of weeks ago, I might have pushed her, might have told her that she *was* family, but she isn't, I know that now, so I shrugged and followed her into the dining room. He was the first person I saw and I was so surprised that it made my heart stop dead in my chest, like a car hitting a brick wall. I didn't think I'd see him and I guess he didn't think he'd see me, either, because I said I'd see him at the wedding. It was such a surprise that I almost stepped on Scarlett's toe.

Olivia was talking to him and clearly besotted, her head tilted and her eyes wider than I've ever seen them (if she was a cartoon character they would have been two huge hearts) as he said something that made her laugh. I suddenly felt very smug at the thought of the string of text messages on my phone, of all the things I knew about him, our private jokes, the x he now added to each one he sent. So when he looked up and his mouth split into a smile, it made me smile, too, and it's silly, because I've known him for months, but it was like seeing him for the first time. I'd even given him a nickname because my mother kept asking who I was talking to – Vivian Darkbloom, the pseudonym Nabokov wanted to publish *Lolita* under, which I figured was apt after our furious exchange over whether it was really an epic love story or just creepy. 'My friend Vivian,' I tell my mother each time she asks, the lie rolling off my tongue, swift and delicious.

He even looked different, younger – *softer* – his hair a mess from where he'd been playing with it too much, and I had to fight the urge to run over to him. I think he did as well, because he took a step forward, then stopped himself and waved instead. I waved back, but when I realised that Scarlett was standing next to me, smiling and waving, too, my cheeks suddenly stung as our arms dropped to our sides in unison. She turned to look at me, more confused than angry, then caught herself. 'I'll get us some champagne.' She smiled sweetly.

But she never came back.

There was no seating plan, so when Scarlett's father invited us to sit down for dinner, she made no move to sit near me and remained at the top of the table, next to Dominic, her glance sweeping towards me every now and then like the arc of a lighthouse warning me to keep back. So I reached for the nearest chair. The table filled up quickly and a moment after I sat down, Mr Lucas put his hand on the chair next to mine and asked if anyone was sitting there. When I told him there wasn't, the old woman sitting opposite me eyed him carefully, clearly questioning his intentions, then softened and leaned a little closer when he asked after my father, making no effort to disguise the fact that she was listening to my response.

'He's much better. Thank you,' I said stiffly, my cheeks flushing a little under her gaze. 'He should be out of hospital soon.'

His shoulders relaxed. 'That's a relief,' he said, pouring me a glass of water, the ice tumbling out of the silver jug with a clatter then landing in the glass with a series of *PLOP*s. When it was full, he held up his champagne glass. 'To his health.'

I lifted my eyelashes to look at him as we clinked glasses. 'To his health.'

'Are we toasting?' I heard Scarlett say and glanced up the table to find her watching us with a curious smile. I don't know how she heard us from the other end of the room – not over the chatter as compliments were exchanged about the flowers – but with that, everyone turned to look and I was so embarrassed I wanted to dissolve into a puddle of linen and lace.

Luckily, Mr Lucas recovered quickly, turning to Edith and Nishad and raising his champagne glass with a smile. 'Look down you gods, and on this couple drop a blessed crown.'

There was a titter of approval as everyone around the table raised their glasses. Edith looked thrilled and turned to Nishad and kissed him to another titter. Her grandmother didn't join in; she plucked a drooping tulip out of the centrepiece and handed it to the waiter as he put a small plate of asparagus down in front of her.

'*The Tempest?*' I whispered when everyone returned to their conversations.

He lowered his voice as well. 'It was either that or *The Simpsons.*' He shrugged. 'Wrong crowd.' I must have looked confused because he did a frighteningly accurate impression of Homer. 'What is a wedding? *Webster's Dictionary* defines a wedding as "the process of removing weeds from one's garden."'

I tipped my head back and laughed, which earned me another look from Scarlett, but I couldn't help it. I never thought I'd hear Mr Lucas quote *The Simpsons*. He chuckled, too, and when we'd calmed down he nodded at my dress.

'Is that a wrapper?'

'It's an African print, but it's just a dress.' I blinked at him, impressed. 'How do you know what a wrapper is?'

'I did some reading about Hindu wedding ceremonies because I was curious about what Edith and Nishad's ceremony would have been like in India.' He pushed his glasses back up his nose and I don't know if he even realised he'd done it, but I almost laughed again. The hopeless geek. Mind you, I probably would have looked it up, too.

'They had a Hindu ceremony?'

'Oh yes.' He paused to take a sip from his glass. 'They're already legally married. All of this is just for their friends and family.'

I looked up the table at Scarlett's grandmother who was talking to the priest and holding her empty glass out for a refill to no one in particular. Olivia obliged.

'But while I was reading about Hindu weddings, there was a link to an article about Igbo ones and I couldn't resist. It was fascinating.' He swallowed another mouthful of champagne. 'Western weddings are very different.'

'It's not my first,' I told him with a smile and he blushed.

'Of course,' he said, suddenly flustered. 'I didn't—'

I raised my hand with a warmer smile. 'It's OK. I know what you mean.'

'All I was trying to say,' he went on after he'd drained his glass, 'is that it's lovely to see someone at a wedding wear so much colour.' He glanced around the table at the men in their neat black suits and the women in their pastel dresses, then smiled loosely. 'You're like a butterfly at a picnic, Miss Okomma.'

When he put down his glass, I arched an eyebrow. 'Are you drunk, Sir?'

He looked stunned, then flushed again when he went to take a sip from his champagne glass and realised it was empty. 'Absolutely not, Miss Okomma,' he said in that way I do when my father asks if the dress I've bought is expensive and I lie and say it was on sale. 'That would be horribly inappropriate, wouldn't it?'

I thought it best to leave it.

'So what happens at a Hindu wedding, then?'

His eyes lit up and while we ate our starter, he told me everything he knew about Hindu weddings between mouthfuls of asparagus (which was an astonishing amount, actually) and concluded that they sounded like the Igbo ones he'd read about.

'I guess.' I told him with a shrug. 'They're just as loud and colourful, but the last few I went to weren't much different to this one.'

He seemed disappointed. 'Really?' There was no wine carrying?'

'What do you know about wine carrying?'

'I know things.' He lifted his chin smugly. 'Like before the wedding, the groom and his elders have to settle on the bride's price with the bride's father –' He was clearly horrified by that and I interrupted with a laugh.

'It's symbolic. *Anaghi alusi nwaanyi alusi*, we say.'

He frowned. 'What does that mean?'

'It means that the worth of a woman cannot be quantified in material terms.'

'Yeah. But you still do it, right?'

'True,' I conceded with another shrug. 'But no one's being sold for a cow.'

'Fair enough.' He chuckled. 'Then there's the wedding ceremony, the *Igba Nwku*,' he sounded so proud of himself. I almost applauded. 'It begins with a dance—'

I stopped him again. 'The boiled eggs are symbolic as well.'

'I know.' He feigned indignation, pushing his glasses back up his nose and he did it on purpose this time. 'The bride selling them to her guests symbolises that she will be able to support herself and her family if needed.'

I laughed and shook my head. I don't know what website he'd found, but he'd memorised it. He sounded like he was reciting his eight times table.

'Then the bride's father gives the bride a wooden cup—'

'What's it called?' I interrupted and I shouldn't have, but I couldn't resist teasing him a little as he stared at me, his lips parted.

'It's a –' he clicked his fingers – 'a –'

'You're going to have to do more than check Wikipedia to get a decent grade, Mr Lucas,' I tutted, parroting what he tells us in class every week.

'It's a –'

'An *iko*.'

He slapped his thigh, furious as the waiter refilled his glass. 'An *iko*!'

'None for you, Mr Lucas.'

'I knew that!' he hissed, knocking back another mouthful of champagne.

'Then what happens?' I said, giving him an opportunity to redeem himself.

His shoulders slumped. 'Then the bride's father gives the bride the *iko*, which is filled with palm wine, while the groom hides among the guests. The wedding isn't official until the bride finds her groom, offers him a sip of the palm wine and he drinks from the cup,' he muttered without as much feeling.

'You forgot the dance.'

'No! I didn't! You just didn't give me a chance.' He pointed at me. 'Then they dance and the guests throw money around them or put bills on their foreheads.'

'Too late. You'd better check Wikipedia again before you speak to Nishad.'

'Dammit! I had this yesterday. Champagne makes me stupid,' he muttered, stopping to drain his glass. 'I'm going to do this tomorrow, aren't I? I'm going to get up to read my poem, completely forget it, then have to do my Homer impression.'

'You should do that anyway.'

'Don't. I'm so nervous.'

'You'll be fine. Just picture everyone in their underwear.'

He laughed. 'That was my first piece of advice when I started at Crofton,' he said, his eyes wide. 'If you get nervous, don't picture them in their underwear!'

He must have said it too loudly because Scarlett's grandmother shot a look down the table at us and he went so red, I thought he might hide under his chair. The old woman sitting opposite me looked horrified as well.

I waited for her to look away, then lowered my voice. 'You're the first white person I've ever met who knows what an *igba nwku* is, by the way.'

He brightened at that. 'Really?'

'I know some Nigerians who don't know what an *igba nwku* is.'

257

'It sounds amazing. Much more interesting than our "I Do" rubbish.'

'I guess. But most couples still have a white wedding as well.'

'Yeah.' He nodded across the table at the overweight middle-aged man guffawing and spilling red wine on his shirt. 'But they're not like *this*.'

I tried not to laugh, but he was right; as Western as they are now, they're still so *Nigerian*. They have all the grandeur – the noise, the colour – and even if the groom is in a tux and sunglasses and arrives in an Escalade, they still reek of tradition. Like the last wedding I went to, it was for a Yoruba couple who had a white wedding a few days after their traditional one. While the bride wore a Kosibah dress Jumoke wanted to rip off her, most of the guests wore Aso Oke wrappers and gowns. Even Jumoke wore a gele, which she doesn't always, but her father likes it when she does. But the bride's mother owned her ass in a red one so tall, I'm sure she had to duck to get in the door.

I had to raise a glass to her, because I still haven't mastered tying them, despite watching my mother since I was a child, in awe of how the fabric would stay up, high and wide around her head, like a silk halo. When I was six, I tried to tie one using one of her Hermès scarves and when she found me struggling with it and whimpering that it wouldn't stay up, she laughed and hugged me until I couldn't breathe.

'Do your parents want you to have a traditional wedding?' Mr Lucas asked, rolling the stem of his empty champagne glass between his finger and thumb.

I could hear Scarlett laughing at the other end of the table, but refused to give her the satisfaction of looking at her. Mr

Lucas didn't either and I was glad because I could just imagine her, eyes sparkling as she waited for us to look, one hand under the table on Dominic's knee or her fingers lingering on the lapel of his suit jacket. So I just held Mr Lucas's gaze as the waiter took our plates away.

'Of course they do,' I told him with a smile I hope Scarlett saw. As liberal as my parents think they are, they want all of that; me in an *akwete* cloth and coral beads, while my father refuses to give me the *iko* and everyone laughs.

'So running off to Vegas isn't an option?'

I chuckled, but before I could respond, I heard someone say, 'Who's running off to Vegas?' and looked up to find Dominic standing behind us with a smirk.

Mr Lucas looked a little uncomfortable, then caught himself and smiled. 'I do believe my glass is empty,' he said, picking it up, then excusing himself.

As soon as he did, Dominic sat in his seat. He put down his Scotch and I shouldn't have been so surprised; not only do the kids at Crofton speak like grown-ups, but they drink like grown-ups as well.

'Aren't you at the wrong end of the table, Mr Sim?'

The corners of his mouth twitched. 'Depends on your definition of wrong.'

My gaze flicked towards Scarlett, but she was distracted, her nose wrinkled as she giggled at something Mr Lucas was saying while he refilled his glass.

'Are you looking forward to the wedding, Miss Okomma?'

'It's going to be a lot of fun.' I looked at her when I said it because I knew she wouldn't be able to resist looking at me, if only for a second. When she did, she smiled smugly, but it wasn't her usual Scarlett smugness, it was a smile that told me

I wouldn't win. Two weeks ago, I would have been mortified and looked away, but something in me finally kicked back, so I raised my glass and gave her a smile that told her we'd see.

Orla wasn't invited to the wedding so I was surprised to see so many people from our year there, especially so close to Christmas. But it seems that I wasn't the only one who made an effort to be there, even the teachers had, and when I stopped outside the church to adjust the strap of my shoe and saw Headmaster Ballard and his wife inside, trying to find a seat, I realised that Orla wasn't being paranoid; Scarlett hadn't invited her on purpose. I had no idea why she was still holding a grudge, but when I walked in and Sam winked at me, I began to wonder.

I think half the village was there, too, so the church filled up quickly. I could hear the pews groaning grumpily as more people tried to squeeze onto them, but I was too late to get on one so stood at the back with a sullen sigh, wishing I'd worn flats. But then Mr Crane saw my heels and graciously offered me his seat and I sat down as the 'Wedding March' began playing.

Edith looked every inch the English bride, her blond hair up and her cheeks pink as she walked up the aisle. Her dress was beautiful; strapless and delicate milk-white lace. It was her something borrowed, Scarlett told me, the dress her mother wore on her wedding day, which, I guessed from the tone of Scarlett's email, she had wanted to wear first.

Nishad glanced back at her and when he saw her, he smiled clumsily. It made my heart flutter suddenly and I found myself looking for him in the church. It took a few moments, but when our gaze met, my stomach burst into a mass of butterflies.

I looked at Scarlett then, she and Olivia were at the top of the aisle in their bridesmaid's dresses, grinning and nudging each other when their mother started crying. But their grand-mother was unmoved and stood stiffly facing the altar, as their father led Edith up the aisle. And it's funny, isn't it? How you can love someone so much that in wanting the best for them, you can't even see what is?

The reception was held in a marquee in the grounds of Scarlett's house. I've been to a lot of weddings with my parents and they're right, they are becoming more and more alike, but thankfully, one tradition that hasn't changed at Nigerian weddings is the food. And while I wasn't holding my breath for any red stew and rice, I think my parents would have liked the food at Edith's wedding – although I'm sure my father would have grumbled that the pumpkin soup wasn't spicy enough. He would have liked the beef Wellington, though, and my mother loves mulled wine, so she probably would have drunk far too much of it. I know I did.

They would have thought the marquee was pretty as well, with the candles and the knots of holly and ivy tied to the back of each chair. The first thing my mother would have done when we sat at our table would be to smell the white camellias in the centrepiece. I could see her taking one and tucking it into her hair or putting one in my father's buttonhole. But I think they would have been bemused by how quiet it was. Even with the string quartet, you could hear the *ting* of everyone's cutlery. There must have been at least three hundred guests – which is tiny compared to a Nigerian wedding – but the hush made it feel much smaller. There was no singing, no fans, no drums, no colour. And it was so dull; most of the men were in black suits and the women in dark-coloured gowns. Nigerian weddings are nothing but colour, swathes and swathes of patterned cloth – oranges and greens and bright, bright blues.

Scarlett must have been really pissed at me, because she sat me next to Molly. I spent most of the dinner nodding and pretending to be shocked as she updated me on what I'd missed while I'd been at home. Scarlett also made sure that he and I were at different tables, but we texted constantly through dinner while we snuck looks across the marquee at one another. He sent me one to ask if Scarlett could have sat us any further apart and it wasn't until we were there, right in the middle of it, that I realised what we were doing, that we were crossing a line. Into what, I didn't know, but after dinner, when the band started playing, I wanted him to take a rose out of one of the centrepieces and ask me to dance. But I knew he wouldn't – couldn't – because then everyone would know that we were, what? I didn't know. Until I did, it was probably best not to dance in front of everyone at Crofton. It would cause so much drama, Molly would faint with joy.

So I settled for dancing with Scarlett instead, who was as drunk as I was (mulled wine and champagne are a lethal combination, it seems) and kept pulling me into photos, her cheekbone digging into mine, like old times. Everyone was having such a good time. Headmaster Ballard's wife danced so much that her hair started coming out of her bun and, when Edith tossed the bouquet, Hannah and Madame Girard collided in their haste to catch it.

I should have known it wouldn't last, though, because an hour or so later, while Mr Lucas and Hannah were showing me how to do the dance to the 'Birdy Song', Dominic joined in. I'd been having so much fun – laughing and almost falling over so many times, that Mr Lucas had to prop me up (which, with hindsight, probably wasn't a good idea given that I was still trying to convince Hannah that I was a serious journalist) – that when Hannah headed off the dance floor, I hesitated. I glanced towards the bar at Molly, who was on tiptoes, her nose in the air as she watched us, when all of a sudden, Scarlett was there.

I heard him calling after us as she tugged me away, but it still didn't register that she was pissed. I thought she wanted to take another photo and waited for her to sling her arm around my shoulders and tell me to smile, but then I felt her nails digging into my arm as she led me into the corner of the marquee, near the table of cupcakes.

When she stopped, she spun around to face me, her dark hair a whir. 'Are you really doing this here?' she hissed and I knew then that she was livid. I'd never seen her like that, so when she took a step towards me, I held my breath. 'You're dancing with him *here*? At my sister's wedding? In front of everyone?'

'Scarlett—'

She wouldn't let me finish and I could see her shaking, her chin trembling as she shook her head. 'Why are you doing this to me?'

'Can we not do this now?' I pleaded, looking around the marquee at half our classmates and teachers milling around. I had no idea where Molly was, but I knew everyone would be talking about this before Edith and Nishad had cut the cake.

'*You're* the one doing it now.'

'Scarlett—'

'You know we're together.'

263

My heart stopped. 'No you're not.'

They weren't. I knew they had a history, but he told me that they hadn't been near each other in months (not like *that*, anyway) and he wouldn't lie. He wouldn't.

'You need to choose, Adamma,' she snapped, and when she changed the subject, I knew that she was lying.

My shoulders fell. 'Choose?'

I stared at her, but before she could respond, I saw her cheeks go red and turned around as Mr Lucas and Hannah emerged from behind the cake stand. My cheeks burned, too, my hands fisting in the skirt of my dress as I fought the urge to hide under the table.

'We were just,' Hannah murmured, holding up a cupcake, then glancing at Mr Lucas, who looked equally embarrassed.

'Excuse us,' he said with a tight smile, and when he led her away, I wanted to die, my blood burning with shame.

'Oh God,' I breathed.

Of all the people to see us squabbling.

I tried to walk away, but Scarlett grabbed my arm again. 'Stop!' I snapped, shrugging her off, then lowering my voice. 'You're acting like a crazy person.'

'You need to choose.'

'Why?'

'Because I can't be friends with you if you're with him. I can't.'

'Stop being so melodramatic.'

'I'm being *real*, Adamma.' I rolled my eyes and when I turned away, she stepped in front of me. 'OK. Fine. We let him choose, but we both know that it'll kill our friendship so let's just shorthand this, OK? Him or me?'

'Jesus, Scarlett,' I said through my teeth. 'You don't even

want him, you just don't want anyone else to have him.' She shrugged as if to say *Yeah. So?* and I threw my hands up. 'How is that fair?'

'None of this is fair, Adamma. You can't compete. We've known each other for years. If I wanted him back, I could have him like *that*.'

Back.

I knew she was lying.

She clicked her fingers and if I wasn't willing to fight for him before, I was then. 'If you thought that for a second then you wouldn't be asking me to back off.'

She stared at me. I don't know if anyone's ever stood up to her before, but she looked at me as though I was a member of staff who'd just answered back. But then she caught herself and crossed her arms. 'How was the play?' she asked with a nasty smile. 'He told me it was boring.'

The blow landed, but I tried not to let it register because he told me that the night at the theatre was nothing; she'd said that she might go when he told her that his cousin was going to be in the play, but it was nothing more than that. So I just rolled my eyes at her again. It obviously wasn't the reaction she was hoping for, because she came at me again. 'You'll always be second best, Adamma.'

That was like a kick in the heart, but as soon as I considered grabbing a cupcake and smashing it in her face, I stopped myself and made myself take a breath.

'Stop it,' I said with a long sigh. 'Just stop it. This is ridiculous. We're supposed to be friends and you have me cornered, screaming at me about some guy.'

'Friends?' She barked out a laugh. 'I know you've been texting each other.'

I felt an itch of anger at that. 'So *that's* why you haven't been in touch.'

She huffed as if to say, *Not this again* and I could feel it coming. Building. I tried to swallow the words back, but I couldn't. I had to get them out.

'Why are you doing this? You don't even want him, Scarlett,' I told her again and I don't know why, whether it was because I really believed it or if I was just trying to make myself feel better. After all, I knew they weren't seeing each other now, but I thought they were that night at the theatre and I still let it happen.

'You don't know what I want,' she said, flicking her hair.

'Because you don't tell me anything!' *Stop*, a voice in my head roared as I took a step towards her. But I couldn't. 'Some friend! You don't tell me anything. You run away to New York and I don't hear about it until your sister calls. My father is shot and I don't even hear from you! You're not my friend!'

I shouldn't have said it – not there, not like that – but it just rushed out of me and she stared at me, too angry to respond, so I looked at the cupcakes, at the pink heart on each one. When she stopped to take a breath, I thought she might cry and say what a mess it was, ask what we should do, but she took a step back.

'We're done, Adamma.'

She walked away and I watched her go, the hem of her pale green bridesmaid's dress swishing back and forth and with that, I guess I chose him. He must have known, because a few minutes later, when I summoned the courage to go back to my table, I saw him on the other side of the marquee, the corners of his mouth curling into a slow smile. I felt something in me realign, not because I was right and Scarlett was wrong, but because I was right about him.

266

I didn't know until then how much I liked him. I liked the way he called me Miss Okomma. I liked the way he said it, how he didn't hesitate, didn't stumble, as though he'd practised it. I thought about it too much, about him too much; the space between each thought getting shorter and shorter until days became hours became minutes became heartbeats and then he was all I could think about.

I looked over at Scarlett, at the bar with Sam, a glass of champagne hanging from her fingers and something told me I was right, to hold on. Actually, it told me to let go, to forget about Scarlett and my parents and whether it was wrong or if we were doomed and just fall down, down, down because it was going to be amazing.

I loved him, I realised then, but it was a reaction, something I hadn't noticed until I was faced with the threat of losing him. I loved him and he didn't need to do anything. He didn't even need to love me back, I just did.

Can you be scared of your heart? I was scared of mine, scared that he might never love me back and I'd still love him. He could go – leave Crofton – and I'd still love him and what would I do? I've never felt anything like that before, that huge, ravenous love I've only read about in books. I guess he felt the same, because when I was walking back to Burnham, I found a note in my coat pocket. He didn't sign it, but I recognised his handwriting, his perfect Os and long, loose Ps, and when I read it, I had to stop and take a breath.

No one's ever picked me.

I turned and headed back to Scarlett's house, his note still in my fist, but halfway down the road, I saw him walking towards me. When he saw me, he stopped then started running, and I don't think I've ever run so hard. I thought my legs were about to give way, but a moment before they did, I felt his cold fingers on my face, then his mouth on mine as we collided in a kiss that made my feet leave the ground.

10 DAYS AFTER

MAY

I didn't move, because I couldn't. But that's me, isn't it? I'm either running or I'm too scared to move. I don't know how long I was sitting there, my back to a gravestone, the chill from the grass bleeding through my skirt. The sun was on my face, but I couldn't summon the strength to move it, then it wasn't, and the relief made me sigh.

'Miss Okomma,' Mr Lucas said and I lifted my eyelashes to find him standing over me in a black suit, his hands on his hips.

'You found me,' I muttered, and I was surprised, not because I'd found a particularly surreptitious hiding place, but because I didn't think he would look for me.

'Mrs Delaney has been looking for you everywhere.'

I brought my knees up to my chest and closed my eyes, letting my head fall back against the gravestone. 'Did you know that if an Igbo woman dies and she doesn't have a son, her body is thrown into a bush?'

'Excuse me?'

'If an Igbo woman dies, she is buried at the home of her son, but if she doesn't have a son, her body is thrown into a bush.'

'Come on, Miss Okomma. Let's go.'

I looked up at him with a frown. 'Doesn't that upset you? Knowing that in Nigeria, they'd just throw Scarlett in a bush?'

'I'm sure they wouldn't be so callous,' he said with an impatient sigh, and he sounded harassed, as though I was drunk and wouldn't get into the back of a cab. 'Besides, Scarlett isn't a woman, she's a *child*.'

Child.

The word dropped to the grass between us like a stone.

When he told me to *come along*, I didn't budge, I just stared at him, at his neat suit and neat shirt and neat hair and thought of the girls at Burnham, chins up and ponytails swinging as they walked through the village to the funeral, concealer caked to the dark patches under their eyes so that no one would know that they'd been crying. I couldn't be so cool, so *contained*. I wanted people to see it, to dance around, to embarrass people with it, make them look away. I wanted to be like Dominic, splashing my grief around like red paint.

'Come along?' I said, fresh tears burning the corners of my eyes.

'Please, Miss Okomma.' He held a hand out. 'We have to go to the cemetery.'

I turned my face away, playing with my necklace. 'Leave me alone.'

'Excuse me?'

'I said,' I raised my voice and looked at him again, '*Leave me alone.*'

He was a quiet for a moment, then said, 'Excuse me, Miss Okomma?'

'Excuse me, Miss Okomma?' I parroted, then rolled my eyes.

I could feel him staring at me, but I ignored him, clambering to my feet and brushing the grass from the back of my skirt with my hands. He took a step towards me, closing the gap between us, but I turned away and looked at the back of the church with my arms crossed so he wouldn't see the tears in my eyes.

I hoped he'd take the hint and leave me alone, but he sighed again. 'I know that you're upset about Scarlett, Miss Okomma,' he said and that was it.

'My name is Adamma!' I spun round to face him, a tear skidding down my cheek as I did. 'It's OK to say it, you know? Why do you always talk like someone from a Jane Austen novel?' I threw my head back and screamed at the sky. 'Jesus. Even Mrs Delaney calls me Adamma sometimes!'

When I looked at him again, I felt another hot tear roll off my jaw, but he was unmoved. He took a deep breath. 'As I said, I know that you're upset about Scarlett –'

'Upset? Scarlett was murdered! The question is: why aren't *you* upset?'

'Will you calm down? Of course I'm upset – everyone is – but I am still your teacher –' he looked nervously around – 'and this is beyond inappropriate, Miss Okomma.'

'Inappropriate?'

'*Calm down*,' he said through his teeth before I could say anything else, looking over my shoulder in the direction of the photographers. 'This isn't the time.'

'This isn't the time?' I laughed, quick and bitter. '*Her funeral* isn't the time?'

He didn't respond, just fussed over a piece of fluff on his jacket, and I lost it.

'I'm in pain! Is that too untidy for you? Is that inappropriate?' I took a step towards him. He took one back. 'I know everyone is being so strong and brave, but I'm not strong or brave and I

271

just need a minute where I don't have to pretend to be. So just let me cry and scream and say that I'm not OK and be a human being about it. I know you can. I've *seen* you be human. So just say something real.' I balled my hands into fists so that I wouldn't shove him. 'Say my name!'

'You want me to say something real?' he said, stepping forward and finally looking me in the eye and I saw it, at last, a flicker of emotion, the tiniest tug of annoyance at the corners of his eyes. 'You're behaving like a brat.' He leaned in, his brown eyes suddenly black. 'Today isn't about you. It's about burying Scarlett, so pull yourself together.'

'You told me not to tell the police,' I spat and I shouldn't have. As soon as I did, I wanted to take it back, like a child sweeping spilt marbles back into a jar.

He frowned. 'Excuse me?'

'I'm sorry.' I shook my head. 'I shouldn't have said that.'

'Well, you have, so go on. I assume you're referring to our conversation about your friend who was *attacked* in Savernake Forest.'

The way he said attacked made my nerves tighten. 'What does that mean?'

'It means that your friend is lying.'

Something kicked at me and I shook my head. 'No she isn't.'

'Yes, she is.'

'And how would *you* know?'

He sighed and put his hands on his hips. 'Because it was me.'

'What was you?'

'It was me who offered to give Chloe Poole a lift that night.'

I laughed. I don't know why, it wasn't funny, but I guess the thought of it was so ridiculous that my body rejected it and I laughed. 'No you didn't.'

He licked his lips and lifted his chin defiantly.

'No.' I had to stop myself taking him by the lapels and shaking him. 'No.'

I waited for him to deny it – waited and waited – but when he didn't, I turned away from him and walked over to one of the gravestones, putting my hand on top of it to steady myself as I felt each of the bones in my legs turn to dust.

'No,' I said again, but then I thought of his car – a dark blue Triumph Stag with its wind-down windows that might look like something James Bond would drive in the dark – and something in me came undone. 'No.'

'I didn't lay a finger on her,' I heard him say, and I wanted to cover my ears with my hands. I couldn't listen. I couldn't listen to any more.

'No.'

'Listen to me,' he took me by the arm and spun me around to face him.

'No.'

'Listen. All of this is Chinese whispers so just listen to what happened.' I tried to wriggle away, but he wouldn't let me, his fingers digging in so hard it hurt, even through my blazer. 'I didn't see her in the forest, it was on the road. I went out for supper with friends and when I was driving past on my way back to Crofton, I saw her staggering out, too drunk to walk, and I stopped, but she wouldn't get in.'

'Let go.'

'That's all that happened.' He shook me so hard it felt like my bones rattled. 'I watched her stumble back to Crofton like a newborn foal, and when I was content that she'd made it back safely without falling into a ditch, I carried on.'

'Let go,' I hissed, finally pulling away, but as I did, I staggered

273

back and fell against a gravestone, yelping as it struck my hip. He reached for me, but I put my arm out. 'Don't!'

He looked horrified. 'What is wrong with you?'

'Olivia thinks it was Dominic, but it was you!' I covered my hands with my mouth.

'I'd choose your next words very carefully, Miss Okomma.'

He said it slowly, *deliberately* – Miss Okomma – and I registered the threat, my scalp shivering, but I couldn't stop. 'It was you. You raped Orla.'

'Orla? What does she have to do with this?'

I shouldn't have said it, but it didn't matter, I'd tell her and she'd tell Bones. But then he realised what I was saying – that she was the other girl I'd told him about – and he grabbed my arm again. 'Are you insane?' It was already tender from the last time and the shock of it, of the flare of his nostrils and his breath against my cheek as he pulled me to him, made my stomach turn. 'I didn't touch her, *either* of them.'

'I don't believe you.' And I didn't; but when I thought of him, tripping over his laces in class and making lame Shakespeare jokes, and being so gentle with me the morning he drove me to the airport in the snow, the thought was so absurd that I recoiled from it as though it was a foul smell.

'Why not?' He suddenly looked inconsolable. 'It's me, Adamma.'

'Molly told me!' I roared, and I don't know where it came from, this blast of anger that made my jaw judder. I guess it scared him, too, because he let go of my arm. 'She told me that Orla was in love with you,' I said more calmly, even though I wasn't at all calm. 'I thought she was making it up, but she wasn't, was she?'

'So you're believing Molly Avery now?'

274

'You're too smart.' I jabbed at my temple with my finger. 'You wouldn't have offered Chloe a ride unless you wanted her to get into your car. No male teacher in his *right mind* would offer a girl a ride, especially at night.'

'You didn't see the state of her. She could barely walk.'

'There were Crofton kids *everywhere* that night. If anyone had seen Chloe getting into your car you would have been fired before you pulled into the car park.'

'I didn't think!'

When I saw his cheeks flush, I remembered the story he'd told me, the one about his friend Charlotte who was raped when she walked home after a party, and it made sense, so I should have softened, but it made me more mad. I could feel my cellphone ringing in my pocket again, but I ignored it.

'Why didn't you tell me? You told me about Charlotte. I would have believed you.'

'I didn't know that. I hardly knew you then.' He took a step forward and when he saw me back into the gravestone, he stopped. 'I was scared. All I did was offer a girl a lift back to her boarding house and by Monday I'd raped her.'

'I told the police. They've been looking for a man in the forest.'

'Exactly.' He looked at the photographers again. 'I couldn't have my name attached to that rumour. What if I was arrested? Stuff like that sticks. Even if it wasn't true, I'd still be known as the teacher who raped a student. I'd never work again.' He leaned in, suddenly too close, his chest almost touching mine. 'If I lose this job, I lose everything. My home, my book deal, my reputation. What am I going to do then? Go back to Sheffield and become a mechanic like my dad? Have three kids by three different women like everyone else I used to go to school with?

275

I have worked too long and too hard to lose everything for a stupid rumour.'

'And you'd do anything to protect yourself, right?'

'What's that supposed to mean?'

'Dominic's car was impounded because a car that "kind of" looks like his was seen in the forest on Sunday afternoon and your car "kind of" looks like his.'

He didn't smile, but he didn't flinch, either. 'Say it if you're going to say it.'

'Did you do it?' I asked and I don't know how my voice sounded so steady because his nose was almost touching mine, his eyes beetle black, and it made everything in me *shake*. 'Did you hurt her?'

I didn't have to say her name, he knew.

My heart was beating so hard that he must have been able to feel how scared I was, to feel the rise and fall of my chest as I struggled to catch my breath, but when he took a step back, I still lifted my chin and looked at him, right in the eye. He walked away and when he did, I thought I might collapse into a boneless heap on the grass, between the gravestones, but I had to find Orla. When I got to the front of the church, everyone was still outside waiting for the cars to take them to the cemetery. Then I saw her and ran, down the path and into the road, forgetting about the photographers as I saw her walking away by herself, her head down and her arms crossed.

I ran towards her, calling her name and she stopped.

'Adamma,' she said with a sob, wiping her cheeks with the heel of her palm. 'I've been trying to call you. Where've you been?'

'I'm sorry,' I started to say, assuming that she was upset about the funeral, but when I saw her shoulders shudder, I realised that it was more. 'What's wrong?'

'I remembered,' she said with a heave and a sob.

'What? When?'

'Just now, in the church. It came from nowhere, like you said. He went to hug me and –' Another sob broke out of her and I waited for her to catch her breath. 'When I couldn't get hold of you, I called Lisa and she told me her husband was working here,' she nodded towards the police station, 'on Scarlett's case.'

'You're going to tell the police?' And I couldn't believe it, my heart stuttering with relief as I hooked my arm through hers. 'Come on. I'll go with you.'

'But what about the funeral? Don't you want to go to the cemetery?'

'Scarlett has the whole village with her. You shouldn't be on your own.'

'Thanks.' She smiled weakly. 'I just feel so stupid.'

'Why?'

'I thought it was some pervert.' She shrugged, eyelashes batting stickily.

When Orla put her hand to her stomach, I knew what she was thinking: that knowing who did it was worse, that he'd seen her every day – in class, walking down the stairs, hugging a folder to her chest – and he knew what he'd done. He must have noticed that she'd stopped wearing make-up, that she'd let her blond bangs grow out so that when they fell forward, they covered most of her face. He must have noticed and he didn't say a word. He was disgusting.

Worse than disgusting.

'I can't.' She stopped suddenly, looking up the road at the police station then put her hands up. 'I know what you're going to say, Adamma, but I can't.'

'Orla—'

'What if I—' she interrupted, then stopped to cover her mouth with her hand as she let out another hiccup of a sob.

I knew what she was getting at and shook my head at her. 'You didn't.'

She took her hand away from her mouth and pressed it to her forehead. 'He knew that I wanted to wait, but I was so drunk. What if I told him we could?'

That threw me, my heart spinning, like a weathervane in a sudden gust of wind. Molly was right – there *was* something going on between Orla and Mr Lucas – and I'll admit to feeling a stab of betrayal, even though I had no right to. Orla and I barely spoke before she admitted what happened to her that night. I'm the one who's been lying to her for the last five months.

'That doesn't matter, Orla,' I said and I wonder if she heard it, the sudden hardness in my voice as I tried to compensate for the shiver of shame. 'Knowing who did it, doesn't change a damn thing. He still hurt you, he still took advantage of you.'

'But there's no way I can prove I said no, is there? He'll just say I didn't. And even if I could, the police won't be able to do anything now. It's been *months*.'

She turned and started walking back in the direction of the village and I knew she was right, but I felt a surge of anger at how resigned she was to it. It wasn't fair.

It wasn't fair.

I caught up with her and stepped in front of her.

She stopped, then crossed her arms. 'I know what you're going to say and *don't*,' she warned, her brow tightening. 'I'm not putting myself through that for nothing. I'm not going to sit there while the police ask me how much I had to drink

278

and what I was wearing so they can tell me there's nothing they can do.'

'But what if he does it to someone else?'

'I said *don't*,' she barked. 'I can't, Adamma. If I tell the police it'll be my word against his and if the police believe him, then it will have been for nothing. Everyone would know – my friends, my dad, Molly *bloody* Avery – and I'll have to see him every day and—'

'It's OK.' I rubbed her arms as she started sobbing again. 'I'm sorry.' I waited for her breathing to settle then said, 'Why don't we tell Mrs Delaney? She won't tell anyone.'

She looked confused. 'Mrs Delaney?'

'I don't know. Maybe she can tell Ballard what happened, find a way to get him fired without anyone finding out why. I'm sure Ballard will be more than happy to make all of this go away as quickly and quietly as possible.'

'Fired?'

'Don't worry about that. This is his fault. He should have thought about that.'

'Fired from *what*? Sam doesn't have a job.'

I stepped back and stared at her. 'Sam?'

'Yeah. Who did you think I was talking about?'

'But Sam couldn't have murdered Scarlett.'

'He wouldn't!' she said with a fierce frown, then caught herself. She looked mortified and I wanted to hug her, tell her that I got it – she'd loved him, it was an instinct to defend him – but she wouldn't look at me. 'Look. I don't know what Sam's capable of any more, but his arm's in a sling so, and I can't believe I'm saying these words,' she shook her head, 'he can't have murdered Scarlett. Unless he strangled her with one hand.'

She was right and with that, everything in my head dislodged and ended up in a different place. All that remained was one question that circled my skull like a fly:

So who did?

104 DAYS BEFORE

FEBRUARY

You know how Charles Dickens said that it was the best of times, it was the worst of times? Well, it's been the best six weeks of my life, and the worst. The worst because I was sure that after what happened at Edith's wedding, everyone would side with Scarlett and I would be the bitch who threw away her best friend for a boy. But when I got back to Crofton in the new year, girls – not all of them, but some, more than I expected – began to gather at my end of the table in the dining hall. The next day there were a few more and the day after that a few more and, by the end of the week – when she made a nasty quip about me in class and not everyone laughed – I began to realise that Scarlett was more infamous than popular.

'The queen is dead,' Molly said, breathless with awe, the first time we watched her walk across the Green to have lunch on her own. It made sense, I suppose. She's been at Crofton since she was eleven and I was the only person she hung around with regularly, the only one she spent exeat weekends with, the only one who went to her house for dinner. She must have had friends before me. I keep thinking about the story Orla told me, how she ran away to Glastonbury with Dominic last summer.

Was there another girl, like me, who didn't hear about it until Olivia called? Who had no idea they were seeing each other? Every time a girl smiles at me in the corridor at school or asks if she can sit with me at lunch, I wonder if it's her. If I'm just one in a long line of Scarlett's best friends.

That's not to say that what happened at Edith's wedding wasn't a scandal, because it was. Our fight is all people have talked about and everyone seems to be divided into two camps: the ones who don't get why Scarlett flipped out and the ones who think I let a boy come between us. There seem to be more in the former than the latter, which is flattering, of course, but that doesn't mean I'm enjoying it. I'm not like her, I don't have to be the prettiest girl in the room. And I don't like being talked about; I'd rather people knew my name because I'm nice or because of the stuff I write for the *Disraeli*, not because I fell out with her. Mind you, as high school indiscretions go, I suppose I got off pretty easily.

But as awkward and embarrassing as it's been, it's still been the best six weeks of my life. It's been almost impossible to be discreet with everyone watching, but we've seen each other as much as we can. I catch myself smiling sometimes and I can't stop.

I'm the one who suggested we hide it and I think that surprised him. He says that I'm not like the other girls at school, that I'm mature. Maybe I am because it's more than not wanting my parents to find out; I don't want to hurt her, either.

I think all of this has kind of forced me to grow up. My father being shot put a lot of things into perspective. I know now what I should hold on to, and what I should let go of. But I didn't used to be like that, before I started at Crofton, before I met him. I used to think that the number of photographs that I was in with other people was a measure of how popular I was, and I'd fret if I wasn't invited to a party. Looking back on it now, I'm almost embarrassed by how much those things used to upset me. I thought it was hilarious when Jumoke would plot the demise of a girl who'd kissed a boy I liked. We'd spend hours and hours discussing it, wallowing in the drama of it until we were lightheaded. But when I'm with him, I don't even think about those things. All I think about is him, about the shape of his mouth and the lines on his palms, comparing them to my own and pressing my hand to his so our love lines touch.

It wasn't like that with Nathan. We didn't sneak around, I didn't skip swimming practice to linger in the backseat of his car, my fingers curled around his tie. Nathan and I went on dates. We'd miss movies because we were kissing so much and eat dinner at restaurants he could walk me home from that weren't two villages away where no one knew us. I could have photos of us on my phone and could tell him that I loved him and not care if anyone heard. And he'd give me gifts: perfume for my birthday and jewellery on Valentine's Day and flowers every Friday. I'd come out of school with my friends to find him leaning against a town car in his St Luke's uniform, a huge bunch of roses in his hand. He could have waited until we were alone, but I would feel a sweet thrill when he told me that he loved me in front of my friends and they gushed, saying that he was the perfect boyfriend.

It was as if it didn't count if they weren't there to see it.

I didn't love Nathan, though. It was as though we were playing house – playing at love. We did everything couples did, but I didn't feel anything for him. That isn't fair actually; I did, but it wasn't love. It wasn't that bone-deep ache that I feel for him when I'm alone in bed, counting the hours until I see him again. I can't lie though, I'm surprised I don't miss it, I never thought that sharing a cupcake he'd sneaked out of the dining room or getting a tatty copy of *Love in the Time of Cholera* that he'd found in a second-hand bookshop would be enough. *More*, even, because he didn't just walk into Chanel and point at a purse like Nathan did, he'd remembered it was my favourite book and inside he'd written it again – *No one's ever picked me* – and *that's* love, I know, those secret moments that are ours, that aren't diluted because I've shared them with everyone else.

It's overwhelming and excruciating, all at once. I can't call him when I want to, can't kiss him when I want to. But it makes things so *intense*. I've had to learn to be patient, to wait, something I'm not very good at, I admit. I can't just throw my feelings around like I used to. I have to hold on to them, save them for him. It's unbearable. I used to spend almost every moment with Nathan, but some days I only see him for an hour. Some days it's just a few minutes during lunch or between classes. If I didn't see Nathan for a few hours, I didn't notice, whereas if I don't see him, it's like I'm *starving*. When I finally see him, I'm shaking, my heart ready to burst, and when he reaches for me, the relief brings tears to my eyes. And when we're together it isn't like it was with Nathan, all sweaty and awkward and unsure. He doesn't keep asking me if I'm OK, and when he touches me, it isn't with wide-eyed curiosity, he knows what's going to happen, even if I don't and oh, it's magnificent.

It's an impossible thing, to control yourself when everything you feel is wild, when you feel untethered. But there's a thrill to it, too, to sneaking around. I'll be kissing him, hands curled around the tops of his arms, tight enough to leave bruises, and ten minutes later we'll pass one another on the way to class without a glance. I'll feel a rush of excitement when we pass, especially when he can't stop himself and his gaze flicks to mine. That moment of weakness is as delicious as any kiss and knowing that I can do that to him, that I can make him lose control like that – if just for a second – makes me feel like I can do anything.

But as frustrating as it is at times, I love how fiercely protective of us he is, as though he and I are a baby bird he has to keep cupped in his hands, too fragile to trust anyone with. There's a thrill to that, too, to how close he holds me sometimes, hearing him breathe *mine* between kisses. He isn't as worried about what she'll do as I am, but I think he's scared that if people know, they'll try to warn me off him, tell me that he's no good. I guess I'm scared about that too, because I haven't told Orla or Jumoke and I tell them *everything*. I don't know why. Maybe it's because I know what they're going to say, that he'll never be the boyfriend I need him to be, that my parents will go nuts, that once the initial excitement of hiding it has passed, he'll get bored and move on.

But it's been six weeks and the joy of seeing him hasn't dampened. We were in touch constantly over the holidays, knocking so many text messages back and forth that my cellphone provider cut me off, convinced that my phone had been stolen. My parents will kill me dead when they get the bill.

This morning, he told me to skip breakfast and meet him behind the library before assembly. It had been snowing all night, so I heard him before I saw him – heard the crunch of his shoes – and my heart leapt into my throat at the thought that it might be someone else. How would I explain why I was lurking behind the library at 7 a.m.? As often as Mrs Delaney

285

encourages us to get fresh air, it was hardly the weather to be languishing outside. But then I saw him. He smiled loosely when he saw me and I had to resist the urge to fly at him. I told myself to stay still, to let him come to me, and when he did, I couldn't resist filling in the last few steps.

It probably sounds cheesy, but Crofton has never looked so beautiful. It's been snowing on and off since the day my father was shot. Not fiercely, but just enough to keep the ground covered and ensure that there was a white Christmas for the first time in years, even if I wasn't there to see it. Everything is perfect, like a holiday card, the green lawns white, the trees drooping under the weight of the snow. The old buildings look like gingerbread houses, their pitched roofs dusted white and their crooked lead windows glittering with frost.

It was so cold that my breath puffed out of me in a great cloud. His did too, so I knew he was struggling to catch his breath as well and it made my heart beat harder. We stood so close that the tips of our shoes were touching, his hands fisted in the back of my coat, mine clinging to the lapels of his. I saw his cheeks get pinker as it started snowing again. We looked up at the sky with a giggle and when I looked at him again, he had snow in his eyelashes. I reached for his hand, but before I could thread my fingers through his, he pulled his away. My heart shuddered to a halt, sure that I'd done something wrong, that I'd misunderstood something, but then he began to tug off my leather glove. When he had done so, he tucked it into the pocket of his coat and reached for my hand again. His fingers were cold and the shock of them against my warm ones made me gasp.

I'm lucky, I know, to see that side of him. I'm sure everyone sees him at Crofton, and doesn't think him capable of such vulnerability. They've never seen that side of him. Never seen him blush. Never seen his hands stutter. They don't know that sometimes, after we've kissed, he's too shy to speak or that he leaves me notes, like the one he left in my coat pocket at Edith's wedding. He hides them between the mail in my pigeonhole or drops them into my open bag as he passes my desk in class. It's kind of old-fashioned, I suppose; he could send an email or a text, but there's a romance to it, to finding one and unfolding it to see the slant of his handwriting, his perfect Os and long, loose Ps.

It's nothing I've felt before. It's changed me, as though my heart has shed its skin and it's all red and tender and new again. I'm nervous around him, as though we've just met. When he calls, I stumble over my words and the last time we kissed, my hands were shaking so much I had to ask him to stop. 'They're supposed to shake,' he told me with a slow smile before he kissed me again.

There's something between us, something I hadn't noticed until right now, as I'm thinking about it. A thread that I only feel when he moves away from me. Whenever he does, I feel a tug in my stomach. I watch him walking away sometimes and I feel it tug and tug until he's so far away from me that the ache is unbearable. I miss him. Even when I'm with him, I miss him. It's as though I can't let myself be with him, because I know that in a few minutes he'll be gone. I don't know when it happened, but *want* became *need* and I find myself brushing past him in the corridor at Crofton sometimes, just for a second, just so I can feel the heat of him next to me. Sometimes, he gives into it too, allowing his fingers to brush against my knuckles while everyone sweeps past us on the way to their next class oblivious that we've even touched as I continue on, my legs weaker.

I wonder sometimes if we still need to be so careful. Some girl just bought a pregnancy test from the chemist in the village, so no one's even talking about me anymore. But I kind of love the melodrama of it: the lying, the hiding. I devour the desperate text messages he sends, begging me to skip class and see him. And I love knowing things about him, secret things no one else knows. His fear of heights, the three moles on his back, the milk-white scar on his knee from when he fell off his bike when he was six. I've never known anyone like that, known their skin, recognised the curve of their mouth, even with my eyes closed. And no one has ever known me like that. I never cried in front of Nathan, never spent an afternoon with him giggling as he tried to count my eyelashes with the tip of his finger.

I don't think I ever even memorised Nathan's cellphone number, but I know his. He bought me another cellphone, one of those disposable ones, one just for us, so we can keep in touch without worrying. I thought it was a little much when he gave it to me, but he told me to pretend we were spies. I enjoy that, too, keeping the phone hidden in my tuck box and charging into my room at lunch to check it. The rush of it is almost too much, knowing that every voicemail is from him, every text message. So while we don't have a relationship like the other couples at Crofton, we don't eat lunch together in the dining hall, don't hold hands on the way to class, we have *that*, and it's just as exciting. It's too much, yet not enough, all at once.

He was right to be paranoid, though, because, last night, Scarlett stole my phone – not the disposable one, my other one, the one that everyone knows about – while we were at Sam's seventeenth birthday party. I thought her 'accidentally bumping' into me was an attempt to spill her drink on my shoes, but when I felt her hand linger on my waist a moment longer than was necessary, I pulled away. By the time I checked the pocket of my tuxedo jacket and realised what she'd done, she was heading out of the kitchen and I chased after her.

'What do you want back, Adamma?' she asked with a smirk. 'Your dignity?'

I told her to go to hell and stormed out, out of the house and down Sam's driveway. I didn't care that she had the phone – it had nothing on it – so she could have it, I just wanted it to stop. I wanted to know when it would stop.

So I walked and walked, drunk and directionless, my cheeks burning despite the chill. I don't know how I didn't slip in the snow, especially in heels, but I passed the pub in the village as DS Bone ambled out with a friend.

'You!' I pointed at him, shaking with rage. 'I need to report a crime.'

He and his friend stopped and looked at one another, then DS Bone turned to me, clearly trying not to smile. 'Hey, Buffy.'

'My cellphone has been stolen!'

'Your phone?' He grabbed his friend's arm. 'Does the Commissioner know?'

'Don't make fun of me, Bones,' I said, and we blinked at each other.

I didn't mean to say it, I was trying to say DS Bone, but it came out as Bones.

I thought he'd be pissed off, but he seemed amused. '*Bones*? I didn't peg you as a *Star Trek* fan, Adamma.'

'*Star Trek*? Ew. No!' I stared at him, horrified. 'Bones, like the television show,' I lied, trying to come up with an explanation other than, *I'm too pissed to speak properly*. 'You know, because you're, like, a cop.'

'That is true.' He nodded. 'I am like a cop.'

'Exactly!' I pointed at him again. 'And a crime has occurred!'

'OK,' he laughed, shaking his head. 'It's freezing. Let's get you home.'

'Via the police station?'

'Yes. Yes,' he said, waving goodbye to his friend, who walked away chuckling, saying that he'd see him on Sunday.

'Why are you here?' I asked as we continued down the road.

'I was having a drink with Bomber.'

'Bomber? That isn't a name. Why is he called Bomber?'

He stopped and looked at me, gaze narrowing at my knee-length dress and heels. 'How do you not have hypothermia?'

'What do you mean?'

'The snow.' He waved his arms around. 'How much have you had to drink?'

'I am not drink.' I stared at him, then corrected myself. 'Drunk.'

'You're, like, totally drink, Adamma. And in front of a policeman.' He tutted and shook his head. 'But I will let the fact that you're only sixteen go because you actually sound like a teenager for once instead of a Crofton clone.'

He carried on walking and I followed him until he stopped in front of his car.

'Oh God.' I stopped and stared at it. I'd forgotten about his car. Even glittering with frost, it was still the ugliest thing I'd ever seen.

'What?'

'What possessed you to buy this thing?'

'Poverty.'

'Do you know it's green?' I asked as he walked around to the driver's side.

He stroked the roof before he opened the door. 'It's the *Green Hornet.*'

'What's a green hornet?'

He looked appalled. 'Do they teach you nothing at that school?'

I glared back. 'I can name each of the bones in your hand.'

'That's useful.'

'You know what else is useful: knowing that this car is Kermit green.'

He pointed at me over the roof. 'Don't even. It's the *Green Hornet.*'

'Don't listen to him, Kermy,' I whispered, stroking the roof.

'Get in the car, Adamma.'

When I did, I frowned. 'Ew. It smells like a bus.'

'What do buses smell like?'

'McDonald's and defeat.'

'Sounds about right,' he mumbled, starting the engine.

He waited for me to put on my seat belt, but I couldn't. 'It's broken,' I told him, with a huff, tugging at it. 'Your seat belt is broken.'

'You can name all the bones in my bloody hand,' he muttered, taking it from me and clicking it in. 'But you can't put on your bloody seat belt.'

'Whatever,' I said, rolling my eyes. I could see my breath and stopped to wonder why I couldn't feel the cold before realising that my hangover was going to be epic. 'So, about my phone,' I went on, as he pulled away from the kerb. 'I know exactly who took it. Scarlett Chiltern. She lives in Langfield House, if you'd like to arrest her.'

'Your friend Scarlett? The one you called me about last year? The who ran away?'

I wish he didn't have to remember *everything*. 'She isn't my friend.'

He nodded. 'What's his name?'

'Whose name?'

'The boy you're fighting over.'

I crossed my arms, furious. 'Of course we have to be fighting over a boy.'

'Look how drink you are. Only love makes you drink like that.'

'I am not drink!' I slapped the dashboard. 'Dammit! *Drunk!*'

'Of course not.'

'And if I am, it's because Scarlett has driven me to it with her batshitness.' I jabbed at my temple with my finger. 'Bones, you don't even know. One minute she's screaming at me, the next she's crying her eyes out. I can't keep up.'

'I know, right? Overemotional teenage girls are, like, totes annoying.'

My gaze narrowed. 'I fear that you're not taking me seriously, Bones.'

He winked at me, then pulled into the long tree-lined road that leads to Crofton. I pointed towards Burnham and when he pulled up outside, he tilted his head at me. 'Do you need help with your seat belt again, Adamma?'

I pressed the button so hard, I broke my nail and he laughed.

'Do you need a plaster?' he asked as I inspected it.

I scowled at him. 'I know what you think of me.'

'You do?'

'Yes. I know everything,' I reminded him, crossing my arms. 'You think I'm another bratty Crofton kid who doesn't give a shit about anyone but herself.'

'Oh yeah?' He nodded. 'How's your friend?'

I sobered a little at the thought of Orla, the memory of what happened to her fading a little each day. I hoped it was fading for her too, but then I remembered how I'd pestered her to tears to go to the party with me and realised that it wasn't.

'Have you heard anything?' I asked, but I knew full well he hadn't. When he shook his head, something in me relaxed and it felt like a betrayal, but as much as I wanted the asshole caught, at least it meant that it hadn't happened to anyone else.

'She's doing better,' I told him with a sigh. 'Your wife was great with her, but she wouldn't speak to the counsellor at Crofton, in the end, because she was scared her parents would find out, but I got her to talk to one of my mother's friends.'

'Is she a psychotherapist?'

'Yeah. She comes up from London and they meet every two weeks at a café in Marlborough. You know the one by the town hall?'

He nodded. 'Did you tell your parents why she needed to see a counsellor?'

'They didn't ask.'

'Must be a bit spendy, though.'

I shrugged. 'My father says it's only money.'

He turned his head to look at me with a smile. 'See? You're such a brat.'

Before I could smile back, there was a knock on the window and we jumped. I won't say that Bones jumped like a girl, but it was a bit girlish. He wound down his window to find Mrs Delaney arching an eyebrow at him and I cursed myself. The vodka had made me stupid and I had forgotten to tell him to drop me around the back so that I could sneak back into Burnham.

'And you are?'

He couldn't get his ID out of his pocket quick enough. 'DS Bone.'

The eyebrow was aimed at me then. 'Care to explain, Miss Okomma?'

'Scarlett Chiltern stole my phone,' I blurted out, hands balled into fists.

She rolled her eyes. 'Get inside. Now.'

11 DAYS AFTER

MAY

Doubt is like rust, once it takes root, it grows, gathering speed until it infects everything it touches. You can file it away, cover it up, but it never goes away, not really. It's still there, still looking for a way out from under all those layers of paint. It makes you hear things differently, remember things differently, and I let it in yesterday, at Scarlett's funeral. I doubted him and I shouldn't have and now he's doubting me because I must have texted him a dozen times to apologise, but he hasn't replied.

My instinct was to call Bones. Orla made me promise that I wouldn't tell him about Sam, so I just said that she'd remembered who did it and when he pressed me for a name, I told him to forget about the man in the forest. He wasn't pissed off, but he didn't sound surprised, either, and it made me feel like a fool. I thought I was being so brave – so *helpful* – the afternoon I charged into the pub to tell him about Orla. I actually thought I was doing the right thing, that he should know about the man in the car, but now I feel like a silly schoolgirl, yapping at him and wasting his time while he tried to do his job. So I stopped there, closing my notebook on what I'd been scribbling since

I'd got back to my room. I'm sure he would have listened, but I've already done enough and I'm not saying another word until I know something for sure and right now I have nothing.

There may be no man in a car trawling Savernake Forest for Crofton girls, but everyone still thinks that there's someone there. That's what I hear whispered at school – in the showers or in the queue for the salad bar in the dining hall – that there's someone in the forest, some mad man who strangled Scarlett. And I get that, I get that everyone wants this to be a passing evil. No one wants to think that they know the guy, that they might have sat next to him at Mass on a Sunday or that they wave at him when they see him in the village.

I do, too, but my mind keeps circling back to him and that's another thing I wanted to tell Bones, but didn't, that if it was his car someone saw driving through the forest the afternoon Scarlett was murdered, it's because he was meeting me. But then I think about the call he got, a few minutes after I heard The Old Dear chug by. *It's a coincidence*, I keep telling myself. But then another voice says, *What if it isn't?*

And what if it isn't?

Dominic wasn't in class this morning and I wasn't surprised, but I still felt sick every time I looked at his empty desk. It wasn't the only one, there were three others including Scarlett's, which sat like a hole in the middle of the classroom. I couldn't stop staring at it so when Mr Lucas walked in, my heart jumped up in my chest as though it had been sound asleep. I held my breath as I waited for him to look at me, but he didn't. He didn't look at anyone, just told us to open *District and Circle* and turn to 'The Blackbird of Glanmore'.

I thought that would be it, but he stopped me after class.

'Miss Okomma, a word, please,' he said as I passed his desk.

'Yes, Sir,' I breathed, my heart banging and banging.

I stopped and turned to face him, watching as he closed his books and slid them into his bag. 'Do you want me to close the door?'

'No.' He picked up his bag. 'Walk with me.'

'Yes, Sir.'

It was a struggle to keep up with him as he strode out of the classroom towards the stairs. The corridor was chaos as usual. Girls called out to one another as they ran down the wobbly wooden staircase to their next class, making it creak crankily, and when a guy crept up behind a girl, then grabbed her, making her shriek, I almost jumped clean out of my skin.

I followed Mr Lucas down the stairs and across the foyer, and when we stepped out into the sunshine, he led me around the fountain towards the path to Sadon Hall.

'I wanted to speak to you about yesterday,' he said tightly when we were far enough away from the cluttered courtyard, his chin in the air.

Panic burned through me like a fever. 'Oh God. I'm so sorry. I know it wasn't you. I can't believe I said that. I'm *mortified*. I'm sorry. I'm so sorry. I'm sorry,' I said all at once and I said it in such a rush that I don't know if he could even understand what I was saying, but I thought that if I said sorry in as many different ways as I could, I'd find the right one.

He waited for me to catch my breath. 'I thought about it a lot last night. I was very angry. I didn't know if I could see you today. I almost called Headmaster Ballard to ask him to take me off the Baccalaureate so I wouldn't have to teach you any more.'

'But—'

'May I finish?' he said tartly, stopping at the top of the path to Sadon Hall.

I stopped, too. 'Sorry.' I pressed my lips together.

'I was so angry, but I told myself to wait until I'd calmed down because this isn't like you, Miss Okomma. I know it isn't, which is why I was so astonished by your behaviour. But grief is a vicious thing.' He stopped, and when he went on, his voice sounded smaller. 'It sends people mad. And what happened to Scarlett was tragic. Utterly *tragic*.' He shook his head. 'But I haven't helped matters because I wasn't completely honest with you about my friend Charlotte.' He lifted his chin and I thought he was going to look at me, but he didn't. 'She wasn't my friend, Miss Okomma, she was my girlfriend, and I should have walked her home that evening, but I was drunk and selfish and stupid.'

His chin trembled and I wanted to touch it with my finger. 'You weren't to know.'

'Maybe not, but I still should have walked her home, Miss Okomma.' He pushed his shoulders back. 'She was murdered that night, Miss Okomma. I didn't tell you that because you were so upset about your friend and I didn't want to alarm you.'

I felt the edges of my heart weaken.

'I'm so sorry—' I started to say, but he wouldn't let me finish.

'I wasn't thinking clearly that evening with Chloe, I hope you understand why now. But I'm not sorry.' He shook his head. 'I'll never understand why it's better to leave a seventeen-year-old girl to stumble home on her own than be seen giving her a lift. Even so, I should have told you, I shouldn't have let you think that there was a madman trawling the forest for teenage girls, so I am as much to blame here. As ashamed as I

am to admit it, you're right, I lied to protect my reputation –
and my job here at Crofton – and for that I am very sorry.'

'It's OK. I shouldn't have—'

'Adamma, please,' he said with an impatient sigh. 'You do
realise that this is part of the problem, don't you? You don't
listen.'

My shoulders fell. 'My father tells me that all the time.'

'He's quite right,' he said, arching an eyebrow at me with a
small smile, and my shoulders relaxed. 'I would never want you
to change, Adamma. You're bright and funny and fearless and
that's what makes you so special, but you have to learn to think
before you speak. You complain that Scarlett was impatient,
but you can be as well, which is probably why you hated it so
much. What is it they say? The things we don't like in other
people are the things we really don't like in ourselves?' He
frowned at me. 'So I do believe that you're sorry, Adamma, but
sometimes you say things that you can't take back, no matter
how many times you say sorry.' I went to say something, but he
held up a hand. 'I'm leaving, Adamma.'

'No,' I interrupted with a sudden sob. 'Don't leave because
of me.'

'I'm not leaving because of you. It's a better job at a better
school.'

'But everyone loves you.'

'I think that may be the problem,' he admitted. 'That's all
I've ever wanted, to be the teacher everyone thought was cool,
but look where it's got me? Our conversation yesterday
reminded me that there's nothing here for me any more, Miss
Okomma. It's time to go.'

He took out a small notebook from the breast pocket of his
blazer and scribbled something down and that was it, I knew.

There was nothing more I could say. I'd already said too much. 'You're going to be late for philosophy. Take this to Mr Crane.'

He handed me the note and as I watched him walk down the path to Sadon Hall and close the door behind him, all I could think was, *What have I done?*

I didn't go to philosophy, so when Mrs Delaney found me in bed, my duvet over me, I thought she was going to tell me off, but she sat down and tugged it back. I waited for her to ask me if I was OK, if I was feeling unwell. Instead she tucked my hair behind my ear with a sigh.

'Can I get you a cup of tea, Adamma?'

'No thank you,' I mumbled, a little petulantly.

'Are your parents still staying at the Castle and Ball?' I nodded. 'It has a lovely restaurant. Why don't you have supper with them there this evening?'

'Thank you, Miss.' I sat up and hugged her so tightly she chuckled.

She rubbed my back with her hand. 'You can even drive there. Someone from the Mercedes garage is on his way with your car.'

'Really?'

'They'll be here any minute.'

'Thanks, Miss,' I said, kicking back the duvet and clambering out of bed.

She tutted, brushing at the sheet with her hand. 'You could have taken your shoes off, Miss Okomma.' She stood up and blinked at me. 'Oh dear. Sit down.'

'What?'

She nodded at the chair by my desk. 'Tuck your shirt in,' she said, when I sat down, then went over to the chest of drawers and picked up a hairbrush. When she came back, she tugged my hair out of its ponytail. I yelped as she began brushing it furiously and looked helplessly at my tub of grease, but before I could ask her to use some, she was done.

'Thanks, Miss,' I muttered, fingers fluttering over my stinging hairline.

She took me by the shoulders and turned me towards the door. 'Don't run,' she said as I bent down to grab my bag.

It must have been lunchtime, because the Green was a mess of sixth formers sprawling like sleepy cats in the sun. As soon as I got to the hill that led down to the car park, I saw my pretty silver car and it was such a relief because it meant that I had somewhere to sit that wasn't the Green or the dining hall, with everyone whispering around me.

I thought it was going to be relatively painless, that I'd sign something then I could sit in my car listening to Asa until I'd calmed down enough to head back into the breach, but when the guy handed me back the keys, he shook his head.

'You might want to tell the police that this wasn't a break in.'

I frowned at him. 'It wasn't?'

'Not unless a brick just happened to fall through the windscreen.'

'A brick?'

'Yeah. We found it while we were valeting. We found this too.' He reached into the breast pocket of his grubby blue overalls and held out a piece of carefully folded newspaper. When I saw what it was, my heart ached as though a song I hadn't heard for years had just come on to the radio: it was a paper ship.

'What's that?' I heard someone say and turned to find Bones behind me.

'Nothing,' I said, snatching it and taking the clipboard from the guy and signing where he told me to. 'What are you doing here, Bones?'

'I came to check on you after yesterday.'

'I'm fine,' I told him, thanking the guy as he handed back my keys.

I put the paper ship in my bag before Bones saw it and as I did, I stopped and stared at the contents – candy wrappers, tissues bruised with half-crescents of lipstick, a pear, its skin punctured by the teeth of my comb, a lidless blue biro that had left a knot of scribbles on the leather – and I didn't recognise it. It made me think of her, of the receipts stuck with gum to her notebooks. Then I thought of her room: the clothes in her laundry hamper that would never be washed, her dressing table with its cluster of perfume bottles. Her house must be so quiet. I guess it always will be. There will be no more slammed doors, no more running down the stairs. She'll never have another birthday; her father will never make another red velvet cake, will never have to make her chicken for Christmas dinner because she hates turkey.

I hadn't thought about it before then. I don't know why. Maybe I was in shock or maybe it was because I was with Orla so I didn't go to the cemetery to see her coffin being lowered into the ground, but until then it felt like she was just *gone*.

I knew then, when I felt that unreachable ache in my chest, that I didn't hate her. I might have said it, I might have thrown it at her when I was too angry to say anything else, but I didn't mean it. Even when she was screaming at me, even when I was delirious with anger, I always thought that someday it would

302

pass and we'd be friends again. I'd have flashes of us, ten years from now, bumping into each other at an airport. We'd hug and laugh about how silly we were. *All of that for a boy*, she'd say, her blue eyes bright. And I'd lie and say, *I know! What was his name again?* But I'm never going to see her again. She'll never forgive me. I will always be the girl who broke her heart. The shame is in my blood now, my marrow. It will never go away. And for what?

All of that for a boy.

I could feel Bones staring at me and shook my head. 'I'm fine.'

'That's two fines.'

I wiped a tear away with the cuff of my shirt, and I hate that he makes me feel like that, like a snotty kid. 'Because it is.'

'It will be. It doesn't feel like it now, but it will.'

'I have to go.'

I wonder if he knew that I didn't believe him, because he called out my name, but I didn't stop, not until I got to the courtyard, when I had to stand by the fountain and take a breath. I stared at it for a few moments, watching the water bubble out the spout and down each of the moss-mottled tiers, like plates on a cake stand, to settle in the basin that was lined with pennies that sparkled in the sun. I stuck my hand out, letting the cold water trip off my fingers and when I saw a small green leaf floating in one of the tiers, I remembered Scarlett's ship and opened my bag.

I shook the water off my hand before I unfolded it, my breath catching in my throat as I peeled back each layer of newspaper to find two words written in red pen:

I WIN

I almost dropped it, the corners of the pages shivering in a sudden breeze as I made myself hold on to it a little tighter, my fingers leaving creases in the paper.

I WIN.

I read the words over and over. *I WIN. I WIN. I WIN.* And there it was again – doubt – but it wasn't slow, *uneasy*, like it was when DS Hanlon showed me the top-up card the police had found in Scarlett's room. It wasn't even like it was yesterday in the graveyard – that creepcreepcreep of dread that I'd tried to ignore and couldn't – it was clear as a bell, ringing long and loud, in my ears, in my bones.

Then I was walking around the fountain and down the path, the note fluttering furiously as I began to walk faster and faster. We're not supposed to go into each other's houses, but we all do, of course. It's for insurance reasons, I think, but it's not something the housemasters and -mistresses enforce with any real vigour, so I've been in her house so many times while she dropped off a text book that was too heavy to lug around or when she'd forgotten an essay, that I knew exactly where the lockers were and I knew which one was hers.

If there's one thing I've learned from her, it's that if I want people to think I belong somewhere, I've got to believe that I belong there first. So I marched towards Rutland House as though I owned it. I only hesitated when I got to her locker. I knew the police had searched it, so I wasn't sure it would still be there and I half expected to find a break in the neat row of lockers – like a bullet hole – but it looked the same, an S painted in the top right-hand corner in red nail polish that she'd half-heartedly tried to scrub off when Mr Crane told her off.

I told myself to leave it, that if there was anything in there, the police would have found it, but my hand was already on the lock. I realised that I didn't know the combination and I was tempted to call Olivia, but then I remembered what she'd said about Scarlett – *She has a brain like a sieve* – and went with the first thing I could think of, hoping that it would be the first thing she would think of, as well: 2105, her birthday.

When I heard the lock *click*, my hands shook as I felt another stab of guilt. I think sometimes that I never knew her – not really – but I did, didn't I? Not all of her, but I knew enough. I thought of him then, of all the lies I've told – to her, to my parents, to Orla – and I realised that I never let her know all of me, either.

As soon as I opened the locker, my hands flew out to catch the pile of books and paper that tumbled out. I managed to get it back in, checking over my shoulder before I began picking through it, the heady smell of decaying banana warning me to watch where I was sticking my fingers. I didn't know what I was looking for, I just needed something else. Perhaps it was denial or maybe I was being careful for once, but if I hadn't already messed things up beyond repair with what I'd said to him in the graveyard yesterday, then I needed to be sure before I threw something else at him. But whatever it was, I kept thinking about what Bones had said the morning we searched Savernake Forest, about everything counting, even the little things, and I began stuffing anything that looked vaguely useful – a couple of letters on Crofton-headed paper, another top-up card, a receipt – into my bag.

Then I saw her notebook and smiled at the battered cover, the sticker she bought in the bookshop in Marlborough in the middle. *She is too fond of books and it has addled her brain.* He said that to me when he saw it, *I'm too fond of you and it has addled my brain.*

I leafed through it to find nothing but her English lit notes and I was about to abandon it, when I heard someone coming and stuffed it into my bag before running back to my room. There was only fifteen minutes of lunch left so I took it all out of my bag and put it on my desk. I reached for the notebook first, examining each page, looking for something that didn't look right – a note scribbled into a corner, something crossed out – but there was nothing, and when I got to the last page, I felt something in me droop, like a young branch under the weight of a plump pigeon.

I looked up and when I saw the time, I jumped, but as I went to close the notebook, my fingers brushed against the last clean page and I shivered as I felt tiny indentations in the paper. It could have been nothing – just the indentations from her notes on *District and Circle* on the previous page, but when I ran my fingers across them, the paper was smooth except for a few words written in the middle of the page. I checked the previous one, which was almost full. Whatever she'd written, she must have torn the page out, so I grabbed a pencil. I sketched it across the blank page – a trick I'd read in a Nancy Drew book, I think – until what she'd written began to appear. I dropped the pencil and covered my mouth with my hand:

You love her now, but you're going to love me for ever.

62 DAYS BEFORE

MARCH

I can't sleep. I've been awake for the last two hours looking at photos on my laptop, trying to work out how this happened. I just went to my old school's website. I thought they would have taken me off by now, but there I am, my photograph next to words I barely recognise. *Valedictorian. Varsity Track. Features Editor.* I look at that girl and I don't know who she is any more, with her smooth hair and neat polished nails. There's a photo of Jumoke and me – drinking coffee on a bench outside the library – and I don't recognise the purse at my feet. Maybe it isn't mine, maybe it's hers – we were always swapping – but I'm looking at the tan Mulberry messenger bag that my father bought me when I started at Crofton, the only bag I have now, and wondering what that girl – the one with the neat nails and the brightly coloured purse – would think of me. I'm sure she wouldn't recognise me, either.

I thought things would be back to normal now. OK, not *normal*, but I thought I would have moved on, but she keeps tugging me back. I know I deserve it – I chose a guy over her – but what's the statute of limitations on screwing your best friend over? It's been three months. I'm trying. It's not like I'm rubbing her face in it. I'm too scared to look at him now. So every time she says something nasty, I want to tell her that. 'I don't even have him.'

That's what I told him last weekend. It was an exeat weekend and my parents were in Lagos, so I told them I'd stay at Crofton because I was working on something for the *Disraeli* and he and I spent the weekend in the Cotswolds. It was amazing until the Sunday, when he caught me trying to take a photo of him on my phone and got mad. The only photograph I have of that weekend is one of our ice creams and it isn't enough. 'I don't know if this is worth it,' I told him on the drive back to Crofton, and I believed it until he parked the car in a lay-by and pulled me into his lap.

I'm doing what he says and trying to ignore it, trying to be the bigger person and not rise to the remarks she makes in class, the looks she tosses at me when we pass in the corridor. I didn't even say anything when she wrote an A on my locker in red lipstick, but today she went too far. My parents were here for the Lower Sixth Universities' Meeting, my mother in a floor-length white and red Duro Olowu cotton dress that made Mr Crane trip and spill his coffee, and my father, impartial as always, in a Cambridge sweatshirt.

My mother saw her before I did, giving her a huge hug before I'd looked up from the Oxford prospectus that my father was trying to prise from my hands.

'Scarlett,' he said, stopping to kiss her on both cheeks.

I almost dropped the prospectus. My parents know that we aren't as close as we used to be, but they don't know why, other than my huffy comments about us 'not having as much in common as I thought'. I'm sure they think it's a fight that we'll get over in a few weeks. They probably wouldn't be so keen to stop and hug her if they knew that she was throwing my secrets around Crofton like handfuls of confetti. Like last week, in English lit when we were talking about *The Price of Salt*, and she told everyone that I'd kissed Jumoke. It was just a peck, when we were nine, but she made it sound like that scene from *Cruel Intentions*.

I eyed her warily, but she just smiled sweetly. 'Mr and Mrs Okomma,' she said, batting her eyelashes, 'have you met Adamma's boyfriend Dominic?'

I hadn't seen him, standing behind her with his back to us, and I don't think he saw us either, not until Scarlett grabbed his elbow. He had a bottle of water in his hand and the water curled out of it in a perfect arc as she spun him round to face us, splashing over our shoes – Mum, me, then Dad. Splash. Splash. Splash.

'Shit,' he muttered, looking down at our feet. 'Shit,' he said again, when he looked up to find me, flanked by my parents. 'I'm so sorry.' He gulped and held his hand out to my father. 'It's a pleasure to meet you, Sir. I'm Dominic Sim.'

Poor Dominic. He obviously didn't hear the boyfriend thing because he looked completely bewildered, and I wanted to slap her. I know why she did it, because she knew how much the parents like to gossip about Dominic. They'd all heard the rumours – about the teacher at Eton, about his fight with Sam, about his car that he tore through Ostley in, music roaring. There isn't a mother at Crofton who hasn't warned her daughter off him, so Scarlett knew full well my mother would freak.

To anyone else's eye, my father didn't flinch, but I knew him well enough to notice the second of hesitation before he took Dominic's hand and said, 'Pleasure to meet you, too, Dominic,' with a smile that didn't quite reach his eyes. And I noticed my mother's gentle nod before she said, 'I've heard so much about you, Dominic.'

'Are you having a good day?' he asked, equally flustered.

'Oh yes,' my mother said, taking me by the elbow. 'Unfortunately, we can't stay and chat. We have a meeting with Adamma's housemistress.'

She didn't let go of my elbow until we were out of the concert hall and heading down the path towards the Green. Then I saw the corners of her mouth drop as she turned to look at me. 'Dominic Sim?' she hissed. 'Of all the boys, Adamma, *Dominic Sim?*'

My father looked confused. 'You have a boyfriend, Ada? Since when?'

'No, Papa. I—'

'Why didn't you tell me?'

'Listen, Papa.'

'You know who that boy is, Uche?' my mother interrupted, nodding back towards the concert hall. 'The one who got that teacher at Eton pregnant.'

'Pregnant?' He stopped and stared at me, then at my mother.

'Yes. One of the mothers told me.'

'It's just a stupid rumour,' I said, a little desperately, but my father was livid.

'A teacher!'

'Listen, Papa—'

'And he gets into fights,' my mother added.

'Fight.' I scowled at her, then held a finger up at him. 'One fight, Papa.'

'No.'

That's all he said as he started marching down the path toward Burnham again – *No* – then he shook his head and he

310

looked so angry I thought that he was going to keel over and have a heart attack.

'Calm down, Papa. I'm not even—'

'No, Adamma.'

'But, Papa—'

'*But, Papa* nothing.' He stopped and held up a finger. 'You are not to see that boy. Do you understand?'

I didn't realise we were at Burnham until Mrs Delaney came out to greet us. 'Mr and Mrs Okomma,' she shook their hands with a quick smile, then gestured at us to follow her inside, 'thanks so much for coming to see me.'

My parents were suddenly all smiles again and I will never not be amazed by that. It's not a gift I have inherited, so I trailed after them, my cheeks stinging. I thought the meeting was an excuse to get away from Dominic. It wasn't until we were in Mrs Delaney's office with the door shut that I realised it might be something more sinister than that.

'I hope you found the Universities Meeting useful,' she said, once we'd sat down. My parents nodded carefully. They're usually great with small talk, they have to attend so many functions after all, but as soon as my school is involved, they have no time for it. Mercifully, Mrs Delaney noticed that and moved on. 'I just wanted to have a chat with you about the letter I sent home with Adamma last weekend.'

I gulped down a gasp and pressed my lips together. The letter. The letter that was still at the bottom of my bag because I hadn't been home. Oh God. I didn't think it was important. I thought it was a flyer for the Easter concert, or something.

I saw it again; my father's second of hesitation then a smile that didn't quite reach his eyes. 'The letter?' he asked, crossing his legs.

Mrs Delaney must have had this conversation with parents before because she didn't flinch. 'I sent a letter home with Adamma last weekend.'

My mother licked her lips, then breathed in through her nose and forced it out again. 'Adamma didn't come home last weekend. She was here at Crofton.'

Don't say it. Don't say it, a voice in my head roared. But of course she did.

'No. She wasn't.'

I waited, hoping that the sun would explode and kill us all, but it didn't, so all I could say was: 'I can explain, Papa.'

'We can discuss that later, Adamma,' he said smoothly, stopping to pick a hair from his pants, then gesturing at Mrs Delaney to go on. 'As we haven't read the letter, would you mind explaining what it says?'

'Adamma has been issued with a written warning.'

Sun. Explode, I prayed. *Now.*

My parents exchanged a look, then my mother muttered something inaudible in Igbo and sat back on the couch. 'A written warning? For what, Mrs Delaney?'

'I've had to give Adamma verbal warnings in the past for going out for a run in the morning without informing me.' My stomach lurched. They were verbal warnings? I thought she was telling me off. 'I realise that as deviant behaviour goes, it could be much worse,' she conceded. 'But we're very strict, as I'm sure you can appreciate. I need to know where my girls are at all times.'

'Of course.' My mother nodded.

'And she's missed prep, too.'

'Prep?' my father asked with a frown.

'After supper, between 6 p.m. and 9 p.m., Adamma should be in her room doing homework. But last week, when I checked, she wasn't, and not for the first time.' I closed my eyes. When she didn't mention it, I thought I'd got away with it. 'She's missed swimming practice too.'

My mother sat a little straighter. 'How many times?'

'Twice.'

It was only once! I almost interrupted but then I remembered that it was twice and thought of us, giggling in the back seat of his car – *One more minute*, he'd breathed, eyes half-closed when I told him that I had to go, then he'd kissed me again.

'And she missed Debating Society last year.'

I had an excuse for that one – it was when I went into the village to tell the police what happened to Orla – but I couldn't tell them that, so I slouched in defeat.

My parents were very quiet for a moment, then they exchanged another look and my mother asked, 'What happens now, Mrs Delaney?'

'As I said, Adamma has been issued with a written warning. If she receives another, she'll be expelled.'

'Expelled?' My father spat the word out of his mouth as though it tasted foul.

Mrs Delaney nodded. 'In the meantime, now that I know you're aware of what's going on,' she said with a smile that told me she knew full well that I hadn't taken the letter home, 'Adamma will be gated for a month.'

My mother flinched. 'What does that mean?'

'She won't be allowed to leave school grounds and will have to sign in with me every hour.'

'Every hour?' my father said, and he seemed satisfied with that, until he sighed. 'I can't tell you how embarrassed we are, Mrs Delaney.' He and my mother exchanged a glance. 'But we can assure you that this won't happen again.'

'Don't be.' She shook her head. 'Adamma isn't a bad child. If you haven't been to a school like Crofton before, it takes some getting used to.'

My mother smiled. 'Thank you for being so understanding, Mrs Delaney.'

'Absolutely.' She stood up. 'I'll give you a moment alone with Adamma.'

As soon as she shut the door behind her, I burst into tears. My father didn't say a word, just got off the couch and walked over to the window. He stood looking outside, his hands behind his back, and when I stopped crying, he walked back over and sat in Mrs Delaney's chair opposite me. 'All of this for a boy, Adamma?'

I couldn't look at him. 'I love him, Papa.'

He was quiet for a moment, then said. 'You're not to see him again.'

I started crying again. 'But, Papa.'

'We had an agreement, Adamma, you can date, but no serious relationships. I was relieved when your mother told me that you hadn't kept in touch with Nathan, but now you're seeing this one?'

'Please, Papa.'

'No, Adamma.' He shook his head. 'That's it. *Enough.* You're too young and relationships are distracting. You're about to go to university and it's a big decision. I don't want you picking somewhere just so you can be with a boy.'

'No. You want me to pick somewhere because *you* went there,' I said before I could stop myself, and I wanted to paw at the air between us and take back the words.

'Adamma!' my mother gasped. 'This is how you speak to your father?' She glared at me until I looked at my hands. 'You

314

see? This boy is no good for you. Look at the way he has you behaving. Disrespecting your father. Skipping class. This isn't you.'

I didn't dare lift my head. 'I'm sorry.'

My father spoke then, his voice harder than I have ever heard it. 'Your trip with Jumoke to Europe this Easter is cancelled,' he said, counting my punishments off on his fingers. 'Your seventeenth birthday party next month is cancelled. The car you were going to get for your birthday will be staying at the Mercedes garage. You will give me your credit cards and your passport and you will spend every exeat weekend at school until you have caught up and when you have,' he stopped and waited until I lifted my chin to look at him, 'we can discuss you getting everything back.'

What about him? I almost said, but I stopped myself this time.

I think that's why I can't sleep, because I keep thinking about that girl, the one with the neat nails and the brightly coloured purse who never missed a class and dated a guy who would bring her mother flowers and chat to her father about Boko Haram when he came to pick her up. Then I walked over to my closet, opened my tuck box and took out our cellphone.

Him and his paranoia, but he was right.

'You'd better be worth it,' I told him with a smile when he answered.

And he laughed.

315

12 DAYS AFTER

MAY

I'm a fool. A fool. They were seeing each other, weren't they? The sneaking around, the disposable phone, the hours in the back seat of his car instead of the back row of the cinema like other couples. Normal couples. I thought it was because of me, because of my parents. I thought I was protecting him. And I actually thought it was *exciting*. I got a thrill from it, from lying, from having him to myself. But I didn't and if he could lie about that, what else did he lie about?

I can't stop thinking about it. Every time I do, I *shake*. It's like a scab that I keep picking at. I think about every call he didn't answer, every lunch break he didn't have time to see me. Was he with her? Would he open his eyes while we were kissing to check his watch? Did he have to think before he said my name? Did they have a song? A place? Did he meet her in Savernake Forest, too, always late, his hair wet?

I used to like it, the way my fingers smelt of shampoo after I ran them though his hair, how his skin tasted of soap. That's the real betrayal: not the lying, not even thinking that he might love her more than me, but the tiny betrayals, the secret ways she knew him that I didn't. I imagined a photograph hidden somewhere in her room, tucked into a drawer, under her mismatched socks, or between the pages of a book he'd given her. A photo of the two of them. The thought of it was like taking off a cheap ring to find a green mark on my finger. And with that it was over.

Broken.

Ruined.

'I know!' I roared at his voicemail after I saw what she'd written in her notebook. I shouldn't have, I was in my room and someone might have heard, but I couldn't stop myself, somewhere between our fight in the graveyard and reading that note, doubt had become fact and when I got his voicemail again, it spilled out of me. I listened to the generic message and cried, not knowing how it had come to this. How it went from him sending frantic texts, desperate to see me, to not answering his phone.

All of this for a boy.

But then I went to bed and I thought of him – him giggling and counting my eyelashes with the tip of his finger, him kissing my wrist and telling me that he could feel my pulse, catching him looking online for apartments in Cambridge – each memory like an ice cube in a glass of whiskey, diluting my resolve.

How did I get it so wrong? I've never thought of myself as gullible, but I guess I am. Did he enjoy it, going between us? He must have. He must have enjoyed those little lies, the tang of them on his tongue, sweet as sherbet. That's who he was going to meet that Sunday afternoon. I see it all differently now – the chug of The Old Dear then the ring of his cellphone, his brow tightening as he answered it. Why hadn't

I put it together? I guess I believed him. He hadn't given me a reason not to until now. That's doubt, it will make you think anything.

I turned on my lamp and reached for my cellphone, but as I was about to call Bones, I stopped myself. What was I going to say? That I thought he had murdered Scarlett? It wasn't the sort of accusation you *threw around*. It would ruin his life. And did I even think that? It's him – sweet, charming, funny *him*. I thought of him at the airport the day my father was shot, at Edith's wedding, lying next to me in Savernake Forest watching the clouds bob by, in class, the corners of his mouth twitching a moment before he dropped a note into my bag, and I kicked back the duvet and walked over to my bookshelf. I pulled off the battered, second-hand copy of *Love in the Time of Cholera* he'd given me and opened it.

No one's ever picked me.

I held it to my chest, my heart singing in that way it does every time I read it and I didn't know what to do. I don't know what happened. I don't know how this happened. I wanted to call my father, but I knew what he'd say, he'd tell me to be honest, but how can I? I am in the middle of this, ingrained in it, deep, deep down.

So I did what I did when Orla told me that she had been raped and I treated it like I was writing a piece for the *Disraeli*. I rolled up a towel and put it against the crack under my door, then went to my desk and pulled out a stack of index cards and a Sharpie and wrote down everything I knew. Everything. Times, dates, facts. I wrote them all on index cards, then sat cross-legged on the floor and spread them out in front of me

319

and I don't know whether it was seeing it all, but I couldn't look at it.

It was him.

I stood up and began pacing. He wouldn't. He couldn't. But what is it that Sherlock Holmes says? When you have eliminated all which is impossible, then whatever remains, however improbable, must be the truth and there it was, in black and white on my floor.

The pendulum swung the other way again and something in me kicked back. Was it black and white? I only had proof that he was seeing her, that he *could have*, that he had the opportunity, but did he have the will? Why would he hurt her? Why? I thought of Orla outside the police station yesterday, defending Sam, and I wondered if I was letting my heart win again as I looked down at the index cards at my feet, but it wasn't enough. I loved him. It wasn't a silly crush. He might have deceived me about her, but not about *that*. I knew him. I knew what he dreamed about, good and bad. I'd counted each of his moles, his birthmarks, his scars. Real things, not words scribbled on index cards. Why would he hurt her? He couldn't.

But what if he did?

I tried to ignore the question, but I couldn't and when I got up this morning, I went back to the pile of stuff I'd taken out of her locker, going through it again. I stopped when I got to the receipt. I don't know why. I didn't even know what it was for – it was just a small square of paper from one of those old tills that didn't even have the name of the store at the top, just the date and time in greying ink – but I slipped it into the pocket of my blazer before I headed down to the dining hall. I've been thinking about it all day. I keep taking it out of my pocket to stare at it – wondering what she'd bought – before I tell myself that it could be from anywhere, given her inability to stay still, and put it back in my pocket again.

My father called as I was heading into my room to dump my bag. He never calls at 3 o'clock because I'm usually harassed and trying to get something filed for the *Disraeli* or cramming for Debating Society. So he calls after 6 o'clock, when he knows I'll be in my room and can talk properly. It was probably a coincidence, but it's moments like that that make me feel like he still knows me, even after all the lies, after everything I've done.

'Ada, *kedu ka i mere?*'

'How am I?' I dropped my bag at my feet and took the receipt out of my pocket again, biting down on my bottom lip as I stared at it. 'I don't know, Papa.'

I shouldn't have said that. I don't even know where it came from, but my head was a *mess* and I think I just wanted him to say something to make me feel better.

'What's wrong?' When I didn't respond, his voice softened. 'Are you OK?'

'No.' I pressed a hand to my forehead. 'Can I say that?'

'Of course you can say that, Ada.'

'I don't know sometimes.'

'I think you should come home with us, Ada,' he said and I pictured him in one of the big chairs at the Castle and Ball, a pot of tea on the small table in front of him.

'Where's home, Papa?'

I shouldn't have said that, either, it must have felt like a splash of hot water on his heart, but when I looked at my bed, I thought of Scarlett's room, of her creased white sheets and the half-eaten chocolate bars she leaves everywhere. There is something missing from her house now. A hole. Then I thought

321

of my bedroom in Lagos with its half-full drawers, and my bedroom in London that I've hardly slept in; then I looked around at my room, at my narrow bed and the closet and desk and chair that were exactly the same as Orla's closet and desk and chair, and Molly's closet and desk and chair, and I realised that I was everywhere and nowhere, all at once. I didn't have bedrooms, I had hotel rooms, places to sleep. When I wasn't in them, no one noticed. No one missed me.

'What's wrong, Adamma?'

I didn't think I'd be able to say it until I heard the words. 'I think I know who murdered Scarlett, Papa.'

He didn't hesitate. 'Tell the police.'

'But I'm not sure. What if I'm wrong?'

That didn't make him hesitate, either. 'Then be sure, Adamma.'

I didn't know where to start, but figured I'd start in Ostley because all the stores had those old tills that dispensed the sort of receipt I'd found in Scarlett's locker. The village only has four stores: a butcher – which I ruled out immediately because they get their meat and eggs from her parents' farm, so there would be no reason for her to go in there; a greengrocer – but she'd spent £10.99 and, after a swift circuit sniffing nectarines and inspecting carrots, I discovered that they didn't sell anything that cost more than £5. I was sure that it was the newsagent – which sold everything from vodka to birthday cards – but when I bought a pack of gum and a Dairy Milk for Orla, I realised that it didn't give receipts, which left the chemist.

The chemist is the smallest – and oldest – store in Ostley. Like the rest of the village, it's postcard perfect. Its name is at the top in gold letters over the dark green-painted door and there's a display of antique scales and medicine bottles in the window that people stop to take a photograph of when they drive through. Inside isn't as impressive. The first time I went in there with her, I thought it had a weird smell, but, like her, I'm a total make-up junkie, so it didn't take me long to succumb to the lure of the make-up stand.

We'd spend ages in there after school, testing sparkly eye-shadows on the backs of our hands and trying out nail polishes, so I knew my way around the store pretty well. I checked my cellphone and realised that I only had twenty minutes before I had to get to swimming practice, so before I wasted time looking for things that cost £10.99, I bought a pack of cough drops. I held my breath as the man behind the counter smiled and handed me my change and there it was: a small receipt just like the one I'd found in her locker.

I had to take a breath before I thanked him, then went over to the make-up stand, checking the yellow price tags on everything – the nail polishes, the blushers, the foundation – to discover with a defeated sigh that nothing on it cost more than £6.99. I checked my cell again with a flutter of panic as I tried to think what she would have bought, going over to check the bubble baths (and resisting the urge to take the lids off and sniff each one) then the lotions and finally the perfumes. But as I examined each dusty box, I realised that as much as my grand-mother loved that stuff – she's had a bar of Yardley lavender soap, still wrapped in the wax paper, in her bathroom for as long as I can remember – Scarlett would never wear it and even if she bought something for someone else, none of it cost more than £10.

I had to get back to Crofton so I started frantically checking everything: cotton buds, aftershave, tubs of Slim-Fast, razors, vitamins. Everything. The guy behind the counter must have thought I was shoplifting, because while I was checking the last thing I could think of – a bottle of lavender water, of all things – he asked if he could help and it made me jump. I told him I was fine and hurried to the door, but on my way out, I passed the one section it didn't occur to me check, the section I would never look at, not in my Crofton uniform.

I glanced at the window, then over at the counter and reached for a pack of condoms. The most expensive pack was £10 and my shoulders fell, but as I was about to leave, I glanced at the counter again and the panic in my fingers stilled as I realised why *she* had bought something from the chemist, and not her poor father whom she tasks with buying everything from hair-removal cream and tampons when he does the weekly shop. Why the receipt was in her locker at school and not on her bedroom floor: because she didn't want anyone to see it.

I marched over to the counter and took a breath. 'I need a pregnancy test, Sir,' I blurted out and he looked a little relieved. I guess it explained my erratic behaviour.

'How late are you?'

'I don't know.' I squirmed, my cheeks burning. 'I'll just take the best one.'

I saw his expression as he turned and picked up a white and blue box from the shelf behind him. He put it on the counter. 'This one. It's digital.'

'How much is it?'

'Ten ninety-nine.'

My heart slammed into my ribs. 'I'm sorry, Sir. I have to go.'

I turned and ran out of the chemist and straight into Bones.

It knocked the air right out of me and when I stepped back with a gasp, he raised an eyebrow at me. 'Either congratulations are in order, Buffy, or you and I need to compare notes.'

29 DAYS BEFORE

APRIL

It took a month of grovelling and a phone call from Mrs Delaney – to confirm that I'd been on my best behaviour – but my father grudgingly agreed to reschedule my birthday party. I was determined not to let Scarlett ruin it, though. Today is Adamma Day. Not Scarlett Day. Adamma Day. She can have the other 364 days of the year, but I want this one.

As always, I was the first up. 'Going for a run on your birthday,' Mrs Delaney said when I told her, stopping to raise her mug of tea at me. 'Now that's dedication!'

If she noticed that my hair was pulled back into a neat ponytail and I was wearing lip-gloss, she didn't think to mention it. And it's funny, because after being too scared to go to Savernake Forest alone after what had happened to Orla, I've never felt more safe there. That's where we meet now. We even have a tree, a crooked beech barnacled with moss that we've carved our initials into.

On the way there, I was torn between getting there as quickly as I could and not arriving in a sweaty mess. In the end, my legs made the decision for me and I ran there so quickly that I was almost sorry my old track coach wasn't there to see me do it. I barely had time to notice the wetness in the air: not a damp winter chill, but a wetness, like running across the hockey field in bare feet after it's been watered. This morning it was fresher, the light yellower as the trees began to shift and stir, bright green buds turning towards the sun, ready to burst. It felt like the end of something, like the start of something, and it made me run faster.

For the first time in weeks, he wasn't late, and I checked over my shoulder before I veered off the road and ran towards where his car was parked.

He jumped when I opened the door, then grinned. 'Hey, birthday girl!'

I didn't wait to be invited, just crawled across the passenger seat and into his lap. He giggled as I put my hands on his shoulders and pressed my mouth to his.

'As fun as this is, Miss Okomma,' he said, pulling back after a moment or two. 'We only have fifteen minutes and I want to give you your present.'

Ordinarily, I would have been pissed – much can be done in fifteen minutes – but I was desperate to see what he had got me. I clapped like a giddy kid as he reached over and opened the glove compartment. My gaze went straight to the small, carefully wrapped box with the pink ribbon, but when he took it out, I caught a glimpse of the letter underneath. It took me a moment to work out how I knew the blue logo, but when I did, I frowned. 'Yale?'

He closed the glove compartment before I could reach for it.

My shoulders sagged. 'But what about Cambridge?'

'It's nothing,' he said with a quick smile. 'Just an offer. We can talk about it later.'

'But I haven't applied to any colleges in the US.'

'Please, Adamma,' he said, pinching my chin. 'Not now. It's Adamma Day.'

He waved the present at me and I pretended to be excited, ignoring the kick of panic I felt at the thought of an ocean between us as I unwrapped it.

'Saint Francis de Sales,' he told me when I opened the black velvet box to find a silver necklace with a small oval medal. 'The Patron Saint of Journalists.'

'Really?' I gasped, bringing my ponytail over one shoulder and turning as much as I could in the cramped front seat so that he could put it on.

'Yeah,' he said, stopping to press a kiss to the back of my neck. 'Although, anyone *you're* interviewing will need the medal. You're kind of scary, you know?'

I turned to face him again with a scowl, poking him in the stomach. 'Hey!'

'So do you like it?'

I pressed the medal between my finger and thumb. 'I love it. Thank you.'

'Vivian Darkbloom has sent you some flowers, too.'

I pretended to swoon. 'Vivian is the bestest friend ever!'

'I'm sorry I can't come to your party tonight, though.'

I felt my smile wilt. 'I know. But we're still going to Paris for our next exeat weekend, right?'

'Oh yeah.' He wiggled his eyebrows and I poked him with my finger until he laughed. 'I just hope that your parents don't find out.'

I must have gone quiet because he kissed me and said, 'Hey. Even if they find out and kill me,' he grinned, his lips a delicious shade of pink from my lip-gloss. 'We'll always have Paris, right?'

* * *

329

Scarlett came to my party. I wasn't even surprised when she swaggered in, blue eyes bright, but I refused to give her the reaction she was hoping for. I just smiled sweetly and gestured at the waiter with the tray of cocktails moving around the room, encouraging her to try one. 'A Nigerian Sling. They're delicious,' I told her with another sweet smile, before I swept off to the bar. She seemed impressed and even raised a glass when she got one as if to say, *touché*.

After that, the only thing I could do was try to pretend that she wasn't there. It seemed to work. We moved seamlessly around each other; when she was on the dance floor, I went to the bar and when she went to the bar, I went back and danced between Orla and Jumoke. Even during the fireworks, when we all ran outside to gasp and cheer, I was aware of her behind me, but I just looked up at the sky, my eyes wide and my heart beating too hard as I pressed the silver medal he'd given me between my finger and thumb with a secret smile.

In the end, she was forced to wait outside the ladies. When I came out, she draped an arm across my shoulders. 'I like your dress,' she said, swaying on her heels. Her mouth was so close to mine that I could smell the rum on her breath. And I don't even know how she got so drunk – the club knew it was my seventeenth so the bar was dry – but then I'm sure she wasn't the only one to sneak something in.

'Thank you, Scarlett,' I said with a tight smile. I would have shrugged her off, but she was all groggy and loose-limbed and would have fallen over if I had.

'It's so pretty,' she said, taking a handful of the pale-green taffeta skirt and fluffing it up, her nose wrinkled, like a little girl playing with her First Holy Communion dress.

'Thank you.'

330

'It reminds me of a bridesmaid's dress I wore once.'

I rolled my eyes, assuming that she was talking about Edith's wedding and waited for another dig. But then she said, 'I was six. I was a bridesmaid and Dominic was a pageboy. That's how we met. Did I ever tell you that?' She poked me in the shoulder with her finger. 'That's when we plotted to run away to Darkest Peru. I told you about that, didn't I?' She stopped to play with the skirt of my dress again. 'About the first time I ran away. Dominic told me to do it, convinced me that Savernake Forest was Darkest Peru. I was meeting him on the other side of the bridge.' She was obviously pleased at how stunned I looked, because she grinned. 'From the moment I met that boy, he's been leading me astray.'

I didn't doubt that.

'Anyway,' she waved her hand, 'that's how we met, at a wedding.'

She leaned into me and if there wasn't a wall behind us, I would have folded. The flocked wallpaper tickled my bare shoulders and it made me shiver. 'I think you should sit down, Scarlett,' I said, out of breath from the effort of trying to hold her up. I looked at the velvet booth nearest us, just past the bar, and contemplated how I was going to get her into it.

'He pushed me into the pool.' She put a hand on my shoulder, tipped her head back and laughed. 'That's the first thing he did after the wedding. He didn't say hello, he didn't tell me I looked pretty, he just pushed me into the pool. Can you believe it?'

I did actually.

'Daddy had to fish me out.'

I slipped my arm around her waist and looked over at the booth. As I did, I saw Jumoke walking towards us and while I needed the help, I was sure she'd just peel Scarlett off me and leave her lying where she fell, so I shook my head and she turned back to the dance floor with a roll of her eyes.

'There I was, Adamma,' Scarlett went on, both arms around my neck, oblivious to the Herculean effort it was taking to keep her upright, 'standing at the edge of the pool in my pretty green bridesmaid's dress, dripping onto my pretty green shoes and Dominic just smiled and said, "You look like a mermaid."'

She leaned closer and I had to put my hand on her stomach to stop her from tipping forward. When I looked at her again, she was staring at me, her forehead creased. 'That's why I'm scared of water, because of Dominic.' She laughed, but not like before. She didn't put a hand on my shoulder, didn't tip her head back. I couldn't look at her and looked at my hand on her stomach instead. 'That's why I'm scared of everything, because of Dominic.'

She looked down at my hand on her stomach and I probably should have moved it, but I left it there. She pressed one of her hands to it – just for a second, her palm clammy against my knuckles – then she moved it away again.

'I don't even know why I'm talking about him,' she said with a regal shrug. 'This is nothing to do with Dominic, is it?'

Before I could respond, she moved on. 'Do you remember this dress?' She lifted the skirt, then let it drop. 'Do you remember what you said about it?'

I remembered. It was my first exeat weekend at Crofton, the one I couldn't persuade Jumoke to come to London for. She bought it in a tiny shop in Chelsea. Everything in the shop was white – the floors, the walls, the couches – and there was Scarlett, dark hair down, twirling around in that green silk dress. Then I realised why she was talking about Dominic: I'd said that she looked like a mermaid.

'You're the only person who will ever know me like Dominic does,' she said, lifting her arm so that both of them were around my neck again. 'I wish I was like you. I wish there was a door in my heart that I could just shut.'

It would have hurt less if she'd punched me. I couldn't breathe.

'I wish I could forget like you, Adamma. Why can't I forget?'

Her forehead fell against my temple and I didn't know what to do. So I just stood there, letting her almost hug me. She smelt of bruised rose petals and I suddenly felt very sad, because I didn't know what perfume it was. It was something new, something I didn't know about her, and it brought tears to my eyes.

12 DAYS AFTER

MAY

I wouldn't tell Bones a thing until he drove me to her house, which he did under duress, scowling and threatening to arrest me all the way.

'They're not here, you know?' he muttered as he pulled into her long driveway. 'They've gone to stay at their house in France.'

'I know,' I muttered back, undoing my seat belt as soon as he pulled up outside her front door, but when I opened the car door, he reached over and closed it.

'Where do you think you're going?'

'I need to check something in her room.'

'Like fuck,' he huffed, reaching over and grabbing the handle of the door as I tried to open it again. 'I'm not letting you traipse through her house.'

'If you want to know what happened to her then you have to let me in.'

'I don't *have* to do anything.' He stared at me and I stared back until he sat back in his seat and sighed. 'Look, Adamma. I know that you've just lost your friend in the most horrific, most public way possible and that you want to help. So I'm trying to be patient and you know how much I hate that,' his gaze narrowed, 'but I'm investigating a murder here. If you know something then you *have* to tell me.'

My shoulders fell. 'I will, Bones. I swear. When I'm sure.'

He stared at me again, but I didn't flinch. I don't know why. I should have told him – I should have told him everything – but some part of me still couldn't believe it. Still held on with both hands. I had to be sure.

'I get that you're trying to be a good friend, Adamma—'

'A good friend?' I interrupted with a bitter laugh, then turned my face away and looked out the window at her front door that opens with a long creak, like something from a horror movie. I brought my hand to my mouth and bit my knuckle to stop the tears I could feel pooling in my eyes. 'It's too late for that.'

I don't know how it came to this, when being friends became so hard. When I was a kid, making friends was easy. On my first day of school, I shared my crayons with Mbeke and that was it, we were best friends. Now it's so complicated. We say things we don't mean, don't say things we do. The words hurt, draw blood.

I thought of him then and asked myself how I had got it so wrong. But I knew, I just didn't want to admit it. She wasn't the only one who wanted the big love, was she? Something to fight for. That's why I was so drawn to her, to her stories about Paris and her parents' second-hand brass bed. I used to think she was restless, but I am too. I'm always moving. 'You make me want to jump,' I told him once, my hands fisted in his shirt. 'You make me want to stand still,' he said, kissing me again. That's why I did it, why I chose him. I shouldn't have, I know that now, and that's something I have to live with, but it was all I'd ever wanted, you know. I've read poems that are so beautiful it hurts, somewhere in my bones, and I wanted that, for someone to love me like that. I'm sorry if that doesn't sound enough. Right now it doesn't feel like enough, either. I can't fix that, but I can fix this.

I can pick her this time.

'Why are you trying to protect him, Adamma?' Bones asked with a softness I didn't think him capable of. 'He isn't who you think he is.'

I swept the tears from under my eyes with my fingers, then wiped them on my skirt. 'Bones, don't.'

'You've worked it out, haven't you – that's why you were in the chemist – that she was pregnant, that she called him that afternoon, the afternoon she went missing, and asked him to meet her in Savernake Forest and when she told him, he strangled her.'

I got a mental image: him with his hands around her neck and her eyes, wide and blue as she looked up at him, and the shock of it knocked something in me loose.

'Stop it.'

'She told him she was pregnant and he strangled her and left her there.'

'Stop it.' I covered my face with my hands, but when I closed my eyes, all I could see was that photograph, the one in the police station, Scarlett with her red, red lips, lying pale but perfect on the forest floor, like Ophelia, a crown of green leaves in her hair.

'And before you think that he just lost his mind, that they had an argument and he snapped, remember that he went back, Adamma. He went back and put lipstick on her.'

I flew out of the car then, leaving the door open as I ran around the side of the house towards the back door. The doormat was already flipped over, the spare key in my hand by the time Bones got to me and he tried to grab my arm, but I pulled away. As soon as I got the door open, I was gone, through the mud room – with its lined-up wellies and wax jackets – into the kitchen, past the shopping list by the fridge and the bowl of browning bananas, into the hall. He called my name, but I was already running up the stairs, taking them two at a time, and he caught up with me as I was about to go into Scarlett's room. He put his arm around my waist and pulled me back. I roared at him not to, but when I saw it, saw her unmade bed and her school skirt in a puddle on the floor, I was glad. I don't think I could have gone in there.

When he saw it, I watched his eyes go wide. 'Did Forensics do this?'

I shook my head.

'No wonder Hanlon couldn't find anything in here.'

I didn't know how we were going to find anything, either. When I looked at all the drawers and dusty corners I realised how many places Scarlett had to hide stuff.

It made me think of last October when she had been in New York, auditioning for that play, and Olivia and I had torn her room apart looking for some clue as to where she was. We'd found a bottle of vodka in one of her riding boots and a pack of cigarettes in her sock drawer, but other than that, there was nothing. Olivia had given up and gone downstairs to check her school bag – which Scarlett had dropped on the kitchen table when she came in from school – telling me to check the bookcase.

I couldn't find a thing and was about to admit defeat, but as I walked across her bedroom to check her hamper, hoping to find a receipt, a note, anything, in the pocket in a pair of jeans,

I walked over her rug. The floorboard beneath it creaked, as it always did, but that day I stopped. I don't know why, but I did and I tugged back the rug to find one floorboard slightly higher than the others.

After failing to lift it with my fingers and breaking several nails, I had grabbed a pair of scissors from her desk and prised it open to find a red leather diary. The shock of it made me let go of the floorboard and it dropped back into place with a puff of dust. When I'd recovered, I lifted it again, reaching for the diary, my hands shaking. I didn't know what to do with it for a moment, but then I thought of Olivia in the kitchen, tearing through Scarlett's school bag, while her father checked his phone again, and I flicked to the last page and there it was, scribbled in her scruffy handwriting:

Hamlet audition, Signature Theatre, 480 West 42nd St

I never told anyone I'd found the diary, not even Scarlett, as though I'd accidentally walked in on her while she was getting dressed and I didn't want to embarrass her by letting her know I'd seen something I shouldn't have. I just called the Bowrey Hotel and she answered on the second ring, laughing when she realised it was me.

It started before then, but that day, when she laughed and said 'Busted!', was the first time I didn't dismiss it, when I let myself question if we were really friends. I felt a sharp pain in my chest as I remembered it, but then I felt another deeper – louder – one when I looked across the room and saw the frame I'd given her for her birthday propped up on her desk. I guess Bones saw it too, because when he edged into the room, gingerly stepping over the piles of clothes cluttering the floor, he stopped and looked at the strip of passport photos she and I had taken our first exeat weekend in London that were stuck to the frame.

I don't know how she knew the frame was from me, but there we were, grinning and blowing kisses. I wonder if Bones read the print – *A ship is safe in harbor, but that's not what ships are for* – because his cheeks were pink when he looked at me again.

'Rug.' I stopped to wipe away a tear with the cuff of my shirt, then pointed at the floor. He nodded and walked over to it, pulling it back. He knew immediately what I was trying to tell him and I held my breath as he struggled to ease the loose floorboard up, the skin between his blond eyebrows pinched. But then he did it and when he muttered 'shit' I knew he'd found it.

He pulled the diary out first. Then, at last, a cellphone exactly like mine.

I was right.

Something in me unravelled then, tears spilling down my cheeks as I watched him switch it on. The screen lit up and he walked over to me, his head dipped as he waited for the menu to load. Once it had, he checked her text messages and stared at the screen.

'What does it say?' I breathed.

He showed me the screen. It was a message from Scarlett to him.

Meet me in Savernake Forest in ten minutes or I'm going to tell.

2 DAYS BEFORE

MAY

Today was one of those perfect May days. The sun finally found the will to punch through the clouds and, as soon as it did, everything was brighter: the air warm with the promise of summer, of heat and watermelon and long, long nights.

I don't think I'll ever get used to going to class on a Saturday, but today was especially excruciating. As soon as our last one ended, we all ran outside. Even Mr Crane had put his book into his bag before the bell rang, and he didn't tell us not to run when it did. As we spilled out into the courtyard, I could hear the day kids tearing out of the car park, the tops of their cars down.

The rest of us ran for the Green, squealing as we peeled off our cardigans. Even Orla took hers off – it's such a little thing, but I don't think I've ever seen her bare arms. It made something in me settle because it's something else she's doing now that means she's getting better. She still hasn't cut her hair, but she does tuck it behind her ears sometimes. It's not much, I suppose, but it's something, because I look at her sometimes and I'm sure I can see the beginning of a spark in her eyes.

We were only sitting on the grass for a few minutes when I got a text from him. He hadn't sent me a message on my phone since he had given me the disposable one, so he must have been desperate to see me and it felt like it did when we first met; Orla rolling her eyes when I told her that I had to go. She's so used to my emergency *Disraeli* meetings and forgotten swimming practices that she didn't say anything. I never thought I was that girl – the girl who leaves her friend to be with a boy – but when I had to stop myself running to Savernake Forest, I realised that I was. As soon as I saw him waiting by our tree, a tartan blanket in one hand and a bottle of wine in the other, the guilt was forgotten, and I ran at him and kissed him until he was breathless.

Perhaps I'm being sentimental, but I don't think I've ever seen the forest look so pretty. Every day it changes; it gets a little brighter, a little fuller. I could feel something stirring around us as we walked under the trees. They felt closer, the gaps between their branches disappearing as clouds of yellow-green leaves filled them, blocking the sky. It made me think of my garden in Lagos, of how it's almost *obscenely* green with neat, neat lawns and spiky palms. Savernake Forest is the opposite: its edges are softer, the grass patchy in places and the trees crooked, their cinnamon bark trunks splitting. This afternoon it looked like a watercolour, washed out and hazy, as the birds sung idly.

'It won't be long until all of this is covered in bluebells,' he told me, waving his hand over the forest floor as we looked for a spot to sit down.

'I can't wait to see it.'

'I want a photo of you in it,' he breathed, his cheeks a little pinker, and when he kissed me again, I thought my heart was going to split open.

342

* * *

We got tipsy on red wine and fell asleep on the tartan blanket. I woke up before him, stretching blissfully, like a cat. I don't know how long I watched him sleep – watched his eyelids flutter and the shadows of the leaves move across his face – but the sky was pink when he eventually woke up and checked his watch. He told me to leave first and I did, walking back to Crofton, dazed from too much sun – and him – smiling to myself as I picked a leaf out of my hair.

I heard The Old Dear before I saw it, wheezing off the road and turning into the forest. My heart stopped and I glanced over my shoulder, hoping that he wasn't in his car. I pulled my cellphone out of the pocket of my blazer and fired off a text, telling him to stay where he was just as The Old Dear pulled up next to me. For an awful moment, I thought it was going to be her, but it was her father who wound down the window with a grin.

'*Kedu*, Adamma.'

'*Kedu ka i mere*, Tom?'

'I haven't said that in a while!' he said, and I smiled.

Whatever I feel for her, her father really is the sweetest man. He's always made an effort to speak Igbo with me or to look up Nigerian recipes on the Internet. He once made *nkwobi* and it was so good, even my father was impressed.

'What are you doing here?'

I thumbed over my shoulder. 'I just went for a walk.'

'Perfect day, isn't it?'

'Yes. It's lovely.'

'I'm setting up for Scarlett and Olivia's party.' He nodded at the pile of boxes in the back seat, bunting and streamers spilling out of them. There was a tangle of fairy lights in one of them that looked beyond unravelling. 'Are you coming?'

I shook my head. 'I don't think I'll be able to.'

'Why not?' He didn't wait for me to answer. 'I don't know what happened between you and Scarlett, but I can tell you this: it isn't worth it, Adamma.' I looked down at my feet and shrugged, but he pushed on. 'Just put it behind you and come.'

'I don't think she'd want me there.'

'She went to your seventeenth, didn't she?'

'I guess.'

'There you go. Besides, it's Scarlett.' He winked. 'Buy her a present and she'll forgive you anything!'

I chuckled.

'See you tonight, then!' he said, waving at me again as he chugged off.

As I watched The Old Dear shudder up the road away from me, I thought about my birthday party, about how she had waited for me outside the washroom – *Why can't I forget?* – and for the first time in a long time, I thought of her, not him.

So I went to her party. She crashed mine, it was only fair, right?

It was held under a tangle of trees near the gates. By the time I got there it was dark, so I expected to slip in unnoticed, but as I approached – following the sound of music from the road – the trees parted to reveal a room of light. I don't know how her father did it, but it was stunning. Strings of light bulbs and Chinese lanterns were threaded between the trees, bright balls of light against the black, black sky.

As I got closer, I could see other things hanging from the branches – some low enough to touch – jam jars of tea lights and milk bottles filled with sunflowers, peonies and ginger-coloured tulips. Through the middle, over the heads of everyone dancing

344

beneath it, was a washing line with photographs of Scarlett and Olivia pegged to it. I recognised some of them – Scarlett in her yellow wellington boots, Scarlett at her drum kit, Scarlett doing a star jump in front of the Eiffel Tower – and I lingered on one of a tiny Scarlett in her bridesmaid's dress, obviously taken before Dominic pushed her in the pool. She looked adorable, all blue eyes and liquorice-coloured ringlets, and I found myself smiling.

I don't remember the last time the thought of her made me smile.

I saw her then, standing next to Olivia by one of the tables, a glass urn of lemonade between them. Olivia saw me first, flicking a filthy look in my direction, before turning back to Scarlett, who seemed amused. She raised her glass – like she had at my party – and I smiled this time, feeling the burn of something familiar in my chest. I don't know what it was, but as I watched her laugh, I smiled again and it felt a little like something repairing itself.

I could have stayed, I suppose, and got drunk on the spiked lemonade, but she looked so happy and I was tired of being the reason she wasn't. I didn't want to bicker, didn't want to pretend not to care when she called me a name. So I added my present to the pile and left. But as I was making my way back to the road, I saw Dominic coming towards me, a champagne bottle in his hand. He was sucking a blackcurrant lollipop. I could smell it when he took it out of his mouth with a POP.

'You look positively ambrosial this evening, Miss Okomma,' he told me with a wicked smile. He looked just like he did my first day at Crofton, all eyelashes and cheekbones and that pink, pink mouth.

But I feigned indifference. 'Ambrosial?'

'It's a word.' He pointed the lollipop at me with an impish grin. 'What are you doing here? You've got more front than Brighton.' I must have looked confused, because he explained it: 'Brighton? Seafront?' He rolled his eyes. 'Never mind.'

I countered with an arched eyebrow. 'I could say the same to you, Mr Sim.'

'True.'

When he tried to put the lollipop back in his mouth and missed, I giggled. 'How long has Drunk Dominic been here?'

'Not long. Not long,' he said, swaying a little. 'But he isn't having any fun.'

'Even with a lollipop?'

'Even with a lollipop.' He took it out and I saw that his tongue was purple.

Molly walked past us then. 'Hello, *Dominic*. Hello, *Adamma*,' she said with a rabid smile, before continuing on towards the party, a bottle in each hand.

I sighed and rolled my eyes. 'Aren't you sick of it?'

'Of what?'

'Of people talking about us?'

'People are always talking about me.'

'Yeah, but,' I lifted my chin to look at him, 'this is different.'

'Is it?'

'Of course it is. You don't need to put up with it. You could tell everyone the truth.'

'True, but honesty is overrated, Miss Okomma.' He shrugged, then grinned. 'Besides, she fucking *hates* it. I love that she hates it. It's just another of our games.'

'I suppose.'

He put the lollipop back in his mouth, then leaned a little

closer, close enough for me to smell the blackcurrant on his breath. 'Do you think she'll ever forgive you?'

'Jesus, Dominic.' I stepped back, my cheeks stinging as though he'd reached across and slapped me. The guilt was sudden and cloying. 'Where did that come from?'

'I was just thinking.'

'Well don't,' I snapped, crossing my arms.

'But seriously, do you think she ever will?'

'I don't know,' I snapped again, the guilt deepening as I remembered my party, her hanging off me, loose limbed and groggy. I turned to look back at the party, at her dancing – arms in the air, her fingers almost touching the string of Chinese lanterns over her head – and when I looked back at him, I shrugged. 'I don't know,' I said again, more softly.

'You're gonna have to be the one, you know,' he said, holding the champagne bottle to his chest. 'She's not as brave as you. You have to make the first move.'

'I know,' I admitted, thinking of my present. I hadn't attached a card because I wanted her to keep it and perhaps that was cruel, letting her get excited, letting her look at it every day and not know it was from me. But I guess some part of me still wanted to be there in her big, untidy room, with its piles of orange peel and dirty plates, even if she didn't know I was.

'She'll forgive you. I know she will,' he said and I don't know if he really believed that, but I didn't realise until that moment that I wanted her to.

I pressed a finger to the medal around my neck and nodded. 'I hope so.'

12 DAYS AFTER

MAY

I didn't say a word on the drive back to Crofton, just looked out the window at the fields rolling by. It felt so final, like the ride to the airport after a vacation, and I made myself memorise everything – every blade of grass, every dandelion, each break in the clouds that exposed the blue, blue sky – holding on to that last moment with both hands – with my fingernails – before I went back to Crofton and everything changed.

I guess Bones thought that was it, that I wasn't going to say another word, because when he pulled up outside the main hall and I got out of the car, he didn't follow. I turned back, stooping down to look at him before I closed the door.

'Come on.' I nodded at the doors.

He took off his seat belt. 'Where are we going?'

'What time is it?'

He checked his watch. 'Almost four.'

'I know where he is.'

When we got to the classroom, he was humming to himself, but when he glanced over to find me in the doorway, he shook his head.

'Please, Adamma,' he said with a weary sigh. 'Not now.'

I guess he didn't see Bones, because he turned back to the whiteboard and I felt an ache in my chest as I remembered our last social, him in the suit he wore to Edith's wedding, me in a dress he told me later was the colour of Dundee marmalade. He made me wait until it was almost over before he approached me, just in passing, just for a moment, and I'd pretended to pout, asking if he'd even seen me. 'You're the only person I see when I walk into a room, Adamma,' he had said with a slow smile.

For a moment it hurt too much to speak, as I stared at him, noting the scuff on his shoes, the missing button on the sleeve of his tweed blazer. I searched for some hardness in his jaw, some blackness in his eyes, but he looked as he always does, awkward and a little flustered, his hair in his eyes.

'I think I made my feelings clear earlier,' he said without looking at me, rubbing away the notes from his Year 10 class.

I stepped into the classroom. 'Daniel, what did you do?'

His hand stilled for a second, but when he recovered, he shook his head and continued running the eraser over the whiteboard. 'For goodness' sake, Adamma, I thought we agreed that—' He shot a look at me as Bones followed me in. 'DS Bone.' He put the eraser down and faced us, his chin up. 'Is everything OK?'

I wanted to fly at him, yell at him, but all I could say was: 'Daniel, what did you do?' again, because they were the only words in my head, churning around and around and around. *What did you do? What did you do? What did you do?*

He looked genuinely bewildered. '*Do?* To whom?'

'To Scarlett.'

There was a moment of silence, her name dropping like ink into water, bleeding – spreading – until the classroom suddenly

350

felt darker. I watched him swallow, his Adam's apple rising then falling again, before he paced over to the door and closed it behind Bones. I wasn't sure what he was going to do, if he was going to turn into a pantomime villain and laugh in my face, grab me by the arm and call me a liar. But he just came and stood in front of me again, his cheeks suddenly too red as he looked at me through his hair. It was the same look he had given me outside the theatre when he had tugged my pashmina over my shoulders and, just like that – as always – we were the only people in the room. Bones wasn't there, there were no desks, no chairs, and he looked so much like the Daniel I knew – my Daniel – young and awkward and unsure of what to do with his hands, that I wanted to press a kiss to his mouth and tell him that it would be OK.

But I took a step back.

'Adamma, I can explain,' he said, his hands shaking as he reached for me.

Even then, I still couldn't believe it and I stepped back. 'No!'

'Adamma, please.' When I wouldn't let him touch me, he pressed his hands together as though he was praying. 'Please. It's me. *Me*. I love you so much.'

'No you don't.'

'I do. I *do*.' He reached for me again and I yanked my arm away.

'No you don't. You were going to leave.' I shook my head and stared at him as I remembered the letter from Yale I'd seen in the glove compartment of his car. They must have discussed going together and he was just going to go without her.

'Just for a year.'

'No! You were running away!'

351

'Adamma, please.'

Something in me gave way and I started crying. 'Daniel, please.' I sobbed and I wanted to reach for him so much, to touch his familiar arms and shoulders, to sweep his hair out of his face with my hand. 'Please tell me you didn't do it.'

'It was an accident.' He looked inconsolable, like a little boy. 'She wouldn't listen.'

'No, Daniel.' I shook my head and took a step back. 'No.'

'She was going to keep it. She wouldn't listen. She was going to ruin everything.'

He tried to reach for my hand again, but I ran out of the classroom before he could.

42 MINUTES BEFORE

MAY

I shouldn't have skipped swimming practice this afternoon, but when he texted, asking me to meet him in Savernake Forest, I didn't hesitate. I should have – Coach told me that I'd be kicked off the team if I missed another practice – but I didn't care. I don't care about anything anymore: about swimming, about my parents getting another letter, about getting kicked out of Crofton. And it's kind of scary, how much you'll give of yourself without realising. Sometimes it feels like I'm not giving, but throwing, pieces away. All I want is him. Him. Him. Him. Everything else can burn. So as soon as I read his text, I didn't think, I just left.

It's moments like that that make me wonder if I have any control over this, that make me feel like an alcoholic hiding empty bottles at the back of closets. I can't remember the last time I told a stammered lie, the last time I felt a sting of shame when my father called and I rejected the call because I was with him. If this is love, then I'm mad with it. Drunk on it. Like today. It was another perfect day, the sun out, high and bright in the sky as we lay on a tartan blanket, the trees arcing over us. I took his hand and counted the bones in his fingers, claiming each one as my own – distal phalanx, middle phalanx, proximal phalanx – while he laughed.

When I'm older, I'm sure I'll think spending a Sunday lying around in the sun is a waste. But today wasn't a waste. Today all we had was time: seconds, minutes, hours, floating around us like dandelion fluff as we looked up at the endless sky, the blanket scratching at our bare elbows as we watched the flimsy clouds float past, pretending each one was a country. ('India! Let's go there. Australia! Let's go there.')

We only stopped when we heard the distant chugchugchug of The Old Dear on the road, somewhere beyond the wall of trees. Usually, it would have ruined the afternoon, the thought of her reminding me of something nasty she had said in class or another rumour she'd tried to start, but I just lay back on the blanket with a sigh.

I think he was surprised. 'So how was the party? You don't have any bruises.'

'Fine.'

He groaned, lying down next to me. 'What did she do this time?'

'Nothing. We didn't even speak.'

He rolled onto his side, taking my hand. 'Do you think that's it?'

'Who knows with Scarlett.' I threaded my fingers through his and looked up at the sky. 'But it's the happiest I've seen her in a long time.'

'Was Dominic there?'

'Yeah.'

'Were they together?' When I shrugged as if to say, *Aren't they always?* he sighed. 'I don't know why he puts up with her. Why he puts up with any of this.'

'He loves her, Daniel.' I turned my head to smile at him. 'You don't know what you'll do for love until you do it.'

354

He smiled back, then pressed a kiss to my forehead. 'Did you talk to him?'

'He told me I should apologise, make the first move.'

'Did you?'

'I took her a present.'

He chuckled. 'Well played.'

'I bought it ages ago. I was going to give it to her for Christmas, but then, you know.' I shrugged again. 'I didn't attach a card so she won't know it's from me.'

'What was it?'

'Nothing. Just a picture frame I saw in a shop in Marlborough.'

I squeezed his hand as I thought about the white wooden frame, the red words: *A ship is safe in harbor, but that's not what ships are for.*

'It's kind of funny. If I hadn't met her, I don't think I would have been brave enough to do this.'

He kissed me, but before I could kiss him back, his cellphone rang. He pulled it out of the pocket of his jeans and looked at the screen with a sigh. I asked him what was wrong, but he just rolled his eyes. 'Crofton. They know not to ring me on a Sunday.'

I groaned before he said it – *I have to go* – rolling onto my stomach to watch him walk back to his car. He was only a few steps away before I felt the tug on the thread between us and I started missing him. I wonder if he knew, because he turned back to smile at me before he disappeared between the trees. When I lost sight of him, I rolled back onto my back with a lazy sigh, a hand on my chest.

Is this love?

I think it is.

ACKNOWLEDGEMENTS

First, I must thank you, lovely reader. Whether you've bought or borrowed this, thank you for reading. I hope this is a story that you will want to read again or, if you're one of those people who read the acknowledgements first, I hope that what I'm about to say will encourage you to go back to the beginning.

Now I must thank the people who worked so hard to put this in your hands. My agent, the delightful and oh-so-patient Claire Wilson, without whom this book would never have been finished. My editors, Hannah Sheppard, Frankie Gray and Sherise Hobbs, without whom this book would be a *mess* and just about Bones. To the incomparable Sam Eades who is not only the best publicist an author could ask for, but always makes sure I have a brew. To the charming Lynsey Sutherland and everyone at Headline, who continue to overwhelm me with their talent and passion. To the booksellers and librarians who have supported me and thrust *Heart-Shaped Bruise* into the hands of so many readers, thank you.

Speaking of *Heart-Shaped Bruise*, this is a great chance to formally thank everyone who read and reviewed it, as well as the judges on the panels of the CWA Daggers, the National Book Awards, the Branford Boase and the Redbridge Children's Book Award, who thought it worthy of nomination. You make me want to be a better writer.

But back to this book, thank you to Funmi Anazodo and Zaina Miuccia for answering all of my many, many questions. Oh and the poor police officer from Wiltshire police who I'm pretty sure thinks I murdered someone. To Godson Echebima for translating the Igbo and Fiona and Claire Hodge and Martha Close for letting me pillage their boarding-school stories. And not forgetting Sarah Genever, who drove me around Wiltshire in the relentless rain as I tried to imagine what Ostley would look like.

On a personal note, I must thank my fellow UKYA Crew – Amy McCulloch, Cat Clarke, James Dawson, James Smythe, Keris Stainton, Laure Eve, Tom Pollock and Will Hill – who have all been so supportive and pretty much kept me sane this year. Particularly Kim Curran, who has fed me tea and cake and told me I could do this while I've ugly cried more times than I care to mention. Much love to my friends Cristin Moor, Jade Bell and Kelly Bignall for just being brilliant, really, and for still being there when I was too busy to call them back or reply to their emails. Thank you, too, to my family – Carly, Martin, my mother and my nephew, Jacob, who has no clue what this writing malarkey is about, but will be bored senseless with stories about it one day.

And finally, thanks once more to you, lovely reader, for persevering through these acknowledgements, which are almost as long as the book. Your dedication is duly noted and very much appreciated. You've earned a cup of tea.